Praise for Mrs. Everything

"You won't want this book to end as you laugh, cry, and root for these characters as if they were a part of your own family. *Mrs. Everything* is Weiner's best book yet."

—*PopSugar*

"Her most sprawling and ambitious work to date."

—*Entertainment Weekly*

"A complex, captivating look at the many different roles women play: daughters, sisters, wives, mothers, friends, and beyond."

—*HelloGiggles*

"Readers will flock to this ambitious, nearly flawless novel. . . . Weiner asks big questions about how society treats women in this slyly funny, absolutely engrossing novel that is simultaneously epic and intimate."

—*Booklist* (starred review)

"Weiner brilliantly crafts this heart-wrenching, multi-generational tale of love, loss, and family. . . . Weiner's talent for characterization, tight pacing, and detail will thrill her fans and easily draw new ones into her orbit. Her expert handling of difficult subjects . . . will force readers to examine their own beliefs and consider unexpected nuances. Weiner tugs every heartstring with this vivid tale."

—*Publishers Weekly* (starred review)

"Jennifer Weiner has created a novel for the ages in *Mrs. Everything*, which is as impressive as it is ambitious. . . . A skillfully rendered and emotionally rich family saga . . . an unapologetic feminist novel, fully fleshing out the pernicious effects of patriarchy . . . Weiner shows that big, expansive social novels are not only still possible in our fragmented society but perhaps necessary. *Mrs. Everything* is a great American novel, full of heart and hope."

—*Shelf Awareness*

"The author of *In Her Shoes* takes a time machine to the 1950s in this story about two sisters growing up in Detroit. You'll laugh and cry (into your beach towel). Par for the Jennifer Weiner course."

—*The Skimm*, a *Skimm* Reads pick

"Weiner is the queen of dreaming up relatable heroines, and we get a double helping with Jo and Bethie Kaufman, the plucky, unlucky sisters at the center of this story."

—*Family Circle*,
"This Summers's Coolest Reads and Chillest Drinks"

"A sweeping, enjoyable novel that takes sisters Jo and Bethie Kaufman from 1950s suburban Detroit to the present day, as each navigates a rapidly changing world of Woodstock and Vietnam, women's liberation, sexual identity, and more."

—*New York Post*

"A sprawling story about two sisters growing up, apart, and back together . . . A poignant reminder of both the strides women have made since the 1950s and the barriers that still hold them back. An ambitious look at how women's roles have changed—and stayed the same—over the last seventy years."

—*Kirkus Reviews*

"*Mrs. Everything*'s flawed but approachable female characters, well-examined friendships and romantic relationships, and often-joyful sex scenes make this vintage Weiner. This is a warm, readable novel about figuring out what it means for a woman to be true to herself, and then figuring out how to act on that knowledge."

—*BookPage*

BOOKS BY JENNIFER WEINER

Jennifer Weiner

Mrs. Everything

A NOVEL

POCKET BOOKS

New York   London   Toronto   Sydney   New Delhi

Pocket Books
An Imprint of Simon & Schuster, Inc.
1230 Avenue of the Americas
New York, NY 10020

This Pocket Books paperback edition January 2021

POCKET and colophon are registered trademarks of Simon & Schuster, Inc.

For information about special discounts for bulk purchases, please contact Simon & Schuster Special Sales at 1-866-506-1949 or business@simonandschuster.com.

The Simon & Schuster Speakers Bureau can bring authors to your live event. For more information or to book an event, contact the Simon & Schuster Speakers Bureau at 1-866-248-3049 or visit our website at www.simonspeakers.com.

Manufactured in the United States of America

10 9 8 7 6 5 4 3 2 1

ISBN 978-1-5011-3348-0
ISBN 978-1-9821-6404-1 (pbk)
ISBN 978-1-5011-3350-3 (ebook)

This is for my mother,
Frances Frumin Weiner

"There is a long time in me between knowing and telling."

—GRACE PALEY

"They tried to bury us. They didn't know we were seeds."

—MEXICAN PROVERB

2015

Jo

Her cell phone rang as they were on their way out of the movies. Jo let the crowd sweep her along, out of the dark theater and into the brighter lobby, smelling popcorn and the winter air on people's coats, blinking in the late-afternoon sunshine. She pulled the phone out of her pocket. "Hello?"

"Jo?" Just from the sound of the doctor's voice, just in that one word, Jo could hear her future. The Magic 8 Ball's truth-telling triangle had flipped from REPLY HAZY or ASK AGAIN LATER to OUTLOOK NOT SO GOOD or MY SOURCES SAY NO. Her chest tightened, and her mouth felt dry. Her wife looked up at her, eyebrows raised in a question. Jo tried to keep her face expressionless as she held up one finger and turned away.

The first time, nine years ago, she'd found the lump while in the shower, a pebble-like hardness underneath her olive-hued skin, once drum-taut, now age-spotted and soft. This time, they'd caught it on one of the mammograms she endured every six months on the breast that remained. *See?* the radiologist had said, tapping the tip of a pen against a shadow on the image. Jo had nodded. *Yes. I see.* It was a tiny concentration of white in the cloudy gray dimness, barely bigger than the head of a pin, but Jo knew, in her bones, the truth of what she was seeing; she understood that she was looking at her doom.

"I'm sorry," said the doctor. Jo caught a glimpse of herself in the movie theater's windows, her face slack, her expression stunned. *Mom's spacing out again!* she imagined Lila cackling. *Leave Mom alone*, her oldest daughter, Kim, would say, and Missy, the even-tempered middle child, would ignore them both and pull a book out of her bag.

The doctor was still talking, her voice sympathetic in Jo's ear. "You should come in so that we can discuss your options," she was saying, but Jo knew that there weren't any options left, at least, not any good ones. The first time around, she'd done the surgeries, the radiation, the chemotherapy. She'd lost her hair, lost her appetite and her energy, lost her left breast and six months of her life. After five years cancer-free, she was allowed to say that she was cured—a *survivor*, in the pink-tinted parlance of the time, as if cancer were an invading army and she'd managed to beat back the hordes. But Jo had never felt like a true survivor. She never believed that the cancer was really gone. She'd always thought it was in temporary retreat, those bad cells huddled deep inside her bones, lurking and plotting and biding their time, and every minute she'd lived, every minute since her fingers had come upon that lump under her wet skin, was borrowed. For nine years she had lived with the sound of a clock in her ears, ticking, louder and louder, its sound underlining everything she did. Now the ticking had given way to the ringing of alarm bells. *Hurry up please, it's time.*

Jo shivered, even though she was wrapped in the puffy purple winter coat all three of her daughters made fun of. Underneath, she wore one of her loose cotton tops and a pair of elastic-waisted jeans that had to be at least fifteen years old, and sneakers on her feet ("I guess those are her dressy sneakers," Jo had overheard Lila say at the big seventieth birthday party Kim had thrown a few years before). Her hair was short, the way she'd always worn it, pale gray, because she'd stopped coloring it years ago, and she never wore makeup, or much jewelry, except for her wedding ring. She wondered what would happen if she let the phone thump to the blue-and-red carpet, what would happen if she started to scream, and found herself remembering the one actual scene she'd made, years ago, in a Blockbuster Video store, when such places had still existed. All those years later, and she could still remember the exact sound she'd made, how her laughter had turned shrieky and wild, the smell of the teenage clerk's spearmint gum, and the feel of the girl's hand on her shoulder as the girl had said, "Ma'am, I'm going to have to ask you to leave." She remembered how Lila's shoulders had hunched up high beside the pale, skinny stalk of her neck, and how Melissa's voice had wobbled as she'd said, "We're going, okay? We're going right now."

Time, she thought, as she gripped the phone in one numb hand. She needed time, as much as they could give her. Time to make sure that she'd done everything she could to make things right with her sister. Time to make Kim believe that she was a good mother. Time to convince Melissa that doing the right thing belatedly was better than never having done it at all. And Lila . . .

well, eternity might not be long enough to solve Lila's problems. But couldn't God at least give Jo long enough to make a start?

She wanted to groan, she wanted to cry, she wanted to throw the phone at the colorful cardboard display of some superhero movie, and the teenagers posing in front of it, snapping selfies, laughing and making faces for the camera, as if they were all going to live forever. She felt her wife slip her small hand into Jo's and squeeze. Jo blinked back tears and thought, *Please, God, or whoever's up there, please just give me enough time to make it right.*

1950

JO

The four Kaufmans stood at the curb in front of the new house on Alhambra Street, as if they were afraid to set foot on the lawn, even though Jo knew they could. The lawn belonged to them now, along with the house, with its red bricks and the white aluminum awning. Every part of it, the front door and the steps, the mailbox at the curb, the cherry tree in the backyard and the maple tree by the driveway, the carport and the basement and the attic you could reach by a flight of stairs that you pulled down from the ceiling, all of it belonged to the Kaufmans. They were moving out of the bad part of Detroit, which Jo's parents said was crowded and unhealthy, full of bad germs and diseases and filling up with people who weren't like them; they were moving up in the world, to this new neighborhood, to a house that would be all their own.

"Oh, Ken," said Jo's mother, as she squeezed his arm with her gloved hand. Her mother's name was Sarah, and she was just over five feet tall, with white skin that always looked a little suntanned, shiny brown hair that fell in curls to her shoulders, and a pursed, painted red mouth beneath a generous nose. Her round chin jutted forward, giving her a determined look, and there were grooves running from the corners of her nose to the edges of her lips, but that morning, her mouth was turned up at the corners, not scrunched up in a frown. She was happy, and as close to beautiful as Jo had ever seen.

Jo wrapped her arms around her mother's waist, feeling the stiffness underneath the starch of Sarah's best red dress, the one with a full skirt flaring out from her narrow waist and three big white buttons on either side of the bodice. A smart red hat with a black ribbon band sat on top of Sarah's curls. Her mother put her arm around Jo's shoulders and squeezed, and Jo felt like someone had pulled a blanket up to her chin, or like she was swimming in Lake Erie, where they went in the summertime, and had just paddled into a patch of warm water.

"So, girls? What do you think?" asked Jo's daddy.

"It's like a castle!" said Bethie, her little sister. Bethie was five years old, chubby and cute, with pale white skin, naturally curly hair, and blue-green eyes, and she always said exactly the right thing. Jo was six, almost seven, tall and gangly, and almost everything she did was wrong.

Jo smiled, dizzy with pleasure as her dad scooped her up in his arms. Ken Kaufman had thick dark hair that he wore combed straight back from his forehead. His nose, Jo thought, gave him a hawklike aspect. His eyes were blue underneath dark brows, and he smelled like the bay rum cologne he patted on his cheeks every morning after he shaved. He was only a few inches taller than his wife, but he was broad-shouldered and solid. Standing in front of the house he'd bought, he looked as tall as Superman from the comic books. He wore his good gray suit, a white shirt, a red tie to match Sarah's dress, and black shoes that Jo had helped him shine that morning, setting the shoes onto yesterday's *Free Press*, working the polish into the leather with a tortoiseshell-handled brush. Jo and Bethie wore matching pink gingham dresses that their mother had sewn, with puffy sleeves, and patent-leather Mary Janes. Bethie could hardly wait to try on the new dress. When Jo had asked to wear her dungarees, her mother had frowned. "Why would you want to wear pants? Today's a special day. Don't you want to look pretty?"

Jo couldn't explain. She didn't have the words to say how she felt about *pretty*, how the lacy socks itched and the fancy shoes pinched and the elastic insides of the sleeves left red dents in her upper arms. When she was dressed up, Jo just felt wrong, like it was hard to breathe, like her skin no longer fit, like she'd been forced into a costume or a disguise, and her mother was always shushing her, even when she wasn't especially loud. She didn't care about looking pretty, and she didn't like dresses. Her mother, she knew, would never understand.

"It's our house," Jo's mother was saying, her voice rich with satisfaction.

"The American Dream," said Jo's dad. To Jo, the house didn't seem like much of a dream. It wasn't a castle with a moat, no matter what Bethie had said, or even a mansion, like the ones in Grosse Pointe that Jo had seen when the family had driven there for a picnic. It was just a regular house, square-shaped and boring red, with a triangle-shaped roof plopped on top, like the one in her "Dick and Jane" readers, on a street of houses that looked just the same. In their old neighborhood, they'd lived in an apartment. You could walk up the stairs and smell what everyone was cooking for dinner. The sidewalks had bustled with people, kids, and old men and women, people with light skin and dark skin. They'd sit on their stoops on warm summer nights, speaking English or Yiddish, or Polish or Italian. Here, the streets were quiet. The air just smelled like air, not food, the sidewalks were empty, and the people she'd seen so far all had white skin like they did. But maybe, in this new place, she could make a fresh start. Maybe here, she could be a good girl.

Except now she had a problem. Her dad had borrowed a camera, a boxy, rectangular Kodak Duaflex with a stand and a timer. The plan was for them all to pose on the steps in front of the house for a picture, but Sarah had made her wear tights under their new dresses, and the tights had caused Jo's underpants to crawl up the crack of her tushie, where they'd gotten stuck. Jo knew if she pulled them out her mother would see, and she'd get angry. "Stop fidgeting!" she would hiss, or "A lady doesn't touch her private parts in public," except everything itched her so awfully that Jo didn't think she could stand it.

Things like this never happened to Bethie. If Jo hadn't seen it herself, she wouldn't have believed that her sister even had a tushie crack. The way Bethie behaved, you'd expect her to be completely smooth down there, like one of the baby dolls Bethie loved. Jo had dolls, too, but she got bored with them once she'd chopped off their hair or twisted off their heads. Jo shifted her weight from side to side, hoping it would dislodge her underwear. It didn't.

Her father pulled the keys out of his pocket, flipped them in the air, and caught them neatly in his hand. "Let's go, ladies!" His voice was loud and cheerful. Bethie and Sarah climbed the stairs and stood in front of the door. Sarah peered across the lawn, shadowing her eyes with her hand, frowning.

"Come on, Jo!"

Jo took one step, feeling her underwear ride up higher. Another step. Then another. When she couldn't stand it anymore, she reached behind her, grabbed a handful of pink gingham, hooked her thumb underneath the underpants' elastic, and yanked. All she'd meant to do was pull her panties back into place, but she tugged so vigorously that she tore the skirt away from its bodice. The sound of the ripping cloth was the loudest sound in the world.

"Josette Kaufman!" Sarah's face was turning red. Her father look startled, and Bethie's face was horrified.

"I'm sorry!" Jo felt her chest start getting tight.

"What's the matter with you?" Sarah snapped. "Why can't you be good for once?"

"Sarah." Ken's voice was quiet, but angry.

"Oh, sure!" said Sarah, and tossed her head. "You always take up for her!" She stopped talking, which was good, except then she started crying, which was bad. Jo stood on the lawn, dress torn, tights askew, watching tears cut tracks through her mother's makeup, hearing her father's low, angry voice, wondering if there was something wrong with her, why things like this were always happening, why she couldn't be good, and why her mom couldn't have just let her wear pants, the way she'd wanted.

Bethie

Her address was 37771 Alhambra Street, and her phone number was UNiversity 2-9291 and her parents' names were Sarah and Ken Kaufman and her sister was Josette and her name was Elizabeth Kaufman, but everyone called her Bethie.

Her sister went to school in the morning and came home for lunch, and ate her sandwich and watched *Kukla, Fran and Ollie* in the living room until it was time to go back, but Bethie had a late birthday and wouldn't start school until next September, so she spent her days at home, with her mother. Tuesdays were wash days. Bethie's job was to help separate the white clothes from the colored ones, down in the basement, and hand her mother clothespins from the Maxwell House coffee can when her mother hung the wet wash on the rotating aluminum hanger in their backyard. On Wednesdays, Mommy would iron, and Bethie would hold the bottles of water and starch, and would sometimes be allowed to spritz the clothes. Mommy would lick the tip of her finger and touch it lightly to the iron, listening for the hiss to see if it was hot enough, but Bethie wasn't allowed to touch the iron, not ever. The radio played in the kitchen all day long, usually big-band music and also the news on WJBK, "the sound of radio in Detroit, fifteen hundred on your dial." Thursdays were marketing. Mommy would push a wheeled metal cart two blocks up to Rochester Avenue, where they would get a chicken or steak or chops at the kosher butchers and dish soap at the five-and-dime. Bethie would follow along, one hand on the side of the cart, watching her mommy squeeze tomatoes and sniff cantaloupes and lift up a plucked chicken's wing to peer underneath, always with a suspicious look on her face, like the foods were trying to trick her. Everyone smiled at Bethie, and pinched her cheeks, and said what a pretty, well-behaved girl she was. Bethie would smile, and Mommy would sigh, probably thinking about Jo, who was a Trial.

Fridays were Bethie's favorite, because Fridays were Shabbat. For breakfast on Fridays, Bethie's mother would use a juice glass to cut out a hole in the middle of a slice of bread. "Wonder Bread builds strong bodies eight ways," Buffalo Bob would say to the kids on *The Howdy Doody Show*. He'd tell them to make sure that their kitchen had the bread with the red, yellow, and blue balloons, but at Bethie's house they ate the bread that Zayde gave them, bread that he'd baked at the bakery where he worked. Mommy would spread margarine on both sides of the slice, then put it into the frying pan, where it would sizzle. On the best days, there'd be a new package of margarine, and Bethie would be allowed to break the capsule of yellow dye and squish it all around until all the margarine was yellow-colored. She'd watch Mommy's hands as she'd crack an egg on the side of the pan and drop it neatly into the hole in the bread. The egg would cook, the bread circle would get toasty-brown, and Sarah would shout for Jo to make her bed and wash her face and come to the table, she was already late. When Jo finally took her seat, the eggs and bread would go onto the plates, and the browned bread circle would sit on top of the egg. That was an egg with a top hat.

When breakfast was finished, and dishes and juice glasses had been washed and put in the drainer to dry, Mommy would make a lunch for Jo to take to school, and Bethie would change out of her flannel nightgown, folding it under her pillow for the coming night. She'd make her bed and get dressed, and her mommy would zip her dress and do her hair. Bethie would hold perfectly still while Sarah combed, parting her hair down the center and dividing it into pigtails, tying them with ribbons to match Bethie's dress. She would watch her mother pull the curlers from her own hair, until rows of shiny brown ringlets hung on each side of her face, before she combed the curls into waves and sprayed them stiff. Mommy would put on a dress and clip nylon stockings to her garters. She would puff perfume out of an atomizer and step through the mist, explaining, "You never put perfume right on your skin, you just mist and step through." Sometimes, when Sarah wasn't watching, Bethie would run through the leftover mist of Soir de Paris, hoping to smell as good as her mommy.

At ten o'clock in the morning, Mae would come. Mae was old, probably forty, but her mother called Mae "the Girl." Mae called her mother "ma'am." Mae had dark skin, a golden brown that was dotted with darker brown moles, and her eyebrows were plucked to skinny arches that she darkened with black pencil. Her hair was shiny and black and lay in gleaming waves against her head and cheeks. Mae would tune the radio to WJLB 1400 and listen to songs like "Blue Shadows," "Fool, Fool, Fool," and "Please Send Me Someone to Love." She'd sing along with the radio while she ironed the Kaufmans' clothes. When the ironing was done, she'd cover her hair with a brightly colored scarf before vacuuming the carpets and mopping and waxing the floors.

Sometimes Mae would bring her own little girl with her. Mae's daughter's name was Frieda. Frieda was skinny as a string bean, with knobby, scabbed knees and the same golden-brown skin as her mother, and she wore her hair in two braided pigtails that stuck out from the sides of her head. Frieda was the same age as Jo, and she was wild. She and Jo would go racing around the backyard, climbing the cherry tree, playing Cowboys and Indians, coming back all sweaty and out of breath, with grass stains on their clothes. Bethie preferred to stay inside and play with her paper dolls, but Jo adored Frieda, and she'd stay in the kitchen with Mae even when Frieda wasn't there, handing Mae things to iron and singing to the radio.

The Kaufmans had two cars, the New Car and the Old Car. The New Car, which lived in the garage, was that year's new-model Ford, purchased with a discount, because Bethie's daddy worked in the accounting office of the Ford plant. The Old Car, parked in the driveway, was the previous model, handed down to Sarah. When Bethie was five, the Old Car was a Ford Tudor sedan, with four doors and a pistachio-green body and a darker-green hardtop roof. On Fridays, Mommy would climb into the driver's seat and lean forward with her hands tight on the wheel as she would drive them carefully from their new home to the old neighborhood, a mile away, where they used to live and where Sarah's parents, Bethie's *bubbe* and *zayde*, still lived, in a three-bedroom apartment on the corner of Rochester and Linwood, where the white-painted walls were stained brown from Zayde's cigars, and the air smelled like tobacco, yeast, and flour, and good things cooking.

Bubbe and Zayde were old and small and wrinkly, their skin the color of walnut shells. They looked like the set of wooden Russian nesting dolls that stood on the mantel at home, because it seemed like every week, they had turned into newer, smaller versions of themselves. Zayde had stooped shoulders, and he wore black pants pulled up halfway to his chest and belted tight and short-sleeved white shirts so thin that Bethie could see the U-shaped neckline of his undershirt. The fringes of his *tzitzit*, his prayer shawl, would hang from the hem of his shirt. Bubbe was even shorter than her husband, even more stooped. Her thin iron-gray hair was pulled back and knotted at the base of her neck, and her dresses were shapeless and black. She would pinch Bethie's cheeks and call her *shayne maidele*, and she'd always be baking something sweet when they arrived. She would slip Bethie little bits of dough, pillowy soft and crunchy with sugar, and Bethie would eat them when her mother wasn't looking.

Bubbe and Zayde were very old. They hadn't been born in America, like Bethie and her mother. They only spoke Yiddish, no English, and so Mommy would do their banking and pay their bills. While Mommy and Bubbe would sit at the dark wooden kitchen table with the checkbook, Zayde and Bethie would make the challah. With smiles and gestures, Zayde would show Bethie how to sprinkle the yeast over warm water and spoon in a little honey to make the yeast bloom. Bethie would tip a cup of oil into the giant wooden bowl. Zayde would crack the eggs and give Bethie a whisk to stir with. Zayde was small, but his gnarled hands were strong. He'd mix in the flour and, with quick motions with the heels of his hands, knead the dough, pushing it this way and that, flipping it over, gathering it up, and kneading it some more. When the bread was back in its oiled bowl, covered up and rising in the warmed oven, Bethie would go to the living room, where Bubbe kept a shoebox full of paper dolls for Bethie to dress up and colored pencils for her to draw with, or Zayde would walk her to the drugstore, where he would buy cigars for himself and Life Savers for Bethie. Back at their apartment, Bethie would study the single framed photograph that hung on the wall. It had been taken shortly after Bubbe and Zayde had come to America. In the picture, Bubbe wore a white shirt with a high, frilly collar and a long black skirt pulled tight at the waist. Her dark hair was piled high on her head. Zayde wore a dark suit and had a beard that fell almost to the middle of his chest. They both were very young, and they both looked very serious. A little girl, who looked just as stern, stood between them. Each of them rested a hand on the girl's shoulders.

"That was you?" Bethie would ask. She could hardly believe that her mommy had ever been a little girl, that she'd ever not been a grown-up.

"That was me," Mommy would say, and she'd explain how Bubbe and Zayde had come from far away, over the seas, from a little village in Russia. The czar of Russia didn't like the Jews. He made them live in ghettos and said that they couldn't do certain jobs. Sometimes, soldiers would come with torches and break the windows of Jewish homes and businesses, or burn them right to the ground, and so Bubbe and Zayde had come to America and sent Sarah to school to learn English and become an American girl. Mommy said the other kids would call her names—"greenie," which was short for "greenhorn," and other names that were probably the same ones Bethie had heard the older boys use on the playground: *mockie* and *hymie* and *yid* and *kike*. Once, she knew, some bad boys had chased her mother home, throwing mud at her dress. Mommy had told Jo the story when Jo had come home for lunch one day with her shirt torn and a note from her teacher. Jo had gotten in a fight because a boy had told her that the Jews killed Jesus. Bethie figured her mother would be mad at Jo for fighting, but instead her mouth had gotten tight, and she'd said, "The Romans killed Jesus, not the Jews. Tell your little friend that." Then she'd told Bethie and Jo about how kids had teased her when she was little. Jo had pestered her for details, like did Sarah tell her parents, and did she tell the teacher and what were the names of the boys and did they ever get in trouble, but Sarah would only shake her head and say, "It was a long time ago."

For lunch at Bubbe and Zayde's, Bubbe would give Bethie a heel of bread, spread with real butter, sprinkled with white sugar, and a bowl of split pea or chicken noodle soup, because Bubbe believed all children needed hot soup to grow, even in the summertime. Her mother and her *bubbe* would have soup, too, and her *zayde* would have pickled herring and black bread.

When lunch was over, Sarah would go run whatever errands required English. Sometimes, Bethie would go to the bedroom and climb onto Bubbe and Zayde's hard bed for a nap. Back in the kitchen, it was her job to punch down the dough. Her *zayde* would show her how to make her hand into a fist, and she'd pull her hand back and then wallop the dough. It would make a whooshing sound, and Bethie would feel her hand sinking into the warm, yielding depth all the way up to her elbow while Zayde smiled his approval. After the second, shorter rising, Zayde would divide the dough into balls and roll the balls out into long strands, pinch six strands together, and braid them, looping them in overlapping patterns, his hands moving fast, like the three-card monte dealer Bethie had once seen on the corner, until he had one, two, three, four loaves. Bethie would brush the loaves with beaten egg and carefully sprinkle poppy seeds on top. Then Sarah would put two loaves onto the cookie sheet she'd brought, cover them with wax paper, and put them into the back of the Old Car for the slow, cautious trip home.

When they arrived, the house would be gleaming, the floors freshly washed, the air smelling of furniture polish and Pine-Sol. Mae would leave a pan of corn bread cooling on the counter, and Sarah would let Bethie have a slice. The challah would stay in the icebox while Sarah prepared the rest of the Shabbat meal: roast chicken and potatoes, green beans and onions, and cholent, a stew of beans and meat and barley that would cook overnight in the heavy orange pot in the still-warm but turned-off oven, until Saturday afternoon, when they would eat it for lunch. Bethie would sit at the kitchen table, or in the living room, looking at her library books, while the house filled up with good smells of roasting chicken and fresh-baked challah. Sarah would bustle around the kitchen, her skirt swishing, her high heels tap-tap-tapping, whisking the gravy, snapping the ends off the green beans, getting out the Shabbat candlesticks, the candles, and the wine. When it started to get dark, Bethie and Jo would have their baths and get into fresh dresses. Daddy would come home and, together, the girls and their mother would make the blessings over the candles. "Good Shabbos," Sarah would say, and give each girl a kiss, leaving a red-lipsticked bow on their cheeks. Bethie would smell her mother's hairspray and perfume and hear the rustle of her mother's dress, and her heart would feel like a balloon, stretched tight, bursting with love. Her father would bless the bread and the wine, and Bethie and Jo would each have a little sip of the sweet red liquor, and the family would sit at the table, beneath its special Friday-night white tablecloth, and eat chicken and gravy and fresh challah with honey, honey cake or rugelach rolled in nuts and sugar and cinnamon and filled with apricot jam for dessert. When it was bedtime, she'd lie in the darkened bedroom, with her face and hands washed and her teeth brushed, with the house full of good smells and her tummy full of good food and her sister in the next bed, close enough to touch. Then the best part of Friday would come. Jo would tell her a story about a princess named Bethie who lived in a castle, where the birds and mice would sew her dresses and help her make her bed. Something bad would always happen. The princess's mother would die, and Princess Bethie's father would marry a wicked woman, who hated Princess Bethie because of her beauty, and she would make Bethie be a servant, or send her into the haunted forest, where, after dark, the trees' branches would turn into arms and reach out to grab little girls.

"Not too scary," Bethie would whisper.

"Princess Bethie ran and ran, until there were holes in her pretty silk slippers, and her long silk dress was ripped," Jo would say. "She ran through the darkness until she found a tall stone tower stretching high up into the sky. The door was shut, but Bethie pulled on the iron handle as hard as she could, and it creaked open, and she began to climb . . ."

Sometimes the princess would climb to the top of the tower, only a thicket of thorns would grow, hiding Princess Bethie from the world, and the birds and mice would have to bring her tiny sips of water and berries to eat. Sometimes Princess Bethie would prick her finger on a poison spinning wheel, and she would sleep for fifty years until a prince's kiss woke her. Sometimes a fairy godmother would grant Bethie her wish for wings, and she'd go flying out the window, soaring high above the kingdom, or the prince would help her onto his horse and they would ride away together, or she would fly away on a dragon that she'd tamed. Whatever came next, however Jo told it, Bethie knew how the story would end. Princess Bethie would escape the tower or tame the dragon. She would marry the prince and inherit the kingdom, she would save her father from the evil witch, and all of them would live happily ever after.

Jo

"Josette Kaufman, get back here right this minute!"

Jo raced down the hall, feet flying, arms pumping, chest tight and her breath coming in short, painful gasps. She ran to the bedroom, slammed the door, and locked it, startling her sister, who was lying on her bed, paging through *The Bobbsey Twins on Blueberry Island*. Before Bethie could ask what was going on, Jo opened the closet, climbed onto the dresser, reached onto the top shelf, and nudged her blue suitcase with its shiny brass clasps until it fell on the floor.

"Jo!" Sarah was hammering on the door, sounding furious.

Jo ignored her, tossing her suitcase onto her bed. The suitcase, made of cardboard and covered in a blue tweedy fabric, had a stretchy pale-blue satin pocket stitched inside for underwear and socks. Jo threw in three pairs of underwear, two shirts, a sweater, her dungarees and socks and sneakers, her brown leather vest with a sheriff's gold star on the front, and her two new library books. She put the robin's egg that she'd found the previous summer and kept wrapped in a handkerchief on the bedside table into the suitcase's satin pouch and clicked the gold-colored clasps shut. As Bethie stared and Sarah banged and shouted, Jo climbed on top of the dresser again, opened the window, pushed the suitcase onto the lawn, then shimmied through the gap between the sill and the screen, scraping her belly as she went, until her sneakered feet hit the grass. She grabbed the suitcase and ran down the driveway, onto Alhambra Street, crossing Clarita and Margareta Avenues, heading toward Livernois. Mae lived on Gratiot Street, in a neighborhood that Frieda said was called Black Bottom. Jo wasn't exactly sure where that was, but she figured if she kept going on Livernois, she'd get there.

After four blocks, Jo slowed from a run to a trot. After five, her arm started to ache, so she switched the suitcase to her other hand. She trudged along the sidewalk, past drugstores and candy stores, feeling her shirt starting to stick to her back. It was May and already hot and humid, the sky a washed-out blue, the trees and grass a brilliant green. The suitcase bumped against her thigh with every step she took. She'd just crossed Thatcher Avenue when she heard a car behind her. When she walked faster, the car sped up and someone called her name. Jo turned around and saw that it was her father. "Hey, Sport," he called through the open window. "Want to go to a Tigers game?"

For a minute, Jo just stared. She and her father had listened to dozens of Tigers games together, on the car radio or in the backyard in the summer as the sky turned orange and gold and the smell of fresh-cut grass surrounded them, but she had never even imagined going to the stadium. Especially not when she was in trouble . . . but maybe her dad didn't know.

"They're playing the Yanks," he said, and looked at her expectantly.

"Really?" She could hardly believe it. A chance to actually go to Briggs Stadium and see Hoot Evers and Vic Wertz in person? A chance to spend an entire afternoon with her father, just the two of them?

Jo decided she could find Mae some other time. She raced around the car, threw her suitcase into the back seat, and jumped into the front seat, next to her dad. Her father handled the car easily, slipping through the rush-hour traffic until they reached the corner of Michigan and Trumbull. He paid a quarter to park behind Brooks Lumber, right in the shadow of the stadium. "Hold my hand," he said, and Jo slipped her small hand into his big one, gripping tight, as they joined the crowd. Jo could smell gasoline and bus exhaust, newsprint from the stacks of papers and hot dogs from the carts. Everyone walked fast, like they had somewhere important to be and were in a big hurry to get there. Her father walked up to the ticket window, and Jo tugged on his sleeve, not wanting to be greedy but knowing she'd kick herself later if she didn't at least ask.

"Do they have seats for right field?"

"You think you could catch a fly ball?" her father asked, and Jo felt her stomach lurch, realizing that, of course, she did not have her baseball glove, the one she'd begged and pestered her parents to buy her for Chanukah so she wouldn't have to keep borrowing from the Stein boys across the street. It was still at home in the toy box at the foot of her bed.

Her father reached into his suit jacket and, like a magician producing a rabbit, pulled out Jo's glove. Jo stared at him in disbelief and jumped in the air, cheering. They walked through the dark, narrow tunnel, then climbed up and up and up through the bleachers, one flight of steep stairs after another. Jo gripped her father's hand in the press of the crowd. The men wore shirtsleeves and hats, or suits and loosened ties; the women had curled hair and lipstick-y smiles. Jo saw a young couple on a date, and watched as the young man took a sip of beer from a plastic cup and handed it to his girl. Down on the field, the lights were dazzling. The grass, far below them, was an emerald green so deep and vibrant that it seemed to glow, and the players, standing in a line, looked no larger than her sister's paper dolls. Jo was overwhelmed with happiness, here, in the place she'd wanted most to be in the whole world, an enchanted kingdom she'd never imagined that she would visit.

She was looking down at the field, trying to see if she could spot Mickey Mantle, the Yankees' new and much-touted rookie, when her father said, "Want to tell me what happened?"

Jo felt her heartbeat speed up and her skin grow cold. Her dad put his hand on the back of her neck and left it there, its warm weight a comfort. He'd taken off his suit jacket and hung it from the back of his chair, and his white shirt glimmered in the afternoon sunshine. "I'm not mad," he said.

"But Mom is," Jo said. The trouble had started when she'd come home from school that day for lunch. It was Tuesday, and Tuesday was a Mae day, and sometimes Frieda would be there, too. Jo had hurried through the door, dumping her books on the living-room floor, racing to the kitchen. There she stopped short. An unfamiliar woman with freckled white skin and a coil of brown braids that wrapped around her head was standing at the sink, filling a bucket with water. The woman was tall and boxy, with heavy arms and big pink hands. She wore a white shirt and brown pants. There was no bright silk scarf on her head, no gap between her front teeth. Instead of music, the radio was tuned to an all-news channel, and Jo couldn't smell corn bread, just Ajax.

"Who're you?" Jo asked the strange woman.

"Josette Kaufman, where are your manners?" Sarah was sitting at the table, pen in hand, making out a grocery list. A cigarette burned from the lip of the glass ashtray.

"I'm sorry," said Jo. She turned back toward the woman. "Excuse me, but who are you?" she asked.

"I'm Iris," said the woman without turning away from the sink.

"Do you know Mae?" Jo asked.

"No'm," said the woman, just as Sarah said, "Mae won't be coming anymore."

Jo whirled to face her mother. "Why?"

"Because she had other work to do."

"What other work?"

"Other work," Sarah said in a tone that let Jo know she wasn't supposed to ask more questions. "And did I hear the sound of someone leaving a mess on the floor?"

Jo went back to the living room, collected her books, and tossed them on her bedroom floor. Back to the kitchen, the new lady was washing the floor with big swishes of the mop. "Is Mae coming back?" Jo asked.

Sarah shook her head.

"Can I go see her?"

"Jo, Mae is busy. She has other families she needs to clean for."

Jo chewed her lip. "What about Frieda?"

Sarah set down her pen and looked at her daughter.

"You have so many nice friends in the neighborhood. Why don't you go play with Sheila? Or Claire? Or maybe Bethie wants to roller-skate with you?"

Jo's face was getting red, and she could feel her insides starting to churn and fizz, like her blood was turning to hot lava. "Because I want to play with Frieda. Can I go see her? I can take the streetcar if you tell me where to go."

"Eight years old is too young to take the streetcar. And Frieda has her own little friends to play with."

"Frieda is my friend. She came to my birthday party." Sarah hadn't even wanted Frieda to come to Jo's party the month before. Jo had seen her frown when she'd asked for Jo's list and Frieda's name was right on the top. "She might have other plans," Sarah had said, and "It's a long trip for Mae to have to make on her day off." Jo had gone to her father, and Ken must have said something to Sarah, because, on the appointed Saturday afternoon, Frieda had been the first one to ring the doorbell, wearing a pink-and-green party dress, with a wrapped present in her hand. They'd played pin the tail on the donkey and duck, duck, goose, and had ice cream and cake, and Frieda had given Jo a fringed buckskin vest with a gold sheriff's badge pinned to the chest. Jo loved that vest. She would have worn it every day if her mother had let her. She'd asked her parents for cowboy boots, which would have matched the vest perfectly, but they'd given her a charm bracelet and a comb-and-brush set instead.

"Come with me," Sarah said, stubbing out her cigarette with a hard twist. "Excuse us, Iris."

"Yessum," said the strange lady. Jo followed her mother into the living room and and stuck out her lower lip as Sarah put her hands on Jo's shoulders and pushed until Jo was sitting on the couch.

"You are making Iris feel unwelcome," Sarah said.

"I'm sorry," said Jo. "Only why did Mae leave? I miss her! I want to see her! I want to see her and I want to see Frieda!"

Sarah pressed her lips together until they were a skinny red line. "Birds of a feather must flock together," she said. "Do you know what that means?"

Jo shook her head. Sarah made her God-give-me-patience face, and Jo heard her take a deep breath.

"Well. *Birds of a feather* mean people who are like each other. *Flock together* means they stay together. So people who are like one another stay with people like them." Sarah looked into Jo's eyes. "Mae and Frieda have their own people. People like them. Their own friends. And you have your own friends too." Sarah looked right into Jo's eyes. "Do you understand?"

Jo did not. "Frieda is like me. She likes to play kickball and marbles and cowboys." Jo felt her eyes start to sting. "Frieda gave me my best present."

Sarah gave an angry sigh and muttered, "I knew that was a mistake."

"Why?" Jo wailed. She couldn't stand the thought of never playing with Frieda again, or never hearing Mae's music coming from the kitchen, or eating Mae's corn bread. "Why?" Jo asked again. When her mother didn't answer, Jo got to her feet. "I'm going to see them," she announced.

"You're staying right here, and you're doing your homework," said Sarah.

"No I'm not. I'm going to see them, and you can't stop me."

"I most certainly can." Sarah's neck was turning red, the flush creeping up toward her chin. "Young lady, you are going to sit right here, and you are going to be in the worst trouble of your life if you . . ."

"You're not the boss of me!" Jo shouted, turning to go. Her mother grabbed her shoulder and slapped her.

For a minute, the two of them stood, breathing hard, staring at each other. Sarah's lips were trembling. Jo's cheek throbbed and stung. She felt her eyes fill with tears, and instead of giving Sarah the satisfaction of seeing her cry, she raced down the hall and locked her bedroom door, and while Sarah pounded and Bethie stared, she'd filled her suitcase and slid out the window.

No matter what Jo did, her mother was angry at her. Jo was always doing something wrong, like leaving her clothes on the floor or pinching her sister, or talking too loudly, or making too much noise when she chewed or even when she walked. Jo lost her library books and broke her toys. She ripped her clothes, she got gum stuck in her hair, and once, she'd kept the money her mother had given her for tzedakah at Hebrew school and had bought candy with it instead, and tattletale Bethie had told on her.

Some rules she understood, but others were mysteries. "Do you have to sit like that?" Sarah would ask when Jo was sitting in a chair with her legs spread apart. "Why does it matter how I sit?" Jo would ask, and Sarah would press her hands to her head, groaning, and say, "Wait 'til your father gets home." When Ken arrived, Sarah would take him into the living room, where she would communicate Jo's latest misdeeds in a low whisper. Ken would sigh, and he'd take Jo to the kitchen. There, he would sit in a straight-backed wooden chair, with his tie pulled loose. Jo would stretch herself out across his lap and pull down her pants or her skirt, and her father would deal out ten measured strokes with the flat of his hand that would leave her bottom pink and stinging. Sarah would watch from the doorway with her arms folded across her chest. When the spanking was done, Ken would say, in his sternest voice, "Come with me, young lady," and Jo, hanging her head, would follow her father out of the house and into the car.

"You okay, Sport?" her dad would ask as soon as the door had shut behind them, and Jo would nod, and he'd sigh and say the same thing every time: "You know, it hurts me more than it hurts you."

Sometimes they would just sit in the car, listening to WXYT broadcast the games: the Detroit Lions or the University of Michigan Wolverines in the fall, the Red Wings in the winter, the Detroit Tigers in the spring. Sometimes they would go for a ride in Ken's new-smelling Ford sedan, which he could steer, to Jo's delight and amazement, just by using his knees. Jo would sit up front on the long vinyl-covered seat as her father drove, sometimes just in circles around their neighborhood, sometimes all the way into downtown Detroit, where he seemed to know every secret place.

He would take her to the National Bank of Detroit, where, in the lobby, there was a glass slipper for the little girls to try on (a bank clerk would give you an Oh Henry! or 3 Musketeers candy bar when your foot proved too big for the dainty little shoe). Sometimes they'd go to the Dipsy Doodle Drive-In, on the corner of 9 Mile and Telegraph, for Double D burgers, or the Mayflower Coffee Shop, where the paper menus read, "As you travel through this life, Brother, Whatever be your goal / Keep your eye upon the doughnut, And not upon the hole," or they would take the car to Jax Kar Wash, whose billboards advised, A CLEAN CAR RIDES BETTER. Jo loved to sit in the dark, feeling the car moving in jerks through the dark tunnel, listening to the brushes slapping and thudding against its roof and sides. Always, on their drives, there was music playing on the car radio. Ken would sing along in a deep and tuneful voice to "The Yellow Rose of Texas," or "Paper Doll," or "It's a Sin to Tell a Lie."

Those were her happiest times, in the car, with her father behind the wheel. On rainy days, the windshield wipers would swish back and forth, making her feel drowsy. In the winter, warm air would blow out from the heater over her knees, and on hot summer days, she'd roll the window down to feel the wind on her face. Her father didn't mind Jo's short hair or her loud voice or her dungarees and her droopy socks, or how Jo's feet were already almost as big as Sarah's and that she'd outgrown her school shoes twice the year before. He didn't care that she was messy or forgetful, or that she was costing them a fortune in late fees at the public library, or that she preferred *Gunsmoke* to *I Love Lucy* or *The Adventures of Ozzie and Harriet*, or that her favorite times were racing through the backyard with Frieda, playing Cowboys and Indians, taking turns shooting at each other with the air gun she'd borrowed from Don Lafferty at school.

When it got late, Ken would turn the car toward home, swing it expertly into the driveway, and he'd keep his hand on her shoulder as he walked Jo into the house. "Listen to your mother," he would say in a deep, warning tone, loud enough for Sarah to hear. Sarah's response was typically an eye-roll and a muttered *You spoil her*, but she wouldn't say it too loud, because at least Ken had gotten Jo out of her hair for the afternoon. *She hates me*, Jo would think, but even that didn't hurt so much, because her father loved her, and she could carry his love, like a glowing coal in the center of her chest, feeling its warmth even in the face of her mother's fury.

In Briggs Stadium, her father put his hand on her shoulder. "Tell me what happened."

"I came home and Mae wasn't there," Jo began. "Mom said she had to go clean for other families and that she was never coming back. I wanted to find her."

"Ah," said her father. "Well. Mae's neighborhood's about a ten-mile walk."

"I don't care." Jo's voice cracked. "She shouldn't get to decide who my friends are." Her eyes were stinging again. "I try," she said. "I try so hard to do what she wants. To be how she wants. But I can't." Jo bent her head. "She hates me," she whispered.

"Ah, Sport," said her father, and gave her neck a reassuring squeeze. "Your mama loves you. And you know I think you're swell." Jo smiled, the way she did when her father tried to talk like the kids did, and blinked away her tears and looked down at the ball game.

In the fifth inning, her father bought a pair of hot dogs, putting just the right amount of ketchup on Jo's. He drank a beer and gave Jo a Red Pop that left her lips and tongue stained crimson. When Joe Ginsberg, the catcher, a Detroit boy who'd graduated from Cooley High, stepped up to the plate, the crowd erupted into wild cheers, and when Ginsberg hit a home run to right field, Jo stretched out her arms and watched as a man just a few rows in front of them caught it.

"So close!" her father lamented, but Jo didn't even care. It was enough, more than enough, to be there, at night, away from her mother, and her mother's anger. Jo drank her Red Pop and let herself imagine what it would be like if, after the final inning, they got in the car and just drove. They could follow the Tigers around the country, going to all the road games until summer's end; they could drive to the Grand Canyon, or to Florida or California, where it was warm the whole year round. They could sleep in motels, or buy a tent and sleep in campgrounds and cook their food over campfires, like Laura Ingalls's family did in *Little House on the Prairie*. Jo could swim in the ocean and wear her buckskin vest with its sheriff's badge every day, and invite whichever kids she liked to her parties, and no one would holler or make her feel like she was too big, or too loud, or just wrong, no matter what she did.

For the rest of her life, Jo would remember that night, when the Tigers had beaten the Yankees, 6–5 in extra innings. She'd remember Joe Ginsberg's home run, and how he'd thrown out two of the Yankee batters. She'd remember the sour tang of the beer that her father let her sip, and feel the ticklish prickle of the foam drying on her lip. She would remember the smell of her father's aftershave as he stood close to her, and the sound of her father's voice, singing along to Nat King Cole's "Mona Lisa" as they drove home.

When they pulled into the driveway, he turned off the car and sat behind the wheel as the engine ticked.

"Did your mom talk to you at all about Mae?" he asked.

"She said 'Birds of a feather must flock together.'" Jo bent her head. "Should've told her I wasn't a bird," she muttered.

Her father looked like he was trying not to smile. "Your mother wants things to be easy for you and your sister," he finally said. "Things weren't so easy for her when she was a little girl."

Jo nodded. She'd heard the stories of how Sarah spoke English while her parents didn't, and how she'd had to speak for them, and how there weren't many Jewish families in her neighborhood, and how some of the other kids had been mean, throwing dirt and chasing her home from the streetcar. "Is that why we moved here?"

Jo asked. "Because almost everyone's Jewish, like we are? Because that's easy, when everyone's the same?"

Her father looked startled, then thoughtful. He drummed his fingers on the steering wheel and finally said, "Being in a Jewish neighborhood was one of the reasons. The schools here are better. The old neighborhood was changing. It wasn't as safe there. And that's a parent's job, to keep kids safe." He sighed and drew Jo close to him, letting her nestle into his warmth and his good smell of clean cotton, hair tonic, and bay rum cologne. "Go inside and tell Mom you're sorry," he told her. "She loves you."

She doesn't, Jo thought. *You know she doesn't.* Instead she said, "I will." Part of her wanted to explain again, about how she did try to be good, that she wanted to follow all the rules, except sometimes she couldn't understand them. And part of her—a bigger part—wanted him to turn the key, to back the car out of the driveway and onto the street, to drive and drive and never bring her home again.

Bethie

By the time she was eleven, Bethie Kaufman knew that it was her destiny to be a star. She had shiny brown hair that her mother curled with rags at night. Her eyes were a pretty shade of blue-green, and her eyebrows were naturally arched, but it was her smile that everyone wanted to see. "Give us a smile!" the hairnetted ladies at Knudsen's Danish Bakery would say when Bethie came in with her mother to buy an almond tea ring, and they'd give Bethie a sprinkle cookie when she obliged.

"Here comes a pretty little miss," Stan Danovich, who owned Stan's Meats on 11 Mile Road, would say, and he'd fold up a slice of turkey or bologna for Bethie to eat. Mr. Tartaglia at the five-and-dime would put extra peppermints in her bag, and Iris, who came to clean three times a week, called her Miss America and brought clip-on earrings for Bethie to wear until it was time for her to go home.

Bethie is a kind and conscientious student with many

friends, Miss Keyes wrote on her fourth-grade report card, in her beautiful, flowing blue script. *Bethie is a gifted musician who sings in tune*, Mrs. Lambert, her music teacher, said. By fifth grade, two boys had kissed her in the cloakroom, and a third had carried her books home for a week, and she'd gotten the solo in the winter concert, where she had sung a whole verse of "Walkin' in a Winter Wonderland" by herself.

Bethie loved being a girl. She loved skirts that flared out when she twirled; she loved the look of her clean white socks against her black and white saddle shoes. She loved the charm bracelet she'd gotten for her birthday. She only had two charms so far, a tiny Eiffel tower and a little Scottie dog, but she hoped to get more for Chanukah.

Bethie was pretty, Bethie was popular, and so it was only natural that when, at Hebrew school, the sign-up sheet for auditions for the spring Purimspiel was posted, Bethie put her name down for the role of Queen Esther, the biggest girl's part in the production.

The Hebrew school students performed the play each year. Bethie knew the story by heart: Once upon a time in the kingdom of Shushan, a not-very-smart king put his disobedient wife aside and found himself in need of a replacement. He held a beauty pageant to find the prettiest girl in all the land, so that he could marry her. ("Isn't that kind of superficial?" Jo had asked, and Sarah had said, "It was how they did things back then.") The winner was a girl named Esther, and her big secret was that she was Jewish, only the king didn't know. After Esther became the queen she overheard Haman, the king's wicked advisor, telling the king that he should kill all the Jews. Only then did Esther reveal herself, and because the king loved her, he let the Jews live, and killed Haman instead.

There were lots of parts for boys in the show—the silly king, whose name, Ahasuerus, sounded like a sneeze, and Mordecai, Esther's cousin, who urged Esther to enter the pageant and then, after she was married, to tell the king the truth, and Haman, the bad guy, who was always played by a boy with a black-eyeliner mustache. Every time Haman's name was spoken, the audience was supposed to hiss or boo, or stamp their feet, or shake their *groggers*, which were homemade noisemakers, paper plates filled with dried lentil beans, folded over and stapled shut.

All of the girls wanted to be Queen Esther, but for two years in a row, the role had gone to Cheryl Goldfarb, who was in sixth grade and whose father was a lawyer. Cheryl lived in an enormous house in Sherwood Forest, where some of the wealthiest Jewish families in Detroit lived. Bethie had never been to Cheryl's house, but her friend Barbara Simoneaux had, and Barbara said that Cheryl had a queen-sized bed with a pink coverlet and a stuffed pink bear that was almost as big as she was. Cheryl took dance lessons twice a week at Miss Vicki's Academy of Dance on Woodward Avenue (Bethie had begged her mother to let her take tap or ballet, and Sarah had sighed and smoothed Bethie's hair and said maybe next year). Cheryl had a white rabbit-fur coat that came with a matching muff, and every time she passed it in the coatroom Bethie would give it a quick stroke, thinking it was so much softer than her own scratchy gray wool. Cheryl had done a good job at the audition, but Bethie had been better. Not only had she memorized every single line of the entire play, but she'd actually cried in the scene where she fell to her knees and begged to King Ahasuerus to spare the lives of her people. "For we may call God by a different name, but all of us are his children," Bethie said, as tears ran from her eyes and Charlie Farber stared down at her, looking alarmed.

When the cast list was posted, Cheryl's face turned the color of a brick. "I should be Esther!" Bethie heard her wailing through the door of Mrs. Jacobs's classroom. "I'm older than she is!"

"You'll make a wonderful Queen Vashti," Mrs. Jacobs said. Vashti was the king's first wife, the one the king put aside after she refused to dance and display herself to the court. Vashti was the only other girl's part in the Purimspiel. The girl who played her got to wear a long, shiny black wig, like Elizabeth Taylor's in *Cleopatra*, and even more eyeliner than Haman. Cheryl should have been happy with that, but instead she just yelled louder.

"Queen Vashti only has one line. One word! It isn't fair!" It sounded like she was crying. *Should've done that for the audition*, Bethie thought, imagining how she would look onstage, with her hair all in curls and a gold foil crown on her head.

The students rehearsed the Purim play for weeks. The morning of the show, Bethie was too nervous to eat even a single bite of Wheatena. "You'll be terrific," her mother told her, brushing rouge on her cheeks, then wetting the curved mascara wand, rubbing it into the black cake of mascara and stroking it onto Bethie's lashes. In the white silk dress with sparkling silver sequins that was kept in the synagogue's costume closet and smelled like mothballs, Bethie thought that she looked beautiful, and very grown-up.

Bethie saw her father tuck a bouquet of carnations into the trunk of the car before he drove them to the synagogue. "Break a leg," her mother whispered, and Jo said, "You've got it made in the shade." Cheryl, in Queen Vashti's red dress, glared at Bethie backstage, but Bethie didn't care. She practiced smiling, imagining taking her bows, and how the crowd would applaud after her song, as Mrs. Jacobs introduced the show.

"Once upon a time, in the far-off land of Shushan, there lived a king and his queen," the narrator, Donald Gitter, said. Charlie Farber, who was wearing what looked like his father's brown bathrobe, with a tinfoil crown, stepped onto the stage.

"His queen's name was Vashti, and she would not obey the king's command to entertain his royal guests," said Donald. That was the cue for Charlie's first line.

"Dance!" said the king. "Or away you must go."

The narrator said, "And to everyone's shock, Queen Vashti said . . ." Charlie turned to Cheryl, who was supposed to walk onstage and say her single line—"No." Instead, Cheryl snake-hipped her way onto the stage, gave Charlie a big, fake-sweet smile, and said, "Anything you want, O my king."

And then, as the members of the court and the audience of parents and siblings watched in shocked silence, Cheryl began to dance. With her arms arched over her head, Cheryl jumped. She spun. She twirled down the stage and leaped back up it. She did a few high kicks, a few pliés, several shuffle-ball-changes, and concluded her performance by leaping straight up in the air and landing in a clumsy split on the floor, right in front of King Ahasuerus, who stared down at her in shock.

"Um," Charlie said. His next line was supposed to be, "Away with you, then, if you will not obey." Except Vashti had obeyed and was looking up at him expectantly, her cheeks flushed and her chest going up and down underneath her red dress.

"See?" she said. "I danced! So now you don't even need another wife!"

Bethie heard laughter ripple through the audience, and a terrible thought flashed through her mind. Cheryl was *stealing the show*. Bethie had heard that expression a million times, but she'd never realized what it felt like, how it was as if something real was being taken away from her, stolen right out from under her nose. *I can't let this happen*, Bethie thought. And so, head held high and her crown in place, she strode out onto the stage, grabbed Cheryl by the shoulders, and pulled her to her feet.

"Kings don't like show-offs." She smiled at Charlie. Charlie, who was obviously waiting to be told what to do, shot a desperate look toward the wings. "Just banish her!" Bethie whispered, and her voice must have been loud enough for the people in the front rows to hear, because they started to laugh.

"Um," said Charlie.

Red-faced, Cheryl put her hands on her hips and said, "I'm his wife and he still loves me!" Turning to Charlie, she said, "I danced for you, didn't I? So you don't need her."

"Um," Charlie said again.

"I'm the prettiest girl in all of Shushan!" Bethie reminded him. It was bragging, which she knew was bad manners, but the real Esther had won the beauty contest, and Bethie couldn't figure out how else to get show-off Cheryl off the stage.

Finally, Charlie decided to take action. Lifting his staff, he said, in his deepest voice, "Queen Vashti, I banish you from Shushan."

"How come?" Cheryl asked. When Charlie didn't answer, she said, "You told me to dance for the court, and I did. So now everything's fine!"

I guess it's up to me, Bethie thought. "The king just

banished you!" she said, giving Cheryl a shove. "It doesn't matter why! He's the king, and you have to do what the king says!"

"You can't marry Esther!" Cheryl wailed, grabbing at Charlie's bathrobe sleeve. "Because she's lying to you!" She sucked in a breath, and Bethie knew what she was going to say before she said it. "Esther is Jewish!" she blared.

"Big deal. So are you," Bethie shot back.

In the front row, Bethie saw one of the fathers laughing so hard that his sides were shaking. A few of the mothers were pressing handkerchiefs to their eyes, and her big sister's face was red with glee.

From the corner of the stage, Mrs. Jacobs was making frantic shooing motions at Cheryl. "Fine!" Cheryl said, tossing her hair. "But you'll be sorry!" She lifted her chin and marched off the stage. The audience began to clap, and even though it wasn't in the script, Bethie turned, gathering her skirt in her hands, and gave them an elegant bow.

When the play was over, Bethie and her parents and her sister walked through the parking lot. Jo was still chuckling and recounting her favorite unscripted moments. "I wonder if Queen Vashti really did say, 'You'll be sorry'?" Bethie was holding her carnations. She felt like she was floating, not walking. She had never been so happy in her life. They had almost reached their car when Bethie saw Cheryl's father, Mr. Goldfarb, standing in front of it with his arms crossed over his chest.

"Ken," Sarah said, putting her hand on her husband's forearm, as Mr. Goldfarb stepped forward. He wasn't a big man, but he looked all puffed up inside his suit, with his bald head almost glowing with rage.

"I'll bet you feel like a big shot," he said in a loud,

angry voice as he waved his thick finger at Bethie. "Humiliating Cheryl like that."

Bethie cringed backward. Ken moved so that he was standing in front of her.

"I think your daughter humiliated herself," he said. His own voice was very calm.

"Cheryl's taken tap and classical dance lessons for five years," said Mr. Goldfarb. "She should've had the bigger part."

"I think the crowd got to appreciate her dancing," Bethie's father said mildly.

"That's not the point and you know it!" Spit sprayed from Mr. Goldfarb's mouth as he shouted.

"Maybe she should have been Queen Esther. I didn't see the auditions, so I can't say for sure. But what I can tell you . . ." Bethie held her breath as her father pulled her forward, settling his hands protectively on her shoulders, "is that my little girl was fantastic."

Mr. Goldfarb muttered some more about favoritism and dance lessons before giving Bethie one final poisonous glare and stomping away.

"Don't let him bother you," her father told her. "You were very good and very funny. Now, who wants to go to Saunders for an ice-cream sundae?"

It turned out that everyone did.

Jo

You did not," Jo said to Lynnette Bobeck as they walked around the track at Bellwood High.

"I did." Lynnette sounded smug. "It's kind of perfect when you think about it. He's happy, and I'm still a virgin." It was Monday afternoon in gym class, the last period of the day, and the girls were dressed in baggy blue shorts and white cotton shirts. Normally, Jo would have gotten the story of her best friend's Saturday-night adventures with Bobby Carver on Sunday, but on that Sunday her mother had woken her and Bethie up early, with her hair tied back with a kerchief and an even sterner-than-usual look on her face. "Spring cleaning," she'd announced, handing them both a pile of rags and a bottle apiece—Jo got Windex; Bethie got Endust. They'd vacuumed all the carpets and scrubbed the oven, dusting the living room and wiping down the plastic that still covered the living-room couch, and at the end of the day, their father had taken them to the Shangri-La for pork fried rice and spareribs.

"Did it taste gross?" Jo asked.

"You don't swallow it, dummy," said Lynnette, as they rounded the bend of the track. For the last thirty minutes, they'd been doing laps under the indifferent eye of Coach Krantz, who coached the boys' football, basketball, and baseball teams and had little patience for girls. The May sunshine was warm on their bare legs, and every time the wind gusted, it sent a shower of dogwood petals raining down.

"First of all, it's got a million calories." Lynnette was short and busty, with hazel eyes and creamy skin that flushed pink whenever she was excited, and she was always watching her figure. Every time she and Jo went out, either by themselves or on a double date, Lynnette would virtuously order a salad, or the Dieter's Plate of cottage cheese and a plain broiled burger, and seltzer water to drink. Jo understood that it was her job to order the French fries and an egg cream or a malted for Lynnette to share. Her friend would sneak fries off Jo's plate or poke her own straw into Jo's glass.

"Was there a lot of it?" Jo was imagining an untended garden hose, thrashing and spewing water into the street.

Lynnette shrugged. "I don't know. I spit it out."

"Where?" Jo asked. "On him?" She was picturing Lynnette and Bobby in the back seat of Lynnette's father's Lincoln Continental, with Lynnette's bra shoved around her neck and Bobby's pants down around his ankles and his penis bobbing around like a candy apple on a stick. She dropped her voice to a whisper. "Did he do it to you?"

"Ew!" Lynnette said. "God! Like I'd ever let a boy put his face down there."

"You put your face down there," Jo pointed out.

"That's different," Lynnette said. "Besides, I don't even think that's a thing, the other way around."

Jo thought that sounded unfair, but decided not to say so. "So how was it?"

Lynnette pressed her lips together. She was wearing Cherries in the Snow lipstick, and her short, dark-blond hair was carefully curled. Jo sometimes thought that the rest of the girls at Bellwood High were like squirrels, plump and sleek and chittering, scurrying this way and that, waving their fluffy tails, racing up trees and down again for no reason at all. She felt like a crow, a big, ungainly misfit, flapping her wings, perching on a power line, sending all the squirrels running. At five foot eight, she was taller than almost all of her female classmates and a not-inconsiderable number of the male ones. Her body was unfashionably narrow-hipped and angular, with long legs made strong from years of running up and down basketball and tennis courts and barely enough bosom for a B cup. On the basketball court, or with a tennis racquet in her hand, Jo was graceful enough, and that was the place where she felt most comfortable. She'd become friends, or at least friendly, with three of the Negro girls who were the team's starters. LaDonna and LaDrea Moore were seniors, identical twins, shorter than Jo, wiry and quick, with freckled, medium-brown skin, French-braided hair, and mischievous smiles that reminded her of her old friend Frieda. Vernita Clinkscale, whose family had moved to Detroit from North Carolina the year before, had a twangy Southern accent and was almost six feet tall, with skin lighter than Jo's, straight, shoulder-length black hair, and a gold cross on a necklace that she kissed before making her free throws.

Negro kids made up less than a quarter of the high

school's population, and the unofficial rule was that they sat by themselves at lunch, but the rule was relaxed somewhat for teammates, and so sometimes, when she and Lynnie didn't have the same lunch period, Jo would sit with the basketball starters. She'd listen to Vernita moon over her boyfriend, who still lived in North Carolina, and to LaDrea and LaDonna, who went to the church where Aretha Franklin's father was the preacher and had met Aretha herself and Rosa Parks. Rosa Parks had moved to Detroit after her arrest for failing to move to the back of the bus in Montgomery, Alabama, and had spoken at the Moore family's church. "She said, 'People thought I wouldn't give up my seat because I was tired,' but that wasn't true," LaDrea said. "She said . . ."

And here her sister chimed in, "'The only tired I was, was tired of giving in.'"

"Wow." Jo tried to imagine being brave enough to do what Rosa Parks had done, to get herself arrested and put in jail. "I bet she's glad to be up here and not down South."

The three girls exchanged a look. "What?" Jo asked.

"You think it's better here?" LaDrea asked, eyebrows raised. "Ask me how many white people live in my apartment building."

"Or on our street," said LaDonna. "Or how many go to our little brother's school."

"Um . . ."

"None. Zero. That's how many. Detroit's just as segregated as any place down South. The only difference is, it's not against the law."

Jo bit a carrot stick, remembering the feeling of her mother's hands on her shoulders, her eight-year-old bottom being pushed onto the plastic slipcovered couch.

Birds of a feather must flock together. "That isn't fair," she said.

The girls exchanged another look. LaDonna rolled her eyes. LaDrea sucked her teeth.

"Can we change the subject, please?" Vernita asked. "Ya'll are making my head hurt. And you know we've got to run suicide drills this afternoon." She leaned forward, so that her cross gleamed in the fluorescent light, and pointed at the lemon bar Jo had brought from home. "You planning on eating that?"

Jo handed over her dessert. She was thinking about Mae and Frieda. "It isn't fair," she said again, but the bell rang, and everyone got up to throw away their trash and get to class.

Later, after practice, LaDrea approached her in the locker room. "You know," she began, "if you're serious about doing something . . ."

"I am," said Jo.

"There are pickets every Saturday at Crystal Pool, on Greenfield and Eight Mile. Crystal Pool's segregated. A bunch of us go." She looked at Jo, her expression neutral. She was holding a basketball tucked against her hip, and a lock of hair had worked its way out of her braid. "We meet here at the school at ten o'clock and carpool over."

Jo nodded. Her heart was beating hard. Her mother, she knew, wouldn't want her at anything like a picket. Her parents believed in equality—at least, that's what they said. "The Jewish people have been oppressed too much to oppress anyone else," Jo's father said. But he'd also moved them away from the old neighborhood, saying it was changing, and Jo was old enough now to understand that *changing* meant *Negros coming in.* Then there was Sarah, who said things like *Don't ruffle any feathers*, and *Don't stir the pot*. Showing up at a picket was nothing if not pot-stirring.

On Saturday morning, Jo got up early and told Sarah that she was going to the high school to practice her free throws.

"Be home by four," her mother said without looking at her, so Jo climbed on her bike and pedaled to school.

"Didn't think you'd be here," LaDonna said, and LaDrea said, "C'mon, you need a sign." There were about a dozen kids, black and white, with squares of posterboard, using black paint to write EQUALITY NOW and INTEGRATE and LIBERTY AND JUSTICE FOR ALL. Jo pulled in a deep breath and dipped her brush in the paint. "Is Vernita coming?" she asked as she wrote the word EQUALITY and hoped her hand wouldn't shake.

"Pssht, Vernita," LaDonna said, waving one of the long-fingered hands that let her grip a basketball so easily. "Forget her."

Jo rode in the Moore sisters' 1959 Mercury. She marched in a circle in front of the pool's chain-link fence as cars drove past. A few would honk in support, but most of them would just look the other way. When it was over, she met Lynnette at the beauty shop, where Lynnie was getting her hair washed and set, teased high in the back, with bangs that curled over her forehead. "What'd you do today?" Lynnette asked as she held a plastic fan in front of her face so the hairdresser's assistant could mist Elnett hairspray from the crown of her head to the tips that curled against her cheeks.

"Oh, nothing," Jo said.

Sometimes Jo wondered if Lynnette liked her because she was taller and ungainly and less attractive, the ugly duckling to Lynnette's swan. The two of them did not have much in common. Jo was a strong student;

Lynnette struggled, especially in math class. Jo was an athlete; Lynnette would get winded the single time each year that Coach Krantz actually did make her run a quarter mile. Lynnette loved clothes—wearing them, shopping for them, talking about the ones she wanted to shop for and wear next—while Jo just grabbed whatever was nearby and relatively clean. What they shared was a sense of mischief, a love of disruption and fun. Lynnette had gotten Jo drunk for the first time when they were both fifteen, and Jo had convinced Lynnette to cut school sophomore year. They'd climbed into Sarah's car with the boy upon whom Lynnette had been bestowing her affections at the time, and one of his tall friends for Jo, and driven to a bowling alley, where they'd ordered pitchers of beer and plates of French fries and laughed about their classmates, stuck back at school for a pep rally. Lynnette sighed over Jo's slender figure—"you can wear anything," she would say—and Jo was similarly appreciative of Lynnette's curves, even when Lynnette despaired about her hips and what she claimed was her double chin. Lynnette had taught Jo how to smoke, and Jo had taught Lynnette how to swim, and they told each other everything . . . except for the increasingly frequent daydreams Jo had been having about their weekly sleepovers, a daydream in which, instead of one of her silk nightgowns, Lynnie would come to bed wearing nothing at all.

"Does he want to go all the way?" Jo asked, careful to keep her voice neutral.

"He tried to put his hand down my pants, but I told him to forget it." Lynnette wagged her finger in Bobby's imaginary face. "I said, 'Mr. Bobby Carver, not until there's a ring on my finger.'" She touched the class ring that she wore around her neck, as if to reassure herself of Bobby's commitment, and how one ring would lead to another.

"Did you like it?" Jo asked. Lynnette tilted her head sideways as she considered.

"It was kind of like brushing my teeth," she finally said. "Or, no, that's not quite it. Maybe it was like clapping. Just, you know. Clap clap clap squirt. Then it's over." Their sneakered feet crunched against the cinders. "I don't know," Lynnette said, sighing. "It was kind of exciting to see how excited he was, you know? To know that I could make him feel like that. But I didn't really feel anything at all." She sighed again. "Maybe real sex will feel better."

"Maybe." Jo was secretly relieved that Lynnette hadn't enjoyed ministering to Bobby Carver. Lynnette interpreted her response as an indication of Jo's frustration over her own lackluster love life.

"It's going to happen for you," she said, reaching up to pat Jo's shoulder. "You'll find the right guy."

Jo shrugged. She'd been out with plenty of boys, usually on double dates with Lynnette. She knew their moves. At the movie shows, the Redford or the Senate, the boy would stretch his arm up high, then casually drape it around her shoulders. At the Bel-Air drive-in, they'd try to get her into the back seat, and at school dances, they'd ask if she needed some fresh air, but their clammy hands on her shoulders, their cool, wormy lips against her mouth had all left her feeling less than nothing.

"Have you ever . . ." Lynnette looked at her, a brief glance from underneath her curled bangs. Jo saw her cheeks blushing pink. "Have you ever touched yourself?"

"Sometimes," she said, after making sure there was no chance that any of their classmates would be able to hear them. A few times, when she'd been fastening a sanitary napkin to her belt, her fingers would drift over the soft triangle of hair between her legs. There was, she had discovered, a tender place right at the top, and when her fingers brushed against it, jolts of pleasure would shoot through her lower belly, making her nipples get hard. The feeling was so strong that it frightened her, and she would hastily take her fingers away. She looked at her friend, gathering her nerve. "Have you?"

Lynnette's lipsticked mouth curved up in a smile, and when she spoke, her voice was so low that Jo could hardly hear. "When I went to Camp Tanuga last summer," she began. Jo moved so close that their shoulders were touching. "One of the counselors there really liked me."

Jo nodded, unsurprised. Everyone liked Lynnette. When she realized what Lynnette meant, about this girl who'd really liked her, she felt her body flush again, this time with jealousy.

"She had something that she let me borrow."

"What?" Jo asked. "What is it?" She felt envious of this counselor, angry that Lynnette had waited all this time to tell her, and, above everything else, desperate to keep Lynnette talking.

"I can't tell you." Lynnette giggled. She'd turned a color past pink, closer to red. "But I can show you. After school," she said, and gave Jo a saucy smile. "My house. I am going to change your life."

Lynnette's family had once lived in a house like Jo's, but when Lynnette was in junior high, her father, who'd been working at an accounting firm in Detroit, got promoted. He moved his family into a much bigger house, a four-bedroom redbrick mock Tudor with a finished basement and an in-law suite. The Bobecks' house had a kitchen with two ovens and creamy white Formica countertops, a living room with a bricked-in wood-burning fireplace and a big color television set, a card table with padded chairs and special lighting where Mrs. Bobeck played bridge. The basement featured pine-paneled walls, a pool table, and a wet bar. Lynnette planned to host the senior class for a party after they finally graduated.

After school, Lynnette and Jo bypassed the kitchen, where normally they would stop for a snack (apples if Lynnette was dieting, cinnamon toast if she wasn't). They went right to Lynnette's bedroom, which had pink and white patterned wallpaper, a dresser, a bookcase, and a nightstand all made of the same painted white wood, and a lacy white canopy over the queen-sized bed. Lynnette locked the door, even though the house was empty—both of her brothers went to the Boys' Club after school, her father worked downtown, and her mom volunteered at the Hebrew Home for the Aged most afternoons. As Jo watched, Lynnette took the chair that sat in front of her desk and wedged it underneath the doorknob. She crossed the room, bent down in front of her record player, and put on a Connie Francis album. Finally, with great care, she slid her hand underneath her mattress and removed something that looked like a handheld eggbeater, complete with an electrical cord and plug. The body was encased in hard tan plastic, but in the space where the beaters should have been there was only a hard rubber disk.

"What is it?" Jo asked, and Lynnette whispered, "It's a vibrator!"

Jo stared. She had only the vaguest idea of what a

vibrator was, thought she'd heard the word but wasn't one hundred percent sure of its meaning, and she'd assumed that something meant for sexual pleasure would be shaped more like a penis than a kitchen utensil. "And it's for . . ." Jo gestured vaguely toward the lower half of her body, feeling the strangest combination of excitement and fear as Lynnette nodded.

"Carla—she was my counselor—she showed it to us, and she told us how to use it, and we decided every girl in our bunk would get a turn. You get it for two weeks, and then you have to wrap it up and mail it to whoever's next on the list."

"You wash it first, right?"

Jo felt like her entire insides were contracting, squeezing tight around the space between her legs, making it throb. There was an ache in her belly, and she wanted to take her friend by her rounded, cashmere-covered shoulders and kiss her. She knew, somehow, that instead of feeling wet and wormy, Lynnette's lips would be firm and sweet, and that instead of feeling faintly revolted, she'd feel happy and content. Had Carla, the camp counselor, kissed Lynnette? *I'll kill her*, Jo thought, feeling jealousy fighting with desire, and both of them at war with shame, because she wasn't supposed to be feeling this way about her best friend, or any girl at all.

"See, look," said Lynnette, unfurling the cord, plugging the little machine into the wall.

Jo's heart was beating hard. "I don't know if we should do this," she said. Her voice sounded hoarse. "Maybe it's, you know, bad for us or something."

Lynnette looked amused. "Just wait," she said, "until you find out how good it feels." With that, she flicked a switch. The little rubber cup began humming. Jo could see that it was, indeed, vibrating, so fast that its motions were almost imperceptible. She imagined how that humming cup would feel against her and felt her lower body contract like a cramp.

"Are you sure the door's locked?" she whispered.

"Yes, I'm sure," said Lynnette. She got on the bed, leaning back against a pile of pillows. "You've really never done anything with a boy? Not anything?"

Jo shook her head. Somehow, the half-darkness made it easier to tell the truth.

"What about with Leonard?" Lynnette asked. Leonard Weiss had been Jo's only long-term boyfriend. They'd dated that winter, during the four months of basketball season, when Jo had been the starting center for the girls' team and Leonard was a guard for the boys. Jo sometimes thought that the only reason she'd stayed with Leonard for so long was that he was one of the few boys at school who was significantly taller than she was. She liked how he made her feel small, how he actually had to bend down to kiss her. But when he did kiss her, it was the same as it had been with Stan and Donald and Paul. She would feel the spit in the boy's mouth, and hear the sound of teeth clicking together, and she'd have to fight to keep herself from shoving away and running immediately for a hot shower and a bottle of Listerine.

"I told you about Leonard," Jo said. "I let him go up my sweater, but that's all."

"Inside your bra or outside?"

"Inside. Once." Jo winced, remembering the way Leonard had fiddled with her nipples, squeezing and pinching them like they were tiny mouths he was trying to shut.

Lynnette widened her eyes in mock horror at Jo's daring, then smiled a wicked, pleased-with-herself smile. "Lie down."

Jo tried for a casual, teasing tone. "I thought this was going to be a visual demonstration."

"This is how Carla showed me." Doubt flickered across her friend's face. "Unless you don't want me to."

Jo had never wanted something so much in her entire life, but she kept her tone casual. "I guess if I'm going to be a writer, I need to have some experiences," she said, lying back on Lynnette's pillows, trying not to appear too eager and scare Lynnette away.

"Take your pants off."

Jo closed her eyes so that she wouldn't have to see her friend's face, and wriggled out of the jeans she'd worn, the ones that her mother despaired of and said made her look like a coal miner. Underneath them, she wore plain white cotton panties. Her legs were smooth—she'd shaved that morning—and already tanned from the spring sun. She felt her belly contract and flutter when Lynnette brushed it with her fingertips. When she felt the rubber cup of the machine thrumming against her thigh, just above her knee, she gasped, jerking up straight.

"Ooh!" Jo said. "It tickles." But Jo could tell that what felt ticklish on her leg was going to feel different, and much better, someplace else.

Lynnette smiled as she turned the disk onto its side and slid its edge up, tracing a line along the inside of Jo's leg. She moved it toward the leg band of Jo's underwear, her pace excruciatingly slow, before pulling it away and running it back along Jo's thigh. Jo found herself squirming as Lynnette continued to drag the vibrator up and down, moving closer, each time, to Jo's underwear, which had to be soaking wet. Jo wondered if her friend could see. Just when Jo was getting ready to say something—*please*—or take her friend's hand and move it between her legs, Lynnette moved the cup over Jo's belly before she pulled it down slowly, until it was almost at the place where her pubic hair began. Jo's hands were clenched into fists, and she was rocking her hips, pumping them up and down, desperate for Lynnette to bring the buzzing cup to where Jo needed to feel it. She could feel sweat gathering at her temples and the small of her back, and her breathing was drowning out Connie Francis.

"Do you like it?" Lynnette's voice sounded a little husky.

"Yes!" Jo managed.

"Want me to keep going?"

Jo nodded, not trusting herself to speak. She grabbed on to Lynnette's comforter with both her hands, spreading her legs wider.

"Okay," Lynnette said, and slid the edge of the cup down from the waistband of Jo's underwear, down to that spot Jo's fingers had brushed a few times in the bathroom, the spot she never let herself touch at night or in the shower.

The effect was electric. Jo felt her body arc off the bed. Her nails dug into the comforter, and she gasped once, harshly, the sound almost like a sob.

"There?" Lynnette asked, sounding very pleased with herself.

Jo took her friend's wrist in her hand and shifted the cup's angle the tiniest fraction. Heat and delicious tension were blooming in her belly and between her legs, the sensation threatening to overwhelm her. She felt her entire body stiffen, in preparation for some delicious release.

"Oh," she said, her voice cracking, her hips lifted. Before she could stop herself, before she could think, she reached up with both arms, wrapping her hands around the back of Lynnette's neck, pulling her best friend down on top of her until they were chest to chest and mouth to mouth. *She'll slap me*, she thought dimly, as the vibrator, trapped between their bodies, tilted at the perfect angle, still thrumming against her. Widening waves of pleasure were rolling out from that place, all through her body. Her toes curled. Her legs locked, muscles shaking, and Lynnette's mouth was as sweet as she'd known it would be, her tongue hot and vital and absolutely necessary, as essential as air as it stroked against Jo's own. Jo felt her hips jerk sharply upward once, twice, then again, and her whole body trembled as bliss swept through her, sharp and sweet and overwhelming.

Jo fell back, breathing hard, and somehow Lynnette ended up tucked beside her, a flushed, sweet, fragrant bundle. *Now*, thought Jo. Now she'll see what is wrong with me. Now she'll tell me to leave. Only Lynnette, giggling and supremely pleased with herself, didn't seem to be in any hurry for Jo to go anywhere. Leaning over Jo's half-naked body to consult the clock on her dresser, she said, "No one's going to be home for another hour."

Jo nodded. As soon as she could catch her breath, she rolled over, pinning Lynnette's arms above her head with one arm. With the other, she pulled off Lynnie's skirt. Her friend squealed, but not in disapproval, and she didn't try to get away. Jo located the little humming device and straddled her friend's thighs, one leg on either side. "Tell me if I'm doing it right," she said, and bent to her task. She wanted to make Lynnette feel what she'd felt, those widening waves of ecstasy, wanted to feel her best friend roll her hips and shake, hear her gasp and sigh, to watch as her fists clenched and her face turned pink and her carefully set curls wilted. Five minutes after she began, Lynnette was gripping Jo's upper arms, eyes shut and gasping. A minute after that, Lynnette pulled Jo down beside her, and, with her eyes still shut, whispered, "I am never ever EVER putting that thing in the mail."

Bethie

When Bethie came home from roller-skating with her friends on an unexpectedly warm Saturday afternoon in March, the house was quiet. There was no smell of roasting chicken or tuna-noodle casserole emanating from the kitchen (Sarah had started cooking on Shabbat, dispensing with cholent years ago, saying she was done being old-fashioned, washing two sets of dishes and following all of the rules). Bethie hadn't seen her father in the driveway, washing his car, the way he liked to do on pleasant Saturdays, and she found her mother in the living room, which was weird, actually sitting on the couch, which was weirder. "Keep your voice down," Sarah murmured before Bethie could say a word. "Your father's got an upset stomach."

Bethie winced. Their house had only one bathroom, with a small window that overlooked the backyard and a noisy ceiling fan that seemed to move the air around more than clear it. Sarah kept a box of kitchen matches on the windowsill and a can of Lysol spray beside it, but when someone in the house had, in their mother's delicate phrasing, "an upset stomach," the entire small house ended up smelling.

"Ken?" Sarah called down the hallway, stretching his name until it was two syllables, her voice rising on the second one: *Ke-en?* No answer came. "Honey? Are you going to want dinner?"

No answer came. Twenty minutes later, Jo's friend Lynnette dropped Jo off. "What's going on?" Jo asked, breezing through the door in blue basketball shorts and a dark-blue T-shirt, as Lynnette backed her parents' car out onto the street, narrowly missing the Steins' mailbox, which she'd already hit twice. Bethie explained the situation as their mother stood in front of the bathroom door, conducting a one-way conversation with their dad. "We'll have a chef's salad for dinner! Does that sound all right?" No answer. Sarah came into the kitchen, looking anxious. "Bethie, why don't you give a knock?"

Bethie did not need to be asked twice. She had plans for the night, a first date with Donald Powers, who was a junior, the student council treasurer, and a member of Key Club. Donald was going to pick her up at seven, to take her to see *Cat on a Hot Tin Roof.* She'd need to shower and use the mirror.

"Daddy?" she called, knocking at the bathroom door and breathing through her mouth, just in case. No answer came. Bethie couldn't hear anything—no words, no bathroom noises, not even breathing.

Bethie knocked again, even harder. "Dad? Daddy?" *Fart once if you can hear us,* she thought, and had to bite her lips to stifle her giggles.

"It isn't funny," Jo said. Her sister's brow was furrowed, and she wore the same look of intense concentration that Bethie had seen when she stood at the free-throw line on the basketball court. That expression gave Bethie her first twinge of unease.

Jo went to their bedroom and came back with a wire hanger. She pulled the curved end straight, inserted the tip into the lock, and twisted it as Sarah stood next to Bethie, both of them a few feet behind Jo. They all heard the sound of the lock popping open. "Dad?" Jo called, and pushed the door open. Sarah gasped.

"Don't look," Jo said, her voice low, but Bethie did, standing on her tiptoes to peek over her sister's shoulder. Her father was sitting on the toilet seat, his pants pulled up, his torso slumped against the wall. His face was a terrible purplish-gray color. His eyes were shut, and Bethie knew, before she heard her mother scream, that her father was dead.

Sarah and the girls didn't get home from the hospital until ten o'clock. When Jo opened the front door that no one had remembered to lock, Bethie saw that Donald Powers, her forgotten Saturday-night date, had left a note tucked into the door jamb. *Guess we got our wires crossed. I'll give you a ring tomorrow.* Bethie stared at the words for a long time. It was as if they had been written in a foreign language, or sent from a different lifetime. She folded the note into her pocket and followed her mother and sister into the kitchen, where Jo filled the kettle, lit one of the gas rings, and pulled out three mugs and three teabags.

Bethie had been the one to call the operator and ask for an ambulance, and Jo had been trying to do CPR that they'd both been taught in gym class when the ambulance finally arrived. The paramedics, two young men in white pants and white shirts, had ordered her out of the room and lifted Ken's body, but even before they'd gotten him onto the couch, and then into the back of the ambulance, a long, white-painted Cadillac that looked distressingly like a hearse, Bethie had known, from the looks they exchanged, that it was hopeless. They'd followed the ambulance to the hospital and been told to sit in the waiting room. Jo had paced restlessly, prowling the floor in her sneakers and shorts. Bethie had tucked herself into a chair in the corner and made up stories. The woman playing solitaire was there because her daughter was having a baby, the fellow who stood by the vending machine, shifting his weight from side to side, was there because his little boy had slammed his hand in a car door. Sarah sat on one of the molded plastic chairs, with her legs crossed at the ankles and her purse in her lap. She seemed perfectly normal if you didn't look at her eyes, or at how her knees were trembling. When the young doctor came out and quietly gave her mother the news, Bethie braced for hysterics, for screaming and tears. But Sarah just nodded and got to her feet, gathering up her pocketbook and her daughters and leading them out to the car.

Now Sarah was sitting motionless at the kitchen table, her face blank, her eyes unfocused. Bethie realized that she could hardly ever remember seeing her mother holding still. When Sarah wasn't on her feet, moving from refrigerator to stove to counters, washing dishes or folding laundry or cooking, she always found something to do with her hands. Bethie must have watched hundreds of television shows, written dozens of papers, and solved thousands of math problems accompanied by the click-click-click of Sarah's knitting needles or the tapping of her heels. That night Sarah just sat, unmoving, with a notebook in front of her and an uncapped pen in her hands.

Jo talked to their mother in a gentle voice Bethie hardly recognized, asking questions that would never have occurred to Bethie. "No," Sarah said, "we don't have plans. We were going to . . ." Her voice trailed off, the way it had been doing since the doctor had knelt in front of her and said *I'm so sorry*. On the way home, a few times Sarah had started to say something—"I should make sure the good dishes are . . ." or "Do you think Daddy would . . ." The girls would wait, but Sarah's voice would just drift off. Jo ended up being the one who'd called the rabbi at Adath Israel, and the funeral parlor, and the newspaper, to request an obituary form. Bethie watched her mother sipping tea, listening to Jo answer questions. *Just a plain pine box* and *We'll bring a suit, and a tie, and his tallis*. When those calls were made, Jo dialed Lynnette. "I'm sorry to call so late, Mrs. Bobeck, but my dad died, and if there's any way I could speak to Lynnette . . ." Bethie couldn't hear the reply, but she could imagine Mrs. Bobeck's shocked gasp, and how she'd murmur, *Oh, of course, dear, I'm so sorry*. Bethie thought about calling Barbara Simoneaux or Laura Ochs or Darlene Conti, but decided to tell them in the morning. *I am a girl whose father died*, she thought, trying on the identity like a new pair of shoes. When she'd fall down on her roller skates, her father was the one who'd dab hydrogen peroxide on her scrapes. When her fingernails needed cutting, her father would pull her onto his lap and clip them. When she was naughty, he'd spank her—a *poch* on the *tuchis*, as he said—but even his spanks were almost gentle; and while Jo was usually the one who went on drives with him, every few weeks he'd bring home a special treat for Bethie, a chocolate tart or a slice of bumpy cake from Saunders. *I am a girl whose father is dead*, Bethie thought again. She wondered if it had hurt, if her father had known what was happening, if he'd been afraid.

By two in the morning, Sarah was asleep on the living-room couch. Jo slipped her mother's shoes off, while Bethie found a blanket and covered her up. The girls took turns brushing their teeth and washing up. Bethie wondered if Jo felt as strange about being in the bathroom as she did, but what could they do? Her parents had talked about adding on to the house, like the Steins across the street had done, building a family room or a big master bedroom and another bathroom, but that had never happened, and now it never would. Bethie waited until Jo was in bed before she whispered, "What are we going to tell people about Dad?"

Jo rolled onto her side. "What do you mean? We're going to tell them that he died. If they don't know already." On Monday morning, they would pin black ribbons to their dresses and the rabbi would cut them, to signify their loss. When they got back from the cemetery, Sarah would set out a bowl of water and a roll of paper towels beside the front door, for mourners to wash their hands before they entered the house. The Jews in the neighborhood would know what that meant, and would explain it to any neighbors who didn't.

"No. I mean about where he died."

The bedsprings creaked as Jo rolled over again. "Do you think people are actually going to ask where it happened?"

"They might." Bethie had already given some thought to the question of how her classmates would react if they learned that her father had died on the toilet. It was shallow, she knew, but Bethie cared about people's opinions in a way that Jo didn't. Maybe it was fine for Jo to just have Lynnette and her friends on the basketball team, and to wear her sloppy jeans and their father's old button-down shirts, not paying attention to what anyone thought of her, but Bethie was different. Bethie did care. And if people found out that Ken Kaufman had died on the toilet, they would laugh. "How about we just say the floor? It's not technically wrong. Because he was on the floor."

"He was on the floor, after the ambulance people pulled him off the toilet."

Bethie sighed, wondering where Jo's unwavering commitment to the truth had come from, and why she herself hadn't gotten it. "Well, I'm telling people that we found him on the floor."

"Say whatever you want," Jo said. "I don't care." Her voice wobbled.

After a moment, Bethie asked, "Do you think we'll be all right? With . . . with money and stuff?" Bethie only had a general awareness about financial matters. Certainly, there were kids whose families had more money than hers did—Cheryl Goldfarb came to mind—but Bethie and her family had enough. They went to Lake Erie for a week every summer; they replaced their Ford sedan whenever the new model came out. With their father dead, without his income, would they still be all right?

The pause stretched out for so long that Bethie wasn't sure she'd be able to stand it. "I guess," Jo finally. "I guess we'll have to be."

At the shiva, their father's mother, Grandma Elkie, and his brother, their uncle Mel, were the first to arrive. Uncle Mel and his wife, Aunt Shirley, their daughters, Audrey and Joanne, and son, Donnie, ages ten, eight, and six, paused at the front door, passing a deli platter the size of a wagon wheel from one to another as each of them washed their hands. Inside, Aunt Shirley hugged their mother and asked her, "What can I do?" while Uncle Mel helped his mother get settled in the living room. Elkie was tiny, frail, almost bald, mostly toothless. That day, she wore a loose, dark-blue dress and a small round hat with a veil covering her sparse white hair. Like Bubbe, she spoke only Yiddish. That afternoon, she didn't speak at all, she just sat there and cried, while the cousins stared at Jo and Bethie, like the two of them were animals in a zoo.

Uncle Mel was eight years younger than their father had been. Ken's parents had left their shtetl in Poland, running from the pogroms in 1908. They'd taken a ship to New York City, then made their way to Detroit because a cousin's friend had promised Chaim Kaufman a job. The part that Bethie could never understand was that they'd left their son behind. Ken, whose name was Kalman then, had stayed with Elkie's parents, whose shtetl was, Bethie supposed, a little safer than the one they'd left, while his father found work as a day laborer moving furniture in Detroit and, eventually, saved up enough money to move out of their cousin's apartment and into one of their own.

Seven years elapsed before they were able to bring Ken to the United States. By the time he arrived, a new baby had been born. Melvin had an American name, and he spoke perfect English, without the greenhorn accent that plagued his brother. Bethie understood that her father had grown up loving his brother and resenting him, too. His parents had pinned all of their hopes on Mel, and Ken had been more like a parent than a sibling, dropping out of school at sixteen to help support the family. Even though he'd been smart enough to go to college, only Melvin had gotten the chance. Bethie's father had worked on the line at the River Rouge plant, taking accounting classes at night, while his brother had finished high school and college, before going on to medical school. By the time Bethie had been born, Uncle Mel was an ophthalmologist. He lived with his wife and three children and his mother in Southfield, in a split-level ranch house with a vast master bathroom, with two sinks with golden taps shaped like swans and a sunken tiled tub that looked as big as a swimming pool. Bethie could remember her mother telling her that she mustn't use the fancy, plush-looking pale-green towels laid out beside the powder room sink, even though Bethie, who had just learned to read, could see the word GUESTS embroidered at the bottom. Sarah showed her how to dry her hands on a piece of tissue instead.

Jo and Bethie and their parents visited the big house twice a year, once for the Passover Seder, where they joined their grandmother, their cousins, and relatives from Aunt Shirley's side of the family for the traditional meal, and again for the first night of Chanukah, when they'd eat brisket and fried latkes, and the children all received gifts.

At dinnertime at Uncle Mel's, a silent Negro girl, short and slim, wearing a black dress with a white apron on top, would carry the roast or the turkey to the table, holding the heavy platter in both hands, bringing it first to Uncle Mel, who'd inspect it and nod his approval before starting to carve. Aunt Shirley had a little silver bell beside her plate, and she rang it to summon the girl, whose name Bethie had never heard. "Where does she eat dinner?" Bethie had asked, as they drove home. "In the kitchen, I imagine," Sarah had said, and Jo had said that she wished she could eat in the kitchen, too, and listen to the radio and not have to sit still and worry about using the right fork, but Bethie had adored her aunt and uncle's dining room. She would smooth her hands over her starched napkin, brush her fingertips against the heavy half-moon-shaped glass paperweight that sat on a side table in the living room, gazing at the branched piece of coral it contained, letting her breath mist its surface, and dream about living in a house like this, with servants to bring her the food and take away the dirty dishes when she was done.

That morning, Mel's eyes were watery and red, and his face was scratchy. Close relatives of the deceased didn't shave during the mourning period. "Bethie," Uncle Mel said when he found her in the kitchen, gathering her into a hug. Bethie had worn the nicest clothes she had to her father's funeral, the navy-blue dress her mother had bought her for eighth-grade graduation, and it had gotten short, and tight under the arms, but, of course, she hadn't wanted to bother her mother to say so. She could feel it straining against her bust as her uncle hugged her. "I'm so sorry."

Why are you sorry? You didn't kill him, Bethie thought. Uncle Mel held her, and she felt his hand drift down her side until it rested on a part of her body that was no longer technically her hip. Bethie froze, almost too startled to breathe. Uncle Mel had never touched her like that before. No one ever had.

Before Bethie could figure out what to do, Uncle Mel removed his hand, kissed her cheek again, and retreated to the living room, where whiskey and schnapps had been set up on a card table. Bethie went to the backyard with Barbara and her other friends, Laura Ochs and Darlene Conti and Patti Jamison, who'd all stayed home from school for the day. She wondered what had just happened and if she'd imagined his hand on her bottom, hoping that if her friends noticed her pale face and her silence, they'd ascribe it to grief.

Barbara asked how she was doing. Laura and Darlene said how sorry they were. Patti said, "If there's anything you need, just tell me." Bethie thought about how nice it would be if, instead of saying *What can we do*, or *I'm here for you*, people would just offer to do something specific. *I will wash the dishes* or *I will fold the laundry* or *I will take your Introduction to Biology final so that you don't have to study*. But, instead of making her friends feel uncomfortable, she just said, "I saw the prettiest formal in the window at Kern's," and the girls seemed relieved to change the subject.

As the day went on, Bethie pushed the memory of what Uncle Mel had done out of her head, telling herself that it had been a mistake, or that maybe she'd imagined it. Uncle Mel disappeared for a while, to take his mother, wife, and children home, but then he came back in the late afternoon and hovered by the schnapps until the rabbi arrived to lead the minyan, the group of ten men who would recite the Kaddish, the prayer for the dead.

Her mother stood in the doorway to the living room, clutching a handkerchief, as the men stood, chanting the Hebrew words. Jo stood behind her, somber and still. "Dear, can you get me a sweater?" Sarah asked Bethie, once the service was over. Bethie went into her parents' bedroom—just her mother's bedroom now, she thought. She'd just closed the dresser drawer when the bedroom door opened, and there was her uncle, red-faced and unsteady on his feet.

"Bethie." His voice was thick. He'd taken off his suit jacket and loosened his tie.

"Hi, Uncle Mel." She tried to edge past him, but he grabbed her elbow and held her tight.

"Do you know Robert Frost? 'The Road Not Taken'?"

Bethie nodded. They'd read the poem in English class the year before, and she thought it was called "The Road Less Traveled," but this didn't seem the time to point it out.

"Two roads diverged in a wood, and I—I took the one less traveled by, and that has made all the difference," her uncle said, and started to cry. He wept and clutched her, enveloping her in his arms and the fetid mist of his breath. She thought that he was saying *My poor brother*, but it was hard for her to understand, because Uncle Mel had buried his wet, scratchy face against her neck and had pressed his whole body against hers. This time, one of his hands brushed against the side of her breast.

Without thinking, Bethie shoved him away, so hard that his back banged into the wall, dislodging a framed photograph of her parents that had been taken on their honeymoon at Niagara Falls. They looked impossibly young, standing on the deck of the *Maid of the Mist*, her father with his arms around her mother's shoulders, and Sarah, in a neat navy-blue suit with a pleated skirt, smiling a dreamy smile.

Breathing hard, speechless with shock at his actions and her own, Bethie stared at her uncle as he bent over clumsily, picking the picture up off the floor. It took him two tries to hook the wire over the nail, and when he let go the picture was crooked. Without a word of apology, he turned and walked out into the hall. Bethie watched him go, breathing hard, wishing she'd grabbed the hand he'd groped her with and slammed it through the nail. She locked the door, then sat down on her parents' bed—her mother's bed, now—and made herself take deep, slow breaths until she stopped shaking. In the bathroom, she ran cold water over her wrists, put a pleasant expression on her face, collected the sweater her mother had asked for, and went to help clear away the uneaten food and pile up the prayer books that they'd use again the next night.

When the house was finally empty, the Kaufman women gathered again around the kitchen table. "So much food," Sarah said. She sounded dazed. Before the minyan, Bethie had overheard Larry Fein, a cousin in his first year of medical school, telling Aunt Shirley that an artery that led to her father's heart had gotten clogged. "The widowmaker, they call that one," he'd said, looking puffed up and proud of himself, before noticing Bethie watching him and quickly looking away.

Jo bustled around the kitchen, covering leftovers in cling wrap—deli platters, plates of pastries, the pan of corn bread that Mae had brought. One of the other cleaning ladies on the street must have told Mae what had happened, because she'd come to the house in a black dress and a hat with a short black veil. *Your daddy's left this world of pain and sorrow,* Mae had said, embracing both girls, and Jo, who'd barely shed a tear, even at the graveside service, had started to cry. Mae had held her, patting her back. *He's gone home to glory.* In her black turtleneck sweater and pleated gray skirt, with hollows under her cheekbones and her new pixie cut exposing her long neck, Jo seemed older, and almost glamorous. Bethie wondered for the thousandth time why her sister didn't do more with herself, why her only makeup was a little bit of lipstick, why she preferred to slop around in jeans and button-down boys' shirts and spent more time with her best friend, Lynnette, than with any of the boys who'd asked her out.

"So," Sarah began, when Jo had finally finished and was sitting at the table. "I should tell you girls a few things." She looked down at her hands clasped on the oilcloth, with its print of red and yellow roses. "Your father had a life insurance policy. Not a lot, but enough so that we won't be out on the street. But you can forget about those East Coast colleges, those Six Sisters," she said sharply, as if Jo had argued with her when, for once in her life, Jo had not.

"Seven Sisters," Jo said. "That's okay. The U of M is fine."

"It'll have to be. And you'll study something practical. Nursing or education, not literature." Sarah shook a cigarette out of the pack on the table and picked up the heavy gold lighter. "I should quit these," she said, looking at the cigarette between her fingers. "And I'll have to get a job. There's the mortgage, and the water and the gas," she said, looking increasingly hopeless. "And property taxes . . . and the heating oil . . ."

Bethie swallowed hard. Some of her friends' mothers worked. Kaye Greenfield's mom did bookkeeping at the grocery store her father owned, and Laura's mom taught nursery school at the synagogue, but none of them had what you'd call a career. Then again, none of them were supporting a family the way she guessed Sarah would be.

"But Uncle Mel's going to help," Sarah said.

At the sound of his name, Bethie flinched, as if her uncle had reappeared in the kitchen and grabbed at her again. Her mother didn't notice. Sarah's lips were pressed so tightly together that they were in danger of vanishing. She breathed deeply, sighed, and said, "Dad and I never told you about this, but once, years ago, your father had a chance to go in on a business opportunity. He and two of his friends were going to buy a Laundromat. Just one at first, and if it worked out they'd buy more. Henry Sheshevsky was one of the fellows. Your father would have been the manager."

Jo was nodding. Bethie could vaguely remember Henry Sheshevsky, who was short and portly and almost as wide as he was tall, with a bald head and small, even white teeth and cheeks that always prickled with stubble. He had been a regular guest, right after they'd moved to Alhambra Street. "Country living!" he would say, climbing out of his car, which would rise a few inches once he'd exited. Henry would raise his head and his nostrils would flare as he took a comically deep breath, remarking on the freshness of the air, the green grass, and the wide-open space. He carried quarters and butterscotch candies in his pocket to give to Jo and Bethie, because he was a bachelor with, as he said, "no little girls to spoil." Sarah would set an extra place, and Henry would join them at the table, sharing whatever they were having— whitefish baked on a bed of onions, or meatloaf and mashed potatoes, or roast chicken and stuffing. Henry Sheshevsky ate daintily, holding his silverware with the tips of his fingers, cutting his food into small pieces and chewing each bite thoroughly, and he never took seconds, not even of mashed potatoes and gravy, Bethie's favorite, which made her wonder how he had gotten so stout.

"All of the men were going to invest some of their own money. Your father didn't have a lot of savings— we'd just bought the house—so he asked his brother for a loan. Not a gift, a loan. He'd pay it back, with interest, but Mel wouldn't agree."

"Why not?" asked Jo.

Sarah looked down at her cigarette. "He said his responsibility was to his mother, that he had to be conservative with his money, so that he could take care of her." Bethie thought about Elkie, who had her own bedroom and bathroom in Uncle Mel's house, and wondered how much care she required. "But he said he wants to do something for us now," Sarah said. She turned to Bethie. "He asked if you could come once a week and help Shirley out. Babysitting, and helping around the house. He'll pay you ten dollars every week. What do you think?"

Bethie knew that she must have looked stunned and stupid. Ten dollars a week was a fortune. Most girls only made twenty-five cents an hour babysitting. And she knew they needed the money. Her mother had made it clear. Bethie turned to her sister, hoping for help, but Jo had gone back to the sink, and was standing with her back to Bethie, and Sarah was looking at her with her eyes wet and her mouth curved in a tremulous, hopeful smile. "Sure," Bethie said, and made herself smile at her mother. "Sure."

The buses in Southfield didn't run as regularly as they did in their neighborhood—probably because everyone there had their own car, Bethie thought—but they did run. After school on a Wednesday afternoon a week and a half after her father's death, Bethie took the bus to the corner of Lahser and Quarton Road and walked up the street to her uncle Mel's house, a single-story ranch-style house that sat on a big lawn on top of a rise halfway up the block. She tucked her schoolbooks under her arm and knocked at the door.

"Bethie!" Aunt Shirley sounded like she was happy to see her. "Come on in!" Aunt Shirley led her past the living room, where her cousins were watching Soupy Sales, and into a kitchen that was big and gleaming and easily twice the size of Bethie's family's kitchen and living room combined. A new pale-yellow Mixmaster stood on the Formica counter. There were potted orchids on the windowsill that looked out over the backyard, and the green linoleum on the floor looked brand-new. Bethie smelled chicken baking. Through the window, she could see the new in-ground swimming pool she'd overheard Uncle Mel bragging about at Passover a few months ago, in the world where her father was still alive. In the dining room she could see the Negro girl setting the table, wiping each fork with her apron before setting it down. In Bethie's neighborhood, there were a few Negro families, with kids who went to Bethie's school, unless they were Catholic and their parents sent them to Our Lady of the Angels, but in Southfield, she suspected that the only Negro people were the ones who worked here and who took the buses back to their own neighborhoods at the end of the day.

"Can I get you a snack?" Aunt Shirley asked. "Something to drink?"

Bethie thought that was strange, because she was there to help Aunt Shirley, not to be waited on, but she was thirsty after the ride and the walk on a warm afternoon. "May I have some water, please?"

Aunt Shirley filled a glass at the sink. She wore a yellow blouse, a few shades darker than the Mixmaster, and a gray-and-cream-colored tweed skirt. Her brown hair looked freshly washed and set. Bethie sipped, wondering what, exactly, she was supposed to be doing, because it seemed like dinner was in the oven, the Negro girl was setting the table, and the TV set was babysitting the kids, but Aunt Shirley was ready with the answer.

"I wonder if you'd mind helping me go through the children's clothes. We can put away all of their winter things and separate the things that they've outgrown." Aunt Shirley led Bethie to the bedrooms, where brightly colored cardboard storage boxes sat empty on the kids' beds. The two of them worked together, emptying the dresser drawers, sorting through the clothes, which took all of thirty minutes. They proceeded to the linen closet in the hall. "We'll put things in three piles: things that are so worn we can just throw them out, things that might have some wear left in them, that can go to the clothing drive at the synagogue, and anything that's a little worn, but still in good shape . . ." Aunt Shirley paused. Bethie knew that those items went to her family. She and her sister had spent their lives sleeping under Audrey's and Joanne's discarded comforters, on top of their cast-off sheets.

"It's fine," she murmured. She carried a stack of washcloths to the girls' bedroom. Aunt Shirley watched from the doorway as Bethie began to sort them, then said, "I'll be in the kitchen if you need me." That project took just ten minutes, with Bethie maliciously slipping a few new-looking towels into the stack that would go to her family. When she found her aunt in the kitchen, Shirley was smoking a cigarette, reading *Woman's Day*, and she looked surprised to see her niece. "You can just wait in the TV room," she said, nodding in that direction. "Mel will take you home."

Bethie hoped that her flinch wasn't visible. "Oh, I'm happy to take the bus."

"Oh, no. And you'll have all of those sheets and towels to take with you. I wouldn't dream of it!"

Crap, thought Bethie, as her numb legs carried her into the TV room, where Soupy Sales had given way to the five o'clock news. *Crap, crap, crap.* She sat on the couch, barely moving, as her three cousins turned their heads to look at her, then turned back to the screen. Her mouth was dry, her heart pounding, as she heard the automatic garage door roll up, the door into the house open and close. "Kids!" her uncle called, and her cousins ran to greet him. Bethie listened to the girls say, "Daddy, Daddy," and the sound of Aunt Shirley's quieter voice. Finally, Uncle Mel came into the living room. "There you are, Bethie!" he said, and opened his arms for a hug. He wore a white lab coat, with his name stitched in blue on one side. His hair was cut short and combed neatly. His face was clean-shaven, and both his glasses and his bald spot gleamed, but when he kissed her, his breath was still foul. She wondered how his patients endured it, how Aunt Shirley did.

"Hi, Uncle Mel."

"Ready to head home?"

"Sure."

Bethie gathered her pocketbook, her schoolbooks, the box of sheets and towels Aunt Shirley had given her. When she climbed into Uncle Mel's boat of a Cadillac, she piled everything on her lap, but when Uncle Mel said, "Let's put those things in the trunk," she didn't know how to refuse. She felt naked, even though she'd worn her least-sheer cotton blouse over her most heavily padded bra, with a sweater on top, even though it was June, and warm outside.

Bethie was worried that her uncle would want to talk, but all he did was whistle along to the radio while he drove through the late-afternoon sunshine, bobbing his head and bouncing the palms of his hand against the steering wheel in time to the songs. "I'll never let'cha go, why, because I love you," he sang, when Frankie Avalon came on. *My father used to sing like that*, Bethie thought, and her heart gave a great, miserable twist. At a red light, Bethie felt Uncle Mel looking at her. She crossed her arms over her chest, turned her head toward the window, and clenched her jaw hard. When they turned onto Alhambra Street, Bethie's right hand was on the door's handle almost before Uncle Mel had put the car in Park, and her left hand was grabbing for the house key she wore on a ribbon around her neck. "Thank you, Uncle Mel," she was saying when Uncle Mel reached across her, pulling the door shut.

"Hold on, now! You don't want to run off before I've paid you!"

Oh, God, Bethie thought. Her stomach twisted. Her mother had sold the Old Car and taken her father's car as her own, and it wasn't in the driveway, because Sarah had gone for a job interview at Hudson's, and Jo was still probably at tennis practice, or at her friend Lynnette's. Her uncle pulled his wallet out of his back pocket and handed Bethie a ten-dollar bill that was still warm from his body. She wanted to pinch it between her fingertips. She wanted to drop it on the floor of the car. She wanted to leap out onto the driveway and run for the front door. Instead, she made herself fold up the bill, slip it into her pocket, and say, "Thank you."

"Bethie," said her uncle. "Poor little Bethie." Once, at a picnic, Bethie had spilled lemonade on her arm. She'd mopped up the mess with a paper napkin and had forgotten all about it until Laura had pointed at her, squealing, and Bethie had looked and seen the tiny black ants seething over the sticky spot, so many of them, packed so densely that her skin looked black, and she'd screamed and screamed and rubbed her arm against the grass, scraping the ants into mush. "How are the three of you holding up?"

"Fine," Bethie said, in a small voice. "We're doing fine."

"Oh, you don't have to be brave with me. I'll bet you miss your daddy, don't you? Poor Bethie. Poor little thing." His voice was thickening. He stretched out his arm. Bethie cringed, leaning away from him, trying to disappear into her car door, but Uncle Mel wrapped his arm around her shoulders and pulled her across the bench seat, until the side of her body was smashed right up against his. "Poor Bethie." He pressed his cheek against the top of her head and held her even more tightly. From the outside, it might have looked like an uncle comforting his niece. That wasn't how it felt. Not with his cheek pressed against her scalp and her cheek squished against his chest, and his horrible stinky breath filling the car with its smell. His hand meandered along the side of her breast, and the point of his chin dug into the top of her head. "Poor little Bethie. I'm so sorry. You must miss your daddy so much. But don't worry. I'm here for you."

"I have to go." She tried to wriggle free, but his arms felt like bars of iron. "I need to start dinner . . ."

"There's no rush. I'll bet you're lonely. And, look, no one's home yet. We have time." He was using his knuckles to rub at the side of her breast, and he had lapsed into a horrible, lisping baby talk. "I don't want my poor widdle Bethie to be all alone in the big dark house."

Bethie hated that the house was empty, that Mel was right, that she would be all alone. She wished, with a panicky desperation, for her mother to come driving down the street, or for her sister to ride up on her bike. She tried to shrink, to make her body smaller. "Please, Uncle Mel, I need to go do my homework."

"My Bethie's a scholar!" He sounded proud of her

as he rubbed his chin up and down against the part in her hair.

"Uncle Mel, I need to go now!" With a great wrench, she pulled away from him, hopped out of the car, kicked the car door shut, and raced for the front door, yanking her key out from underneath her blouse. For a minute, she imagined that she could feel his breath on the back of her neck. Her hands were shaking, and it took her three tries to fit the key into the lock, but she finally got it there, just as she heard the sound of Uncle Mel's footsteps behind her, like a monster in a horror movie. Bethie turned, reluctantly, and saw that he was holding her books and the cardboard box of towels. "Don't want to forget these!" His voice was cheery, and his expression was pleasant, like he hadn't done anything wrong. And maybe he hadn't done anything wrong. He'd hugged her, rubbed the top of her head, brushed the side of her breast, but maybe by accident? Or maybe she'd imagined it? Bethie examined her memories, hearing Uncle Mel whistling again as he strolled back to his car. As he drove past her, he tapped the horn, giving two cheery honks— beep, beep! Bethie jumped and turned, just in time to see him waving and hear him call, "See you next week!"

She walked into the empty house, setting the towels by their own, far less spacious linen closet, dumping her schoolbooks on her bed. She left Uncle Mel's money on the kitchen table. In the bathroom, she stripped off her clothes and stood under the hot water and she scrubbed until her skin was bright red. She still felt dirty, like there was an oily residue all over her skin, sticking to her like cling wrap, like she would never be clean again.

In the kitchen, she seasoned a chicken, feeling her stomach roll as she touched its pimply skin and pulled the pinfeathers out of its wings. She and her mother and her sister would have roast chicken for dinner, chicken salad for lunch, and chopped-up cooked chicken baked under a coating of Velveeta cheese or cream of mushroom soup for dinner the following night. Bethie scrubbed two baking potatoes, pricked their skins with a fork, and put them in the oven, and she cut up the remaining quarter head of iceberg lettuce that Sarah had left in the crisper. In the very back of the refrigerator was a bowl of chocolate chip cookie dough. This was Jo's treat. Jo loved chocolate chip cookies, and on weekends she'd make a double batch of dough at Lynnette's house, bring it home, and bake a few cookies every night. With all the exercising she did, Jo could eat all the dessert she wanted and not see it show up on her thighs, but Bethie and Sarah both watched their weight, and the most Bethie ever ate was one.

That night, Bethie pulled the bowl out of the refrigerator and a mixing spoon out of the drawer. She scooped a walnut-sized glob of dough out of the bowl and shoved it in her mouth. Almost before she'd swallowed that bite, she'd scooped out another, working to force the spoon through stiff, cold dough. She sat at the kitchen table, with the spoon in her hand and the bowl tucked between her arm and her body, scooping and eating and scooping and eating and scooping and eating some more, the spoon moving faster as the dough warmed up, filling her mouth with the cloying sweetness of sugar and chocolate, swallowing in breathless gulps, trying to cram herself so full that there would be no room left for her confusion or her rage or her shame.

Every Wednesday, for the whole summer—June, July, and into August—Bethie went to Uncle Mel's. Each week she would try to find the words to tell her mother what was happening, and each week she'd lose her nerve. The one time she tried to say something, Sarah had stared at her. Her mother had been dressed in a new maroon-colored rayon skirt and matching bolero jacket, with the bright morning sunshine illuminating the new dark circles beneath her eyes. Her face was exhausted as she'd stared at Bethie, finally shaking her head and repeating what Bethie had said. "Hugging you too long? What do you mean?" Sarah had asked, and the words had shriveled up and died inside of Bethie's mouth. She would have told Jo, had her sister been there to tell, but Lynnette had gotten Jo a job as a counselor and tennis instructor at Camp Tanuga. Jo had packed her duffel bag and gotten on a bus three days after school ended. Nor had Bethie failed to notice the haste with which Sarah had grabbed the first ten dollars that Bethie had left on the table. That had erased any doubt Bethie might have had about whether her family needed the money. She thought about writing to Jo, but what could Jo do, two hundred miles away in the Upper Peninsula? Go to the camp director and say, *Sorry, I've got to go home, my uncle is hugging my sister?*

All summer long, every Wednesday morning, Bethie would push her spoon back and forth through the bowl of cornflakes that she'd pour herself, waiting until the cereal turned to mush, knowing that if she said she wasn't hungry, Sarah would have questions. Her mother would rush off to work, and Bethie would be left alone in the house. She'd do the laundry. She'd mop the floors. She'd defrost whatever they were having for dinner. She'd vacuum and dust and fold things that didn't need folding, none of which filled the hours that dragged by, until it was three o'clock and time to take the bus to Uncle Mel's.

Each week, Bethie would arrive by four. Aunt Shirley would let her in and assign her some task that would never take more than thirty minutes. Bethie would empty her cousins' toy chests, sorting through what was broken or abandoned, or she'd take the plates off a shelf in the kitchen or dining room, wash the plates, dust the shelf, then dry the plates and stack them back where they'd been. Once her work was done, she would sit in the air-conditioned living room, watching TV by herself, because her cousins had gone to a camp of their own, and she never saw her grandmother. "Elkie's not feeling well," Shirley said, the one time Bethie had asked. She would wait, not watching the television, feeling her stomach squeeze into a ball at the sound of the garage door opening and Uncle Mel's too-hearty greeting to his wife. Every week she would offer to take the bus, and each week Uncle Mel would say, "No! No! I insist!" After the second week, instead of pulling into the driveway of their house on Alhambra Street, Uncle Mel would cruise past the empty house and park at the very end of the block. At first he was satisfied with pulling her against him. By July, he was settling her on his lap. Bethie would close her eyes, taking sips of air through her mouth, as his horrible breath filled the car and fogged the windows and his hands roamed over her chest and her hips and her bottom, pinching and grabbing. As bad as that was, it got worse when he'd start talking about her father while he touched her, in his horrible, lisping baby talk. *Poor widdle Bethie, do you miss your daddy? Poor Bethie must miss her daddy so much.* He'd rock against her, faster and faster, his stinky breath coming in agonized pants against her neck, until, finally, he'd thrust himself against her so hard that it hurt, and shudder, then wilt back into his seat, before handing her the money and letting her go.

Bethie would scramble out of his car and run home through the summer twilight and the air that smelled like barbecues and fresh-cut grass. A twirling sprinkler would send sprays of water arcing onto the Steins' lawn, and she'd hear car doors slamming, kids laughing or arguing, and moms calling their children in for dinner. It felt like another world, a lost paradise, like all of Bethie's previous summers, when her dad had been alive. The Dubinsky girls would be playing hopscotch; the Stein boys would have their bats slung over their shoulders as they ran home for dinner. Andy Simoneaux, her friend Barbara's little brother, would ride past her on his new bike. He'd used clothespins to clip playing cards to the spokes, and they made a whirring sound when he pedaled, calling, "Hi, Bethie!" She would wave at Andy, hurrying for her own front door, praying it would be dark enough so that no one would see the wet spot on the back of her jeans. She'd leave Uncle Mel's money on the kitchen table, underneath the white china sugar bowl with its chipped lid and its gold rim, and peel off her clothes and stand under the shower, first with the water scalding hot, then icy cold. She'd cook dinner and pick at her food, and sit in front of the television set with her mother, who no longer had the energy to knit or mend or even fold the laundry. After dinner, Sarah would sit, nodding off halfway through *Leave It to Beaver* or *The Andy Griffith Show*. Her mouth would fall open, and she'd snore. In the glare of the television set, she looked old, and frail, and powerless. After her mother had gone to bed, Bethie would slip into the kitchen, padding on her bare feet, plucking a mixing spoon out of the drawer, opening the refrigerator and shoving whatever she could find down her throat, anything that was soft and yielding. Cookie dough was best, but she'd eat ice cream and sherbet or cottage cheese, bread or cold rice or mashed potatoes, raspberry jam or chicken gravy that had solidified to jelly. Anything that was soft, anything that could be scooped up and gulped down without her even tasting it. Anything to fill the hole that had opened up inside of her, anything to fill the void, until there was no room left for bad memories or anger or guilt or shame.

By August, she'd put on ten pounds. Her skin was broken out, with angry red pimples spattering her forehead and cheeks, and her breasts had grown two cup sizes so that all her bras squeezed. Sarah didn't say anything about the vanishing supply of food, which she surely must have noticed. All she did was snip a copy of a seven-day grapefruit-and-hardboiled-egg diet out of *Ladies' Home Journal* and leave it at Bethie's spot on the kitchen table after she'd left for work, murmuring, "When you're short, with a small frame, every pound shows."

Bethie avoided her friends, who were spending their summer days sunning themselves by the public pool or who, if they were old enough, had part-time jobs babysitting or scooping ice cream or waiting tables. She wasn't old enough to work, and she couldn't stand the thought of putting on her swimsuit, which no longer fit, and lying on a towel on the concrete around the pool, with so much of her body exposed. She said she was busy when Barbara Simoneaux asked her to doubledate, and missed Laura Ochs's Sweet Sixteen. *Under the weather,* she'd say, which was code for menstrual cramps, or she'd say, *My mom needs me at home,* and who could argue with that?

Finally, one Wednesday night in August, Uncle Mel pulled down Alhambra Street and, oh thank God, the lights were on in the house, shining through the window.

"Uncle Mel, I have to go," Bethie blurted, and had her feet on the ground almost before the car had stopped. She ran across the lawn, fumbling for her key on its ribbon, hurrying through the door, and Jo was there, Jo had finally come home. She was standing in the kitchen, her legs tanned underneath her white camp shorts, her shoulders broad and strong beneath her green-and-white Camp Tanuga T-shirt. The light above the stove was on, giving the shabby room a warm glow, and the radio was tuned to the Tigers game. Jo was cracking eggs into a bowl, the scuffed pale green plastic one they always used. Bethie saw a startled expression on her sister's face as Jo took her in, before her sister asked, "How about breakfast for dinner?" Bethie was so relieved, so glad to see her sister, so glad not to be alone, that she started to cry. Jo put her arm around Bethie's shoulders, pulling her close.

"Hey, what's wrong? Are you okay?" Bethie couldn't answer, couldn't speak. "Is it Dad?" Jo asked, her voice warm and sympathetic. Bethie leaned against her, the scent and the solidity of her sister's body reassuring and familiar. "I know. I miss him, too."

"It's not that," Bethie managed to say through her tears. "It's something else."

Jo looked down at her. "What?" she asked. "What's wrong?"

"It's Uncle Mel," Bethie whispered. She inhaled, squeezed her eyes shut, and said, all in a rush, "He's touching me."

After Bethie told Jo everything, Jo's lips turned white around the edges and she started walking like she couldn't keep still. *I'll kill him*, she kept saying. *I'll kill him.* She paced the length of the living room with her tennis racquet in her hand, looking ready to start smashing things. Bethie was the one who calmed her down, the one who said, truthfully, that Uncle Mel had never touched her underneath her clothes, or made Bethie touch him under his. *He'd just say that he was comforting me, or that I was misinterpreting things*, Bethie said. *And Mom needs the money. You know she does.* Jo paced, and glared, and told her, *We have to come up with a plan. We need to get him to leave you alone, and we need his money.* That night, for the first time in months, Bethie ate her dinner and did not sneak out of bed to eat, and Jo told her a story, not about Princess Bethie in the dark woods in search of a magic chalice, or in the high tower, but Princess Bethie in Uncle Mel's house on a quest for cash, and the sisters talked late into the night.

The next night, Bethie and Jo waited until six o'clock, when Uncle Mel was sure to be home, and drove to Southfield. Jo parked in the driveway, and the sisters walked to the door. Shirley's expression went from annoyed to surprised when she saw that both sisters were there.

"Is Uncle Mel at home?" said Bethie. "Jo and I need to speak to him." Her hands, her knees, even her neck, everything was quivering, but her voice was clear and steady. Shirley gave them a curious look, but she said, "Of course," and led the girls into Uncle Mel's office, which had bookshelves full of medical texts, and an imposing dark wood desk, where a fancy black and gold pen rested on a leather blotter. A minute later, Uncle Mel, in his suit pants and white lab coat, walked in.

"Well, isn't this a nice surprise! What can I do for you young ladies?" he asked.

Bethie's stomach felt fluttery, the way it did when her teachers handed out exams facedown, in the minutes before they said, "Begin." She wanted to get up and run, out of the office, past Aunt Shirley and her cousins, through the gleaming kitchen, all the way back to the car. As if she'd read her mind, Jo took her hand and gave it a squeeze, and Bethie forced herself to breathe and tried to remember all the stories her sister had told her. Princess Bethie had faced the dragons and the wicked queen. She'd tamed the wild stallion and ridden on its back; she had hacked her own way through the forest of thorns before the prince ever showed up.

Uncle Mel was looking at her. Bethie swallowed, then started to speak. "You talked to me about 'The Road Less Traveled' at my father's shiva. Remember? 'Two roads diverged in a yellow wood'?"

Uncle Mel gave a cautious nod. Bethie felt her belly uncoil. The sick, sinking feeling she'd carried all summer was evaporating. What was left in its place was rage. Her chest and throat and cheeks felt hot. She kept her face still and made herself smile, and tilt her head, and speak sweetly.

"Our father didn't choose, though. He didn't get to choose. Your parents chose for him. He didn't get to say, 'Maybe I'd like to finish high school and maybe I'd like to go to college.' He had to drop out of school and go to work, to help the family. To help you. It wasn't his choice to die before he turned forty-five." She paused to take a breath, before delivering her final blow. "Or to have his daughter get pawed by his brother once a week."

Uncle Mel's face darkened. He raised his hands. "I think you misunderstood—"

"I think she understood fine," Jo interrupted. "You ought to be ashamed of yourself. We should report you to the board in charge of eye doctors." Jo glared at him. "Or maybe your wife."

In his study, behind his gleaming desk, Uncle Mel's

mouth was moving soundlessly. "I didn't mean . . ." he finally managed. He gulped, then said, "I was distraught!"

"I bet Aunt Shirley would be pretty distraught if I told her what you were doing." Uncle Mel was squirming. Bethie could see beads of sweat gleaming through the coarse hairs of his mustache, and how he couldn't look either one of them in the face.

"What do you want?" he asked.

"A while back, our father asked to borrow money. Remember? He wanted to open a Laundromat with Henry Sheshevsky. And you told him no."

"Only to protect your family!" Mel said, his voice loud and self-righteous. He looked toward the door, lowered his voice, and continued, "Your father . . . he didn't have a *kop far geshefte*. No head for business. He'd have lost my money, and whatever he'd invested of his own."

"Maybe," Bethie said. Jo was glaring across the desk with her hands in fists. Bethie knew that her sister probably hated hearing her father insulted that way, like he was dumb, or incompetent. She could feel her heart pounding, the sound of it in her ears. "Or maybe we'd be the ones living in Southfield with a swimming pool in our backyard. We'll never know. That's the road not taken, right?" She gave Uncle Mel her prettiest smile. "You can't go back to where the road diverged. But I bet you'd feel better if you helped my mother out." Bethie squeezed her hands together so that he couldn't see them tremble. "Whatever my father asked to borrow from you. I want you to write our mom a check." She sat back, her stomach twisting again, her palms sweaty and her mouth dry. *Now*, she thought. *Now he'll tell me that I made the whole thing up. He'll call my mother and tell her I'm a liar. He'll start yelling, and he'll throw us out.*

Instead, her uncle sighed and bowed his head. After a

minute, he opened the top drawer of his desk. He wrote out a check and put it in an envelope with his name—Dr. Melvin Kaufman—and his office's address embossed in the upper-left-hand corner, and put it into Bethie's outstretched hand.

"I'm sorry," he said . . . and, to Bethie's horror, he did sound genuinely sad. Whatever else he'd been, whatever he'd done, he had been her father's little brother. As much as she hated to think it, he had lost someone, too. She tucked the check into the zippered pocket of her purse. Jo stood up, and the two of them left Uncle Mel without a word. Bethie was hurrying toward the door, planning on leaving without even a "goodbye" to Aunt Shirley, but as she passed the dining room, she saw the Negro girl humming as she stood in front of an ironing board with a stack of white napkins piled on one end. Bethie stopped, so suddenly that her sister almost walked into her back. When the girl looked up, with her face immobile and her eyes wary, Bethie thought she'd used up all the courage she had for that day, for that week, maybe for the rest of her life. Then she remembered her uncle's hands on her, the horrible stink of his breath, and that her sister was standing behind her. It made her brave enough to step forward.

"What's your name?" she asked.

"Coralee, ma'am," said the girl. Up close, Bethie could see that she was older than she'd thought, in her twenties at least. Her face was small and heart-shaped. Her two front teeth overlapped slightly, and her eyelashes curled up at the tips.

"I'm not a ma'am," Bethie said, and shook her head. Her eyes were stinging. "I'm just a kid." She stepped close to the young woman, lowering her voice. "Does he ever touch you?" she whispered. Coralee's eyes got wide.

She shook her head. "If he ever does . . . if he ever tries anything . . ."

Bethie didn't know what to say next, but her sister did. "We're his nieces. Jo and Bethie Kaufman."

Coralee nodded. "I remember."

"We live on Alhambra Street. Our number's UNiversity 2-9291. Call us if you need us."

The girl nodded, and Bethie turned again toward the door. In the living room, there was the heavy glass paperweight with its piece of coral inside. When she was little, Bethie had loved the heft of it, the smooth curve of the glass against her palm. On her way out, she fell a few steps behind Jo and picked it up and slipped it in her pocket, next to the check. She walked out the front door and she and Jo hurried down the gentle slope of her uncle's front yard, to where the car was waiting.

Jo

Jo and Lynnette looked at each other across the microphone in the school's front office that would broadcast their voices over the PA system. Smiling, Jo mouthed
the words "Three . . . two . . . one," and Lynnette bonged
out the introductory notes of "Mister Sandman" on the
xylophone they'd borrowed from the music room. The
two of them leaned forward and sang, in credible har-
mony, "Fellow classmates . . . bring us your dues. / We
need your money, for our senior cruise. / A night of
dancing, and plenty to eat / Will keep us out of all those
car back sea-ats / Classmates, our savings are low / Can't
throw a party, without any dough / So please, don't make
us have the blues . . . / Fellow classmates, bring us your
dues!"

Mrs. Douglass glared at them, the way she glared at
everyone, before allowing herself the tiniest smile and
saying, "Not bad, girls." Jo and Lynnie made it through
the door, with its wire-reinforced glass window, and
were out in the hallway when they thrust their hands

in the air in triumph and collapsed against each other, laughing.

"Oh my God, I was sure you were going to do it!" Lynnette said.

"Do what?" Jo asked, her face innocent. The previous week, Jo had proposed all kinds of lyrics, from funny to disgusting to obscene, with increasingly offensive rhymes of "dues" and "Jews," until Lynnette begged her to stop, leaning against the bedroom wall with tears on her cheeks, saying, "I'm going to pee my pants!" As class secretary, Jo was responsible for collecting the class dues of five dollars apiece. The money would pay for a double-decker boat that would take the kids on a post-prom cruise along the Detroit River in May.

Giddy and breathless, Jo walked down the hall with Lynnette, who looked extra-adorable in her maroon and cream cheerleading uniform, with its short, pleated skirt. The summer had been bittersweet, wonderful and strange. Jo spent her days in the sun, at the lake or on the tennis court, the hours so full that there was little time to grieve. At night, she and Lynnette would slip down to the beach and slip out of their clothes and skinny-dip in the warm lake water, sometimes with the other female counselors, sometimes alone. "I love you," Jo had whispered, and Lynnette had said it back. But as soon as they'd come home, Lynnette had started right up again with Bobby Carver, as if the summer had never happened. Bobby Carver, football-team captain; Bobby Carver, who, someday, would own his father's dealership, Carver Chevrolet. "The Saturday Night Fights," Lynnie had taken to calling their dates, shaking her head as she told Jo about how every night ended with a wrestling match in the back seat of Bobby's car. She'd describe Bobby's wet kisses, his octopus-like hands, the way he was always attempting to grind his erection against her, without seeming to particularly care which part he was grinding against. "Is it even dry-humping if he's, like, pushing it into my arm?" Lynnette wondered, and Jo told her, solemnly, "I believe that Plato and Socrates had debates about the exact same thing," without letting her face show how it sickened her to imagine Lynnette and Bobby that way. She was brave enough to tell Lynnette that she loved her, but not, it seemed, brave enough to demand that Lynnie end things with Bobby.

"Funny," Lynnette said, elbowing Jo in the ribs and looking up at Jo fondly, in a way that made Jo's heart do a flip-flop in her chest. "You're so funny. You should have a TV show, like Lucille Ball."

"Only if you'll be my Ethel," Jo said. Jo had no desire to be on TV. She dreamed of being a writer, or a lawyer, like Perry Mason. That wasn't an ambition shared by many of her female classmates, and Sarah had scoffed the few times Jo had brought it up. Lynnette, meanwhile, didn't even want to go to college. Jo thought that Lynnie wanted a life exactly like her own mother's—a big house, a few kids, enough money to pay for help with the cooking and cleaning so that she could spend her afternoons playing bridge or mah-jongg or doing volunteer work. As much as she loved her Lynnie, as much as she wanted to believe that they could be together forever, Jo wasn't so starry-eyed that she couldn't see the truth. Making a life with a woman would be hard. And Lynnette, her sweet, slightly daffy, lazy friend, Lynnette of the strawberry-sweet lips and clever tongue, Lynnette who never read a book that hadn't been assigned in class and never finished her own homework when she could get Jo to do it, whose knowledge of current events and the world did not extend past the campus of Bellwood High, was not made for the struggle. She would not try—or even want—to remake the world. The idea of turning down Bobby Carver's marriage proposal and running away with Jo would be as alien to her as planning to live on the moon.

"What are you doing this weekend?" Jo asked as they walked down the hall, by which she meant, *What are we doing this weekend?* Most Saturday nights, the girls would double-date, the two of them plus Bobby Carver and one of his friends. Over the years, Jo had earned a reputation as a prude, a girl who wouldn't even let her dates go up her shirt and barely had enough of a chest for a boy to bother. "A carpenter's dream," was the joke they made, about her chest being flat as a board. Jo didn't care. She hoped that, eventually, boys would stop asking, but the longer Jo held out, the more boys she pushed away, the more determined some of them became.

So every Saturday, she and Lynnie and Bobby and whoever was currently trying to break down her defenses would go to a movie, or a record hop, or to a football or basketball game at a rival high school, where the action would be enlivened by the flask that someone would invariably pass around. Bobby Carver would drive to the Bobecks' house. Jo would go inside, and after Lynnette finally pried herself away from him, she'd join Jo in the kitchen for a snack, then in the bedroom. Jo would pull out the trundle bed, muss the blankets, in case anyone looked, and shuck off her clothes in ten seconds flat. Once she was in her pajamas, she'd spend half an hour watching Lynnette go through her pre-bedtime ritual. Lynnie's saddle shoes had to be unlaced, wiped off, and put into their cubby in her closet; her nylons had to be unclipped from her garter belt. "Unzip me," she'd request, and Jo would slowly pull her zipper down, sometimes planting a kiss on Lynnie's neck or her shoulder. The dress's sides would part, revealing a long-line bra and a panty girdle that left welts on the white skin of Lynnette's hips. "Why do you wear those things?" Jo would ask, easing open the hooks, and Lynnette would sigh and examine herself in the mirror, turning from side to side, sucking in her stomach and her cheeks and saying things like "I wish I had more neck," until Jo would take her by the shoulders and march her to the bathroom. There, Lynnette would commence a lengthy routine involving Pond's cold cream, cotton balls, and witch hazel, and brushing her hair a hundred times. Jo would lie on her back in Lynnette's bed, staring at the canopy, making appropriate sounds of assent or denial as Lynnette talked about the movie, or the dance, or asked if Jo had liked Allan Gross or Louis Ettinger any better than the boys she'd been out with before. Lynnette would still be chattering and patting her face dry when she came to bed, dressed in one of her peach or pale-blue nighties. "Roll over," she'd say, elbowing Jo out of the warm spot. Jo would wait for Lynnette to pull up the covers, waiting for her friend to issue the invitation. "Cuddle me?" Lynnie would ask in a babyish voice. Or, "Scratch my back?" She'd hum as Jo held her or ran her short fingernails over the satiny skin of Lynnette's back, before turning to Jo, eyes half-closed, mouth open for a kiss.

Jo stayed at Lynnette's house as long as she could every Sunday, doing homework, watching TV, dragging out the day until she couldn't stall any longer and would have to go back to the grim, silent house on Alhambra Street. Before her father's death, they'd all eaten dinner together every night. On Sundays, which Sarah called "the cook's night off," they'd order Chinese takeout, spare ribs and egg rolls, chop suey and egg foo yong. Jo's father would pick up the food, and they'd watch TV in the den, *The Ed Sullivan Show* and *What's My Line?* Now Sarah worked on the weekends and rarely came home before eight o'clock. It was the girls' job to make dinner, and they ate by themselves, leaving a covered dish in the oven for their mother.

In the hallway, the late bell trilled. "Can you sleep over tonight?" Lynnette asked.

"Tonight?" asked Jo. "What about tomorrow?"

Lynnette held her books tightly against her chest. "It's our anniversary," she said, looking both proud and shy. "Bobby's taking me to dinner, and dancing at Cliff Bell's. And after . . ." Lynnette rattled her fingertips against the cover of her algebra textbook, mimicking a drumroll. Jo felt coldness creep over her skin.

"You don't have to," Jo blurted, feeling her chest get tight. *Why would you want to do anything with Bobby Carver when you have me?* "You don't have to do anything you don't want to do."

"We've been going steady for almost two years, Jo." Lynnette's voice was calm and matter-of-fact. She could have been reading the list of ingredients on a cereal box. "He says he loves me."

I love you, Jo thought. "Do you love him?" she asked.

Lynnette didn't answer. "And the thing is . . ." Her voice trailed off.

"What?" asked Jo. When she heard the sharpness in her voice, she made herself smile. "What's the thing?"

Lynnette looked down at her saddle shoes. "Bobby says whenever we go out I spend more time talking to you than to him."

"Well, if Bobby had any conversational topics besides football and himself—" Jo began.

Lynnette put her hand on Jo's forearm, stopping her.

Her voice was very soft. "He says I like you more than I like him."

Jo's chest felt tight, her head spinning with a giddy mixture of pride and fear. "Well, honestly, who wouldn't?" she said, struggling to keep her tone light as her cheeks flushed.

Lynnette's pretty face was troubled. "You don't get it," she said, shaking her head.

"What, Lynnie?" asked Jo. "What don't I get?"

Lynnette grabbed Jo's elbow, pulled her into the girls' room, and walked her all the way to the last sink in the row, checking for feet under the stall doors along the way. Jo could smell disinfectant and the ghosts of a thousand cigarettes as they stood in the shaft of smoky light that came in through the single high window made of bubbled, milky glass. "He says that people are starting to talk about us," Lynnette whispered. "They're saying that we're . . ." She dropped her voice to a hushed whisper. "Lesbians."

Jo's tongue felt frozen. "Well, isn't that what they call women who love women," she finally said.

Lynnette waved her free hand dismissively, making a face. "I don't love women. I just love you. And it's different. We're not . . . you know . . . mannish," she said. "We don't cut our hair off and dress like boys."

"Have you even seen me?" Jo touched her short hair, trying to keep her voice light, even as she felt icy bands tighten around her heart. Did people think she was mannish? Had they guessed her secret? Instead of seeing her as smart and sporty, a standout student and the managing editor of the school paper, did they think she was a deviant?

"Oh, but that's just your style," Lynnette said, waving her hand again. "You've got the best legs of all the girls in the senior class. You're pretty! You'd be even prettier if you'd let me pluck your eyebrows." She stood on her tiptoes to brush the ball of her thumb over Jo's left brow. "Seriously, your only problem is that you haven't met the right guy yet."

"I am never going to meet the right guy." Jo hoped she didn't look the way she felt, which was like she'd been punched. She knew what she was. She'd gone out with enough boys to know that their kisses, their bodies, their stubble and their smells, did not arouse her. She'd also taken *The Well of Loneliness* out of the library and she'd ridden the bus all the way to Birmingham to buy *Odd Girl Out* from a spinning wire rack of pulp titles in a drugstore. The book's cover depicted a dark-haired, violet-eyed, crimson-lipped woman giving a hungry look to a pretty blond co-ed. *Suddenly they were alone on an island of forbidden bliss*, the cover read, as if there was any doubt about the plot. In the drugstore, Jo had buried the book in a pile of things she didn't need—mouthwash, a bar of Ivory soap, a box of Tampax. Still, she imagined she felt the woman behind the counter smirking as she rang her up. She'd barely made it home before devouring the tale of innocent Laura, who fell for her beautiful roommate Beth. Her heartbeat thundered in her ears and she'd felt a heavy, insistent throbbing between her legs as she read the author's description of the girls' first time: *Laura's hands descended to their enthralling task again, caressing the flawless hollows, the sweet shoulders. She was lost to reason now.*

That was how Jo felt around Lynnette. *Lost to reason.* The novels had been a solace, a confirmation of what she was, and that there were other women like her. She was a lesbian, she loved Lynnette and wanted to find a way to be with her forever . . . only, to Lynnie, Jo was a pleasant diversion, a naughty secret, an experiment, and ultimately a dead end. Bobby Carver was the path forward, the only road that Lynnette could see.

"Don't be such a dummy." Lynnette punched Jo lightly on her arm. "Of course you'll find the right guy. And when you do, we'll have a double wedding, and we'll live next door to each other. You can come over and borrow a cup of sugar."

Jo made herself smile, even though she wanted to cry. Lynnette knew that Jo's dream was to become a writer and live in New York City, and yet, in Lynnie's fantasies, Jo was right here in Detroit, wearing an apron and baking. She made herself smile. "And you'll come to my house?"

"Anytime you want me." Lynnette flashed her a smile, licked her lips in a way that usually made Jo's knees go wobbly, and bounced out of the girls' room on her way to Remedial Math.

Jo went to the Bobecks' house that night. In Lynnette's bed, the sex was as enthralling and the cuddling was as sweet as they'd ever been. But when her friend woke up on Saturday morning, pulling out dresses and asking Jo what she should wear for Bobby, Jo's chest felt so tight that it was hard to breathe.

"Are you okay?" Lynnette asked for the fourth time, after Jo failed to give an opinion about whether Lynnette's blue-and-white-checked skirt with a pale-blue sweater or her daisy-patterned cotton dress with its circle skirt and boat neck was a better choice.

"I'm fine." Jo wanted to ask how Lynnette was. Excited? Nervous? Looking forward to sex with Bobby, or dreading it, and just determined to lose her virginity before she collected her diploma? Jo wasn't sure which answer was worse. "Actually, you know what? My stomach's killing me."

"Cramps?" asked Lynnette sympathetically. They spent so much time together that of course Lynnette knew that Jo's period was on its way.

Nodding, Jo said, "I think I'll go home and lie down."

Lynnette kissed her and told her to feel better. Before Jo had even closed the bedroom door, she saw her beloved back at the mirror, holding up dresses against her body, her cheeks flushed, her expression pleased. Jo rode her bike the long way back, pedaling hard, desperate to find a way to outrun her own thoughts. At home, her mother had taken the car to work. Bethie was gone.

She called up Vernita, who was on the tennis team with her, and convinced her to meet her at the high school court. After two hours, Vernita, flushed and exhausted, begged off. "Are you okay?" she asked Jo. "You're hitting that ball like it did something bad to you."

"I'm fine," Jo said. It was only four in the afternoon, three hours until Bobby would pick up Lynnette and take her dancing at Cliff Bell's. Back on Alhambra Street, the house was empty, her mother's car was still gone. Jo took a shower and changed her clothes. On the top shelf of the pantry, she found a dusty bottle of liquor that must have been sitting there since her father's shiva. She carried the bottle to her bedroom, held her nose, and wincing at the burn, swallowed gulp after gulp of schnapps, until the room started to spin and her limbs felt too heavy to move. She lay back, closing her eyes, and she must have fallen asleep, or passed out. When she opened her eyes again, the early-morning sun was stabbing at her eyes, and her sister was giving her a sympathetic look. "Drink this," she said, handing Jo a fresh glass of water. "And take these." Bethie gave her sister two aspirin.

"Mom?" Jo's voice was raspy. It hurt to talk. It hurt to breathe, to think. Everything hurt.

"You were passed out when I got home. I told her you had the flu. And I hid this." Bethie reached under Jo's mattress and pulled out the mostly empty bottle of schnapps. "Want to talk about it?"

Jo's tongue felt like it had grown an inch-thick coating of moss, her head felt like invisible demons were kicking at her temples with steel-toed boots, and her shoulders and forearms and thighs ached from all the tennis. What would happen if she told her sister that she was in love with Lynnette? Would Bethie recoil? Would she flinch in disgust? Did she already know? "No," Jo said, because shaking her head would hurt too much. "But thanks. I owe you one."

Bethie gave her a thoughtful look, and seemed to be on the verge of saying, or asking, something more. But all she said was, "You took care of me with Uncle Mel," before closing the door with an almost silent click. Jo shut her eyes. It was ten o'clock in the morning. Whatever had happened with Lynnette and Bobby had happened. All that was left, she thought glumly, was to hear about it, to make herself smile, to say *I'm happy if you are,* when what she really wanted to say was *Run away with me, somewhere that we can be together, forever.*

Bethie

Bethie had been in the restroom, her saddle shoes looking, she supposed, like every other pair of saddle shoes underneath a stall, when she'd heard girls whispering about her.

"Have you seen Bethie Kaufman?" asked a voice she thought belonged to Winnie Freed. "She used to be so cute!" Bethie couldn't tie the responding giggles to anyone she knew as she sat there with a wad of toilet tissue in her hand, her face burning with shame. Tryouts for the school musical, her first high school musical, were the first week in October, and Bethie knew that at her current size, she'd never have a shot at the lead.

It was time to take action. That afternoon, with Sarah's grudging permission, she had Jo drive her to the drugstore, where she used some of Uncle Mel's money to purchase twenty-eight cans of Metrecal.

"Let me know what you think of that stuff," the cashier said when Bethie had paid. Bethie nodded. She'd seen the diet drink advertised in Aunt Shirley's *Ladies'*

Home Journal and on TV. Bethie could recite that entire ad by heart. "Here come the slim ones," the announcer intoned, as skiers in skintight bodysuits made their way down the mountain. "Here come the trim ones. Here comes the Metrecal-for-lunch bunch!"

The text on the cans recommended replacing lunch with a can of Metrecal, and eating sensibly for the rest of the day. "Two Metrecal meals a day, lunch and dinner, and you can lose weight steadily. As for three a day, talk it over with your doctor first. You might disappear." Disappearance sounded just fine to Bethie, and she had no intention of discussing her plans with Dr. Sachs, who had a pushbroom mustache that matched his salt-and-pepper hair and still handed out lollipops after her checkups. She figured that if she eliminated all solid food, drank three Metrecals a day, and added some exercise, she might be able to shed fifteen pounds in less than a month, which would take her back to what she'd weighed at the start of the summer.

Bethie carried the cans into the kitchen, stacked them in the cupboard, then took her first can, shook it, and poured it over ice.

"How's it taste?" Jo asked, hooking a package of Wonder Bread out of the bread box and pulling a jar of peanut butter out of the pantry.

Bethie took a sip and tried not to wince. Jo held out her hand for the glass. She sniffed it, raised the glass to her mouth, and took a swallow. "Ugh!" she said. "This stuff is putrid!"

Bethie thought it was icky, too, but she wasn't going to say so.

"It tastes like chalk," said Jo, peering at the words on the can. "'With the taste and texture of a milkshake,' my aunt Fanny."

"I got a few different flavors," Bethie said, holding her hand out for her glass. "Maybe they'll be better."

Jo rolled her eyes. "Why are you doing this, anyhow?"

"Because," said Bethie, "I need to slim down for the auditions."

"So why not just stop eating dessert for a while?"

"Because," said Bethie, with exaggerated patience, "I don't have a while. Auditions are in three weeks."

Jo hoisted herself up to sit on the kitchen counter, a move Sarah never permitted. "Who says Nellie Forbush has to be a skinny Minnie? Besides, nobody in the whole school can sing like you can."

Bethie shook her head and sipped her Metrecal. Jo would never understand how it felt to walk around with her skirts barely fitting and the buttons of her sweaters straining over her bust; with boys' eyes skipping over her, like she was part of the furniture or, worse, a teacher. Beauty was power, and Bethie wanted her power back.

You may experience hunger pains for the first few days on the Metrecal plan, the labels had warned. Bethie quickly learned that *hunger pains* was putting it mildly. Her first morning on the diet was fine. She got up, did a routine of sit-ups, leg raises, and jumping jacks that she'd found in *Seventeen* magazine, showered, drank her shake, and went to school. At lunchtime, she sat in the cafeteria, virtuously sipping her shake, as Denise and Barbara commiserated and Suzanne turned her back to eat her French fries. By the bus ride home she was dizzy, and at home the smell of the minute steaks Jo was preparing made her want to cry. Her stomach growled and her mouth filled with saliva, and so, instead of coming to the table, she stayed in bed, telling her sister that she had a headache. A few hours later, when she smelled cookies baking, she groaned, and covered her head with her pillow, certain that Jo was trying to kill her.

She was hungry the next morning, but she pushed through her exercises. At lunch, as she was sipping from another can, this one butterscotch-flavored, Suzanne asked if she'd ever tried the Hollywood diet, which Suzanne's mother had completed with great success.

"You have half a grapefruit for breakfast, then consommé, I think," she said, and Bethie had snapped, "I'm doing this one, if that's quite all right with you." She'd hoped the butterscotch flavor might be better than the Dutch chocolate, but her hopes had been in vain.

By two o'clock, she was ready to pass out. "Miss Kaufman, are you with us?" asked Mr. Blundell, her math teacher.

"Yes," said Bethie. Her voice was faint. She'd been thinking about what she'd eat once the auditions were over. Rib roast was expensive, she knew, but maybe she'd buy one with her babysitting money, cut little slits into the fat cap, and stuff slivers of garlic inside, and roast it for hours in a slow oven, until the whole house smelled good. She'd make twice-baked potatoes, mashing the potato flesh with cheddar cheese and sour cream, and have raspberry trifle for dessert, with vanilla pudding, made from scratch, and heavy cream that she'd whip herself.

Just twenty days, she told herself . . . and when she weighed herself the next morning, she found that she'd lost three pounds. That achievement gave her the strength to survive another three-shake day. The next morning, she'd had her breakfast shake, but halfway through her first twenty sit-ups on the living-room floor, she'd gotten so dizzy that the room had wavered in front of her and she'd had to lean against the edge of the couch. When she'd opened her eyes again, her sister was staring down at her, holding the empty can of Metrecal in her hand.

"You're going to make yourself sick," said Jo.

"It's none of your business," said Bethie. "How about you make like a tree and leave."

"This is stupid," Jo said. "Are you eating any actual food? Because you're only supposed to have the shakes for lunch, right?"

"Well, today I felt like having one for breakfast. Now make like a drummer and beat it," Bethie asked. She got to her feet, collected her lunchtime can of Metrecal, put it in her purse, and went outside to wait for the school bus. Only two more weeks plus two days. She could get through that.

Except when she got home, the Metrecal was missing from the cupboard. "Jo!" she hollered. Of course, her sister wasn't there. She was probably at field-hockey practice, racing up and down the grass, with her hair all sweaty and her rubber mouth guard stretching her lips into a fierce grin. Jo didn't have to worry about her figure, and even if she did, she wouldn't. Jo didn't worry about anything.

It isn't fair, Bethie thought, and, before she could stop herself, she'd hurled the glass she was holding, the one she'd meant for her Metrecal, against the wall, where it shattered into nasty glittering shards that of course she ended up having to pick up. When she'd done that, she went looking for shakes in the bedroom that she and Jo shared, reasoning that her sister wouldn't have just dumped them down the drain. It took her a while, but eventually she found them, up in the attic, next to the boxes of baby clothes that their *bubbe* had knitted, a broken radio, a box of old records, the sled she and Jo had used when they were little, and a box she didn't open labeled DAD'S STUFF.

After ten days, Bethie had lost eight pounds and she could button almost all of her skirts again. She'd stopped being hungry and started feeling airy, as if a balloon was expanding inside of her. At lunch, she could stare at Suzanne's French fries without feeling even the tiniest bit of desire for one, and at home when there was whitefish or meatloaf or burgers or croquettes, she'd move the food around the plate, chewing each bite over and over until it was a tasteless paste, eating just enough to keep her mother from getting on her case. Nights when she worried that she'd eaten too much, she'd go for a walk. There was an empty house at the end of the street, where Uncle Mel used to park, and in the empty backyard she'd lean against a tree, stick her fingers down her throat, and kick dirt over whatever she vomited up, so as not to attract bugs or raccoons. Lines from the Metrecal ad tolled like a bell in her head. *As for three a day, talk it over with your doctor first. You might disappear.*

Could she? Bethie would wonder at night in bed, her fingers exploring the contours of her torso, the rise of her ribs beneath her skin, the jut of a hipbone here, the new ridge of a clavicle there. Probably not, but she could turn into something else, something that looked like a girl but was just pure steely will.

"You look good," her mother told her, paying her a rare compliment after Bethie had completed two and a half weeks on the Metrecal plan. Jo just scowled and shook her head. Bethie stuck her tongue out at Jo when her mother's back was turned, and Jo raised her middle finger.

"Oh," said Bethie. "Very mature."

"Stop fighting, girls," said Sarah without looking at

them as she picked up her purse and walked out the door. At the auditions, her voice was as clear and as expressive as it had ever been. Her hair was shiny, her eyes were bright, and she wore a narrow belt cinched tight around the waist of her skirt. "Wonderful," said Miss McCullough, and even though the cast list wouldn't be posted until the following Monday, Bethie could see on her face that she'd done well, that she would get the leading role, as expected. "Wait here." Miss McCullough raised her voice. "Harold! We're ready for you!"

The boy who walked out from the wings looked desperately uncomfortable. His head was bent and his broad shoulders were hunched inside his varsity jacket, as if he were trying to make himself invisible. *Good luck with that*, Bethie thought. He was big, maybe a little taller than six feet, with a broad chest and wide shoulders, reddish-brown skin, close-cropped, tightly curled dark-brown hair, and sparse eyebrows, like an artist had started to sketch them in and had gotten called away on something else. He had full lips, an aquiline nose, and brown eyes that tilted up at the corners. The wooden crate he was holding looked no bigger than a lunchbox as it dangled from his hand.

"Hey," he said, and stopped squinting in the direction of the seats long enough to remove his free hand from the pocket of his khaki pants and extend it to Bethie. "Hi. I'm Harold Jefferson."

Bethie nodded. She knew that Harold was a senior and the star of the football team, but if he'd ever set foot in a drama club meeting before that afternoon, Bethie hadn't heard about it.

"Just stand there, Harold," said Miss McCullough. "On the mark." Harold looked lost, so Bethie pointed to the taped X on the floor.

"Are you auditioning?" she whispered.

"Um," he said, and Miss McCullough said, "Bethie, can you hop up on that box for me?"

Harold and Bethie looked at each other. Harold set the crate down, and Bethie climbed on top.

"Hmm. Try it on its short end," Miss McCullough said. Harold did as she requested. Again, Bethie hopped on top.

"Okay, Harold. I need you to hold her by the waist, lift her up, and put her down."

Harold looked apologetic. Bethie felt sick. Had they had to recruit an extra-strong guy because she had let herself get so big? She hoped that Harold couldn't tell how ashamed she was. Gently, he put his hands around Bethie's waist. "Ups-a-daisy," he said. She smelled his cologne—Old Spice, she thought—and then she was swooping through the air, first up, then down, with Harold settling her gently on her feet.

"Great! Now, lift her while you sing the line."

Harold ducked his head. Bethie saw his throat work as he swallowed. But on Miss McCullough's cue, he put his hands on Bethie's waist, lifted her up, opened his mouth, and sang in a tuneful and startlingly low voice, "There is nothin' like a daaaaame."

"Oh, wow," Bethie said when she was on her feet again. "Did you swallow Enrico Caruso?"

Harold looked, if possible, even more ashamed. "I can't do this," he whispered. "I feel like a fool."

Bethie's question must have been obvious from her expression, because Harold said, "I got in trouble with Coach. He said I could audition for the show or get benched for three games." He looked down at her hopefully. "Did a lot of guys try out?"

"Um." Bethie didn't have the heart to tell him that

only a handful of guys had auditioned, that Carl Berringer would get the lead, and none of the others had anything close to Harold's bass voice, or his good looks, or his presence. Instead, she asked, "Have you ever sung in public?"

"Just in church. And that's only because my father's the preacher." Harold looked sick. "If I'm in this play for real, the whole team's going to turn out and razz me. And my sisters." He looked even more sick.

"How many sisters do you have?"

"Four. Three older, one younger."

"Thank you!" Miss McCullough called. "The cast list will be posted on Monday morning."

"I better not get it," Harold muttered, and Bethie shook her head and smiled, hoping that he would.

By the end of October, rehearsals were progressing. As Bethie had predicted, Harold had been cast in the role of Billis, and every afternoon, four days a week, Bethie would feel his big hands around her diminishing waistline as he lifted her and lowered her. During rehearsals, she fished for details about what kind of trouble Harold had gotten into with the football coach, but Harold wouldn't say. He was more forthcoming on the topic of why he'd never auditioned for any of the school shows, even with his voice.

"Stage fright," he said. "I don't like doing things in front of people."

Bethie had laughed, and Harold, looking chagrined, had said, "What? It's true!"

"You play football! How can you be on a football field in front of hundreds of people—"

"That's different," Harold said. "I'm wearing pads,

and a helmet, and a uniform. I'm part of a team, not out there all by myself. And I'm not—you know—" His lips twisted as he spoke the hated word. "Dancing."

"What's wrong with dancing?" Bethie asked.

"I don't know." Harold considered. "It's not very manly, I guess."

"You dance at school dances, right?"

"Not in front of everyone." Harold was frowning, picking at the skin around his thumbnail. "Not as a performance. Can we stop talking about it? Please? It's just making it worse."

Bethie asked, "Would it help if you pictured everyone in the audience in their underwear?"

Harold looked shocked, and Bethie remembered that his father was a preacher. Maybe he wasn't used to girls talking about nakedness.

"Or if you pretended you could tackle the other actors?"

Harold smiled. "Maybe."

"Just not me."

"Okay," he agreed. "Just not you."

At first, Harold was quiet around the other drama club kids who could, Bethie knew, be a cliquey bunch. Harold was both the only Negro student in the show and the only football player, and the rest of the cast treated him like a curiosity. Gradually, there was a thaw, prompted by an improv game Miss McCullough had them play. "It's so hot," she'd begin, and the kids, standing in a circle, would shout, "HOW HOT IS IT?" Then Miss McCullough would point at one of them, and that boy or girl would have to come up with a comparison: *So hot that you could fry an egg on the sidewalk; so hot I saw a funeral procession pulling into Dairy Queen.* Harold often had the funniest comebacks. *Hotter than a goat's butt in a pepper patch. Colder than a well-digger's belt buckle. So ugly you'd hire her to haunt a house. So stupid that if he ever had a thought, it'd be lonely.* They were his father's sayings, Harold said. "He's got thousands of them."

Bethie thought he was cute, but she knew that, if her mother hadn't wanted Jo playing with a Negro girl when they were children, she certainly would not have wanted Bethie dating a Negro boy. *Birds of a feather must flock together.* Not that it mattered. Harold, she learned, was going with Jo's basketball teammate, Vernita Clink-scale, who'd thrown over her boyfriend in the navy when Harold had asked her to homecoming. Besides, Harold wasn't the least bit interested. He treated Bethie with a kind of casual, offhand affection, like she was one of his sisters. And, as if that wasn't depressing enough, her weight loss had stalled. She'd lost eighteen pounds, even more than she'd initially planned, but she wanted to keep going, and so she cut her daily intake down to two shakes a day and water with a squeeze of lemon in between. In the mornings she would wake up at five, slip down to the basement with a basket of laundry, and do jumping jacks and sit-ups for half an hour, down where no one could hear her. When she wasn't feeling dizzy, she felt wonderful, full of energy, as slim and sharp and keen as a fencer's blade. She wondered what would happen if she only had one shake a day, or even one shake every other day. How much weight could a girl shed while still going about her daily business? When would she stop being a body altogether and just float away, up into the sky?

Dodie Sanders, the senior who was in charge of props and costumes, took in her khaki skirt and shirt, and the Ban-Lon swimsuit she'd wear for "Wash That Man Right Outta My Hair," and clucked her tongue as she pulled the measuring tape tight, but Dodie was heavyset, with coarse dark hair on her forearms and her upper lip. Bethie didn't care what Dodie thought. "Don't go getting too thin on us," Miss McCullough called the next day as rehearsal was letting out, but Bethie ignored her. Was there such a thing as too thin?

"I want you to stop with this," Sarah told her that night. "You're making yourself sick." Bethie promised that she was done with Metrecal, that she was having only one shake for lunch, just to finish up what she'd bought.

"Do they go bad?" Jo asked innocently. "I thought you could just keep them forever."

Bethie glared at her. Jo stared back, her face innocent. "Girls, stop fighting," said Sarah, and looked meaningfully at Bethie's plate. Bethie ate baked fish and half of a sweet potato, hating every leaden, greasy mouthful, imagining the fat and grease polluting her pure, cleaned-out self. On Monday afternoon, at rehearsal, she was singing about being in love with a wonderful guy when the world wavered, and the stage seemed to roll, like the wooden boards had turned into waves on the water. That was the last thing she remembered until she woke up in the nurse's office, looking up at Harold Jefferson's back, hearing her sister's voice. "She's been dieting," she heard Jo say, and Bethie struggled to push herself upright.

"I'm fine," she insisted.

"You're not," Harold said. His sparse eyebrows were pulled down over his eyes, and he'd shoved his hands in his pockets. "You fainted."

"You should call your family doctor," said the nurse, and Jo promised that she would. "Come on, I've got the car," she said, and insisted on keeping her arm around Bethie's waist as she led her into the parking lot.

Bethie sat in the passenger's seat as Jo drove them

back to Alhambra Street. The house was dark and quiet. On Mondays and Tuesdays, her days off, Sarah rested as much as she could, napping in the bedroom until the last possible minute when she'd get up and sit with them for dinner.

Bethie tried to go to the bedroom, but Jo grabbed her by the shoulder and held her firmly in place.

"At least let me take my makeup off," Bethie said, trying to keep her voice light.

Her sister shook her head. "Come to the kitchen," she said, and Bethie couldn't see a way out. In the kitchen, Bethie sat at the table. Jo reached into the refrigerator and pulled out bread and cheese. Bethie shook her head.

"I had a bunch of chips at rehearsal. Lynn Friedlander and Dodie Sanders brought snacks for everyone."

"You didn't have any potato chips. You'd rather die than eat a potato chip," said Jo. She was putting more things on the counter. Bethie saw pickle chips, and a stick of real butter that Jo must have bought herself. Bethie watched as Jo put a pat of butter in the frying pan and spread more on each side of the two slices of bread. When the butter was sizzling she put the bread in the pan, layering two slices of cheese on each piece and sat down at the table.

"I know you aren't eating."

Bethie opened her mouth to protest. Jo held up her hand. "Just listen for a minute." She looked Bethie right in the eyes. "If you keep hurting yourself, he wins."

Bethie squirmed on her chair. "I don't know what you're talking about."

"Yes, you do."

"Nobody's winning anything, Jo, I just needed to lose a few pounds for the show."

"And now you have." Jo got to her feet, flipped the

sandwich over, and set it on a blue plate. The kitchen was full of the good smells of toasty bread, melted butter, and cheese. Jo used a fork to fish a few sweet pickle chips out of the jar. She cut the crusts off the sandwich, sliced it in half, diagonally, then into quarters, and she set it down in front of her sister.

"Jo, I'm really not hungry," said Bethie.

"Just have a few bites, and I promise I'll leave you alone." When Bethie didn't answer, Jo said, "Bethie, you passed out. A bunch of people saw you. And you've lost, what, twenty pounds?"

"Eighteen," said Bethie, feeling pleased that Jo thought it was more.

"It's enough. Please. Don't let him win." Bethie shook her head and opened her mouth, ready to say something flip, but she saw that Jo's brow was knitted, and that her sister, who never took anything seriously, looked as if she was going to cry.

She lifted one of the sandwich quarters, feeling its warmth, the yielding melted cheese between the buttery slices of bread. She knew how it would feel when her teeth shattered the crisp crust, when the warm cheese poured over her tongue, how it would feel to chew a mouthful, and swallow, and how her mouth would pucker when she took a bite of sweet, briny pickle and felt it crunch against her teeth. It would be so good. She wouldn't be able to stop.

She put the sandwich down and wiped the butter off her fingers. "Jo, I'm sorry, but I'm just not hungry." She could wait it out. In a few minutes, the bread would cool, the butter and cheese would congeal, the sandwich would stop looking so delicious and smelling so good. "Besides, aren't we having dinner soon?"

Without answering, Jo turned back toward the stove.

She turned the flame on under the pan, added more butter, pulled two more slices of bread out of the package, and spread more butter on them. When the second sandwich was set in front of her, Jo looked at her again and said, "Please." With a crooked smile, she added, "I feel like you're going to disappear."

That's what I want, Bethie thought. *Don't you understand?* But Jo was looking at her with stubborn insistence, and Bethie knew her sister well enough to understand that Jo wouldn't let up, that she'd make another ten sandwiches, sit here all night and into the morning until Bethie gave in.

Gingerly, she used her fingertips to lift a quarter of the sandwich. With the very edges of her teeth, she took the tiniest nibble. The bread crunched, the cheese oozed, the butter flooded her mouth with its taste of uncomplicated goodness. Bethie took another nibble, and another, then a bite, and when she'd finished the first quarter, she ate a pickle, and sipped from the glass of juice that Jo had poured.

"Okay?" she asked.

Jo shook her head. With great ceremony, she removed the last four cans of Metrecal from the cupboard and poured them, one after another, down the sink. "I don't want you going anywhere," she told her sister.

"Fine," said Bethie. Her belly was unsettled, she felt uncomfortably full, and her throat ached as she watched Jo pour her diet shakes down the sink, one can after another, until every last drop had swirled down the drain and disappeared.

Jo

Thanksgiving had always been her father's favorite holiday. He'd liked the Jewish holidays, eating apples and honey on Rosh Hashana, leading the Passover Seders, but he had cherished holidays where the Kaufmans were the same as everyone else in Detroit and America, not the ones that only underlined their difference. He'd hang an American flag by the front door for the Fourth of July and Memorial Day and Veterans Day. They were always the first family with a pumpkin on their stoop in October, and every November, Ken would pull the steps down from the attic and retrieve, from a cardboard box marked THANKS-GIVING, the paper-plate turkey centerpieces that the girls had made in kindergarten. Her father did not cook, but on Thanksgiving, he would take charge of the turkey, putting it in to roast at just after six o'clock in the morning, crouching in front of the oven's open door to baste it every fifteen minutes with his secret marinade that Jo knew was made of melted margarine, orange juice, and teriyaki sauce. The house would fill with the smells of roasting

turkey, nutmeg and ginger and cinnamon, and Sarah's famous Parker House rolls. At ten o'clock, Jo and Bethie
would be bundled into their winter coats, even if it was
still warm outside, and their father would take them to
Woodward Avenue to see the Thanksgiving Day Parade.
He'd lift Bethie onto his shoulders, and Jo would hold his
hand. They'd stand as close to the curb as they could get
and watch the procession of bands, baton twirlers, balloons, and the Big Heads, marchers wearing giant heads
made from papier-mâché. At two o'clock, the turkey
would emerge from the oven and sit on the counter to
rest. Jo would stare, wondering if anyone would notice if
she broke off a wing tip to nibble, while her mother began
to heat the side dishes she'd spent all week making, deftly
sliding dishes in and out of the hot oven, shifting the
plates and platters to make space. Her dad would drive
into Detroit to pick up Bubbe and Zayde, and at four
o'clock they would sit down for a feast.

Now, everything was different. Hudson's was closed
on Thanksgiving Day, but staffers who wanted to earn
overtime could come in, starting at seven a.m., preparing
the floor for the holiday shoppers who would show up
first thing Friday morning, lists in hand. *Just so they could
lord it over the last-minute people*, was Sarah's opinion.
She couldn't afford to turn down time-and-a-half pay, so
she'd signed up for an eight-hour shift. Jo thought about
going to the parade—she could invite Lynnette, who had
two younger brothers—but the thought of being there
without her father made her feel like crying. Going to
their uncle's house was out of the question. So, together,
the sisters came up with a plan.

"How would it be if we invited some people for
Thanksgiving?" Jo asked on a Friday night in early November. The Shabbat dinners they'd once enjoyed had

turned into makeshift affairs, with Bethie preparing the chicken, Jo setting the table, and Sarah picking up bakery challah on her way home from work. The store-bought bread was never as good as the bread Zayde had made, but Zayde had finally retired.

Her mother stared at her across the kitchen table, a vertical line cutting a groove between her eyebrows. "People like who?"

"Maybe the Steins. And the Simoneaux could come."

Sarah looked from one daughter to the other. Jo was dressed in her Bellwood High sweatshirt and her long cotton basketball shorts; Bethie had on a blue-and-gold kilt that used to be Jo's, a blue blouse with a pointed collar, saddle shoes, and a dark-blue rayon cardigan, bought on sale and already pilling. Sarah had on her green faille wool dress and a leather belt. She had taken off the pumps she wore to work, the ones that left a red line across her instep, and was rubbing one foot with her thumb, sighing as she sat at the kitchen table, with a notebook and a nubbly plastic box of recipes, written in her large, looping handwriting on index cards, in front of her. The dress's dark fabric absorbed the light, emphasizing Sarah's pallor and the circles under her eyes.

"We'll be eating leftover turkey for a month if it's just us," said Bethie.

"We could ask Henry Sheshevsky," Jo said.

Sarah looked startled, then thoughtful. "Henry Sheshevsky. Now there's a name from the past."

"Come on, Mom," said Bethie. "It'll be fun!"

"And we'll do the inviting," said Jo, who thought appealing to Sarah's sense of, or appetite for, fun was a losing battle. "And clean up when it's over."

"I can't afford to stay home and cook . . ." Sarah said, but Jo could see that her mother was wavering.

"We'll cook," said Bethie. Sarah gave them an incredulous look. "I'll cook," Bethie amended.

"Hey! I can cook!" said Jo. Her mother and sister both looked at her with identical expressions of disbelief. Jo bit her lip. It was true that she'd endured some notable failures during the home economics classes that all girls at Bellwood High were required to take. In her defense, Lynnette had been distracting her the day she'd left the eggs out of a pound cake, and she was pretty sure that she'd been tripped the time she'd dropped a pan full of unbaked popover dough on the floor a few weeks later.

"How about Jell-O?" Bethie suggested.

Jo bit her lip. They'd always had Jell-O on the Thanksgiving table. Jo remembered how her father would plop a slice on his plate and perform the jingle. "Watch it wiggle, see it jiggle," he'd sing. The girls had loved it when they were little, but they had gotten increasingly embarrassed by the singing as the years had gone on. Jo cringed, remembering how, last year she'd rolled her eyes when he began. What she'd give to hear his voice again, she thought, even if he was singing a silly Jell-O ditty.

"Do you think you can handle that?" Sarah asked, giving Jo a hard look. "And be home at four o'clock? In a dress?"

"So can we ask some people?"

Sarah heaved another sigh. "As long as it doesn't end up being more work for me," she said. "You'll have to help cook, and clean, and set the table."

"We will," Jo and Bethie promised, and Sarah finally, wearily, nodded her assent.

On Thanksgiving morning, the Kaufman ladies got up early. Sarah put an apron on over the skirt and blouse she was wearing to work that day and spooned Bethie's stuffing into the turkey. Bethie, who was wearing her own apron, began sifting flour, salt, and baking soda for the rolls, while Jo set up the ironing board in the living room. She ironed their good white tablecloth and draped it over the three folding tables that they'd borrowed from the Steins. There would be fifteen at the table this year, the three of them, Bubbe and Zayde and Henry Sheshevsky, who would drive Sarah's parents; their neighbors Don and Beverly Stein and Tim, Pat, and Donald Junior; and Mr. and Mrs. Simoneaux, with Bethie's friend Barbara and Barb's brother, Andy. Jo was looking forward to the crowd, conversation, and laughter, not long silences and bad memories. The Steins were bringing desserts, three kinds of pie and fresh whipped cream, and Henry Sheshevsky was bringing wine and schnapps, and the Simoneaux were bringing a cheese ball and crackers. Jo only wished that Lynnette could be there, but Lynnette hadn't been able to convince her parents to forgo their annual trip to Grand Rapids.

Jo folded the ironed napkins at each place and set out the white china plates and the crystal wine and water glasses Sarah had purchased with her Hudson's discount. The previous afternoon had been a half-day at school, and, on her way home, Jo had purchased a bunch of yellow and orange gerbera daisies from a florist on 10 Mile Road. The guy behind the counter had flirted with her and thrown in some ferns and baby's breath, and Jo turned the bouquet into three small arrangements, each in a cleaned glass jar that had once held mustard or honey. She set them on the table with a satisfied smile. *Maybe I can't cook*, she imagined telling Lynnette, *but not all of the womanly arts are lost on me.*

In the kitchen, the green beans and the sweet potatoes sat on the counter in their baking dishes, coming to room temperature before they went back into the oven. The rolls were rising, the turkey had been stuffed and trussed, and Sarah was off to Hudson's.

"If it's okay, I'm going to go to Lynnette's for a while. I'll make the Jell-O there," Jo said.

"We're starting at four," Sarah reminded them. "Put the turkey in at ten, take it out at three to rest." She gave Bethie a kiss, gave Jo a hard look, picked up her handbag, and walked out the door.

Pedaling to Lynnette's, Jo thought about Thanksgiving and why it mattered to her mother. Maybe Sarah would never have a four-bedroom house in Southfield or Bloomfield Hills, or a colored girl in a uniform to help serve and clear; maybe she no longer had a husband and had to spend her days on her feet, cruising through the dressing rooms, calling, "Can I get anyone a different size?" or patiently telling women that even if a garment still had its tags attached, it could not be returned for a refund with visible perspiration stains underneath the armpits. In spite of it all, the Kaufman ladies could still get Thanksgiving dinner on the table; they could offer their guests a delicious meal; they could dish out turkey and stuffing and Parker House rolls and look like every other family in America.

Jo rode along, enjoying the exertion, the feeling of the muscles in her thighs working as she pedaled. Lynnette's parents were leaving early for Grand Rapids, and Lynnie was going to drive herself and the boys at three, thus minimizing the amount of time that rowdy, clumsy, big-handed Randy and Gary Bobeck would spend in her grandmother's house, which was full of fragile china figurines, breakable *objets*, and white wall-to-wall carpeting. "Besides," Lynnette had told Mrs. Bobeck, "Jo needs help with her cooking."

She parked her bike by the garage and knocked on the door, and Lynnette opened it, wearing her soft pink bathrobe, with her hair still damp and her skin still pink from the shower. "Come on," Lynnette whispered, grabbing Jo's hand. She smelled like Camay soap and Prell shampoo, and Jo wanted to kiss every bit of her, from her little toes to the crown of her head. They'd hurried, giggling, through the house, which smelled, as always, of floor polish and pickling spices, through the living room, where the new sofa, with its skinny gold legs and turquoise-blue upholstery, sat in front of an enormous wood-paneled television set, proceeding straight to Lynnie's bedroom. *Isn't this better than it is with him?* Jo wanted to ask, as she nibbled the pale skin of Lynnette's throat and brushed her fingertips against Lynnette's breasts. Lynnette hadn't told her much about what had happened with Bobby Carver, but Jo felt as if Lynnette's lost virginity had turned their bedroom activities from pure delight into a contest every bit as competitive as a volleyball match or a basketball game. Hearing Lynnette sigh, seeing the rosy flush that suffused her chest and neck, watching her hips arch off the bed as her heels pushed against her pink-and-white flowered sheets, Jo would think, *Isn't this better than it is with him?* But she never let herself ask, instead applying herself wholeheartedly to Lynnette's delight, hoping her friend would come to that realization all by herself. *And what if she does?* Jo thought, as she cupped Lynnette's head and kissed her. *She'll break up with Bobby and run away with me?* It would never happen. Lynnette wasn't built for that kind of life. Jo wasn't entirely certain that she herself was, either.

"Stop teasing," Lynnette said, as Jo brushed her fingers, ever so lightly, over the curls between Lynnette's legs. Ignoring her, Jo moved her hands down to Lynnette's plump and quivering thighs, caressing until they fell open, revealing her most secret place. Jo bent her head, using just the tip of her tongue, as Lynnette squirmed and sighed, rocking her hips from side to side, grabbing for Jo's hair, trying to pull Jo's face more firmly against her. "Oh, God, oh, God, ohGod," she chanted, as Jo slipped one finger inside of her, flicking her tongue, keeping her free hand pressed on Lynnette's belly to keep her in place, wishing that she could stay there forever, in that bedroom, in that bed, with Lynnette warm and sweet and willing underneath her.

When Lynnie was done with her, Jo flopped onto her back, and once she'd caught her breath, Lynnette reached over Jo and picked up the copy of *Amy Vanderbilt's Complete Book of Etiquette* that she had on her bedside table, next to a white poodle with a transistor radio in its belly. Lynnette's grandmother had given her the book as a gift for her sixteenth birthday, and Lynnette's latest favorite postcoital activity was to find ridiculous passages and read them out loud in ostentatiously plummy tones.

"Listen to this," Lynnette said. She was still flushed splotchy red, from chest to chin, and her hair was half-dry, curling around her forehead and her cheeks and flat against her back. She cleared her throat and warbled, "'Occasionally in business it is necessary for a woman executive to pay entertainment or other bills for men clients or to take their share of checks when lunching with men business associates. In all cases (for the sake of the man) a woman tries to avoid a public display of her financial arrangements. Even if she is lunching a junior executive, it is courteous to allow him the dignity of seeming to pay the bill.'"

Jo half listened to Lynnie's performance as she stretched her arms over her head. She felt wonderful, her body loose and relaxed, like she'd moved out of her head and entirely into her skin, where she didn't have to worry about her mother, or her future, or how much it would hurt when things with Lynnette were over.

"Does your mother ever lunch with anyone at her job?"

Jo shook her head. "And even if she did, it wouldn't be a man." All of the people her mother worked with, her boss and her fellow salesladies, were all women. *The girls*, Sarah called them. Some of the girls actually were just past girlhood, young women, some of them single, biding their time before marriage, some married, saving money before babies. Other of the girls weren't girls at all, they were women in their forties and fifties, working to supplement a husband's income, and some of them were widows like Sarah. There were even two divorcées (Sarah pronounced the word "divor-sees"), supporting themselves and their children, all on their own. Jo had heard her mother speak respectfully of her boss, Mrs. Lyons, and a young Negro woman named Toby Pettigrew, who'd worked her way up from seamstress to a sales position in Better Dresses, but she'd never invited any of her colleagues to the house, and Jo and Bethie had never met them.

"Or there's this," Lynnette said, flipping pages. "'It's hard to face this, but no woman can find happiness in putting career ahead of her husband and family,'" she read. "'Once she has taken on woman's natural responsibilities, whatever work she undertakes must be done in a way that deprives the family the least. Everywhere we meet women who seem to overcome the difficulties of the dual role, but the hard truth is that more women with young children fail at making happy homes while working full-time than succeed.'"

"Woman's natural responsibilities," Jo mused, and wondered if her mother had felt happier when she'd been a housewife, with a husband who brought home a salary, or if she enjoyed being part of the working world. As far as she could see, work made her mother no happier than keeping house ever had. Sarah's mouth was still compressed in the same tight line, her face permanently set in its expression of displeasure whether she'd spent the day cooking and cleaning at home or selling dresses at Hudson's. "I don't think she cares too much about making a happy home," Jo said.

"She doesn't have young children," Lynnette pointed out.

"True. But I think she likes having somewhere to go every day. Something to do."

"Maybe it keeps her from thinking about your father," Lynnette suggested.

Jo drummed her fingers on Lynnette's soft sheets. "I'm actually not sure she misses him."

Lynnette looked shocked. "Of course she does!"

"I'm not sure," Jo repeated. She believed that her mother enjoyed the independence widowhood had conferred, not to mention the power over the checkbook, the car keys, and the decision about where—and if—Jo would go to college.

"Are you still going to that thing on Saturday?" Lynnette asked, rolling onto her side and pulling the sheet up to her chin.

"That thing is a picket." Jo felt a brief flare of annoyance. "And yes, I am." Since her junior year, Jo had spent one Saturday a month picketing somewhere in Detroit. In March, she and a few other kids from Bellwood High had driven to Lansing to participate in an NAACP demonstration for housing equality on the steps of the statehouse building. For months, she'd tried to get Lynnette to come with her. First, she'd tried to make the case that, in a world where everything was equal, they'd be able to date each other. Lynnette had just stared at her, looking shocked, so quickly, Jo had said, "Just keep me company. It'll be fun!" "I'll see," Lynnette said, but every weekend she had an excuse, saying that she had to help her mother with the boys, or study for a test, or wash her hair. "I'm sure you'll have great stories!" she told Jo, and indeed, Jo came back full of tales of how Al Hymowitz had spent the entire ride in both directions quoting from *The Communist Manifesto*, and how Deenie Altshuler had seen a photographer from the *Detroit News* and had gotten so upset about her parents possibly seeing her picture in the paper that she'd dropped her sign to throw her hands over her face.

Lynnette rolled onto her back, lifting her arms over her head in a way that made her breasts rise enticingly. "Remind me again why you care."

"Because," Jo said, bending to plant a row of kisses from Lynnie's shoulder to her neck, "I believe in fairness." She kissed one cheek. "I believe in equality." She kissed the other. "And I think that people should be able to eat, or swim, or go to school wherever they want to." She pulled down the sheet and blew a raspberry on Lynnette's belly. Lynnette shrieked, then tried to push Jo's head away.

"You know what I think?" Lynnette said, once she'd caught her breath. "I think you just like making your mom see red."

"It's a nice side effect." Lynnette knew the story of Mae and Mae's daughter Frieda. She also knew about the time Jo and Bethie had gone to the public swimming pool on Belle Isle on Memorial Day weekend the previous summer. The pool was scheduled to open at ten o'clock, and families had gotten there early to stand in line, mothers laden with tote bags and snacks and towels wrapped in rubber bands, fishbelly-pale kids running around in swimsuits that had gotten too small over the winter, or in ones that had been handed down from an older brother or sister and flopped around their legs or gaped loose at their chests. On the opposite side of the fence, four black boys had stood, with their fingers hooked through the chain link, watching quietly as the gates opened and the white kids whooped and cannon-balled into the water, ignoring the lifeguard's shouts and their parents' pleas to slow down and be careful and watch where they were jumping. The kids hadn't said anything, and of course they hadn't tried to get into the pool, but the look of longing on their faces had stayed with Jo all through the summer. When she'd told Lynnette about it, Lynnette had shrugged, asking, "They've got their own places, right?"

"Come on," Jo said. She set her feet on the pale-pink carpet that was a few shades lighter than the pink-patterned wallpaper and bent down to collect her clothes. "Time to cook."

Lynnette groaned, but got to her feet, pulled on her robe, and rummaged around until she found a magazine on her desk. "I have a plan. Your mother thinks you're incapable, right?"

"You know she does," said Jo.

"Well." Lynnette was smiling, visibly pleased with herself. "Sarah's not going to think you're a failure as a woman if you come home with . . ." She opened the magazine to a page she'd marked, and beamed. "Strawberry Pineapple Ring!"

"Mmm," said Jo, because "Mmm" was part of the recipe's official name. She and Lynnette read it out loud, together: "Strawberry Pineapple Ring! Mmm!"

"I don't have any pineapple," said Jo.

"Well, today must be your lucky day," said Lynnette, skipping downstairs to the kitchen and producing a can of pineapple from her mother's pantry. Jo studied the label, thinking that this did not sound like a good idea. Experimentation was not her strong suit. "Maybe we should just keep it simple? Besides, I bought cherry Jell-O, not strawberry."

Lynnette shook her head. "You're overthinking. It's red, isn't it?" When Jo nodded, Lynnette pulled the magazine out of her robe's pocket and continued to read. "Fresh strawberries. Got 'em. Pineapple syrup." She frowned, then shrugged. "I'll bet we can just use maple." Quickly, she and Jo assembled the dish, adding hot water to the powdered Jell-O, pouring it into a plastic mixing bowl, and mixing in the canned fruit and the cut-up strawberries, as well as the lemon juice the recipe called for. Jo stirred and poured at Lynnie's direction. After she slid the pan into the refrigerator, Lynnette looked at the clock and gave her a slow, saucy smile. "So now it's got to thicken. Want to take a shower?"

Jo did. They stayed in the bathroom until the hot water ran out. When Jo flicked at Lynnette's bottom with a rolled-up towel, Lynnette squealed and went racing out of the bathroom naked, with only a shower cap on her head, and Jo, wearing only a towel, in pursuit. Laughing, Jo rounded the corner to Lynnette's bedroom and almost slammed into Randy Bobeck, who'd just come up the stairs. Randy held up both of his hands in front of his chest in a warding-off gesture. His eyes and his mouth were both opened wide as his gaze moved from Jo to his sister and bounced back to Jo again.

Lynnette screamed—for real, that time. She put one arm over her breasts and stuck the other hand between her legs. "Randy, you fink!" she shrieked, before slamming her bedroom door. "'Scuse me," Jo muttered, hurrying back to the bathroom, hoping that Randy wasn't looking, imagining that probably he was.

A few minutes later, Lynnette knocked on the bathroom door. She was dressed in her new Jonathan Logan double-knit dress, dark brown, scattered with red and pink flowers, along with hose and shoes. "Did he see anything?" she whispered, stepping inside. Her face was pale; her eyes were enormous.

"No." Jo tried to sound confident, when the truth was that she didn't know what Randy saw, or what he might be thinking. Two girls, mostly naked, laughing and chasing each other. Would Randy think it was just the kind of thing girls did if they were very good friends? Jo swallowed hard. "Don't worry," she told Lynnette. "We weren't doing anything. He didn't see anything. It's fine."

Lynnette shook her head. She still looked terrified. "If he says something to my parents . . . if this gets out at school . . ."

"It won't. Because we weren't doing anything. It's fine," Jo repeated. Lynnette gave a single, tight-lipped nod, and she barely looked at Jo as she handed over the button-down shirt and dungarees that Jo had worn over.

Downstairs, Jo took the Bundt pan out of the refrigerator while Lynnette called her brothers.

"Randy! Gary! We have to go now!"

The whole way back to Alhambra Street, Jo could

barely breathe. She listened to the boys in the back seat talking about the prospects of the Detroit hockey team, as opposed to how Randy had seen their big sister cavorting naked with her best friend.

"Bye," she said to Lynnette, who'd gotten the car moving again almost before Jo had slammed the trunk shut. Jo rolled her bike into the garage, went to the kitchen, and slid the pan into the refrigerator, noticing, as she did, that the Jell-O seemed to be a little watery, wishing there was a way to check and see if it had set, knowing that all she could do was hope.

"Hi, Mom," Jo said. The house smelled delicious. The wineglasses sparkled, the flowers brightened the room, but Jo still felt sick, her chest so tight she could barely manage a full inhalation.

"You're late," Sarah said. Her tone was clipped, her mouth compressed. She was still in her work clothes, with a frilly pink apron tied at her waist. The turkey, now cooked, was cooling on a cutting board next to the oven. "Go change."

Jo waited until her mom was in the living room, then transferred her Jell-O from the refrigerator into the freezer, reasoning that colder temperatures would help it to set more quickly. In the bedroom, she pulled on a dark-gray wool shirtdress with white trim on the long sleeves and the collar, and slipped her feet into a pair of black flats, shoes her mother only deemed acceptable because, in heels, Jo towered over almost every man she knew. She did what she could with her hair, backcombing and spraying, in an effort that would at least show her mother that she'd tried, before pulling it back with a plastic tortoiseshell headband.

When she returned to the kitchen, Sarah was in front of the stove, whisking cornstarch into the gravy. "Fill the water glasses," she told Jo without lifting her eyes from the pot. Jo was carrying a pitcher of water to the table when Bethie hurried through the door.

"I'm sorry!" she said. "I went to Denise's house." She sounded a little out of breath, but Jo's quick glance did not reveal anything immediately amiss. Underneath her cardigan, Bethie's light-blue blouse was buttoned correctly, tucked into her blue-and-green kilt. Her hair was neat and her lipstick was freshly applied. Jo looked at her sister and felt an ugly flare of jealousy, knowing that Denise's older brother was home from college and that it was possible Bethie had spent her afternoon with him. Knowing, too, that even if Bethie had looked like she'd just rolled out of bed, she wouldn't have gotten in the kind of trouble Jo and Lynnette were facing, because she'd have been in that bed with a boy.

By five o'clock twilight was gathering, the sky deepening from blue to indigo outside the windows. All down the block, Jo could see lights shining through doorways and spilling onto the street, could hear the sounds of car doors closing and welcoming calls of "Glad you made it!" and "Come on in!" and "Happy Thanksgiving!" "Let's turn the lights off," said Bethie, and the darkness made the room look even more elegant, with the candlelight sparkling off the crystal and silver and the glass flower jars, making the white tablecloth seem to glow.

"You did a nice job on the table," Sarah said, giving Jo a rare compliment, as Bethie pulled a tray of rolls out of the oven and used tongs to put them into a napkin-lined wicker basket.

Henry Sheshevsky, still short and heavyset and light on his feet, arrived first. He ushered Bubbe and Zayde into the house, took Bubbe's coat with a courtly bow, and with great ceremony, handed Sarah two bottles of

Lancers wine. "For a special occasion! I'm so glad you're inviting me to your luffly home!" The Simoneaux came next. Henry helped Barbara and Mrs. Simoneaux with their coats—"Such beauties!" he exclaimed. "I'm surrounded by beauties!," while Jo put the heralded cheese ball and cut-up carrots and celery and dip on the coffee table, along with a stack of small plates and forks. The Steins came trooping across the street, with each boy carrying a pie and Mrs. Stein wanting to know if she could put the metal bowl and the beaters into the freezer, so they'd be cold when it was time to whip the cream. The house was warm and crowded and noisy, full of overlapping voices and laughter.

Mr. Stein took the boys out back to throw a football around, and Mr. Simoneaux and Andy joined them. Henry Sheshevsky poured Sarah a glass of wine, and when she waved him away, he cajoled her, eventually pressing the glass into her hand. Mrs. Stein and Mrs. Simoneaux complained about the Krinskys at the end of the block, who didn't keep their grass cut, and about the Perrinaults, whose new basset hound howled at five in the morning when the milkman came, and Mr. Simoneaux went back down the street to get his new electric carving knife. Jo watched quietly from the kitchen, wishing that her father could have been there. He would have bantered with Henry, and flattered Sarah's mother, and made Barbara blush by telling her how grown-up she looked, and made sure Jo got the drumstick, and not minded if Jo ate it with her hands.

Finally, Sarah called everyone to the table. When the guests were seated, Sarah stood and said, "Thank you all for coming. I'm so glad to have friends around us today. And I'm grateful to my daughters." The candlelight smoothed out the lines around her eyes and softened the grooves that descended from her nose to the corners of her lips that had deepened since her husband's death. In the flickering dimness, with her wineglass in her hand and a tentative expression on her face, her mother looked almost young and almost pretty.

"Mazel tov! Now let's eat!" said Henry, clapping his hands and bouncing up from his chair to fill the wineglasses. Sarah beckoned Jo and Bethie close, and surprised Jo by taking their hands.

"I know this hasn't been easy," she said. "Losing your dad, and having me working." She looked up. "Bethie, I wish I could come to all of your performances."

Bethie murmured a demurral.

"And, Jo, I'd like to see more of your games."

I doubt it, Jo thought. Sarah would occasionally come to Jo's tennis matches—*probably because I have to wear a skirt to play*, Jo thought—but had skipped every volleyball and basketball game, even the ones on Mondays and Tuesdays that she theoretically could have attended. Jo suspected her mother hated the sight of her racing up and down the court, or crouching in front of the net; that she hated the knee pads and the mouthguards, the uniforms that left her sweaty limbs bare. *It's so rough*, Sarah had said once, shuddering, after enduring the sight of Jo exchanging hand-slaps with her teammates after they'd won a tough match.

"So thank you," Sarah said. Her eyes seemed to glitter. "Thank you both."

"You're welcome," Jo said, and Bethie added, "There's nothing you need to thank us for."

"No. I'm grateful. You did a wonderful job."

Jo thought of the Jell-O and shuddered, wondering if her mother would notice if she just never brought it to the table.

Mr. Simoneaux and Mr. Stein went to the kitchen to carve the turkey. "Jo, get the cranberry sauce," said Bethie. Up close, Jo could see a suck mark on the side of her sister's neck. Sarah passed around the side dishes, the green beans and the rolls, the mashed potatoes and the sweet potatoes that Bethie had baked and run through a ricer with heavy cream, nutmeg, and real butter and a pinch of orange rind before spooning them into a baking dish and decorating the top with an intricate, spiraling pattern made of bits of glazed pecans and miniature marshmallows. That was Bethie, Jo thought. Everything she touched came out perfectly.

Jo helped herself to stuffing, reached for a drumstick, saw her mother's face, and took a slice of white meat instead.

"Jo," Sarah said brightly, "don't forget your Jell-O!"

"The famous Jell-O!" said Henry Sheshevsky as he clapped his hands.

Slowly, Jo got to her feet, sending up a silent prayer to whatever god guarded careless teenage lesbian sex fiends. She carried the Bundt pan to the table and turned it upside down on a clean plate. She tapped it gently. Nothing happened. Feeling everyone's eyes on her, Jo gave the pan a little shake. Still nothing. Jo raised the pan, shaking harder. There was a horrible slooping sound, and a flood of half-liquefied Jell-O and chunks of fruit poured out of the mold and flooded the plate, pouring onto the white tablecloth, and directly into Mrs. Stein's lap.

Mrs. Stein shrieked and shoved her chair back, out of the path of the deluge. "Oh, my God, I'm so sorry!" Jo said, as she tried to scoop up as much of the fruit and solid Jell-O as she could, but it was clear that Mrs. Stein's dress was ruined, and the tablecloth, and maybe the carpeting, too. She bent to shove napkins over the worst of the damage while Bethie ran to the kitchen for seltzer water and baking soda and paper towels. At the head of the table, Jo heard her mother pull in a slow breath and let it hiss out of her nostrils. Jo bent back down, scooping up the fruit, scrubbing at the stains, listening to her mother breathing, postponing the inevitable as long as she could, until finally she straightened up so that Sarah could see her. "I think this is as good as it's going to get right now."

Her mother said nothing.

"I can try putting vinegar on the stains . . ." Jo's voice trailed off. Sarah still did not speak.

"I'm so sorry," Jo said. "I don't know what happened!" She felt laughter, like poison gas, bubbling up in her chest—had it been just a few hours ago, at Lynnette's, where she'd thought things couldn't get worse?—and she had to bite her lip to keep it inside.

"Not to worry," said Henry Sheshevsky. He patted Jo's back. "It's a little spill, not the end of the world!"

Sarah ignored him and kept her eyes on her daughter. "You have to make a real effort to ruin Jell-O, so maybe I should be impressed that you found a way," Sarah said. Her voice was calm. "What is wrong with you?"

"I don't know," Jo said. She was telling the truth. She didn't know what was wrong with her, or why she was different, or how to make it right. "I really don't."

"Well, whatever it is, you'd better fix it. Because, you have my word, no man is going to want a wife who can't even manage Jell-O." She sighed, the weary exhalation of a woman who had burdens too heavy to carry, and who knew she'd never be able to set them down, and lifted her fork to cut a sliver of white meat from the slice of turkey she'd set on her plate. Jo picked up her own fork and knife. Bethie was still in the bathroom, trying to save Mrs. Stein's dress. The Stein boys were all eating quietly. At the far end of the table, Bubbe and Zayde had their heads together and were murmuring in Yiddish, and Barbara Simoneaux seemed too shocked to even breathe.

Across the table, Henry Sheshevsky, her father's old friend, gave Jo a sympathetic look. Jo missed her father so much in that moment, she felt such a deep, sorrowful ache that she wasn't sure that she'd be able to breathe. Gently, she set down her own silverware and looked at her mother.

"Why don't you just be honest," Jo said. "Say you hate me. That's the truth, right?"

"Hey, so who thinks the Tigers could go all the way this year?" asked Henry Sheshevsky, his voice loud and hearty. Jo kept talking.

"I can't cook. I won't do my hair. I hate wearing dresses. I'd rather hit a ball or shoot a basket than prance around a stage and sing. I'm not the daughter of your dreams, but I'm the only one in this family who even misses him." Jo knew it wasn't true, knew that Bethie, at least, missed their father, but it was as if some demon had taken possession of her tongue. She couldn't have stopped talking if she'd wanted to.

"That's a lie!" Sarah's voice was high and trembling.

Jo stood up, hands clenched. "I'll bet you wish I was the one who died. Or maybe both of us. That way, it'd just be you and your perfect little princess."

Bethie, who was just coming back to the living room, gasped. Jo saw her mother stand up, pulling her hand back. She felt time slowing down as she saw her mother's lips press together until they'd all but disappeared. As Sarah's body turned, Jo could have leaned back, or run, or even turned her face away, but she didn't. She just stood there, frozen and immobile, knowing what was coming and unable to avoid it.

The sound of her mother's palm on her cheek was like an explosion. It was the first time her mother had struck her in anger since that awful day they'd fought about Mae.

For a moment, Jo stood, unmoving, feeling the blood rush to her face. She could see the people at the table, but it was like she was looking up at them from the bottom of a lake. Their faces and voices were distorted and seemed very far away.

"You're a bitch," she finally said, and she heard Barbara Simoneaux gasp. Bubbe said something short and sharp in Yiddish.

"Here, now!" Henry Sheshevsky roared. "Here, now! That's enough!"

Sarah raised her chin. "And do you know what you are?" she asked. "You think I don't know about you?" Sarah had dropped her voice to a whisper, low and dangerous. "You think I don't know about you and your little girlfriend? You're unnatural."

Jo felt like she'd been thrown into a frozen river. Her chest was tight, her mind was whirling. What did her mother know? What had she seen? Had Lynnette's brothers told their parents, and had the Bobecks called the house and told Sarah? Or was her mother just guessing, stitching together supposition and paranoia, and coming up with the worst? Except, Jo thought, the worst was true. Something was wrong with her. She was broken, she was twisted, she was unnatural, like her mother had said. She would never be fixed or made right.

Jo turned and ran, only this time, instead of going to her bedroom, she went to the front door. The car keys were on the credenza. She grabbed them, jumped behind the wheel of the car, and backed out of the driveway, burning rubber as she stomped on the gas. She hit fifty miles per hour on her way down Evergreen Terrace, and turned onto Route 10. Route 10 would take her to I-75, which would take her to the Windsor Tunnel, down underneath Lake Erie. Her father used to drive through the tunnel with her, having her watch for the dividing line that showed when they'd passed from the United States into Canada. Jo would always hold her breath, imagining that she'd be able to tell, that something would feel different when she was in another country. Of course, nothing ever did.

She drove through the darkness, her foot heavy on the gas and her hands tight on the wheel, all the way to Ambassador Bridge Street. There, she pulled to the side of the road at the last possible instant before the traffic would have swept her through the tunnel. She sat behind the wheel, underneath a streetlamp, with her fisted hands pressed against her eyes. She could drive to Canada, all the way to the northernmost provinces, all the way to the ends of the earth, and the truth would never change. Lynnette would forget her. Her mother would never love her. Her father would still be dead.

Jo opened the car door and stepped out into the darkness. She hadn't worn her coat, and the wind off the water cut through the fabric of her dress. Cars sped by, cars with happy families inside of them, dads behind the wheel, moms with Saran-wrapped leftovers in their laps, little brothers, stuffed full of whipped cream and pie, in the back seat, next to teenage big sisters who'd close their eyes and dream about boys, the way girls were supposed to.

Jo's breath caught in her throat. She remembered her father taking her to see the Tigers play, pulling her baseball glove out from under his jacket, like he was performing a magic trick. She remembered his hand on her head, and how he'd call her Sport, and how she'd wanted to run away with him, to go somewhere safe, somewhere better.

"Dad," she whispered. No voice answered. The wind whipped at her hair and battered her face, freezing her tears, and the cars rushed past in a heedless stream, none of them stopping or even slowing down.

Jo stood until her body ached from the cold, until her face and toes and fingertips were numb. Back in the car, she pressed her cheek against the vinyl of the seat cover, hoping she'd be able to catch the ghost of her father's scent, the starch of his shirts and bay rum cologne, but all she could smell was Sarah's hairspray and perfume. She cried until her eyes burned. *I am going to leave here*, she thought. I am going to read, and I am going to write. I am going to find a girl who is brave enough to love me, and I am going to have the kind of life I want, and as God is my witness, I'll never eat Jell-O again.

The thought made her laugh a little, and then she was laughing and crying all at once, making weird, hiccupping sounds, with the pain of missing her father as fresh as if he'd died the day before. She cried until there were no tears left, until she was empty and aching, and when the tears were gone, she pulled a wad of paper napkins from the glove compartment, wiped her face, and blew her nose. Finally, because there was no place else to go, she drove back home.

It felt like an entire night had passed since the fight, but in reality, just over an hour had gone by since Sarah had slapped her. The front door was unlocked and the table still set, the candles still lit, the house still full of the smells of Thanksgiving, but all of the guests seemed to have gone home. Sarah was sitting on the living-room couch. She'd taken off her shoes but was still wearing her skirt and her blouse. "Bethie," she called, "put the pie in the oven, please, and turn the heat on under the gravy."

Jo swallowed. "Hi, Mom."

Her mother raised her head. She looked smaller, shrunken and pale, with all the anger drained away. "Are you hungry?" Sarah asked, as if Jo had just come home from school or basketball practice.

Jo didn't know what to say. In her whole life, she could count the endearments Sarah had used on one hand and have fingers left over. Sarah couldn't manage an *I love you*, couldn't find time to watch a basketball game, barely spoke Jo's name if she could help it. She thought that Jo was unnatural, and had probably felt that way for a while. But she could ask if Jo was hungry, and fill her plate with something good. It wasn't the kind of affection Jo craved, the love she'd gotten from her father, but it was something. Lots of people went through life with less.

Bethie carried a basket of rolls to the table. "Do you want whipped cream?" she asked. Jo reached for her sister's hand.

"I'm sorry," she said. Her throat felt tight, and her eyes were burning again, remembering what she'd said. Bethie gave Jo's hand a squeeze as she passed, and went back to the kitchen for the whipped cream and pies. Sarah gave Jo a plate of turkey and gravy and stuffing, and set a wedge of pumpkin pie on a dessert plate. Jo understood that she was being offered a chance, an opportunity to defend herself, to set the record straight and say, *Lynnette and I are just friends* or *I'm not unnatural*, or *Don't worry, I like boys, I just haven't met the right one yet*. But Jo didn't say those things. Instead, she sniffled, wiped her nose with her napkin, and said, "Maybe I am different. But being different isn't the worst thing." That was as close as she could come to *Mom, I like girls, and I'll never get married.* It was closer than she ever thought she'd get.

For a minute, there was silence. Then Bethie ate a bite of pie. Sarah poured a splash of wine into her glass and looked at Jo searchingly. Her expression wasn't angry, just puzzled, like Jo was an exotic animal, some ungainly, awkward creature, an ostrich or a giraffe that had folded itself through the front door and sat down at the table, and Sarah was wondering what to feed it, or how to make it disappear.

"You think I'm mean," Sarah finally said. "But all I want is for you to be happy. I want you to find a man who loves you like your father loved me. I want you to have children. To have a regular life."

"Maybe I don't want regular," said Jo.

"You don't know. It's hard being different." Sarah turned toward the window that looked out at the street. Jo wondered if her mother was thinking about her own parents. All her mother ever wanted was to fit in, to have a real American family whose members would look and sound and behave like everyone else.

"Well," said Jo. "I guess I'll find out."

"I guess you will," Sarah said, and tried to smile. In the candlelight, with her curvy figure, her clear skin and shiny hair, Bethie glowed. Sarah looked thoughtful and sad. Jo suspected that she and her mother had endured their last big blowup. They'd told each other the truth, and maybe things would be easier between them. The air smelled of vinegar, and pumpkin pie, and cinnamon and cloves, fresh rolls and Henry Sheshevsky's wine.

"Look at us," Jo said. "The Kaufman ladies."

"We'll be fine, Mom," said Bethie, and Jo nodded and took Bethie's hand, repeating what her sister had said. "We'll be fine."

PART

two

1962

Bethie

Have a good weekend, Beth," called Mrs. Miller as Bethie made her way down the hall of Bellwood High. "You, too," Bethie said. Mrs. Miller—aka Killer Miller—taught the sophomore Honors English class, which Bethie had aced.

"Bye, Bethie!" chorused three freshmen cheerleaders as they sat on the waist-high brick wall in front of the school. Bethie gave them a wave and strolled through the parking lot, hair bouncing, skirt flipping around her knees. She was going to visit her sister in Ann Arbor for the weekend. She had a plaid overnight bag packed with pajamas, her toothbrush and face cream, pedal-pushers and a blouse, and her prettiest party dress, sleeveless taffeta with a blue-and-white floral print, and a matching blue-and-white headband. The dress's bodice nipped her in where she was the slimmest; the full skirt covered up her thighs.

Jo had offered to meet her at the train station, but Bethie wanted to walk through the campus by herself.

She got off the train on an overcast Friday afternoon in October and headed uphill to join the flood of kids making their way around the Diag. The U of M was big, even as state schools went, with more than forty thousand undergrads, and it was easy to get lost in the swirl. Bethie walked, staring up at the hulking buildings, some made of red brick, others of brownstone, many covered in a latticework of ivy, some big enough to span entire blocks. When she could, she snuck glances at the students. Most of the girls dressed in the kind of clothes Bethie wore, skirts or Bermuda shorts, sweater sets and double-knit dresses and Ship 'n Shore blouses, with lipstick and hair teased and sprayed into bouffants or flips. But, here and there, Bethie saw girls in long, loose dresses that looked like something a pioneer woman crossing the prairie in a covered wagon might wear, or loose-fitting jeans and sweatshirts, without a stitch of makeup and with unstyled hair tumbling past their shoulders. A few of the Negro students, male and female, had hair that stood out like puffy crowns around their heads, and one boy wore a pin on his jacket: U.S. OUT OF VIETNAM. Bethie felt her eyes widen as she passed a boy with straight dark hair so long that it tangled with his chest-length beard, and gave a startled smile as he nodded at her and flashed two fingers, spread in a V. She looked down, blinking, confirming that he was indeed barefoot, even though the temperature was in the fifties and the slate had to be cold underneath his feet.

She saw two white boys throwing a Frisbee. She saw, beneath one tree, a Negro boy wearing glasses with tiny round, dark lenses, strumming a guitar and singing about John Henry, and beneath another, a girl with a sketchpad, occasionally stretching out her hand and studying the bend of her wrist before returning her attention to the page. Someone handed Bethie a leaflet about a meeting of Students for a Democratic Society, and someone else handed her a flyer for a luncheon hosted by the Foreign Students Alliance, and a tall, slender woman in jeans and a University of Michigan T-shirt walked toward her. The woman's dark hair was cut short and tucked behind her ears, her expression was alert and curious, and her tanned skin glowed. People watched the girl pass, her long legs making short work of the distance, drawing appreciative glances from some of the boys. She was almost right in front of her before Bethie realized that the stranger was her sister.

"Hey!" Jo gave her a hug, picked up her bag, and said, "How was the train?"

"It was fine," Bethie said, feeling childish and dowdy as she hurried after Jo, taking two steps to every one of her sister's.

"Are you hungry? I thought we'd get a bite to eat."

Jo took her to the Union, a four-story redbrick building. In the basement cafeteria, they bought a burger for Jo, a chicken-salad sandwich for Bethie, and two cups of coffee.

"What's on the agenda?" Bethie asked, automatically removing the top slice of bread from her sandwich.

"Want to sit in on my literature class?" Jo asked. "It's a survey course on British poetry." She smiled, gesturing like a game-show host. "Keats! Yeats! Byron! Auden!"

"Parties, Jo," Bethie said. "I want to go to parties."

Jo gave her a fond, indulgent smile. "Tomorrow's the game, of course. We'll want to leave early, for the tailgating." Bethie knew that thousands of students and even more alumni descended on Ann Arbor for football game-day weekends. They'd park their cars in the lot near the stadium, they'd dress up in the team's colors, maize and blue, and set up their grills and barbecues to cook brats and burgers, and they'd drink, and drink, and drink some more. Sometimes, Jo said, rolling her eyes, they'd even manage to put down their beer steins long enough to go into the stadium and watch the game.

"How about tomorrow night after the game?" Bethie asked.

"We can go hear some music. And on Sunday, I'm going to a demonstration with some friends."

Bethie nibbled a lettuce leaf, wondering why, with all the things she could be doing, Jo was wasting her time walking in circles in front of a department store with a picket sign. Was that really the best thing she could think of? Or was it an excuse, so that she could go do something else, something she didn't want Bethie to know about?

Bethie took a last bite of her sandwich and said, "I'll skip the class. If it's okay, I'll just walk around for a while." Jo gave her a hug, and a key to her dorm room, and they made plans to meet there at six o'clock that night.

After an hour's stroll around the campus, staring at the girls with limp, lank hair in sack-like dresses, or the ones in bell-bottom jeans, Bethie found her way back to Stockwell Hall. She climbed three flights of stairs, unlocked the door, and stood in the doorway of Jo's room, breathing in her sister's familiar scent. After Jo moved out, Bethie had taken over the closet they'd once shared and had transformed the bedroom as best she could. She'd convinced Sarah to buy a pink and white braided rug for the floor. New wallpaper was not in the budget, but Bethie had covered the walls in layers of posters of the school's drama productions, photographs of herself, Barbara, and Linda at the swimming pool, *Seventeen* magazine articles called "The New Eat-for-Beauty Diet," and "How Much Do You Want to Be Pretty?" along with ads for dresses she wanted to buy, or patterns she'd try to sew someday. Her bed was piled with pillows that she'd made from fabric remnants; her desk was stacked with schoolbooks and magazines. She'd draped her bedside lamp in a red rayon scarf to give the room a soft glow after she'd read about a character in a novel doing that, and she'd bought a full-length mirror to hang on the back of the door. It was undeniably a girl's room, undeniably hers. In contrast, Jo's dorm room, with its mostly blank walls and meticulously neat desk, could have belonged to anyone. It was like a prison cell, the home of a girl whose inner life was a secret and who was taking pains not to give any part of it away.

At least, at some point during the last few years Jo had learned how to make her bed. There was a dark-blue spread on the bed, a single pillow in a white case, a triangular U of M pennant and a poster of the Ronettes tacked on one wall and a Kennedy campaign poster on the other. Underneath the window, Jo had stacked plastic orange crates and set her record player on top. Jo's records were stored in one crate, her paperback novels and hardcovers from the library, *Hawaii* and *The Invisible Man* and *On the Road*, in another. A desk and chair made of the same varnished yellow wood stood against one wall, a free-standing closet rested against the other, and Jo's bathrobe and towel hung from a hook on the back of the door. Bethie surveyed her sister's belongings. She didn't see any signs of a boyfriend—no boys' clothes in the closet, no razors or shaving cream on the dresser, no records in the crate that couldn't plausibly belong to her sister. When her first search was complete, she went through everything again, looking more closely for signs of a girlfriend—a different brand of deodorant or perfume on the dresser, the smell of a different shampoo on the pillowcase. She couldn't find a thing.

You're unnatural, Sarah had said, and Jo hadn't denied it, but Bethie wasn't sure that meant that Jo was really a lesbian. Her sister and her mom had been at war for so long that Bethie could imagine Sarah flinging the accusation in a moment of rage, and Jo throwing it back in Sarah's face just to make her mother even angrier. It was also possible that Jo didn't know herself, one way or the other. But Bethie remembered how her sister looked at Lynnette, with a kind of fierce, protective tenderness that suggested more than friendship. Lynnette was married now—Bethie had seen Jo's friend at the new A&P, pushing a shopping cart, her stomach a bulging half-moon underneath her maternity blouse. Had Jo found another girl, a friend, or more-than-friend, to replace her?

Bethie slid her hand underneath Jo's mattress. There she found a book that wasn't on display in the crate, a pulpy novel with a lurid cover and the title ODD GIRL OUT. *Ah*, she thought, and read the first three chapters about a girl named Laura who was in love with an older classmate, a sorority sister named Beth. Maybe she should have been horrified, she thought, as she read the breathless prose of the sex scene. Certainly her friends would have been horrified, and maybe even afraid to be alone in a room with Jo, and Sarah would be furious and ashamed, more than she already was. Bethie examined herself for revulsion or disgust and found none . . . only sympathy. She understood that the world would make room for her in a way it might not ever accommodate her sister, and a sense of her own good fortune.

Carefully, Bethie replaced the book in its spot underneath the mattress. She lay down on her sister's bed, settling her head on her sister's pillow, gazing up at the ceiling. She felt sorry for Jo, but also sorry for herself; a little lonesome as she lay there, listening to the sounds of the dorm, feet on the stairs and in the halls, laughter and bits of music whenever another door opened. She and her sister were growing up. Jo had always been Bethie's anchor and protector, and now they were moving in different directions, away from each other. It was as if Jo had bought a ticket for a trip Bethie couldn't take; like she was already on her way to a country where Bethie would never become a citizen, where she would always speak the language with an accent. Bethie would possibly be able to visit, but she'd always have to leave, to go back to her own place, to stand at the border and wave and mouth *I love you* across the divide.

Bethie was waiting in the dormitory's lobby, surrounded by students sitting at tables studying, or talking, or playing cards, when she heard a familiar deep voice calling her name.

"Bethie? Is that Bethie Kaufman?"

She turned. "Why, Harold!" Harold Jefferson had changed since high school. His hair, previously a neatly cropped cap of tight curls, had grown into a thick mane that stood up and out a few inches from his head. Instead of a football jersey or a varsity jacket or an Arrow button-down, he wore a cream-colored shirt that fell past his hips and had gold embroidery around the notched collar, and a pair of bell-bottom jeans (both the shirt and the jeans, Bethie noticed, were meticulously clean and perfectly pressed). His long, narrow feet were bare.

Bethie could see their high arches and his long toes, and how they were paler underneath than on top.

"You up here for an interview?" Harold asked.

"I'm visiting Jo," Bethie said. From behind him, Bethie heard the girls at the table laughing, and one voice rising over the giggles, calling, "Harold, we're lonely! Come back!" Peeking over his shoulder, she saw glimpses of the girls at the table: a glint of long red hair, a lit cigarette in a dark-skinned hand with oval nails painted red. Someone had set up speakers, from which Bob Dylan's plangent, droning voice declaimed, *I'm out here a thousand miles from my home / Walkin' a road other men have gone down.*

Bethie shook her head, thinking about how, back in Detroit, the kids were still mostly listening to Frank Sinatra, or Elvis singing "Crying in the Chapel." She wanted to join those girls, to sit cross-legged on the floor, and smoke cigarettes, or whatever else they'd inhaled that made everything so funny. "Har-old," called one of the girls in a teasing singsong.

"Hey," he said, ignoring the girls' protests, keeping his eyes on Bethie. "You want to go for a walk?"

"So, do you play football?" Bethie asked ten minutes later as she strolled through the Diag with Harold beside her, trying not to stare at everything she saw.

Harold smiled, shaking his head. "I might've been a big shot in high school, but here? I'm barely good enough to be the water boy."

"So then . . ." Bethie gave him an innocent look from underneath her lashes. "Drama club?"

"No, no, no," Harold said, shaking his head. "Once was enough for me."

"But you were so good," Bethie said. It was true.

Harold had brought down the house in *South Pacific*. Even his football buddies, and the sisters he'd said had only come to laugh, had been on their feet by the end.

They walked along the sidewalk, through the throngs of other kids, all of them cheerful, nobody looking lonely or out of place. It made Bethie feel optimistic. Here was a place to start over, a place where nobody—or at least only the kids from high school—would remember how Bethie had packed on fifteen pounds one summer, or would instantly know her as a girl whose father had died. Here, she could begin again.

"You never even asked me why I was in trouble with Coach," Harold said as they turned onto Division Street. "Never once." His voice was teasing, and every once in a while he'd come so close that Bethie could almost feel his hip bump against hers, or she would catch a whiff of his cologne. She was so happy she barely noticed feeling hungry, and these days her hunger was a constant presence, like a pet that followed her everywhere. Bethie weighed herself every morning, and if the scale crept up by more than a pound, she'd have nothing but lemon water for breakfast and lunch that day.

"That's not true. I asked you all the time!"

"Is that right?" Harold looked like he was trying hard to remember. Bethie balled up her fist and punched his bicep. Harold rolled his eyes.

"Maybe you just forgot because you were so preoccupied with Vernita," Bethie said.

"Ah, Vernita," Harold said, his expression turning comically dreamy.

"Why were you in trouble?" Bethie asked.

"You know how seniors are in charge of putting messages up on the marquee?"

Bethie nodded. There was a large rectangular marquee on the lawn in front of the high school, usually displaying banalities like CONGRATULATIONS GRADUATES or BACK-TO-SCHOOL HEALTH FORMS DUE SEPTEMBER 9 or ENJOY SPRING BREAK.

"Well," Harold said. "The situation was, on Monday the school would put up whatever message the administration wanted, but on Friday, the seniors got to pick. Doug Fitzgibbons—you remember Doug?—he was in charge of putting up the messages. But Doug was what you'd call undermotivated."

"Lazy," Bethie supplied.

"Indeed. So he left your faithful friend Harold Jefferson in charge. Gave me the keys to the supply closet, told me what the marquee should say. You know, 'Go Spartans,' or 'Congratulations, Homecoming Court.' That kind of stuff. So I'd do it. Except I started stealing the *E*s."

"You did what?"

Harold looked both slightly ashamed and pleased with himself. "The letter *E*s. I just started taking them. The first one was an accident. I'd taken out too many *E*s, and I just put the leftover one in my pocket and didn't even realize it until I got home. The next week, I took one on purpose."

"Because your accidental *E* was lonely?"

Harold nodded, and said, "There's nothing sadder than a lonely vowel. So then I had the two, and I guess it started to feel like a challenge. And I wanted to see what would happen, of course."

"Was your plan to eventually just use them? Have the sign just say 'EEEEEEE'? Like it was screaming?" Bethie asked. "Or were you going to branch out to the *A*s and the *I*s?"

Smiling, Harold shook his head. "I never got that

far. I just kept stealing *E*s. So eventually, Coach Krantz had to put up something about a Future Farmers meeting, and you need *E*s in 'Future' and 'Farmers.' Week after that, there was a Debate Club meet, and you can't spell 'Debate' without *E*s. So he just wrote 'Farmrs' and 'Dbat,'" Harold said, spelling them out. "And I guess someone in the administration noticed, and told Coach that it was a bad look for a school to have a big misspelled sign right up front."

"I see their point," Bethie murmured.

"Coach called Dougie and the rest of the class officers down to the gym, and he just lost his mind and started screaming, 'WHO IS TAKING THE GODDAMN *E*S?' And I guess I was overheard in the caf that afternoon, repeating the phrase and, ah, displaying my loot to some of my brothers in arms. Next thing you know, ol' Harold's dressed up as a Seabee, prancing around onstage." He shook his head in mock sorrow.

"You were good," said Bethie, her voice soft and sincere. She felt herself blushing and wished that Harold would reach for her hand. Too soon, they were back in front of Jo's dorm.

"You got any plans tonight?"

Bethie shook her head. "Jo wants to take me to hear some music, but nothing's official."

"Want to come to a party?" he said, and Bethie, grinning, said, "I thought you'd never ask."

Dinner in the dorm cafeteria was some kind of sliced meat under a blanket of thick gravy, mashed potatoes, steamed green beans, and surprisingly tasty carrot cake, served in the noisy, echoing, high-ceilinged dining hall. After they'd eaten, Jo took Bethie to a church a few blocks off campus. HOOTENANNY TONIGHT, read a hand-drawn sign, with an arrow pointing toward the basement door. Jo put some money in a coffee can with a hole cut into the lid and found them two metal folding chairs a few rows back from the stage. A single spotlight on spindly metal legs cast a circle of illumination on the microphone. Behind it, two boys sat on metal chairs, tuning their guitars.

Bethie stifled a sigh and tried to get comfortable. She had worn her best blue-and-white dress and had dabbed a little perfume behind her ears, thinking about meeting Harold later that night, half paying attention to the music, hearing the crowd laugh and clap when the boys sang the line about not working for Maggie's pa no more, because "he puts his cigar / out in your face just for kicks / His bedroom window / It is made out of bricks / The National Guard stands around his door." When they were done, a girl with creamy skin and long, wavy blond hair in a turquoise minidress, high-heeled white boots, and a strand of beads around her neck took the stage. Eschewing the guitars, she clasped her hands at her waist, closed her eyes, and sang, a capella, "Masters of War."

The evening ended after that performance. Students, Jo included, clustered around the stage. Bethie waited for a gap in the conversation before saying, "I ran into Harold Jefferson this afternoon. Remember him?"

"Sure. I know Harold. He's in SDS with me."

Bethie knew she was supposed to care what SDS might be. She decided that she didn't. "He said there's a party tonight." Jo's eyes were on the girl in the turquoise-blue dress, who was heading toward the door. Bethie saw her chance and grabbed it. "If it's okay, you can go with your friends, and I can go check out the party with Harold. I won't stay long, and I've got your key, so I can let myself in."

Jo was frowning. "Are you sure?"

"I'll be in college myself next year," Bethie pointed out. "I'm going to go to all kinds of places on my own. And Harold's a good guy."

"Don't stay out too late," said Jo. "Don't drink too much."

"Got it, Mom." Bethie rolled her eyes, but Jo had already turned around, swept up in the crowd of beards and beads and bell-bottoms, all of them talking about Sunday's "action." Bethie followed them onto the street, where Jo's crowd turned east, toward College Avenue, and Bethie headed west, toward the address Harold had given her.

Since she'd started high school, Bethie had been to sock hops and school dances, record parties at the VFW Hall or the Masonic Lodge, and house parties in pine-paneled basement rec rooms in Bellwood's nicer neighborhoods, where kids dumped pints of pilfered booze into the punch bowl on the sly and parents stepped away from *The Huntley-Brinkley Report* long enough to stick their heads down the stairs and holler at the kids to keep it down. She knew, as soon as she found the address Harold had given her, that this would be a different kind of affair.

The house, a two-story brick structure, was fronted by a sagging wooden porch. Three steps and a splintery railing led to the front door, which stood wide open. In-side, most of the lights were off, and all of the furniture had been shoved against the walls. The room was packed with people and full of smoke and a thick, skunky-sweet smell that Bethie figured had to be marijuana. Boys and girls were dancing, except instead of doing the Shag or the Twist or the Hully Gully or any of the dances Bethie knew, they were just pressed up against one another, swaying in the darkness.

In her blue-and-white flower-print party dress, with her hairband and a pair of white pumps, Bethie felt ridiculous. All of the girls wore jeans, or long dresses, or colorful, embroidered skirts, and all of them seemed completely at ease in these costumey clothes. Quickly, Bethie pulled off her hairband and ran her fingers through the curls she'd taken such pains to style, thinking that she couldn't do a thing about her clothes, but she could at least make her hairdo less conspicuous.

"Hello, Alice."

Bethie spun around to see a boy smiling at her, and she felt her heart leap into her throat. The boy—not a boy, a man, she thought—had dark eyes, a mustache, and a sharply trimmed beard that came to a point on his chin. His long, dark hair fell to his shoulders, and his white skin had golden undertones, as if he'd spent months in the sun. Her first thought was that he looked like Jesus, but there was nothing remotely holy about the gleam in his eye. *He looks like a pirate*, she decided, imagining him with a hoop through one ear, a scar or two on one high cheekbone, and a parrot perched on his shoulder.

"My name's not Alice."

He gave a lazy shrug. "And here I was, all ready to welcome you to Wonderland."

Bethie made a show of looking around. "Is that what you call this place?"

He smiled. His teeth, she saw, were very straight. "Rose-colored glasses, child. Let me fit you with a pair of rose-colored glasses. I can make the world beautiful."

"With glasses," Bethie repeated.

"Of the chemical variety," he explained.

"Do you live here?"

"That I do," he said, and tipped her a wink.

"Do you go to school?" He seemed too old to be an undergrad, and far too disreputable to be studying medicine or law.

"I am a student," the man said, as if that answered her question.

"Dev, leave her alone." Finally, Harold Jefferson appeared, wearing the same shirt he'd had on in the dorm. His crown of hair bounced and waved with each step. "Ixnay on the ailbait-jay."

"I am not jailbait," Bethie said, her voice high and childishly indignant, belying her words.

"Okay," the man said indulgently, smiling, as if Bethie had told him a joke instead of her age. He reached down and set his hand on Bethie's girdled hip, drawing her close, as if he had a right to her body, as if he'd known her forever.

"Is this a friend of yours?" Bethie asked Harold, who nodded.

"This is Devon Brady. Devon, Bethie Kaufman, a friend from back home."

"Alice," said Devon, with a grin that was almost a smirk. "I've named her Alice."

"I already have a name," Bethie said. Part of her was indignant, and part of her recognized her indignation as a pose, like she was playing the part of the good girl, pretending to be Alice, before Alice slipped down the rabbit hole. Except Alice had taken her tumble unwillingly. Bethie, on the other hand, was excited to go. She wanted to be different, now that she was almost a college girl. She wanted to see what the world looked like upside-down.

"So have another." Dev's expression was paternal. Bethie didn't want that. She didn't want him feeling fatherly; she wanted him feeling desire. "Names are important. We ought to be able to choose our own. Once we've decided who we are." Bethie watched, feeling almost hypnotized, as he reached into his pocket and pulled out a spotless white envelope, folded in half. With great ceremony, he unfolded it and shook something out into his hand. Bethie saw what looked like a square of pale-brown cellophane, a quarter of the size of a normal stamp.

"Dev." Harold's voice held a note of warning. Ignoring him, Dev leaned in close, with the cellophane square pinched between his fingers. He had a woodsy scent, unfamiliar but pleasant, a little like a cookout in the forest, with undertones of fire and moss.

"Our friend Harold here is a P.K. Know what that is? A preacher's kid." Bethie nodded. At rehearsals, back at Bellwood High, Harold would do imitations of his father, Reverend Luther. "In or out?" Harold would holler, pretending to be his father, yelling at the kids. "Am I paying to air-condition the whole doggone street?" Harold would demand, with his shoulders back and his chest out, assuming what Bethie imagined was the reverend's posture. "You shut that door before I slap you into next week, have you looking both ways for Sunday."

"As such," Devon continued, "Harold is naturally more cautious about certain mind-expanding substances."

"They use wine in church, right?" Bethie felt like she was being hypnotized. At her side, Harold made a disgusted noise.

"Holy Communion." Dev reached one finger toward her face. Bethie thought that maybe he was going to tap the end of her nose, like she was a little kid, but instead he touched his finger to her lips.

"Open up," the pirate said. "I'm going to show you all the wonders of the world."

I shouldn't do this, Bethie thought. But that was the voice of her mother, the voice of Vice Principal Douglass, the voice of scared-little-girl conformity. Bethie might have to be young and female, but she didn't have to be scared, and she didn't have to conform. She could be like her sister, on her way to some exotic destination. This small brown square could be her ticket.

Bethie opened her mouth. "Bless you, my child," Dev said, and laid the square of whatever-it-was on her tongue. "Hold it there. Let it dissolve." He smiled, before reaching out with his long-fingered hands, cupping her head in a gesture that felt almost like a blessing. "Welcome to Wonderland," he said.

Bethie let Dev lead her to the plaid couch pockmarked with cigarette burns, which had been shoved against the wall. On one side of the couch was a boy and a girl, their pale arms and legs entwined. On her other side was a curly-haired, golden-skinned boy who lay on the couch, looking like a prince who had fallen in battle, with his head thrown back and his mouth wide open. Bethie sat between them and held the square on her tongue, listening to a song about purple people eaters. The smoke got thicker, and the music got faster, and the dancing became more urgent to the Beach Boys, the Chiffons, Lesley Gore and Brenda Lee. Bethie watched male hands cup and caress the curves of female bottoms, female hands gripping men's waists and shoulders. In the dim light, through the haze of smoke, all of the girls were beautiful, all of the boys were handsome, and Bethie felt her skin dissolving, her body floating away, somewhere up near the ceiling, a high perch from which she could look down at herself and the party. She peered through the smoke, looking for Harold, but couldn't see him. At one point, the sleeping prince shook himself awake and stumbled off, and one of the dancers flung herself down in the space the boy had left empty. The girl had a wild, loose tangle of light-brown hair and pale white skin that glistened with sweat. She was barefoot, not thin, her hips wide above fleshy thighs, but she hadn't seemed to be worried about her problem areas, as she spun in ecstatic circles, arms spread wide. Bethie had watched her in admiration, wondering how it felt to take up room like that, to force other people out of your way, to claim so much space for your own. Bethie's father was dead, her mother's life was small and predictable, her sister was moving on, heading toward a world Bethie couldn't inhabit, and sometimes—a lot of the time—it felt like her skin no longer fit her, and her body was only a collection of flaws to be fixed or at least disguised, an endless source of despair. But now, it was as if her spirit was rising, leaving her body, and her pain, and her silly party dress behind. She felt like she was pure joy, excitement and anticipation and desire. She wanted to move on, too. She wanted to be born again, in this new place. She wanted to dance.

"Hey, little sister," the dancing girl said. Bethie turned to answer her and felt her mouth fall open. The walls were expanding and contracting, but gently, like lungs, breathing in time to the music, which pulsed through the room like a wave.

"The walls," Bethie tried to say. She lifted her arms, intending to point, but her limbs felt like they'd turned into some kind of very soft, heavy metal. She could imagine them bending and drooping, like petals full of rain. "The walls are breathing."

"Cool," said the other girl, not unkindly. She reached behind the couch and, like a magician pulling a rabbit from an empty top hat, produced a blanket, the kind of knitted afghan that Bethie's *bubbe* had once made. Gently, the girl spread it over Bethie's curled-up legs.

"You're tripping. Just stay calm," said the girl. "Enjoy the ride."

In the months that followed, Bethie would learn that Devon's woodsy smell came from the patchouli incense that he burned in his bedroom, and that Harold's style of shirt was called a dashiki, and that the cellophane-looking square that Dev laid on her tongue was blotter acid, high-quality stuff that Devon, who once upon a time had studied chemistry, made in the U of M's own labs. She would learn the lyrics to all of Bob Dylan's songs, and "Like a Rolling Stone" would become her friends' anthem when she arrived on campus nine months later. She would learn, too, that it was fortunate that no guy tried to touch her as she lay sprawled on the couch, watching the walls billow and retreat. Other nights, she wouldn't be as lucky. But that night, Bethie stared at a poster of the beach that was thumbtacked to the wall, imagining that she could taste colors: the sharp acidity of yellow, the soothing cool of blue. The green was tangy and astringent, like an unripe banana, and the yellow was a rich ribbon of butterscotch. She tried to explain it to Harold when he appeared beside her on the couch. Harold listened, then repeated what the dancing girl had said: "You're tripping." Harold looked considerably less amused than the girl had been. "Let's get you home."

Tripping, Bethie thought. She had never been on trips, except in the summertime, to a cabin on the shores of Lake Erie, when her father had been alive. She remembered sunshine in her hair as a canoe went gliding through the water; the feeling of piercing a worm's body with a fishhook, how it would squirm and then be still. "Was it weird to be a preacher's kid?" It was hard to get the words out correctly. Her tongue felt as heavy and droopy as her arms had.

"It was different," Harold said. "People look at you differently. They hold you to a higher standard, I'd say. Oh, and there's no getting out of church. Ever." He had his arm around her waist. Leaning against him felt like leaning against a very warm wall.

"You're strong," Bethie told him. Before Harold could respond to that, she asked, "What's it like, knowing your Messiah's shown up already?"

"What's that, now?"

"Jesus," Bethie explained. "Like, your Messiah's already come, and now you're waiting for him to come back, right? Is that weird? Does it feel like there was a great movie and you missed it?"

"Ah, not exactly," Harold said.

Bethie said, "See, if you're Jewish, you wait. Because the Messiah hasn't come yet. Could be anyone." She made a show of looking around at the kids walking around campus. "Could be . . ." She paused, then pointed at the least-likely person she saw, a shrimpy pale-faced red-haired boy with a sunken chest and a rabbitty overbite. "Him!"

Harold chuckled.

"Could be me!" Bethie said. She stopped in front of a wooden bench, climbed on top, and said, "I could be the Messiah!" A few kids clapped, a few more stared.

"Come on," Harold said, and put his hands on her waist, lifting her down the way he had in the show. "Keep moving."

The night air was cool, and it felt good against her flushed cheeks. Bethie wanted to ask him about being a

Negro, if he felt different all the time, or if it was more like being Jewish, where you could go for long stretches mostly fitting in, feeling the same as everyone else, until something—a store clerk wishing you "Merry Christmas," or a casual exclamation of "Jesus Christ," or someone saying, "I jewed him down" when he'd gotten a good price on a used car—would remind you that you were different. She wanted to ask if he was the kind of Christian who thought that Jews were all going to hell, or if he believed in hell, or God at all, but before she could decide how to ask it, Harold had walked her through the door of Stockwell Hall, up the stairs, down the corridor, past a half-dozen open dorm-room doors from which a half-dozen different kinds of music could be heard, and into Jo's cell-like chamber. Bethie lay back on Jo's bed, feeling Harold fumble with the straps of her shoes. He spread a blanket over her and turned off the light, and Bethie shut her eyes, thinking that there was more to the world than she'd ever imagined. She pictured the dancing girl, arms spread wide, hair flaring out as she spun and spun, at ease with her own size, her own power, forcing people to make room for her, and how she still felt like she'd somehow left her body, like she was pure feeling now. *I want to be brave like that*, thought Bethie, as sleep washed over her and carried her away.

Jo

Even at a school as big as the University of Michigan, it was statistically probable that most students' paths would cross at least a few times before graduation. The same face would appear in lecture halls, on the Diag, at the Student Union, or in the stadium for the football games. So it was that Jo Kaufman had seen Shelley Finkelbein three times, and knew exactly who she was, before they ever spoke.

The first time was in Introduction to Philosophy, her freshman year. Jo had taken a seat in the middle of the hall, and Professor Glass had started his lecture when the door banged open and a slender, dark-haired girl with luminously pale skin and light eyes fringed with thick, dark lashes came hurrying down the aisle, leaving the fresh scent of something floral trailing in her wake. "Sorry, sorry, sorry," she murmured, taking a seat, easing an expensive-looking trench coat off her shoulders and tossing it negligently on the chair beside her. Her hair was stylishly arranged, teased up high around her head, hanging long and loose in the back. Professor Glass raised his bushy eyebrows. "And you are?" he inquired. A few kids laughed.

"Shelley Finkelbein," said Shelley. Her voice was low, but confident, and if the professor had expected her to squirm or apologize, he was disappointed. After a brief pause he launched back into his discussion of the Ancients. Shelley's dark head bent over her notebook as she wrote. Jo made herself look away, keeping her attention on her own notes. Two days later, when the class met again, Shelley was a no-show, and when she didn't reappear the following week, or the week after that, Jo figured she must have dropped the course.

The second time she saw Shelley, Shelley was on-stage, standing atop a plywood tower, playing Juliet in a production of *Romeo and Juliet* put on by MUSKET, the campus theater troupe (MUSKET, Jo had learned, stood for "Michigan Union Shows, Ko-Eds Too," which was what the formerly all-male theater troupe had renamed itself in 1956). Shelley was almost unrecognizable at first in a long blond wig, until Jo recalled the curve of her cheek and the contrast between her pale skin and dark brows. "Deny thy father and refuse thy name, and I'll no longer be a Capulet," she said, in the low, thrillingly assured voice with which she'd addressed the philosophy professor. Jo wasn't sure if Shelley was a good actress, or if it was her own predilections that made it impossible for her to take her eyes off the other girl.

"She's rich," said Rachel, an SDS friend with whom Jo had gone to see the play. When Jo described Shelley's single visit to philosophy class, Rachel nodded and said, "Sounds like Shelley. I've heard she's changed majors four times." Rachel knew more stories: how Shelley had shown up in Ann Arbor with a red Karmann Ghia, with a monogrammed gold plate by the driver's-side door, and how she'd ruined the engine because she hadn't known enough to change the oil. Jo, who'd grown up watching her father care for his cars, had winced, and Rachel had nodded. "I hear her folks just bought her a new one." Jo learned that Shelley was the only female participant in Sigma Alpha Mu's weekly poker game and that she won, more often than not, and that Shelley had dated the fraternity's president and dumped him for the local television weatherman, a man of thirty-two.

"Is she still with him?" Jo asked, disappointed but unsurprised.

"I've heard things," Rachel said, but wouldn't say what.

The third time Jo saw Shelley Finkelbein had been in a picture on the front page of the *Michigan Daily*. "Dean of Women Confronted Over Policies," read the typically bland headline, but there was nothing typical or bland about the photograph. The dean, with her cat's-eye glasses and Mamie Eisenhower bangs, had been sitting behind a table, her expression grim. In front of her, arm extended, finger pointing and mouth opened, stood Shelley Finkelbein. "Miss Finkelbein, a junior, lives off-campus in a league house," the name for non-dorm residences where women could live. "When her landlady refused to allow Miss Finkelbein's date, a Negro, up to her room, Miss Finkelbein took her case to the dean." The dean had told Shelley that landlords were permitted to make their own rules. Shelley had argued that they should be forced to abide by the same regulations as the dorms. Jo had read the article all the way to the end, before going back to stare at the black-and-white picture. Even with her face contorted, like she'd been photographed mid-yell, Shelley Finkelbein was lovely.

Lovely and politically aware. She wouldn't be like Lynnette, another pretty, dim, head-in-the-sand girl who didn't care about the world around her.

On a Friday afternoon in late November, Jo was in her World Anthropology lecture, half paying attention to the lesson, half thinking about her plans for the weekend. Professor Fleiss was standing at the front of the class, asking, "What are the three principles of natural selection?" when a boy ran into the lecture hall, shouting, "The president's been shot!"

The students looked at each other. Jo assumed that the boy was talking about Harlan Hatcher, the president of the U of M, but the boy, whose name Jo never learned, was quick to clear that up. "Kennedy!" he said. "He was in Dallas, in a motorcade. A sniper shot him. He's dead."

No, thought Jo. *It can't be.* The previous June, back home for the weekend, she had watched when Kennedy had given his civil rights address, sitting next to her sister on the plastic-covered couch as the president, in his broad Bostonian accent, proclaimed, "we preach freedom around the world, and we mean it . . . but are we to say to the world, and much more importantly, to each other, that this is the land of the free except for the Negroes?"

"Seems to me that the Negroes are doing just fine," Sarah observed from the kitchen, where she was ironing sheets.

"The Negroes are not doing fine," Jo said, and her sister had muttered, "Oh, boy, here we go."

"All I'm saying is that nobody made any special laws to help the Jews," said Sarah.

"I think that things were a little easier for the Jews. Insofar as nobody brought us to this country as property," said Jo.

"Maybe we weren't slaves, but I certainly don't remember anyone throwing us welcome parties. Remember the M.S. *St. Louis?*"

Jo nodded. It felt like every week of Hebrew school they'd gotten lessons on the Holocaust, including the story of the ship of nine hundred Jewish refugees that had been turned away from the United States in 1939 because the government believed the passengers were spies.

"I've told you what it was like for me as a girl. Kids calling me names. Throwing things at me. And nobody made any laws to make it easier for Jews to find jobs or houses," Sarah said, pointing her spray bottle of starch at Jo for emphasis.

"Right," said Jo. "You know what it's like to feel discrimination. So why would you want anyone else to suffer?"

"I don't want anyone to suffer. I want everyone to have the same chances."

"That's all these laws will do. Give Negroes the same chances."

"No," Sarah said, setting her iron down with a thump. "It's giving them more." She raised her chin. "Negroes could work hard and have all of that, too. If they wanted."

"That's like saying you could win a marathon if you had to start five miles behind everyone else. And then told if you didn't win, you just weren't trying hard enough. Don't you see the way everything's set up to keep Negroes from getting ahead?"

Sarah sent the final sheet billowing into the air and began to fold it in precise squares. "I see that the Steins sold their house to the Johnsons. And now our house is worth ten thousand dollars less than what it used to be. That's what I see." With that, Sarah had gone to her bedroom, closing the door behind her.

"Dead?" Jo said. At the desk beside hers, a girl named Norma Tester was crying, and Professor Fleiss's normally robust bass voice was almost too quiet to hear when he said, "Class is dismissed."

Jo went out to the Diag, which was funereally silent, cutting through the crowds of weeping classmates, looking for a television. Kids were clustered six deep around the sets in the Union, so thickly that it was impossible to see. "It is true?" Jo asked, and the curly-haired boy in front of her nodded grimly, saying, "Cronkite just confirmed it."

"His poor wife," said someone, and someone else chimed in, "She just lost that baby, you know."

"It doesn't seem real," Jo said, half to herself. She felt a creeping numbness, the constriction in her chest that she remembered from her worst fights with her mother. All around her, girls were sobbing, boys were shaking their hands and saying, "I can't believe it," all of them looking at one another, asking, "What happens now?" Jo felt a wave of longing, the loneliness that she'd trained herself to ignore. *I don't want to be alone*, she thought. She wondered if Lynnie had heard the news. That was when the girl in front of her turned around. She'd looked up at Jo and said, in a low, familiar voice, "Will you walk with me? I need to walk. I think if I don't start moving, I'm going to explode."

Jo nodded. She felt exactly the same way. Together, the two of them turned and made their way back outside.

"I'm Shelley Finkelbein," said the girl, and Jo, who hadn't recognized her yet, said, "Oh."

"Have we met?" Shelley asked, glancing up at Jo.

Jo shook her head. "You were in my Intro to Philosophy class for about a minute."

Shelley waved her hand, dismissing philosophy.

"And I saw you in *Romeo and Juliet*."

"Oh," said Shelley, her cheeks turning pink. "Well. At least it wasn't *Carousel*. A disaster for the ages."

"Is that the one where everyone was naked?" Jo asked, remembering what she'd heard about that performance, which ran for three nights in a church basement and had been the talk of the campus.

"Lightly clad," said Shelley, with a slight smile. "It was not a dramatic triumph." She fell into step next to Jo, the top of her glossy head barely reaching Jo's shoulder. Jo wanted to stare but contented herself with a peek.

Shelley Finkelbein was of average height, but delicately built, with light eyes and dark brows and small, uptilted breasts the size and shape of teacups underneath a soft sweater, its color somewhere between lavender and gray. She wore a pair of fitted pedal-pushers that zipped on the side and clung to the swell of her hips, and were cropped to display her dainty ankles, and a pair of pristine white sneakers. Up close, Jo could see that her brows rose in peaks at their center, giving her a quizzical look, and that her eyes were a pale, luminous gray. She had a narrow nose, slightly upturned at the tip, and lush pink lips, the lower one much fuller than the upper one, and skin that looked dewy. Even with her lipstick chewed away and her stunned, sorrowful expression, she was lovely.

"Hey, can you slow down a little?" Shelley asked. Jo stopped, looked down, and saw that, in spite of everything, Shelley was smiling. "Not all of us have legs a mile long."

"Sorry," said Jo. Even in her distress she felt her face flushing at the thought of Shelley noticing her legs. She slowed down. Shelley pulled a pack of Parliaments and a heavy gold St. Dupont lighter from her brown leather purse. She shook one cigarette free, tapped it on the pack, lit it, raised it to her lips, tilted her head back, and blew a pair of perfect smoke rings, one inside of the other, into the cloudy sky. "What do you think we're supposed to do now?"

"I don't know," Jo said. "Something. We have to do something."

"You go to those demonstrations, right? SNCC, SDS?" Shelley pronounced the acronym for the Student Nonviolent Coordinating Committee as *Snick*, the way students in the know did. Jo nodded. Just like in high school, she'd protested most Saturdays, carrying an EQUALITY NOW sign outside of Woolworth in Ann Arbor, marching in a circle with maybe fifty other kids.

"Take me with you?" Shelley looked up at Jo. Her eyes had sooty rings of mascara underneath them, and Jo found herself, in spite of everything, noticing how sweet she smelled, and that Shelley's cheeks were faintly freckled.

"Sure," Jo said. "Sure."

"Attention!" Doug Brodesseur had a high, nasal voice, pale skin pitted with acne scars and curly black hair, and was all of five feet, three inches tall. Doug was hosting the first meeting of the executive committee of the University of Michigan's chapter of the Student Nonviolent Coordinating Committee that had been convened since Kennedy's assassination. Instead of the usual dozen students, almost a hundred kids had crowded into the living room of his off-campus apartment to listen.

Shelley had called Jo on the dormitory's phone that morning, and had met her out on the Diag, in front of the Undergraduate Library, affectionately called the UGLI, dressed in a burnt-orange corduroy skirt and a white wool turtleneck sweater. A brown leather belt cinched her waist, and her knee-high brown suede boots matched the shade of her belt exactly. In her right hand was a cigarette; on her face was her typically amused look. "Howdy, Stretch," she'd said, as Jo approached, and Jo had smiled.

"My dad used to call me 'Sport.'" Up close, Shelley's breath smelled like mint and tobacco. Jo wished she'd gotten dressed up, that she'd chosen something more flattering than jeans and a loose white shirt with blue stripes. Jo and Shelley had walked together to the house that Doug shared with three other guys, an off-campus residence that was easily the filthiest place Jo had ever visited. Dirty footprints and clumps of cat hair dotted the carpet, which had probably been cream-colored at one point and was currently the gray of sidewalks after the rain. Dozens of empty beer cans and pop bottles, some half-full, with cigarette butts floating in the liquid, stood on or near the coffee table. A stack of pizza boxes and newspapers teetered in one corner. A fly buzzed around the box at the top of the pile, and one of the walls looked like someone had punched a hole through it and patched up the damage with . . . Jo squinted to confirm that it was, indeed, crumpled-up pages of the *Daily* and duct tape.

Most of the meeting's attendees were white boys. Jo recognized some of them from previous pickets or actions or meetings. Some of them were sitting on the cream-and-orange plaid couch. Others sat on folding chairs that had been set up around the edge of the room, with their feet planted on the floor and legs spread wide. Jo and Shelley found places toward the back of the living room, by the door. "In case we need to make a quick getaway," Jo said. She watched Shelley smile and lean against the wall, and pull away as soon as her shoulder touched the knotty pine paneling. Jo knew, from experience, that the walls were sticky; that everything in the house seemed to have been lightly coated in spilled pop.

"Okay!" called Doug. "Now, more than ever, it's important for us to stay the course and not back down. We need to show the rest of the country, the rest of the world, that they can kill our president . . ." He gulped, and his voice, which had been trembling, got steadier. ". . . but they can't shake our commitment to civil rights, or slow the wheel of progress. No matter what." This prompted murmurs of assent, nods, and a smattering of applause. "We're going to talk about the action we've got planned for this coming Saturday at Woolworth.

"Now, last week we only had about seventy-five people show up." His voice became louder and more aggrieved. "There are twenty-four thousand people on this campus. What does it say that only seventy-five of them can be bothered to stand up for racial equality?"

"That you aren't very good at your job?" Jo heard someone mutter.

"I want every person in this room who's planning to be there Saturday to commit to bringing at least two new people with them!" said Doug. "And I need someone to volunteer to type up the flyers!" His eyes, small and close-set underneath his high forehead, moved over the room, finally arriving at a woman in a corduroy jumper, who sat perched on the couch in a manner suggesting she was trying to keep as much of her body away from the fabric as possible. "Marian, how about you?"

Marian nodded.

"Moving on," said Doug. "We need to talk about the bigger picture. Summer's going to be here before you know it. The Freedom Rider Coordinating Committee is asking for new riders," he continued. "The rides begin in Washington, D.C., and end in New Orleans."

"Or jail," someone muttered.

"Many universities have had students participate," Doug continued. "It would be great if the U of M could have a representative on one of the buses."

A dark-haired white fellow with heavy stubble and dark-rimmed glasses raised his hand to ask if arrests showed up on your academic records. "Is going to jail going to keep me out of medical school?" he asked. The crowd offered competing, contradictory answers about how an arrest for civil rights activism might affect one's future.

Jo stood close enough to feel the warmth of Shelley's body, listening as the boys discussed the putative consequences of riding a bus and registering voters while their less fortunate, poor, and Negro counterparts were being beaten by cops or set upon by dogs or shipped off to die in Vietnam. She and Shelley and the other girls who had come stood quietly until, finally, Doug deigned to acknowledge them with a smile that displayed his overbite.

"Hey, you know what? If a few of you gals want to get dinner started, there's spaghetti and sauce in the kitchen."

"So that's the movement."

"I can't believe that," Shelley said, with a disgusted

roll of her eyes. She and Jo had left the meeting and were walking through campus in the twilight, moving fast, with the empty paths providing fresh air and space to complain. "I can't believe he expected us to make copies and make them dinner!" A few steps more, and Shelley said, "I can't believe we did!"

Jo made a noncommittal noise. She'd washed her hands, but she could still smell jarred tomatoes and oregano underneath her nails.

"Are you planning on being a politician?" Shelley asked.

"Who, me?"

"Yes, you," Shelley said, and playfully bumped Jo's hip with her own. Jo felt herself smiling. "You're all commanding and committed."

"That's the only time I've ever spoken up in a meeting. I care about the world, but I don't want to go into politics."

"So what, then?" asked Shelley. "I can tell you're a gal with a plan. What's your major?"

"English," said Jo. Her face, her whole body, was flushing with pleasure at being the subject of Shelley's regard. She couldn't remember the last time someone had complimented her, or been interested in her future. "I'm going to get a teaching degree, so I'll be able to support myself. But what I really want is to be a writer."

"Books?" Shelley asked, as if Jo had expressed a perfectly reasonable wish, like wanting a burger for lunch. "Or journalism? Do you want to write for newspapers or magazines?"

"I want to write books," said Jo, and wondered how long it had been since she'd given voice to that dream. She'd told Lynnette, but had Lynnette believed her? "Maybe for children. When my sister and I were little,

I used to make up stories for her." Jo looked down at
Shelley, gathering her courage. "Hey. Do you want to
come to my dorm room and listen to some records?"
She could feel her heart beating, body thrumming
with an excitement that she couldn't ascribe to simply
making a new friend. "Or, if you've got homework to
do . . ."

"Music," Shelley said, and smiled up at Jo. "Music
sounds good."

The cinder-block walls in Jo's dorm room were the
pinkish-tan of a Band-Aid, and there was barely space
for a twin bed, a dresser, and a desk with bookshelves
above it. As she opened the door Jo was overwhelmingly
aware of how small the space was; how close to Shelley
she would be.

"Welcome," she said, as Shelley sashayed her way inside. A Michigan pennant, a calendar, and a red, white,
and blue Kennedy poster with the slogan LEADERSHIP
FOR THE '60S hung on the wall. Jo sat on the bed before
deciding it was too suggestive, so she got up and strolled
casually across the room to take a seat at her desk.

"Dorms," Shelley murmured, looking around. With
her lipsticked pout and her cheeks still pink from the
walk, Shelley looked delicious. "I haven't been in one in
forever." Shelley knelt gracefully and flipped through Jo's
albums, stacked in a plastic crate, as Jo cringed, holding her breath, hoping that her taste in music was up to
Shelley's standards, only exhaling when Shelley selected
a 45 of "Be My Baby." She showed it to Jo, eyebrows
raised. "Okay?"

Jo nodded. Shelley slipped the record out of its paper
sleeve and lifted the phonograph's needle. When the

song began, she took a seat on Jo's bed, toeing off her boots and letting them fall to the floor. She looked up at Jo from underneath the dark fringe of her lashes. "Okay if I smoke?"

Jo nodded, and found the metal peanut-butter lid that she used as an ashtray, on the rare occasion when she had guests. Shelley pulled her cigarettes and her gold lighter from her skirt pocket and went through the ritual of shaking a cigarette loose, tapping it and lighting it. Jo's mouth felt dry as she watched.

"I'm glad we went tonight. In spite of the b.s.," Shelley said. She blew smoke rings toward the ceiling, a group of three that descended in size as they went: large, medium, small. Jo wondered how much practice it took to become that proficient a smoker.

"So how about you?" Jo asked.

Shelley laughed a musical laugh. "Oh, Lord, please don't ask what I want to be when I grow up. It changes every week. Every day. I might just stay in college forever. Just never make up my mind." She looked at Jo, and again Jo flushed, thrilled and disconcerted by Shelley's attention. "So how'd you get involved in civil rights stuff?"

"Well, Kennedy," Jo said.

"Of course," Shelley answered, her eyes still fixed on Jo. "Only you've been at it awhile."

"Since high school," Jo replied. "We had a cleaning lady when I was a girl. Her name was Mae, and her daughter, Frieda, was my friend. My mom didn't like that we were close, so she fired Mae." Jo could still remember how she'd felt, coming home to find a stranger in the kitchen, the all-news station on the radio, realizing that her mother had banished Mae and Frieda, and that Jo wouldn't see them again.

"So that's what got you started?" Shelley drew on her cigarette, watching Jo.

Jo nodded. "I think people should be able to be who they want to be. Be friends with who they want to be friends with. Live where they want to live. How about you?" she asked Shelley. "When was your big epiphany?"

Shelley looked up at the ceiling, exposing the slim column of her throat. "We have help, too. A woman named Dolores, who lives in and cooks and cleans, and basically raised me and my brothers, and a man named Davis, who drives my father and does yardwork. My parents aren't cruel to them. They pay them well. It's more that they treat them like they're pets."

Jo winced, recognizing the truth of what Shelley had said; the way her mother and other women she'd known could be polite, kind, even generous to the women who washed their dishes and cooked their meals and rocked their children to sleep, without ever treating them as entirely human. Shelley got to her feet, looking moody as she stared out the window. "I remember when I was twelve, there was a huge snowstorm. Davis had shoveled the front walk, but not the back. Dolores's daughter Trish was helping that day—my mother had a bridge party, or a tea for the Hadassah ladies, or something—and when it was time for Trish to go, she went out the back. I remember standing in the kitchen, watching her wading through the snow that came up to her hips and asking my mom why she couldn't use the front door, and my mother telling me that it wouldn't look right." Shelley's voice was bitter. She blew twin plumes of smoke from her nostrils, before bending over the record player and starting the song again. "The party wasn't for another hour, so it wasn't as if there was anyone there to see. The neighbors, maybe. It made me sick."

"You'd think the Jews got here and forgot all about the ghettos and the pogroms," Jo said.

Shelley rolled her eyes. "My mother's family's been here since the 1870s. They're basically the Pilgrims of the Jews. My mother grew up rich, and now she's even richer. Which I guess she thinks gives her license to behave like she was raised on a plantation." Shelley straightened her shoulders and stubbed out her cigarette. "So, I'll come to this picket. Maybe I'll get my picture in the paper. God, my parents would die." She seemed pleased at this thought, smiling as she went back to the bed and pulled her knees to her chest.

"You don't get along with your folks?" Jo asked.

Shelley shook her head decisively. "Leo's fine, but he's never home. Davis drives him to work at six in the morning and brings him home at eight at night. He's extremely busy making a fortune, so he's not around enough for me to really despise, and Gloria . . ." Shelley curved her fingers, wrapping them around an imaginary glass that she raised to her lips.

"Oh," said Jo. Lynnie's father had been a martini drinker. Mrs. Bobeck would mix up a pitcher of gin and vermouth, and meet him at the door with his first drink, which he'd swallow almost before he'd set his briefcase down. But she hadn't known anyone with a real drinking problem.

Shelley tilted her head, flashing Jo her pretty gray eyes. "And how about you?"

"You mean, do I make my cleaning lady walk through the snow?" Jo wrapped her hand around her own imaginary wineglass. Shelley picked up Jo's pillow and heaved it at Jo's head. Laughing, Jo caught it and said, "Okay. My mom and I don't get along. I've got a kid sister who's a freshman. My father died when I was sixteen."

Jo waited for the exclamations of sympathy that typically followed the dead-dad reveal, but Shelley simply said, "Tell me what happened."

Jo explained, giving Shelley more of the story than she usually shared. "He wasn't sick, and he hadn't been in any pain. But it happened so fast that I never got to say goodbye to him."

Shelley nodded. Instead of telling Jo that she was sorry, or worse, that she understood, she knelt down to inspect Jo's books before returning to her spot on Jo's bed, and patted the space beside her. "Come sit with me," she said. When Jo hesitated, she said, "Come on, Stretch. I won't bite."

Jo stood up, still holding her pillow, and crossed the room, a journey that seemed to last at least a week. It was dark outside, the Diag loud with students' voices, shouts and laughter, and the Ronettes were singing "Baby, I Love You," and Jo could hear the bedsprings creak when she sat down next to Shelley, who leaned against her, settling her head on Jo's shoulder as if that was a perfectly normal thing to do. Jo could smell Shelley's shampoo and hairspray, tobacco and toothpaste and Shelley's flowery perfume. Jo could barely breathe. She wondered if she dared to move her arm, to drape it over Shelley's shoulders and pull her close. But what if she'd misread things? What if Shelley screamed, or shoved her away, or called her sick or perverted? Jo was seventy-five percent sure that Shelley wanted Jo's arm around her, but in that remaining twenty-five percent lay the possibility for embarrassment and expulsion and a lot of trouble with her mother.

And so, instead of pulling the other girl close, like she wanted, like she thought Shelley wanted, Jo gave

Shelley's shoulder a quick squeeze and got to her feet. Shelley blinked up at her, looking startled. "I should study," Jo said. "I've got a ten-page paper for my lit seminar, and two problem sets for economics."

Shelley pushed herself lightly off the bed and crossed the room on her small, stockinged feet. "Want a ride to the picket?" she asked. Jo's mind was telling her to stay away, not to risk it, that Shelley Finkelbein probably just wanted a comrade in arms and a friend, but her traitorous mouth, denied the kisses it craved, opened up and said the word, "Sure."

"Cool beans." Shelley bent over for her boots. "I bet I can get my boyfriend to come, too."

In that instant, with that word, Jo felt as wounded as if Shelley had pulled a stiletto out of her suede boot and plunged it into Jo's heart. Of course Shelley had a boyfriend. What had she expected? Jo's face felt frozen, her lips were numb, as she made herself ask, "Who's your boyfriend? Anyone I know?"

"Denny Ziskin. He's a great guy. He graduated last year—he's over in London, he's a Fulbright Scholar—but he's home for the holidays." Shelley explained the strange English term system as Jo stood and listened, feeling as stupid as she'd ever felt in her life. "See you tomorrow, Stretch!" Shelley said, with a wink that made Jo's heart leap. Then she was gone.

Saturday dawned gray and drizzly, but the rain had tapered off to a fine, freezing mist by the time Shelley parked her car, the legendary Karmann Ghia, with a monogrammed nameplate that read REF by the driver's door handle.

"No boyfriend?" Jo had asked when Shelley showed up alone. Shelley answered with a headshake and an enigmatic smile. She and Jo had put their posters in the trunk, and Jo carried them both as they made their way to a group of about fifty people, most of them white, a few of them Negroes, who were walking in a slow circle in front of the store's front door. "Two, four, six, eight, Woolworth's needs to integrate!" Doug Brodesseur called through a megaphone. Shelley pressed her lips together, like she was trying not to smile. "Maybe I'll just watch for a bit," she said, and so Jo stood by her, at the edge of the sidewalk. Jo's sign read EQUALITY NOW. Shelley's read LIBERTY AND JUSTICE FOR ALL.

"Do these ever get, you know, violent?" Shelley asked as an older white woman in a raincoat, with a plastic bonnet tied under her chin, gave an angry sniff and pushed through the picketers on her way to the revolving door.

"The only blood I ever saw was when Kathy Coslaw tripped and cut her knee," Jo replied. A black woman holding a little girl's hand bent her head and slipped through the picket line next. Shelley's gaze followed her into the store. "Now what was that about?" she asked.

Jo shrugged. "Like Doug will be happy to tell you, this Woolworth's doesn't discriminate. Maybe that lady needed toothpaste or dish soap, or her daughter needed a pencil case for school."

"It's weird," Shelley said. "You think they'd be . . ." Jo saw her swallow the word "grateful," perhaps realizing how it sounded. She started again. "I guess I don't understand why anyone would shop at a chain of stores that doesn't treat them as equal."

Jo found that she didn't want to discuss it. She wanted to hear more from Shelley. She wanted to know all about Dolores, who cooked her breakfast, and about her brothers and her mother. She wanted to know what her bedroom at home looked like, and who her first best friend had been, and if she'd gone to sleepaway camp and if she'd ever kissed a girl.

"You want to march?" Jo asked Shelley, who lit another cigarette and took a slow drag.

"Why don't you go ahead? Don't worry, I won't leave without you."

"Come on," Jo pressed, and Shelley smiled.

"Okay, then. Can't have you thinking I'm all show and no go." They marched together, with Jo taking care to put herself on the edge of the sidewalk closest to traffic, the way her father always did when he'd walked with her. She was pleasantly aware of Shelley beside her, of the presence of Shelley's body, her faint, flowery scent, and the way her hips swung when she walked. After their third circuit, a driver passed them, leaning on his horn and speeding up to send plumes of cold water splashing at the picketers. He was shouting something out his window. Jo couldn't make out any words, but the waving, clenched fist and contorted face sent the message.

"Oh, very nice," Shelley said. Her slacks were plastered to her legs and her cuffs were dripping. She stretched her arm out of her trench coat's sleeve and looked at the time on a slim rectangular watch that Jo suspected was real gold and probably cost more than all of Jo's possessions combined. "Hey, Stretch. We've given this an hour. How about we go home and get dry?"

"Sure," said Jo, who had never, never once, left a picket or an action before it was over. Her chest felt tight, like breathing required extra effort. "Let's go."

•   •   •

In the car, Shelley suggested they go back to her place, an apartment on the third floor of a three-story brick house a few blocks away from College Avenue. They walked through the entryway, a high-ceilinged, dimly lit space with a faded green-and-gold rug on the floor and cubbyholes for mail against the wall. Upstairs the rooms were airy, with high ceilings and walls painted creamy-white. There was a kind of parlor, with a couch upholstered in soft gray mohair, and a coffee table made of ornately carved and polished wood, and a rug, apple-green with ivory fringe. "My mom's hand-me-downs," Shelley said with a negligent wave. "She redecorates and I get the cast-offs." A television set, with antennae stretching halfway toward the ceiling, sat on a carved wood stand in the corner. A desk, made of the same dark, polished wood, was piled high with textbooks, with a pale-blue Olivetti typewriter beside them. Jo saw *The Norton Anthology of English Literature*, volumes of poetry, a battered, bathwater-swollen copy of *Wuthering Heights*. A wheeled cart with glass shelves stood against the wall, carrying neat rows of wineglasses, martini glasses, highballs and tumblers, half a dozen bottles, and a glass ice bucket. The bar cart was Shelley's first stop, after a detour to the kitchen to collect a metal ice-cube tray, which she deftly cracked and decanted into the bucket. The glass and the ice bucket were both engraved with REF, the same monogram as the car. "Rochelle Elise," Shelley said, noticing Jo noticing. "You got a middle name, Stretch?" Using gold-plated tongs, she plonked ice cubes into two short glasses, adding a generous splash of amber liquid from a decanter before turning to Jo, eyebrows lifted. "Manhattans okay by you?"

"Sure. And no, no middle name."

"So are you a Josephine?" Shelley was using a smaller

pair of tongs to retrieve a maraschino cherry from a jar. "A Joan? A Joanne?"

"Josette." Jo's throat felt thick. Shelley handed her a glass and raised her own.

"Rochelle and Josette," Shelley said. "Well. Shall we toast to nicknames?"

"To nicknames," Jo repeated. She felt like she'd walked into an old black-and-white movie, where an elegant couple sipped drinks and tossed witticisms at each other. Her first taste of the Manhattan was closer to a gulp than a sip. She could taste the sweetness of the cherry and feel the burn of the liquor tracing a fiery line down her chest, glowing in her belly like a lit bulb.

"I'm going to get out of these wet things," Shelley announced. She eyed Jo up and down and said, "I'll bet I've got some pajamas that'll fit you."

Shelley had taken her shoes off by the door. Jo watched as she padded, barefoot, toward the back of the apartment. By the time she reappeared in a soft pink robe, with a set of flannel pajamas in her hand, Jo had finished almost half of her drink, and her head was starting to spin. Shelley's toenails were the same pink as her robe. The pajamas were size small, still with tags attached.

Shelley noticed her noticing and winked. "I'm not actually a pajama gal." She raised her arms, and the robe lifted, revealing the slim ivory curves of her calves. She was standing so close that Jo could see her pupils, the dark ring around her pale-gray iris, so close that Jo could feel Shelley's exhalations against her own skin.

Do not do this, Jo told herself. Shelley has a boyfriend. She doesn't like you that way. You could get in trouble. You could get expelled. People will talk. But she could feel all of those sensible thoughts floating away like smoke rings, erased by the alcohol and by Shelley's proximity. She was certain that Shelley had nothing on underneath that soft pink robe, and that she wanted Jo to know it.

"You know what I think?" Shelley's expression was teasing, and when she leaned close Jo could smell perfume, Camay soap, and maraschino cherry. "I think you like me."

Jo's head spun with desire and confusion. "You've got a boyfriend," she said.

Shelley stood on her tiptoes, wrapped her arms around Jo's shoulders, and kissed her, very lightly, on the mouth. "I'll tell you a secret," she whispered, so close that Jo could feel the puff of Shelley's breath as she formed each word against her own lips. "I like boys. I like girls, too. A lot of times . . ." She dropped her voice to a beguiling whisper. "I like girls better." She tilted her head up, looking at Jo with those dizzying gray eyes. "So what's your story, Stretch?"

"I like girls, too," Jo whispered, all in a rush. It was the truth, as true as it had been the day she'd made the same confession to Lynnette, and she'd been so lonely for so long; without a girlfriend, without even female friends, because Jo didn't want to do anything that would cause the girls in her dorm or her classes to become suspicious. She'd kept to herself her entire time in Ann Arbor, and instead of being free, away from her mother's scrutiny and suspicion, she'd just been lonely.

"Well, then." Shelley cupped the base of Jo's head in her hand, stroking gently. "And do you like me?" Shelley stood on her tiptoes and brushed Jo's lips with her own. They kissed, softly at first, then more deeply. Shelley's lips parted, and Jo brushed the tip of her tongue against

Shelley's, hearing the other girl sigh, feeling her sway against her.

"This way," Shelley whispered, taking Jo's hand, and Jo let herself be tugged along, down a shadowy hallway, hearing Shelley humming sweetly as she fell backward onto the bed, pulling Jo down with her.

Bethie

Summer school?" Sarah asked, as she sat at the kitchen table in her yellow rayon housecoat. The month's bills were piled in front of her, and her checkbook and calculator were at her side. The table was covered, as usual, in an oilcloth, this one with red roses on a green background. A wooden spice rack, with the same half-dozen bottles of oregano and sage and thyme, parsley and basil and fossilized-looking bay leaves that had been there for as long as Bethie could remember, hung on the wall by the sink, beneath the calendar that came free from the National Bank of Detroit. A clock with black numbers on a white face ticked next to the window, which was covered in the curtains that Sarah had sewn when they'd moved to Alhambra Street. Once a cheery yellow-and-white check, the curtains had faded to the same dingy yellow as Sarah's housedress.

"Summer school," Bethie confirmed. Insofar as it was going to be summer and she was, technically, going to be at school, she didn't feel like it was a complete lie.

"What classes will you be taking?" Sarah asked. Her squint and her skeptical expression suggested that she wasn't as convinced as Bethie wanted her to be, but Bethie was ready for her.

"A course in modern music appreciation, and a humanities requirement." It was, Bethie thought, a neat way of describing her summer plans, which included hanging out with her friends and, eventually, traveling in Connie's van to the Newport Folk Festival in Rhode Island. She would hear, and appreciate, modern music. She would see humanity. And in between, she would work. She'd snagged a job on campus, cataloging books at the University of Michigan law library. "And Jo will be there to keep an eye on me."

"At least until she leaves," Sarah said. Soon, Jo would be flying to London with her best friend, Shelley Finkelbein. From London, the girls would take a bus to Turkey and start out on the Overland Route, trekking into India and Nepal. Sarah had refused to let Jo travel to Washington for the Freedom March. ("It won't be safe," Sarah had sniffed, "and if you think I'm in a position to help you buy your schoolbooks because you decided not to work all summer, you can think again.") Jo had never forgiven Sarah for keeping her from being there on that momentous day. She'd spent her senior year begging and pleading and finally announcing that she was over twenty-one, technically an adult, and that she could get a passport and go wherever she wanted to go, with or without Sarah's permission. Sarah did not approve of Shelley Finkelbein, or of Jo's planned trip—"Why would you want to spend your money to go to countries where the people are so poor that they'd do anything to come over here?" she'd asked. But Jo had pestered and persisted and even cried, and eventually Sarah had grudgingly given her permission, announcing that at least India was better than going to organize down South and getting herself arrested, or even killed.

"And these classes are . . ." Sarah peered at Bethie and groped for the terminology. "Requirements for your major?"

"Part of the core curriculum," Bethie said, knowing her mother might not even know what a curriculum was, or how the word "core" might apply to it. She felt bad about lying to Sarah, who had dropped out of school after tenth grade in the midst of the Depression. But if Bethie's choices were a summer in Ann Arbor, having adventures with her friends, or three months in Detroit, sleeping in her girlhood bedroom, having dinner every night with her mother in this sad, dark kitchen, and selling ties or silverware all day long at Hudson's, Bethie would lie, and probably also cheat and steal to make sure she got to leave.

"Where will you stay?"

"I rented a room in an off-campus apartment in a house where some of my friends already live." Bethie waited for her mother to start probing—*which friends? Off-campus where? How will you be paying for this?* But all Sarah did was sigh.

"I should be used to it by now." Sarah's mouth folded itself into a tight-lipped frown as she used a silver letter opener to slit the throat of the envelope holding the gas bill. "Jo stopped coming home for the summers, and now you won't, either."

"It's easier to find jobs in Ann Arbor," Bethie said.

"Hudson's is always hiring," Sarah replied. Bethie could see strands of gray in her mother's dark-brown hair as Sarah bent over the checkbook at the table that still had four chairs around it. Her mom reminded her of a rubber band that had been snapped so many times until all of its resilience was used up, and it just hung there, stretched out and useless and limp. Those fights with Jo had been the animating force of Sarah's life. The back-and-forth of the battle had given her a reason to get up in the mornings. Anger and frustration and hope that she could turn Jo into someone else had powered her through her days, and had probably given her plenty of sleepless nights. Now that Jo was gone, and her husband was dead, and Bethie, too, was leaving, what did Sarah have to keep her going?

Bethie felt her heart give a sudden, painful twist. She had people. She had Devon, and Flip and Marjorie and Connie, and the rest of her friends. She had boys to dance with, boys to flirt with, boys who would loan her their copies of *Last Exit to Brooklyn*, and *Howl* by Allen Ginsberg. Jo had Shelley, and their crowd of activists, Doug Brodesseur and Marian Leight and Valerie Moore, a stunning girl with high cheekbones and glossy dark skin whose Afro made her almost six feet tall and who, it was whispered, was a member of Detroit's Black Panthers. Who did Sarah have? Bethie looked at the four chairs around the kitchen table, the scuff marks on the walls. There was a bare spot in the red linoleum in front of the sink, and it was probably the exact size of the space Sarah's feet occupied when she stood there, washing dishes. The radio in its plastic case stood on the counter, probably still tuned to WKMH, the "Keener Thirteen-er," the station her dad listened to when they'd broadcast the Tigers games. Bethie wondered if anyone besides her mom, herself, her sister had been inside the house since that fateful Thanksgiving when she and Jo had insisted on having guests. Her mother had never been a great one for making friends. *My family is all I need*, she would say, along with *We keep ourselves to ourselves*. Her companions had been her own sisters, Ellen and Iris. In the summer, all three sisters would come to the cabin on Lake Erie; Ellen with her husband, Max, whom nobody liked, and their sons, Jerry and Alan, and Iris, the glamorous unmarried sister, who wore red lipstick and smoked mentholated cigarettes. Iris would bring Bethie and Jo candy wax lips, and Ellen would take a rowboat all the way out to the middle of the lake, telling everyone that she was going fishing, when they all knew that she was trying to get away from baby Jerry's crying and her husband's requests for sandwiches and bottles of beer.

Eventually, Ellen and Max had moved to St. Louis when Max got some job there, and Iris died of breast cancer, two years after Ken. Bethie had heard her mother talk about "the girls" at work, but she'd only ever heard them described as a single, nameless mass, not as individuals. Sometimes Sarah met the girls for drinks, and once or twice a year, they'd go out to dinner, but Bethie was almost positive that Sarah had never invited any of the girls to her house.

"I'll come home whenever I can," Bethie promised, feeling sad and sorry, because that, too, was a lie. The next morning, Sarah dropped her at the bus station on her way in to work. By ten o'clock, Bethie was back in Ann Arbor. By noon, she was naked, in Devon Brady's bed, with her head resting on his chest. "How'd it go with your mother, little Alice?" Devon asked, reaching across her for the pipe he'd packed before she'd arrived. He lit it, inhaled deeply, and pressed his lips against hers, blowing smoke into her mouth.

"Summer school," said Bethie, when she could breathe again. She didn't want to tell Dev how small and worn her mother had looked in the kitchen, and how even the air had felt old and stale. "I told her I was going to do summer school."

Dev slipped his warm hands underneath her bare bottom, pulling her up closer. "Adult education."

Dev was only six years older than she was, but he seemed more worldly than other boys Bethie had known. He called himself a student, but he was really a businessman, with a lucrative industry selling a product that was popular, albeit illegal. She thought of Dev as the Candyman, with an endless supply of treats. There was pot, of course, which he acquired by the garbage-bagful and sold by the joint or by the lid or by the ounce. There were mushrooms, dried-up and wrinkled, some of them looking disturbingly like body parts, amputated ears or lips gone gray and shriveled. There was Dev's famous and much-sought-after acid, guaranteed to provide the smoothest high, the most vivid trips, and the gentlest come-down, and there were assorted pills of varying sizes and colors, in glass bottles, lined up in Devon's dresser drawers. Once, Bethie had asked Dev if he was worried about having all that stuff in his place. He'd given her his slow, sly smile, the one that made her feel like she was made of melting ice cream, and said, "I've got prescriptions. Or at least, someone does."

Most of the boys' dorm rooms and apartments Bethie had visited ranged from disorganized to sloppy to so filthy they felt hazardous to her health. Dev's garden apartment, on the lower floor of a Victorian on Church Street, was scrupulously clean. His hardwood floors were immaculate, swept in the morning and at night. In the living room, one wall was covered with bookshelves made of raw lengths of lumber and cinder blocks, and the shelves were full of books of philosophy and poetry and political history, biographies of generals and presidents, martyrs and saints. Above the bricked-over fireplace he'd hung a poster of a red-and-white woodcut image of a woman with a serene expression and flowers in her hair and the words MAKE ART NOT WAR. A couch was draped in Indian-print fabric. In the bedroom was a brass bed covered in a patchwork quilt, with squares of corduroy and velvet, striped and patterned cotton. Dev's grandmother had sewn it for him. "This was my jacket, when I was a little boy," he'd told Bethie, pointing to a square of denim. "This was my mother's favorite dress," he'd said, leading her hand first to a square of red polka-dotted cotton, then sliding it beneath the quilt.

"This is my favorite," Bethie whispered, touching his penis, stroking it the way he'd taught her. With his clothes off, Devon was wiry, his chest and arms muscled, with a patch of surprisingly soft dark hair over his chest. His toes were almost as long as fingers, and he would sometimes amuse Bethie by picking up a pen and writing her name with his foot.

She'd imagined that Devon would have a history to match his piratical appearance, that he'd been born at sea, or that he'd grown up traveling with a circus. But his background could not have been more prosaic. His parents were third-generation Michiganders. His father was a dentist, and his mom worked in his office as a dental hygienist. "Well, at least your teeth make sense," Bethie had said, after Dev had concluded his disappointing origin story with a gleaming smile. Devon had three older sisters, all of them with husbands and, presumably, excellent teeth.

"They're housewives," Dev told her, his voice rich with scorn. Whenever he played Pete Seeger's song "Little Boxes," he'd talk about his sisters, each of them in a small, square starter house that sounded, in his descriptions, very much like the house on Alhambra Street where Bethie had grown up. One sister had married a banker, one had married a lawyer, and the third, the youngest, had married a friend of Devon's who'd been in art school when they'd met. He'd been planning to be a potter, but Dev's sister Melinda told him that would be no kind of life. Now he was in law school, too, and Melinda was expecting.

"Someone has to have the babies," Bethie pointed out when Devon told the story of his poor buddy Randall the ex-potter, now lawyer-to-be. "Someone has to clean people's teeth. Someone has to live in those houses, and do those jobs."

"Not me," Devon told her, kissing her lightly, once on each eyelid. "Not us."

When she'd arrived on campus, Bethie worried that Devon wouldn't remember her, or worse, that she wouldn't be able to find him at all. For three weeks, she went to every party she could find with a blue band in her hair, like Alice in *Alice in Wonderland*, so that if Dev saw her, he'd remember. Boys asked her to dance, boys offered to walk her home, but Bethie didn't want them. She wanted her Candyman, her magic man, the man who could, with a little bit of something on her tongue, take her out of her body and out of her head and let her forget every bad thing that had happened.

One night, at another church-basement concert, she ran into Harold Jefferson. "Why, hello, Harold!" she'd said. His Afro had gotten bigger since she'd last seen him, but his smile was the same.

"How's freshman year treating you?" he'd asked. He wasn't wearing a dashiki, but there was a peace-sign pin stuck on the front of his jacket. "Boys giving you the rush?" They'd chatted about people they knew in common back home, and which sororities Bethie was considering. At a Sunday-night hootenanny, nobody stared at them, but Bethie knew that, at certain fraternities, people would have noticed a white girl talking to a Negro boy. Just like in high school, there were Negro kids at the University of Michigan, but they were a definite minority, and except for the places where there was overlap—the sports teams and, lately, the civil-rights groups—they kept to themselves. But Bethie was comfortable with Harold, who smelled good, the way he always did, and felt familiar, right up to the minute when Harold asked, "Who are you looking for?"

"No one," Bethie said, feeling herself blush as she realized that she must have been looking over his shoulder while they'd talked.

"C'mon. You know what my daddy would say." Harold pushed his chest forward, spreading his legs wide, turning into his father before her very eyes. "'A closed mouth don't get fed.'"

Bethie ducked her head, blushing. She didn't want to tell Harold that she was looking for Devon. He wouldn't approve.

"Go on, then. I'll let you go find whoever it is you're looking for," he'd said. So Bethie had gone, and she'd looked and looked until finally, on the first Saturday in October, she saw Devon again, in the corner of the Sigma Mu house's common room, watching the dancers with a bemused look on his face as he leaned, loose-limbed, against the wall. Bethie wanted to run right over to him, to open her mouth and stretch out her tongue, but she made herself hang back, watching, noticing how boys would approach Dev, in groups of two or three. There would be a brief conversation; hands would move to and from pockets. She waited until Devon was alone before approaching, feeling her heart lift as he smiled. "Hello, little Alice," he said, opening his arms. Bethie stepped into his embrace, pressing her head against his chest, letting him hold her, smiling as she felt him ease her headband off her head and run his fingers through her hair, smiling even more widely when he tilted her chin, opened her mouth, and put one of those magical cellophane squares inside of it.

Bethie went home with him that night. In his bedroom, when he began to undress her she helped him, without hesitation, unhooking her bra, slithering out of her girdle, lifting her arms over her head so he could pull off her dress. The walls and the ceiling hadn't started their magical pulsing, but she felt the sensation she remembered, like she'd left her body and was floating far above, watching as Devon laid her on the bed, moving her limbs and her head to suit himself. For a long time, he just touched her with his fingertips, stroking from the tops of her breasts down to the swell of her hips, moving his fingers slowly toward the center of her body, until he'd eased her legs apart and was touching the slick seam at her center. Bethie sighed, spreading her legs, lifting her hips, murmuring, "More." She was done being a good girl, done being anyone or anything at all. She was just feeling, nameless, skinless sensation, watching the action from somewhere up near the ceiling as Devon kissed her neck and her shoulders and fondled her breasts, clasping and suckling and even slapping them gently. His beard tickled and scratched her skin as he moved his face against her, licking here, kissing there, nipping at her breasts with those strong, white teeth. She watched as Devon shed his own clothes, observing his skin, smooth and olive, the triangular patch of dark hair on his chest and another between his legs. His penis was long and slender, matching the rest of him, and Bethie didn't resist when he instructed her to touch it. "Here," he said, and took her hand. "Like this." She wrapped her hand around him, pumping gently, hearing his breath catch. After a few minutes, he pushed her hand away and again worked his fingers between her legs, pushing one, then two fingers inside of her. Bethie sighed and wriggled, murmuring her pleasure.

"You're a virgin, little girl?" he asked. She wondered if it was something he'd touched with his fingers or something he'd seen on her face that gave it away.

"Yes," said Bethie, "but I don't want to be anymore." She felt his hands on her legs, spreading them wide, his mouth on hers, his penis nuzzling against her, and Bethie shut her eyes and prayed that the drugs would never wear off, that Devon would want to keep her around, that she would rise up from his bed transformed, with all of the old pain and sorrow behind her. She did things she thought he'd like, tossing her head, moaning in appreciation, chanting, "So good, so good, so good" in time to his thrusts. She wanted to give her body, the most secret parts of herself, to this man, instead of having them grabbed and groped and taken. The next morning Bethie woke up in his bed, with Devon smiling at her and starting to touch her again. When they finally got hungry enough to leave the bed, Bethie abandoned her crumpled party clothes on the floor and didn't bother with her curlers. She borrowed Devon's toothbrush and one of his denim work shirts, found a pair of bell-bottom corduroys at a thrift shop on College Avenue, and began her college life, reborn.

Since that first October, she was Dev's girl. She joined MUSKET and had appeared in the chorus of *Medea*, and had played Tuptim in *The King and I*, and understudied Alexandra Del Lago in *Sweet Bird of Youth*. She attended enough lectures and turned in enough of her work to maintain a C average. She saw her sister once or twice a week, for pizza dates at Pia's, where Jo worked, or for lunch at the Union, and on Sunday nights they'd make a phone call home together, usually from Jo's friend Shelley's rooms, because Shelley had her own phone and would discreetly leave when they were talking. The rest of the time, Jo was busy with her demonstrations, and with Shelley. Bethie had her suspicions about that relationship, but she never asked, and Jo left her alone about Devon, after one unpleasant conversation where she tried to tell Bethie that her boyfriend had a little bit of a reputation, to which Bethie had scornfully replied, "Oh, and who doesn't?"

There was a not-insignificant amount of overlap between Devon's customers, Jo's fellow activists, and the theater people Bethie fell in with, a crowd of vivid, chatty, bright, amusingly neurotic young women (and a few young men who Bethie suspected were homosexual) who talked endlessly about themselves and who were unafraid to dress how they pleased, to take up space. Because Bethie was Dev's girl, she was treated with admiration and respect, and received all the advice she could wish for about what clothes to wear and where to buy them and how to do her hair. By Thanksgiving, Bethie had swapped her kilts and cardigans for bell-bottom jeans and loose cotton caftans with billowing sleeves, and long skirts with colorful embroidery. She put away her rattail comb, her hot rollers, her curling iron, and her economy-sized can of Elnett, grew her hair past her shoulders, and let it hang, wavy and unstyled, the way Devon liked it. It was funny, she thought. He complained about his sisters and their small, conformist lives; he made fun of their little houses and their safe suburbs, but he liked it when she looked like all the other girls in their crowd, and he liked having dinner on the table at seven o'clock. Bethie didn't mind. She was happy to dress for him and cook for him. She learned to fry burgers on his stove, how to make pasta the way he liked it, al dente, so that the noodles still had a little starchy stiffness when you bit them. She would wash their clothes at the Laundromat, and iron Dev's shirts on the kitchen table. In return, Devon kept her safe. He slept curled around her at night, the big spoon to her little spoon, and during the daytime, he gave her what she needed, pills when she had to stay awake and study, pills when she wanted slow, lapping waves of euphoria, pills to go up, pills to come down, and acid to take her out of her skin and out of the world entirely.

"We should start packing," Devon said, and Bethie, who understood that *we* meant *her*, got out of bed and went barefoot to the closet. The plan was for them to do the first half of the drive, from Ann Arbor to Pittsburgh, on Wednesday, arriving in Rhode Island on Thursday afternoon in time for the shows.

"Can you throw some stuff in a bag for me?" asked Devon, hopping onto the floor with his usual limber grace.

"Sure," Bethie said. She pulled on one of his T-shirts, found a duffel bag at the bottom of the closet, and had started to fill it when someone knocked on the door.

"It's your sister!" Dev called. Bethie found her skirt, smoothed her hair, and trotted into the living room. A shopping bag stood by the door, and Jo was examining Devon's library.

"Have you read this one?" she asked, holding up Ken Kesey's *Sometimes a Great Notion*.

"Not yet," Bethie admitted.

"Says here it has the mythic impact of a Greek tragedy," Jo said, reading from the copy on the back.

"I'll bring it with me." Bethie held out her hand, but instead of handing her the book, Jo gave her the brown paper shopping bag.

"It's for your birthday," she said. "Sorry it's late."

Bethie pulled an oversized shoebox out of the bag. "I hope you like them," Jo continued. "Shelley helped me pick them out." Bethie lifted the lid to reveal, tucked into a nest of crumpled white tissue, a pair of soft red leather cowboy boots, ankle-high, with pointy toes, embroidered with green vines and flowers in shades of blue and gold and purple.

"Oh, my goodness," Bethie said. "They're gorgeous!"

"Spanish boots of Spanish leather," Dev said, peering over her shoulder and into the box.

Jo launched into some story about how they'd been in Chicago, because Shelley said there weren't good shoes available in Detroit, but Bethie was barely listening. She was hearing, in her head, the song lyrics that must have inspired the purchase, whether Jo was aware of them or not. *Oh, I'm sailing away, my own true love / I'm sailing away in the morning / Is there something I can send you from across the sea / From the place that I'll be landing,* Bethie had heard Bob Dylan singing in her head. *Take heed, take heed, of the western wind / Take heed of the stormy weather / And yes, there's something you can send back to me / Spanish boots of Spanish leather.*

"They're beautiful," she told her sister, feeling her throat tighten. Soon, her sister would be leaving Ann Arbor, leaving Michigan, leaving the United States. Jo would be leaving her alone. "I'll wear them for the rest of my life."

Her sister looked at her closely. "Are you all right?"

"I'm fine." Bethie widened her eyes and tilted her chin, hoping she looked innocent and that she didn't smell of pot. She was high a lot of the time, which did not make her unusual among her group, or Jo's, for that matter. She smoked pot most nights, and sometimes in the morning, and reserved uppers for test and paper-writing time, the downers and the acid for weekends. Mondays were miserable, but usually, just the knowledge that, in a few days, she'd be able to drift away from her skin, her body, and her memories was enough to keep her on the straight and narrow during the school week, and she was careful to be straight (or mostly straight) when she saw Jo, knowing that Jo would worry.

"You're too thin," said her sister. Bethie preened, even as Jo frowned. Among his treasure trove, Dev had prescription-strength diet pills. Bethie would take a few whenever she felt her clothes getting tight, or when she spotted the hint of a double chin in the mirror. The pills sent her flying. She wouldn't even think of food for days, and she'd have so much energy that she could clean the entire apartment and still have pep to burn.

"Jo, I'm fine." Bethie braced for a fight, but Jo wasn't going to give her one.

"I've got to go," she said. "Shelley's waiting."

Bethie hugged her sister, thanked her for the boots.

"Be careful," said Jo, and kissed her cheek. "Be good."

Back in the bedroom, Bethie considered a stack of underwear and bras; Devon cruised by with his wicked grin and put them back into the dresser drawer. Bethie smiled at him, unable to help herself. She put her boots in the bag first, thinking that she'd changed enough to leave most, but not all, of her previous life behind.

·   ·   ·

The five of them left on Wednesday morning, an hour later than planned, because Marjorie hadn't filled the Vanagon's tank and Connie had forgotten to pack her allergy pills.

When they finally got on the highway, the first leg of the trip was easy. They sang along with the radio and listened to the news reports: President Johnson named Supreme Court Justice Arthur J. Goldberg to succeed Adlai E. Stevenson as the United States' representative to the United Nations. Defense Secretary McNamara said the situation in South Vietnam was getting worse. ("Big surprise," Flip hooted.) Congress was expected to pass the administration's Medicare–Social Security bill.

By five, they were outside of Pittsburgh. Dev pulled off the two-lane road onto a dirt driveway, dragging a plume of dust behind it. As they got closer to the farmhouse, where they'd be spending the night with Devon's friends, Bethie saw a man standing on the porch, barefoot in denim overalls with no shirt on underneath. A little boy, maybe two or three years old, was hanging on to his leg. The boy had curly hair and pouty lips, and he was naked, with a milky-white belly and sunburned shoulders. He stared and sucked his fingers, unimpressed with the sight of five young adults piling out of the van, all of them disheveled and smelling of pot. On Dev's orders, they hadn't smoked in the car—"That's all we need, the Man pulling us over," he'd said. But there had been rest stops, and Marjorie had hidden a dozen neatly rolled joints in a gold cigarette case. One of them would keep watch while the remaining four huddled behind the bathrooms, giggling between tokes.

"I'm Scout," said the man, hugging each of them in turn. He smelled like freshly turned dirt and unwashed armpit. Bethie made herself smile and tried to breathe through her mouth. "And the little fella's name is Sky."

"Well, aren't you a cutie!" Marjorie said, clasping her hands at her chest and bending down to look him in the eye. Sky stared back at her before taking his little penis in grimy fingers, aiming, and peeing on her sandal and her bare toes. Marjorie screeched and hopped backward. Scout laughed. "I don't think he cares for your shoes." While Marjorie hopped off in search of a hose, Sky inserted his index finger into his right nostril, rotated it, pulled it out, and stuck it in his mouth. Bethie shuddered, burying her face in Dev's shirt, which smelled like patchouli and her sweetheart's warm skin.

The farmhouse's first floor was a series of big, barely furnished rooms, with walls stained brown from woodsmoke. Bethie looked down and saw holes in the wooden floors that let her peer straight down to the basement, and the chairs and couches all looked like they had been picked up off the curb on trash day. Bethie picked her way through the living room and found the kitchen, where a woman standing over the sink introduced herself as Blue. She wore a dirty peasant blouse with red-and-gold embroidery around the neck, and jeans. She had lank dark-blond hair, bare feet, dirt under her fingernails, and the same milky skin as Sky. "I hope everyone likes pasta," she said, her mournful voice suggesting that probably nobody did, and that she'd be in trouble for serving it. Bethie and Marjorie and Connie worked in the kitchen, helping to chop mushrooms and onions and garlic, and wash a bushel basketful of a dark green leafy vegetable that Blue told them was kale. While the pasta boiled, Bethie removed dirty dishes, books, broken crayons, newspapers, and a copy of *The Hobbit* from the long wooden table, and wiped off the crumbs and smears of sticky stuff underneath, and Connie brought over chipped, mismatched plates, silverware and glasses and cloth napkins. There were only seven forks, and eight of them, but Blue told them that Sky didn't count because he mostly ate with his fingers. Bethie shuddered again, thinking of the places that those fingers had been, and hoped the little boy's parents made him wash up before he started eating.

Over dinner, she learned that Blue's name had once been Bonnie, and that she'd grown up outside of Cleveland and attended OSU. Scout had once been Scott, and he and Devon had been graduate students at the U of M together before, as Scout put it, "we chose another path." Bethie also learned that Scout's main crop on the farm wasn't corn or zucchini but marijuana, and that there was a lab set up in the basement where he was manufacturing acid, using the recipe that he and Dev had perfected in Ann Arbor. Bethie picked at her pasta, wishing the cavernous dining room were a little more brightly lit so that she'd be able to tell exactly what she was eating, and what was a mushroom and what was a dead fly. ("Hey, it's protein," Scout had said, after a slightly hysterical Connie told everyone that she thought she'd swallowed a beetle.) After dinner, the guys went down to the basement. Bethie could hear conversation and laughter floating up through the holes in the floor, while the girls did the dishes. Blue explained in an apologetic tone that they were a little short on beds and blankets and pillows, and there was only one functioning toilet in the house. "'Functioning' is a little generous, babe," Scout said, climbing up the stairs with a joint burning between his fingertips. "Honestly, if you've just got to whiz, the woods are a better bet."

Bethie tried to smile as Dev took her hand. "Come

on," he said, walking her toward the backyard. "There's a tent." Bethie followed him out into the darkness, hearing a mosquito whining in her ear, and almost tripping over an abandoned rake. *You could be home right now, with a real bed and a functioning toilet, and a summer job selling sheets and towels at Hudson's,* she thought, and tried to tell herself that this was an adventure. When they rounded the corner, she saw that the tent was wonderful, like something out of a children's book, a tall white triangle, its circular base covered in rugs and pillows, its canvas walls sheer enough to admit the moonlight's glow. Bethie and Dev sat on a blanket, underneath the star-shot sky, smoking a joint. Dev laid a tab of acid on her tongue, and when they made love, Bethie could feel the world swirling around her, the dirt warm beneath her back, the silvery moon and the stars moving, in a stately waltz, above her head. The darkness hid the farmhouse's peeling paint and broken shutters and the way the doors didn't quite line up with the frames. Warm golden light shone through the windows, and in an upstairs bedroom, Bethie could see Blue holding Sky against her chest, sitting in a rocking chair, her lips moving as she sang him to sleep.

"Beautiful," she murmured, as Dev rolled off her, taking her hand.

"What's beautiful, Alice?" he asked.

"Everything," she said, her voice dreamy, and Dev laughed and rolled her against him, tucking her into his arms. It was wonderful, being with Dev. Better than wonderful; it was fair. With her uncle, sex had been a thing taken from her. She and Dev took from each other and gave to each other in equal measure. It was just the way it should be. When he woke up, she would tell him that. She'd explain what had been done to her, and tell him how much he meant to her.

"I love you," Bethie whispered, finally giving voice to the words she'd said in her head a hundred times. Devon held her, and didn't answer. When Bethie rolled on her side to look at him, she saw that he'd fallen asleep. His eyes were closed, his mouth was open, his black hair tangled. Bethie combed her fingers through it and eased a pillow underneath his head. She knew that he loved her, even if he'd never said so. He told her she was beautiful all the time, and in the clearest sign of his affections, he never made her pay for the drugs he gave her, a courtesy she'd never seen him extend to anyone else.

Bethie decided that she would gladly abandon her dreams of fame and fortune as long as she could be with him, wherever he went. They would be wanderers, travelers, moving lightly through the world with nothing more than backpacks on their backs. Anyplace there was a college or a university, anyplace there was a concentration of young people who wanted to open their minds, Dev had friends, or could make them, and Bethie would be at his side. She couldn't imagine being without him. She loved his lean body, his black beard, his glittering eyes, his smell. She loved how he called her Alice and pulled her onto his lap, as if she were no bigger than a doll. She loved how he had looked past her sprayed curls and her starched party dress and seen her adventurer's heart. She loved him, and she would make him love her, if he didn't already, and they would be together forever.

When Bethie woke up in the morning, the air in the tent was humid, and her skin was unpleasantly sticky. Devon was gone, the tent's flap was open, and Bethie opened her eyes to see Sky staring down at her dispassionately. Someone had given him a shirt, a men's undershirt that hung down past his knees. "I like your shirt," Bethie said.

"It's a dress," Sky said disdainfully, and wandered off. *Well, at least he didn't pee on me*, Bethie thought. There was that.

Bethie pulled on her own dress and inched into the sunshine. Connie hurried over to whisper, "You do not want to go in that bathroom. Believe me." She gave a dramatic shudder, and Bethie went into the woods to do her business before joining Connie and Marjorie, who'd found a garden hose. The girls rinsed off for as long as they could stand it underneath the icy blast. The men were already piling things into the van. Scout gave them each an apple, "grown right here, on the land," before they all climbed aboard and set out for Rhode Island.

On the first day, when there'd been five of them, they'd been tight but relatively comfortable. With seven adults and a squirmy toddler, the van felt unendurably crowded. Flip wanted to listen to music, like they had on the first leg, all of them singing, but as I-95 brought them closer to New York City, Devon insisted on the all-news station that delivered traffic reports every ten minutes. ("Isn't it funny," Connie murmured, "you put a guy behind the wheel of a car and he instantly turns into your dad?") Two of the men sat up front, Dev behind the wheel and Scout in the passenger's seat, riding in comfort while everyone else was shoulder to shoulder, thigh to thigh, with Sky in the very back of the van, on top of a pile of luggage, with his T-shirt hiked up to his waist, dreamily tugging his penis toward his feet, letting it snap back, and doing it again. ("I guess they don't believe in giving him toys," Connie whispered when Bethie alerted her to the situation. "He's just making do with what he's got.") Bethie sat in the third row, in the middle seat, with her arms pressed tight against her body, smelling clary and lavender oil, marijuana and body odor. In spite of the smells and her discomfort, the pot and the pills Dev had given her that morning suffused her limbs with a pleasant heaviness, making her drowsy and content. She felt like a cat basking in the sunshine, and couldn't wait until they arrived. Dev said they'd be able to pull a blanket up close enough to the stage so that they could hear. Bethie imagined it, being close enough to touch Odetta or Joan Baez as she curled up next to Dev, with his body warm against hers and his clever fingers combing through her hair.

Traffic slowed once they got off I-95 outside of Providence and made their way along the back roads to Newport. Dev steered the van through heavy traffic, over a suspension bridge that carried them over the water, toward the sprawling fairgrounds and the city's downtown, and Bethie felt her heart speed up, eager for a glimpse of the Atlantic, which she'd never seen. She'd pleaded with Devon to drive them past Newport's famous mansions, and he'd agreed, but from her seat in between the three other women she saw the grand summer houses in pieces—a glimpse of roof here, a peek of lawn there, a sliver of the glinting water, then just more cars. The sidewalks were full of people, some of the men in tie-dyed T-shirts or chambray work shirts, some of the women with bare feet and long dresses, or crowns of flowers in their hair. *My people*, Bethie thought. She couldn't wait to jump out of the car and join the throngs. The drugs were still working, giving everything a honey-dipped glow, and everywhere she looked there were young people playing guitars or harmonicas, banjos or fiddles or even blowing into jugs, singing, repeating lyrics back and forth, trading songs. As soon as Devon stopped the car, Bethie could hear the music, and feel it, too, the thudding of the bass and the pounding of the drums, through the windows and right up through her feet.

"C'mon," she said to Marjorie, grabbing the other girl's hand. They left the men to sort out the tents and found a concrete bathhouse with a row of stalls and sinks and mirrors made of polished metal. Bethie breathed through her mouth while she used the facilities, washing her hands and splashing water on her face. Marjorie stripped off her purple cotton tank top. She wasn't wearing a bra, and Bethie saw her breasts, small and almost triangular, set far apart on her chest, with nipples that pointed toward her belly. Marjorie grabbed paper towels, squirted soap from the dispenser on top, and scrubbed her breasts, the back of her neck, and her underarms. "Ugh! That farm! That kid! That bathroom!"

"We're here now," said Bethie, feeling a smile stretch her face. Outside, the crowd swept them up and carried them toward a makeshift-looking wooden stage. And there was Joan Baez, surprisingly small and slender, with her wavy hair blowing and her dark eyes wide and intent, standing in front of the red-and-white-striped backdrop, singing "Long Black Veil." "Look what I've got," Marjorie whispered, reaching into her pocket. Marjorie had wide hips and narrow shoulders and big, slightly bulgy blue eyes that made her look a little like a frog. *But a friendly frog*, Bethie thought, as Marjorie opened her hand to reveal two squares of acid, both of them stamped with a cartoon likeness of Goofy.

"Is it Dev's?" Bethie asked. Marjorie nodded. Without hesitation, Bethie slipped the tab on her tongue. The bitterness should have been the first hint that something was off—Dev's blotter was normally tasteless, or even slightly sweet. This stuff made her face crinkle, and she had to struggle not to spit it out, but Marjorie seemed fine, so Bethie let the tab dissolve and waited for the drugs and the music to take her somewhere wonderful.

Time passed. Bethie could not have said how much. Instead of feeling the familiar upswelling of bliss, she felt a rising unease, the sourness in her mouth gathering into a sensation of foreboding in her belly. When she felt hands grabbing at her from behind, she turned around. "Hey!" The man who'd touched her raised his hands, grinning at her, palms out in the universal gesture of apology. He had bare feet, crusted with dirt, and blue jeans, but on top of them he wore a white lab coat, and above that Bethie saw her Uncle Mel's face, floating in the twilight. Her mouth dropped open. Uncle Mel reached out and squeezed her breast, hard enough to hurt.

Not real, Bethie thought. Dev had told her what to do if she ever ended up on a bad trip. *Breathe. Keep calm. Go somewhere safe. Hold still and wait. I'll find you, and I'll take care of you. Remember that nothing you are seeing is real.* Bethie breathed in and out slowly, once, twice, three times, before turning to her right, looking for Marjorie. But Marjorie wasn't there. In her place was Cheryl Goldfarb, wearing Queen Esther's crown. "I was better than you were," Cheryl said, through her red-lipsticked mouth. "They only gave you the part because everyone felt so sorry for you because your dad was dead." Of course, that didn't make sense—Bethie's father hadn't been dead when she'd been Queen Esther; he'd been at the performance, cheering for her. Bethie turned away, pushing through the crowd, as someone whispered *slut* and someone else whispered *fat-ass*.

Bethie kept moving, eyes down, ignoring the voices that called her names, who said that she was a whore and a liar and not as talented as Cheryl Goldfarb. The air felt thick and clinging and hard to breathe. A black cat with green eyes and white socks on its forepaws began to follow her, padding along at her side. A gray-and-black calico cat joined in behind the black cat, and an orange tabby fell in line. Next came a sleek gray cat with a white shield on its chest, and a fluffy brown cat with its fur wild and tangled. Bethie stopped, turned around, and looked at the cats, blinking. The cats sat down in a row and blinked back.

Not real, she thought, walking more quickly, until she was jogging, then running, and every time she turned there were more cats, dozens of them, an army of cats following her on their little feet, which so cunningly hid their claws. *Queen of the cats*, she thought, and remembered the Cheshire Cat in *Alice in Wonderland*. He told Alice he would see her again when she played croquet with the Queen.

Bethie stopped to catch her breath and looked around, trying to remember where the van had been. Somehow, she finally found a tree that looked familiar, and a car she recognized, a little VW Bug painted cheery blue. Three rows past the Bug was the Vanagon, with Sky standing guard by the driver's seat. He was naked again, his white T-shirt puddled at his feet, and he stared at her with his dirty fingers plugged into his mouth. Bethie pressed her hand against the stitch in her side, trying to catch her breath. "Hi, honey," she said, when she could speak again. The little boy stared at her blankly. Or maybe he was looking behind her. Bethie was afraid to turn around to see if the cats were still there. "You took off your dress."

"It's a shirt," said the boy, lifting his nose disdainfully into the air.

"Do you know where Devon is?" She realized, as soon as she'd spoken, that the boy was unlikely to even know who Devon was, let alone where. Sky gave an indifferent shrug. Bethie reached for the van's door.

The metal handle was feverishly hot against her palm as she gripped it. Bethie dragged the door open, feeling it grind on its tracks. A cloud of smoke came billowing out into the open air, along with the scent of pot and sweat, but when Bethie peered into the van's dim interior, no one was there. Bethie turned, looking left, then right. Sky had vanished and she was all alone. She kept walking, head down, pushing past the barefoot girls and boys with harmonicas and tambourines. Johnny Cash was singing, still. "A, B, C, W, X, Y, Z, the cat's in the cupboard but he don't see me." The music was moving all around her, it was twining like vines around her ankles and wrists and waist and throat, it was tripping her, choking her, and Bethie could taste blood in her throat, like hot copper. *I want my mom*, she thought. *I want my sister. I want someone to save me. I want to go home.*

"Hey!"

A boy fell out of the sky and landed in a crouch right in front of her. Bethie gave a little scream, jumping backward, and the boy straightened up, laughing. "Don't be scared, I was just . . ." He pointed up. Bethie followed the path of his finger. There was a tree, and the tree was full of people, boys and girls who'd climbed up to straddle the branches, to get a better view of the stage.

"Oh," she said. The boy put his hand on the small of her back, smiling. In the glimmering near-darkness, Bethie saw white skin, dark eyes, and beads around his neck. "Come with me," he said. "You look like you could use some taking care of." Bethie let him move her past the tree into a field, where there was a tent, and a group of boys, and sleeping bags, unzipped and spread out on the ground.

All she wanted to do was lie down, close her eyes, and wait for this terrible night to be over. "Don't worry," the boy was saying, "you'll be fine. Bad trip? Bummer," he said, when she nodded. She went with him, following along, weak with gratitude, letting him help her into a spot on the sleeping bags, as two, three, and finally four boys dropped out of the tree and came to join them. She shut her eyes, willing the world to stop spinning. It wasn't until the first boy had her dress off, one hand over her mouth, clamping off her screams, and the other hand working between her legs that Bethie realized she'd made a terrible mistake.

Jo

Jo woke to the feeling of something shaking her in the shoulder, and Shelley's insistent voice saying, "Look at this." When Jo didn't open her eyes, Shelley rolled the magazine into a tube and poked Jo's shoulder and the side of her head.

"Five more minutes," Jo murmured. She was still half-asleep, her eyelids heavy, her limbs warm and relaxed in the warmth beneath the covers in the bedroom of Shelley's apartment, which her parents had allowed her to keep over the summer. In her dream, there'd been an old woman, a rambling mansion with turrets and towers and gingerbread trim. Was the mansion her prison? Was it a paradise she'd worked her whole life to obtain? Was the house somehow magical, letting her live different versions of her life from start to finish, then sending her back to the beginning again? In her head, Jo began to gather the threads that she could tie into a story, maybe one she could submit to the school's literary magazine. After Shelley poked her again Jo sat up and looked at the page Shelley held open. It was an ad for the Peace Corps, black text on a yellow background. NOW THAT YOU HAVE A DEGREE, GET AN EDUCATION, it read.

"Shelley," Jo said, struggling to keep her voice steady, even when what she wanted to do was rip the magazine out of Shelley's hands and throw it at the wall. "We have a plan. Remember?"

Jo was ready to move to New York and start her life as a writer, with Shelley at her side, but Shelley had sidestepped and made excuses and had finally announced that what she wanted to do was travel; to take one big trip and see the world before they settled down. "My treat," she'd insisted, and Jo had agreed to let her pay for the tickets. On August 14, they'd take their backpacks and board the plane to London. They'd see India and Turkey and Iran and Nepal; they would stay in an ashram in Goa and climb mountains in Tibet and float together in the sunshine in the warm waters of the Indian Sea. They had their tickets, a timetable for the buses, and reservations for three nights at a guesthouse in Istanbul recommended by one of Shelley's fraternity pals' older brothers. After that, they had no set agenda. They'd go where they wanted to go, and stay until they were ready to come home. Jo hoped it wouldn't be for months, maybe even as long as a year. The world wouldn't look twice at two young women, recent college graduates and best friends, traveling together. She and Shelley could share a room, even a bed, without arousing anyone's suspicion, and if someone did get suspicious they could pack up and move on to another city, even another country. Jo planned to try to do some travel writing— she had made a list of magazines, with names of editors to whom she could submit pieces. She figured that she could make money teaching English, in a pinch, and if even that didn't work out, she could wash dishes or clean houses, doing whatever it took to keep them afloat.

"I know we have a plan," Shelley said, sitting back on her heels, pouting adorably. She wore Jo's extra-large U of M T-shirt, which fell down past her knees, with nothing on underneath it, and her long, dark hair was still disheveled from sleep. "Only now I'm wondering if it's selfish. I mean, aren't we just indulging ourselves, when we should be using our college educations to help people?"

"How about this," Jo said. "When we come back from our trip, if you still want to join the Peace Corps, I will seriously consider it."

"Oh, you'll seriously consider it," Shelley said, widening her eyes and deepening her voice as she repeated Jo's words. Jo opened her mouth, preparing to argue again in favor of their trip, as Shelley snuggled up beside her, kissing her cheek and her nose. It was hot outside, a sunny July day, the temperature already in the seventies, but the thick green leaves of the oak trees that lined the street formed a canopy over the house. Looking out the bedroom windows, all Jo could see was green, with sunshine filtering through, and she could hear cars and voices, but they sounded very far away. It was as if she and Shelley were in their own private tree house, the two of them alone together in their own sunny, summertime cocoon.

"I will," said Jo. "But first, we are going to the Grand Bazaar and the hammams in Istanbul." She flipped Shelley onto her back and bit her—not gently—on her neck. Shelley squealed, and sighed, spreading out her arms and legs, unfurling underneath her like a flower. "And then, we are going to the ruins of Ephesus." Jo sucked gently at a spot underneath Shelley's ear, loving the way Shelley wriggled underneath her. "We are going hiking in Cappadocia, and we are going to see the whirling dervishes in Konya."

"Whirling dervishes." Shelley sounded slightly breathless.

"Then we're going to India." Jo kissed her way down Shelley's neck and chest, taking Shelley's teacup breasts in her hands. "We'll go to an ashram in Udipalya and learn yoga. We'll take a bus to the beaches in Goa and sit on the sand in the sun." Jo kept kissing until Shelley gripped her head, trying to push her down, but Jo would not let herself be pushed. She stopped and sat up, leaning back on her heels. Shelley whined, groping for Jo's hands, and Jo let Shelley hold them but would not let Shelley pull her down.

"And then what?" she prompted.

"No fair," Shelley panted.

With one fingertip, Jo stroked a line from the sweet indentation of Shelley's navel, down through the silky black curls, and pressed the pad of her finger against the kernel of pink flesh. Shelley writhed, gasping. "What next?" Jo asked.

"The Village!" Shelley said. Jo rewarded her by moving her finger, very slightly, up and down. "We'll have an apartment . . . and we'll live in the Village . . . and I'll act in plays, and you'll write for magazines, and you'll learn how to cook, and I'll have a window seat so I can watch all the people, and we'll go dancing . . . oh," she sighed as finally Jo bent her head toward Shelley's sweetness and gave her lovely girl what she wanted. It wasn't fair, she thought. But if sex was what it took to get Shelley to agree with Jo's plans, to get her to admit that Jo was who she wanted, Jo would use sex. She would be ruthless, if ruthlessness was what was required.

When it was over, Shelley curled on her side, giving Jo her back, lying quiet and thoughtful, while Jo got up to shower and dress. She'd gotten used to this by now. For the last six months, Jo and Shelley had been together constantly. They weren't taking any of the same classes, but at least once a day, they'd manage to meet up. In the library, they'd sit across from each other, with their books open on the table and, underneath it, the tips of Jo's toes resting against Shelley's instep or her calf. At the Student Union, where they'd have coffee or lunch, Shelley would brush her hand against Jo's at the table as she gestured, making a point, or Jo would touch Shelley's shoulder or the small of Shelley's back as they left, steering her past a group of boys. Shelley would watch Jo play intramural basketball or volleyball, clapping when Jo made a basket or scored a point, and they'd walk back together through the twilight, Jo glowing and sweaty, Shelley dainty and neat, beside her.

They slept together almost every night, most of them at Shelley's place. Her room was easily three times the size of Jo's, and she had a queen-sized bed with a carved-wood headboard and footboard, a matching desk and dresser and vanity, a bookcase for her textbooks and a table for her record player. Her walls were covered with paintings framed in glass, reproductions of Monet's water lilies and Degas's ballerinas, interspersed with posters for Phil Ochs and Dylan that were just thumbtacked to the plaster. Above the bed hung Shelley's prized possession, a Beatles poster from Sweden in cheery shades of red and pink that read HJÄLP! A pink-and-white rug covered the floor, and Indian-print fabrics covered the love seat. It was a reflection of Shelley, Jo thought; the room of a girl who was trying to make up her mind.

Some days Shelley talked about joining the Peace

Corps. "I need a dose of reality," she'd declare, and Jo would point out that there was reality all around them, much closer than Tanganyika. Some days, Shelley would talk about going to Europe—"the grand tour, they used to call it." Her parents would pay, she said, and Jo would explain, again, that she wasn't comfortable taking the Finkelbeins' handouts. On a Monday she would want to move to Washington; by Wednesday she'd be thinking about getting a graduate degree in fine arts, or going to the Yale School of Drama, or going to the Rhode Island School of Design and learning to make sculpture and jewelry. Her voice, low and confiding, was perfect for radio, and her face was pretty enough for TV. Shelley could do any of it, and every day, Jo would listen, patient and amused at first and, eventually, frustrated and angry, as Shelley spun one version after another of the future. She could move to Hollywood and wait to be discovered! She could go to WWDT in Detroit and ask her ex-boyfriend for an audition! She could go to New York City and find a gallery to sell her bracelets!

Jo knew what she wanted for herself. At her mother's insistence, she'd majored in elementary education and had graduated with a teaching certificate, but she'd taken every literature class she could fit into her schedule. If it was up to her, she would have applied to every graduate school she could find, and attend the one that offered her the best scholarship, and get a PhD in literature. She'd read all day, novels and poems, all the classics she hadn't gotten to in college, and she'd write all night, working on her own fiction. She would write, the way she'd always dreamed of doing, and if she couldn't find a way to support herself as a writer, she'd teach, and she'd have a life surrounded by stories.

Her lit professors had encouraged her. They'd given

her As on her papers, praised her reasoning and her prose, told her that she should pursue writing as a career. "I'm an education major," Jo had said shyly, as her Modern British Literature professor had urged her to think about graduate school and pursuing a PhD. "Maybe I could teach literature?"

"Or you could study it." Professor Klaas was one of a tiny handful of women on the Michigan faculty. She wore her hair cut short, and dressed like her male colleagues, in button-down shirts and tweed vests, only with skirts instead of pants. Professor Klaas lived with her research assistant, a buxom blond woman named Donna, and the rumors were that the two women were more than just friends. Jo had heard the ugly words that kids whispered about the professor—*dyke* and *bull dagger* were a few—but if Professor Klaas knew what people said about her, it didn't seem to trouble her.

"You have a gift, Miss Kaufman." She'd cocked her head in an inquisitive, birdlike way, examining Jo with her bright brown eyes. "I don't see a class ring anywhere. Or one of those dreadful fraternity pins."

"No," Jo said.

"Not going to rush out of here and into wedlock?" Professor Klaas asked. "Trade your graduation gown for a white dress? Earn your MRS degree?"

"No," Jo said again, thinking that if she could marry Shelley, she would.

"So why not, then? There are scholarships available, here in Ann Arbor and elsewhere. Some are even earmarked for female students who show particular promise."

"I'll think about it," Jo said. And she had, telling herself that when Shelley finally made up her mind, whether she agreed to New York City or someplace else, Jo would find a way to keep reading and writing.

But for long months, Shelley had refused to commit. Her moods were as changeable as the spring weather in Ann Arbor. Sometimes, she would disappear, for a day or even a weekend, telling Jo that she was needed at home, to sign some papers having to do with her trust fund, or to attend some family function, a wedding or a bris. Sometimes she would sit in silence on her love seat, staring out the window, smoking, with an ashtray balanced on one knee, and she wouldn't want to talk or even leave the room. "Stop crowding me!" she'd snapped once, when Jo had stopped by the library, the way she'd done a dozen times before without incident, only that night Shelley had yelled at her, in a voice loud enough that three or four students bent over their work had looked up to stare. Startled and hurt, her face burning, Jo had gone back to her dorm room, where two hours later, Shelley showed up with a bouquet of roses that she'd bought somewhere, all apologies and kisses. "Don't be mad at me," she'd begged. "It's that time of the month."

Jo knew that Shelley got terrible menstrual cramps, and would gather her hot-water bottle and the bottle of pills from her doctor back home and crawl into bed until they passed. She suffered from migraines, and she'd have to lie in her darkened room with a wet washcloth over her eyes for hours. Jo loved her intramural basketball and volleyball games, and loved taking long, aimless walks around the campus. Shelley didn't even like walking through a parking lot, and her idea of exercise was carrying a few bags of new clothes up the stairs. Shelley would call her parents every Saturday morning, and she'd be in a terrible mood afterward, pacing around her room and muttering things under her breath. "Why do you love me?" she'd asked Jo once, after a Saturday of sulking and smoking over something her mother had said. "I'm no good for you." Jo would hold her and tell her that she was wonderful, funny and smart and irresistibly sexy, and that she wanted to be with her forever. She'd comb Shelley's hairspray-sticky hair with her fingers, and massage Shelley's shoulders, and the back of her neck. And finally—finally—after weeks of discussions, and consulting maps and travel guides, Shelley had settled on the trip.

In the bedroom, Shelley curled on her side with her eyes shut. "Ten more minutes," she mumbled. Jo pulled the covers back down. "Come on, lazybones."

While Shelley grumbled and pulled the covers over her head, Jo walked to the window, thinking about her sister, who was most likely still with her friends, making her way back from Newport. In high school, in her kilts and her bobby socks and sweater sets, with her hair bobbed and curled, Bethie had looked like the rest of the pretty, popular girls. At Michigan, with her long hair hanging past her shoulders, in one of her long dresses with strappy leather sandals on her feet and beaded earrings dangling from her ears, she also fit in perfectly, right down to her glazed expression and the roach clip in her pocket.

Jo thought sometimes that Bethie liked to play at being a rebel, when the truth was that her sister had a genius for conformity, for making herself the best, most stylish example of whatever version of femininity was currently in fashion. That, along with her accommodating personality, meant that things would be easy for Bethie. Jo had felt equal amounts of admiration and envy as she'd kissed Bethie's cheek and given her one last hug, inhaling her scent of patchouli incense and pot.

"Okay," Shelley grumbled, and finally got out of bed. Jo pulled up the sheets, smoothed the comforter, and plumped the pillows. They were leaving their little cave of sunshine and green and going to Shelley's house for the day. Shelley's parents and her brothers were up north, at the family's vacation home in Charlevoix, the staff had all been given two weeks off, and Shelley and Jo would have the house in West Bloomfield Hills all to themselves. They could sun by the pool (naked, Jo imagined, feeling a pleasant shiver at the thought of Shelley with her hair wet and sleek, rising from the water), and get Shelley packed for the trip (Jo was sure Shelley would want to bring everything she owned).

Jo had been to Shelley's house once before, for Passover the previous spring. She'd been excited, and a little scared, nervous about meeting Shelley's family, worried that she'd commit some terrible breach of etiquette at the table, or wear the wrong clothes, or accidentally blurt out something about Shelley's mother's alcoholism, or the truth of their relationship. It hadn't helped that Shelley had gotten more and more moody as the day of the visit approached, swinging between snappish and solicitous. "You won't hate me, will you?" she'd asked when they pulled onto Shelley's street. "Once you see how I grew up?"

Jo promised that of course she wouldn't, but it made her wonder what Shelley was ashamed about; what she wanted to hide. College was a great equalizer, where everyone wore the same sweatshirts, purchased from the university bookstore, and everyone took the same classes, read the same textbooks, and ate the same burgers at the Union, but there were occasions when Jo was forced to consider how her own upbringing differed from Shelley's, whose parents had thrown her a Sweet Sixteen for three hundred guests ("two hundred and eighty-five of their closest friends, and fifteen of mine,"

Shelley joked), and had taken her to Europe instead of Lake Erie. Shelley had grown up riding, while Jo had barely seen a horse. Shelley's brothers attended boarding schools on the East Coast, where they rowed crew and played lacrosse. Shelley's mother went to Paris or New York City like Jo's mother went to Kresge's or to the butcher shop.

Jo had promised herself that she wouldn't gawk at Shelley's house, or make the mistake of calling it a mansion ("it's just a house," Shelley had said sharply on the one occasion that Jo had used the word), but when they turned into the gravel driveway, she couldn't stop herself from staring. Set half a mile off the road, in a copse of manicured woods, the house looked like some kind of institution, a small museum or a dormitory at an old English college. It was a sprawling structure, three stories of cream-colored half-timbered plaster, with a slate roof and a paved path leading to the enormous front door, a slab of oak that had a gigantic iron ring set in its center, instead of a knob.

Jo stared up at the grays and browns and cream-colored tiles of the roof, the huge iron ring on the door. "Eh," she said, feeling grateful that her voice sounded steady. "My house is bigger."

Then the door swung open and Shelley's brothers, Tom and Pete, had come pelting down the stairs, bounding around like puppies, arguing over which one would get to carry Jo's bags, their voices overlapping as they recounted for their big sister their triumphs on the lacrosse field and the story of the new turtle that Pete had gotten for his birthday. Jo had met Shelley's mother, Gloria, a petite blond woman in what Jo thought was a real Chanel suit, the same kind Jackie O had worn. Gloria looked almost as young as her daughter, until you got up close and saw the network of fine wrinkles that webbed her face. Shaking Gloria's hand, Jo felt its tremble, and saw how all of the woman's makeup was the tiniest bit askew, the lipstick extending past her lips, one eye lined more heavily than the other. Jo knew, because Shelley had told her, that Gloria Finkelbein had been to half a dozen discreet and costly facilities to dry out, and that so far it hadn't taken. When Shelley was little, Gloria had hidden bottles of wine and pints of vodka in her boots, in the pockets of her coats, in the boathouse and in the toilet tanks, and Shelley and her brothers would find them and pour them out, like it was a scavenger hunt or a game.

"Since the last place, she's got it in her head that she can't be that bad if she's not drinking during the daytime," Shelley said, speaking quietly as they climbed the stairs to the second floor. "So she sits, and she waits, and she watches the clock. I bet sometimes she sneaks something into her tea."

"I'm sorry," said Jo, knowing how inadequate the words were. At school, Shelley had hardly ever talked about her family. The visit had let Jo fill in some of the blanks. She wondered if Shelley or her brothers had ever come home from school or baseball practice to find their mom reeling, or passed out, and if a drunk mother was worse than a permanently enraged one.

"Don't be." Shelley shrugged. "I'm used to it. There's plenty of people here to make sure everything gets taken care of. She doesn't really have any responsibilities except looking pretty. And I made my dad get Tom and Pete out of the house, so at least they're away from the worst of it." Shelley had flopped on her bed. Her childhood bedroom was actually a suite of rooms, with a private bathroom and dressing room and a window seat that looked over the lawn and the lake, and Jo had wished fiercely that she was a boy, so that she wouldn't have to worry about the door being locked before she could take Shelley in her arms and kiss her and tell her that she was brave and smart and strong and a wonderful big sister.

Shelley's father had shown up late to the Seder and had come bounding into the dining room after they'd all been seated. Leo was as short and disheveled as his wife was cool and elegant, with stains on his tie and shirt buttons straining over his belly. He was bald, with a jutting beak of a nose and floating wisps of white hair that danced around a pink skull, and he spoke with a heavy Yiddish accent that reminded Jo of her own father. She could tell that he adored his daughter. "My Shelley, the scholar," he called her, the last word sounding like "skah-lah," and Shelley had smiled at him fondly, waving the compliment away. Leo had held Jo's chair out with a flourish, introduced her to their family friends, the Adamses, Morrie and Bev, their daughter, Leah, who blushed every time fourteen-year-old Peter looked her way, and their little boy, Richard, who wore shorts, knee socks, and a shirt with a tiny bow tie. "And of course my luffly wife you're already meeting." Gloria had given Jo a glassy nod, extending her hand as if they hadn't already met. As the Seder progressed, Jo noticed the way Gloria seemed to cringe every time her husband opened his mouth. *German Jewish*, Shelley had explained. Gloria's relatives were German Jews, who'd made their way to the United States in the 1880s and were as close to the aristocracy as Jews in America could be. Leo had come over as a teenager, in 1921, not knowing a word of English, after his parents had died in Poland. He'd moved in with cousins and started off selling remnants of fabrics and trim from a cart when he was fourteen, saving enough to open his first store at twenty, franchising the business at twenty-eight. By thirty, he was rich enough to woo and marry the youngest and loveliest daughter of one of Detroit's oldest Jewish families. Now there were seven Forest Fabrics in Detroit and its suburbs, and the business had expanded into Ohio. New York State, Shelley had told her, would be next. Jo carefully spooned up her matzoh ball soup, wondering if either husband or wife was happy with the bargain they had made, and what Shelley thought of her parents' marriage, and how their choices would inform her own.

The air had turned humid, and the campus was quiet as they walked to Shelley's car. Shelley handed Jo the keys, and Jo drove, delighting in the warmth of the day, Shelley's presence beside her, and the anticipation of their trip and all the days they'd have to spend together. Forty-five minutes later, they were crunching up the gravel driveway. "Are you sure nobody's here?" Jo asked, as Shelley said, "Don't be such a scaredy-cat," and Jo followed her through the house, out back to the pool, where Shelley turned, lifting her arms, causing the hem of her pink cotton minidress to ride up high on her thighs. "Unzip me." Underneath the dress, Shelley had nothing on but a pair of lace-trimmed panties. She kicked them off, gave Jo a grin over her shoulder, and dove into the water, with the clean form of a girl who'd spent her summers at sleepaway camp, where swimming lessons were taught twice a day. Jo pulled off her own shirt and shorts, leaving her bra and underwear on before jumping in the water and scooping Shelley in her arms. Shelley closed her eyes, humming happily as Jo held her, bouncing her a little, walking from one side of the pool to the other.

"This is perfect," Shelley said, without opening her eyes. "I want a house with a pool."

"We'll have to figure out how to get one," Jo replied . . . and did she imagine it, or did Shelley's body stiffen, ever so slightly, in her arms? Before she could decide, Shelley wriggled free, slipping away and swimming underwater toward the deep end with her long, dark hair trailing behind her. Jo swam after her, grabbing her ankles, pulling her, wriggling and laughing, into her arms, covering her wet skin with kisses, thinking that she'd never been so happy.

After a little while, Shelley got bored in the water, so Jo swam laps while Shelley lay in the sun, wrapped in a towel, leafing through *Vogue* with her wet hair gathered into a braid. After half an hour, Jo came to sit with her. She took Shelley in her arms, letting Shelley's head rest on her shoulder.

"It's so beautiful here." Jo had decided to confine her remarks to the present, and the obvious—the sunshine, the green grass, the water. *Can't you just enjoy things?* Shelley had asked, like a refrain, all through the spring, when Jo would press her about the future, demanding certainty, demanding answers. *Can't you just be happy being with me now?*

"I wonder if my mom was ever happy." Shelley's voice was low and musing.

"You don't think she ever loved your dad?"

Shelley shook her head. "I think, for her, it was more like taking a job than falling in love. If you've been bred to marry a rich man and have his babies and basically be decoration, and you have no skills and no idea how to support yourself, how many options do you really have?" She reached down for her cigarettes and her lighter, which were always within grabbing distance. "I think Gloria can barely stand my father, but she knows that she wouldn't be able to live without him."

"What do you mean?" Jo asked.

"I mean if you took everything away from my mother, and told her she had to support herself, cook her own meals and pay her own bills and balance her own checkbook and wash her own lingerie, I guarantee you she'd be dead in two weeks. She could never live without help. Without . . ." Shelley gestured toward the house. ". . . all of this."

Jo was thinking about Sarah, who had been brisk and competent even before her husband's death. She didn't think Sarah liked her much, but she and Bethie had both gone to college, the way her father had always wanted, and Sarah's hard work had made that possible.

"And what about you?" Jo swallowed hard, and made herself ask, "What do you want?" Jo knew that she could dream of a life abroad, or in the Village, in New York City, but could Shelley live like that? Or would she want a life like her mother's, with a big house, a new car every year, live-in help, and a regular mah-jongg game? Shelley would have to decide for both of them. Shelley would pick a city, New York or Washington or Los Angeles or anywhere in between, and Jo would follow, finding a teaching job and a graduate school.

Whither thou goest, I will go, too. Jo reached for Shelley's hand, which rested limply in hers. Shelley's dark-brown hair curled against her pale, faintly freckled skin, and her long lashes lay against her cheeks.

"We need more towels," Shelley mumbled, without opening her eyes. It was and was not an answer to Jo's question . . . and it was as much as she could hope for, Jo thought.

"I'll go get them." Jo pulled her shirt and shorts on over her wet underwear and bra. Barefoot, she walked through the kitchen to the house's echoing tiled entryway, up the grand, carved staircase, with the stairs covered in soft blue carpet and washed with light filtered through stained-glass windows, into Shelley's bedroom. There was a linen closet in the bathroom, stacked with fluffy white bath towels and hand towels and washcloths, all with the REF monogram that Jo had first seen on Shelley's car. She piled towels in her arms and then, thinking that Shelley might want a fresh shirt or a sundress to pull on once she was dry, she opened Shelley's closet. The racks were full of blouses and dresses, arranged by color, from light to dark. Those everyday clothes had been pushed aside to make room in the center for a single garment: a long white satin dress, swathed in a zippered bag of clear plastic that read *Bridal Fashions by Marcile* in fancy gold script.

No, Jo thought. Her mind was whirling, spinning in a search for explanations. *It's someone else's. One of Dolores's daughters. It's Gloria's old wedding dress. They're storing it here to keep it safe.* But as she let herself look at the dress, really seeing it, the truth hit her, hard and undeniable. It wasn't just a wedding gown; it was Shelley's wedding gown, the heavy silk cut to flatter Shelley's petite frame. The neckline would show off her shoulders and the delicate architecture of her neck, the bodice would emphasize her tiny waist. It was Shelley's style, with no frills or ornamentation, not a single seed pearl or sequin or scrap of lace. Just yards of lustrous satin, cream-colored, with the faintest undertones of pink.

Jo stood in front of the closet as pieces clicked together in her mind: the times Shelley had disappeared, the excuses she'd had at the ready, stories about parties, or her parents, or a pair of shoes she needed to retrieve (*You've got shoes here*, Jo had said that night, and Shelley had rolled her eyes at her fashion-backward girlfriend and said, *Not the right ones*). Last Friday, her mother had needed her to drive her to a synagogue Sisterhood meeting. The Wednesday before that, there were forms that the family accountant had asked her to sign, and she'd been gone all afternoon. Jo remembered how she'd come to the apartment and found Shelley moody and quiet, smoking on her window seat with her legs pulled up to her chest, and how Shelley's kisses had an almost frantic quality, how she'd grabbed onto Jo like she'd had something to prove.

A rage stronger than anything she'd ever felt suffused her, flushing her face, curling her hands into fists, making her feel like her skin was going to split. Before she knew what she was doing, Jo grabbed the dress, gathering it into her arms and holding it against her as she ran down the stairs.

By the time she got to the pool, Shelley was sitting up, squinting at her, one hand shading her eyes. When she saw what Jo was holding, she cringed, as if Jo had struck her. For a moment, Jo just glared. In a voice that sounded raspy, she asked, "When's the happy day?"

"January," Shelley whispered, with her eyes cast down. "New Year's Day."

"And who's the lucky guy?"

"Dennis Ziskin." Shelley's voice was barely audible. Jo remembered the name, the boy Shelley had called her boyfriend when they'd first met, the one who she said was overseas, studying in London.

"Of course. Good old Denny. Good for him." Jo's voice was high and sounded brittle. She sounded, she thought, like her mother. "When were you going to tell me? On our way to the airport? On the plane?"

"I thought . . ." Shelley wrapped her wet towel around her shoulders, gripping the edges tightly. "I thought we could have our trip. I wanted to see the world with you, like we planned. I thought I could have that."

"And then you thought you'd come home and get married?"

"I wanted to tell you." Shelley sounded like she was crying, but Jo couldn't bring herself to look. "I hated lying. I tried, a hundred times."

"So what was the problem? Why didn't you just say it?" Jo asked. "Why couldn't you tell me the truth?"

"I didn't want to hurt you. I didn't want to lose you. I wanted to have . . . what we have . . . for as long as I could." Shelley's hands were twisting in her lap, and her expression was anguished.

"Why not forever?" Jo asked. "Why do you have to get married? Why can't we be with each other?"

Shelley's voice was flat. "You know it can't be that way."

"Why not?" Jo asked. She was trembling with anger, and with fear, and with the growing certainty that this was the end, the final hours she would spend with the girl she loved. She felt like her world was splitting open, sending everything spinning and flying away. How could she go through her days, brushing her teeth and putting on clothes and talking to other people, now that this had happened? How could she survive this kind of pain?

"Because that's not how the world works." Shelley's voice cracked as she said, "I love you, Jo, you know I do, but I'm not brave like you are. I couldn't live with people staring at me and whispering about me and not wanting their kids around me."

"It doesn't have to be like that. You know it doesn't. We talked about this." Jo heard her voice cracking. "We could go . . ."

"Go where?" Shelley demanded, sitting up straight, tossing her braid over her shoulder. Her neck and chest were flushed, her hands were fisted on the towel's hem. "Tell me. Tell me where could we go where two women could live together and people would be okay with it."

"New York," said Jo. "Or San Francisco. There're places, Shell, you know there are!"

Shelley was shaking her head. "My parents would disown me. I wouldn't be able to explain it to them, or my grandparents. My brothers . . ." Shelley let the towel slide down her shoulders as she buried her face in her hands. "I'm sorry," she cried, in a terrible, broken voice. "I'm sorry, I'm sorry, I'm sorry." She lifted her hands and looked at Jo, her face miserable, her eyes filled with tears. "I want to be with you, more than anything. I love you, Jo, I do. I thought I could be brave. But I can't."

"But you promised." Jo's voice was a little kid's whisper, a little girl who'd been told she could trick-or-treat until eight o'clock and whose mother had changed the curfew and pulled her inside at seven-thirty. She hated herself for sounding like such a baby. She hated herself for believing that Shelley ever intended to make a life with her.

"I know." Shelley bent her head, not arguing. "You probably hate me. You should hate me. I'm awful."

Jo stared at her, stunned and numb. Her beautiful Shelley, with her damp hair and flushed cheeks and silvery gray eyes full of tears . . . and then, without planning it, without considering her action, or its consequences, she gathered the heavy satin dress in her arms and heaved it, as hard as she could, into the water.

The next day, the first day of her post-Shelley life, Jo collected her belongings from Shelley's apartment and left her key on the kitchen table. She walked from her dorm room to the Army-Navy store on Dearborn, where she bought a rucksack with a metal frame, a heavy cotton sleeping bag, a tent, and a length of mosquito netting. She bought a canteen, iodine tablets to purify the drinking water, a flashlight with spare batteries, a toothbrush with a built-in plastic case, and a travel-sized tube of Crest. She packed khaki shorts and wool socks, bras and underwear and a pair of jeans and loose, short-sleeved men's cotton button-down shirts. On the appointed day in August, Sarah drove her to the airport, and she flew, for the first time in her life, first from Detroit to New York City, and from New York City to London. She'd wondered if the seat beside her on the airplane, the seat where Shelley was supposed to have been, would be empty, but another girl sat down beside her, a girl with blue eyes and freckled cheeks who was going to be a senior at Macalester College and who mentioned her boyfriend four times in five minutes. Jo nodded politely and turned away, closing her eyes. When they landed in London, Jo joined a group of students, some from Michigan, some from Ohio, and some from Madison, Wisconsin. They piled onto double-decker buses and toured London. Jo saw Buckingham Palace and the Changing of the Guard, and spent a yawning, sandy-eyed hour at the Victoria and Albert Museum, looking at carved wooden tigers and jeweled tiaras, and ate fish and chips, wrapped in newspaper, sprinkled with malt vinegar, and drank pints of ale with lemon squeezed onto the foam. By six in the morning she'd boarded her bus.

Jo slept and woke and slept and woke again, trying to read from her copy of James Michener's *The Source* as the bus bounced along for almost two days, stopping for kids to board or disembark, making its way east to

Istanbul. When they finally arrived, the boys hurried off to buy hash. Jo joined a group of girls who, she'd discovered, had also made reservations at the guesthouse in Sultanahmet that she'd chosen for herself and Shelley. The air was dusty, the streets full with people, many of them young and white, like Jo, others darker-skinned, the men bearded, the women in veils. Jo pulled her collar up over her face, rubbing at her gritty eyes, staring at her map until she and her new friends figured out which way to walk.

The girls' names were Katherine and Melinda and Gina. Katherine was tall and blond and busty, with flushed cheeks and a high-pitched voice, and Melinda had heavy glasses and a quiet, self-contained manner, and Gina was petite, with short black hair and a quick smile. *Stay away*, Jo told herself as they sat in a teahouse for a meal of fiery lentils and rice. In the guesthouse's communal bathroom, Jo took a long, hot shower, listening as Katherine, who was dressed in a bathrobe and leaning against the sink, read from a guidebook about the squat toilets.

"I guess that they're basically holes in the ground, with a pitcher of water to rinse off after."

"Ew," said Melinda, and Gina shrugged and said, "Can't be worse than my summer camp."

The beds were narrow, six of them in rows of three in one little room, and the sheets were stiff and scratchy, smelling strongly of bleach, but Jo was so tired that she didn't care. She brushed her teeth and was asleep as soon as she'd closed her eyes. Twelve hours later, when she woke up, the room was full of sunshine and was empty except for Gina, who was standing at the window. "You're up!" Gina called, when she saw that Jo's eyes were open. "Want to go to see the Hagia Sophia? The lady at the desk says it's a three-minute walk."

Jo sat up slowly. She could smell bleach and dust and curry, and even the quality of the light looked different than it had back home. *I'm somewhere else*, she thought, still hardly believing that she had made it halfway around the world . . . and that she'd left Shelley behind. *Stop it*, she told herself, the way she'd done it every time she found her thoughts wandering in Shelley's direction. It was like a wound she couldn't make herself stop probing. She wondered if it would ever stop hurting.

"I need to make a stop first. I need to go . . ."

". . . to the American Express office." Gina's slim build and sleek hair made Jo think of an otter, some graceful creature just as at home in the water as on land. "Melinda and Kat already went. I think we all promised our parents the same thing. Come on, I'm starving! Let's find out what they eat for breakfast here."

Jo pulled on loose pants, a long-sleeved white blouse, remembering what she'd read about modest dress in Muslim countries, and a pair of sandals she'd bought in Ann Arbor and had never worn before. The clerk sent them to another teahouse, where they ate triangles of soft white cheese, soft-boiled eggs, olives, white bread and apricot jam, along with cups of strong tea. Fed, rested, dressed in clean clothes, with a new friend beside her and plans forming for the next few weeks, Jo felt the faint stirrings of excitement. She promised herself that she would keep moving forward, distracting herself with new places and new faces.

They found the American Express office at the intersection of two main streets with unpronounceable names, and gave the woman behind the counter their names and the address of the guesthouse. The woman held up one finger—*wait*—and disappeared behind a wall. Jo looked at Gina, who shrugged and said, "Want to see the bazaar after the church?"

"Sounds good," said Jo as the woman came back, holding a telegram with Jo's name typed on the front. Jo's heart was in her throat as she unfolded it. EMERGENCY COME HOME NOW YOUR SISTER NEEDS YOU, it said. Jo leaned on the counter, staring at the words, and she must have made some noise, because Gina was there, patting her back, saying, "Breathe. Don't worry. We'll figure out how to get you home."

Bethie

For the first week after she came back from Rhode Island, she felt so sick and sad, so used and dirty, that she could barely find the strength to leave her bedroom. Because she realized she'd have to say something, she told Sarah she'd been mugged at the folk festival. Sarah had sniffed, muttering under her breath about how she wasn't surprised. "And that boyfriend of yours?" Sarah asked, standing in the bedroom's doorway. She knew who Devon was, had even met him once, on campus, at Jo's graduation, but she'd never said his name out loud. Bethie wasn't sure what part of him she found the most objectionable: his age, his religion, or the way he so obviously lacked anything that could be called a job.

"We broke up," Bethie said, in a tone she hoped would preclude additional questions. By the time she'd made it back to the van, the sun was coming up, and Devon was looking at her like she was toilet paper stuck to the bottom of someone's shoe. She'd tried to explain what had happened—the bad trip, the boys in the trees, and what they'd done to her—but the only part of it Devon seemed to understand was that she'd been with someone else that night. He'd been cold to her the whole way home, dropping her off at her rented room without a kiss, or a word of goodbye. Bethie knew, without having to be told, that she wasn't his girl any longer. She'd packed up her things and slunk back home to Alhambra Street.

"Well. Finally, some good news." Bethie had curled back onto the bed, her eyes closed. That was Sarah's cue to leave, but she didn't take the hint.

"You can't just stay here and do nothing for the rest of the summer," she finally said.

"Just let me rest," Bethie begged.

"I can ask at Hudson's—"

"Mom," said Bethie. "Please. Just give me a few days to get myself together."

Sarah had grumbled, but she'd finally agreed, and Bethie had dragged herself under the covers like a wounded animal returning to its den. She felt feverish. Her head ached constantly, and it burned when she peed. *I'm just tired*, she told herself, *just worn down*, but the pain kept getting worse. Eventually, she was forced to call her old pediatrician, Dr. Sachs, after her mother had left for work. "I think I have an infection," she whispered to the receptionist, who said that Doctor could squeeze her in that afternoon. Bethie took the bus to his office, took off her clothes and put on a gown, and lay on her back on a narrow, padded table covered with crinkling white paper. Cartoons of Mickey and Minnie Mouse, Donald Duck and Goofy cavorted on the walls. A glass jar of lollipops stood by the sink, for good little boys and girls who were brave when they'd gotten their shots. Not too long ago, Bethie had been one of them herself.

"Hello, hello!" said Dr. Sachs, bustling into the room. He was short and pink, with a head bald and shiny as a peeled egg. He'd tended to Bethie and Jo since they were little girls, treating their chicken pox and their ear infections. Bethie felt almost sick with shame as she whispered her symptoms. The doctor's face became carefully neutral as he listened. "I'm going to do an exam," he said, calling the nurse into the room before showing Bethie how to put her feet into the metal stirrups and let her knees fall open. Bethie squeezed her eyes shut, trying not to feel or hear.

"We should wait until that comes back," the doctor said. His voice was sympathetic but detached. "But, my dear, I'm about ninety-nine percent certain that you have gonorrhea."

Bethie lowered her eyes. Her face was burning.

"It's lucky we caught it," Dr. Sachs said. "For women, where it goes undiagnosed, it can cause all kinds of trouble. You could end up sterile."

The word, and the thought that followed it, struck Bethie like a fist hitting her midsection. She bit her lip to keep from gasping, and she counted backward, sorting through the dates, trying to remember the last time she'd gotten her period.

"Doctor," Bethie managed to whisper, "what if . . ."

Dr. Sachs must have followed the progression of her thoughts. He backed toward the door, one hand holding her chart, the other aloft. "I'll call you when we have the results," he said. "I'll prescribe a course of antibiotics. I'll call them right into the pharmacy for you to pick up. You should be fine," he said, and managed a smile before vanishing. The raised hand, the haste of his exit, filled in the rest of the blanks: *Don't ask me to help you. I won't do it.*

Back at home, Bethie huddled on her bed, knees pulled up to her chest, rocking as she finally let herself consider the symptoms she'd been trying to ignore. Her breasts were tender, she'd thrown up two mornings in a row, and the last period she could remember had been almost three months ago. She'd have to find a way to learn for sure if she was pregnant or not. If she was, there was no way she could stay that way, no way she could convince Devon to marry her, even if she was one hundred percent certain that the baby was his. She needed to end this, to get this thing out of her, and for that she'd need money. Money and a name.

Dev would know someone, but when she called his apartment in Ann Arbor, the phone just rang and rang. She called Marjorie Bronfman at school and at home in Plymouth. "I think Dev went back to that farm." Marjorie's voice was somber and respectful. She knew that Bethie and Dev had broken up, even if she didn't know why.

"Do you have a phone number?" Bethie asked.

"I don't think they've got a phone there," Marjorie said, and Bethie squeezed her eyes shut, remembering the stained walls, the holes in the floorboards, the filthy little toddler, and groaned.

"I really need to talk to him."

"I wish I could help, kiddo."

"You could," Bethie began. She was trying to remember what Marjorie had told her about her life before college, if she came from money, if she'd have any connections. "Listen," she said. "Do you know anyone who helps . . . you know . . . girls in trouble?"

"Oh, Bethie." Marjorie's voice was low. "Oh, jeez. I can ask around," she said. "Do you ride horseback? I have a friend who has a friend who was in trouble. She rode a really wild horse, and let herself get thrown. I guess that did the trick."

"I don't ride," said Bethie. She felt so exhausted, so dirty and ashamed, and the thought of figuring out where to even find a horse left her feeling even more weary.

"Let me see what I can do." The next day Marjorie called Bethie with what she said was a medical student's number, but when Bethie dialed, the number just rang and rang. Bethie hid in her bedroom, telling Sarah that she was sick, making phone calls all day long while Sarah worked, calling every friend, every friend of a friend, searching for help and finding none. Her friend Flip's older sister told her that if she had five hundred dollars she could get it taken care of in a clinic in Tijuana, but Bethie didn't have five hundred dollars, or a way to get herself to Mexico. A sorority sister of Bethie's freshman-year roommate had a number, but it turned out it was the same disconnected one that Marjorie had passed along. After five days of dead ends, Bethie had almost decided to try to take care of it herself, with a knitting needle. She was trying to figure out how much she'd need to drink to keep it from hurting too much without getting so drunk that her hands would be unsteady. *Tomorrow*, she thought. *I'll do it tomorrow.* That morning, her mother figured it out.

"You're pregnant." Sarah's voice was flat as she stood in the doorway of Bethie's bedroom, backlit by the morning sun. Instead of answering, Bethie rolled onto her side and buried her head in a pillow that had gotten just as greasy as her hair. "How could you do this?" Sarah's voice rang out, loud and angry and hurt, and Bethie wanted to explain, she wanted to say that this wasn't something she'd done, that it was something that had been done to her, and that she was still her mother's good girl.

"Was it that Devon?" asked Sarah. Bethie didn't answer. "Have you told him?" she demanded. "Will he marry you?"

Bethie said, "I don't know where he is." She paused, gathering herself, before she said, "And anyhow, I'm not sure it's his."

Sarah sucked in a breath. Bethie couldn't see her mother's face, but she could imagine it, forehead wrinkled, brows drawn, lips pursed in disgust. "Well," Sarah said, "this is a fine mess. A fine mess you've gotten us into." For a moment, Bethie thought that her mother would come sit by the side of her bed, to touch her hair, to tell her that she would help, she would fix things, she'd take care of Bethie and everything would be fine. Bethie wanted that, so badly. She wanted a grown-up to swoop in and clean up her mess, but her mother did not seem to be in a swooping frame of mind.

"I'm going to telegram your sister."

Bethie sat up straight, panic lancing through her. "No! No, don't do that."

"Jo has money," Sarah said, as if Bethie hadn't spoken. "And that rich girlfriend of hers might know someone who can help you."

"Mom, don't call Jo. This isn't her problem. She's my sister. You're my mom." Bethie hoped that saying it would help Sarah put it in perspective, that she'd let Jo have her adventure and find a way to help Bethie herself, but Sarah had already turned to go. Bethie could hear the tap of her high heels on the floor, the front door opening and shutting, the car as it pulled onto the street.

"Mom, wait," said Bethie. She pushed herself out of bed, feeling her greasy skin, her filmed teeth. She hurried down the hallway, racing for the door, but her mother was already driving away, gripping the wheel tightly in both hands. Across the street, Mrs. Johnson, their new neighbor, stopped watering her rhododendrons long enough to give Bethie a wave. Bethie waved back and went inside. She plodded back to her bedroom, collapsed onto her bed, shutting her eyes, feeling the hot tears drip down her cheeks. She kept the shades drawn and the lights off and the covers pulled over her head, so that it was always dark. Three days after telling Sarah her news, she woke up and her sister was standing next to her bed.

"Hi." Bethie pushed herself upright and, to her shame, began to cry.

"What's wrong?" Jo asked. "Mom wouldn't say."

Bethie pulled a pillow against her midriff and started to cry harder. She heard her sister sigh.

"Okay," said Jo. She touched Bethie's shoulder and stroked her hair. "Okay. Don't worry. We'll figure it out."

"I'm sorry," Bethie said again. "I told Mom not to tell you. I didn't mean to ruin your trip." She wiped her face with a corner of the pillowcase. "I tried to take care of it. I asked everyone I could think of, but I just kept getting the same name, and that guy's phone's been disconnected. Then I guess Mom heard me getting sick in the bathroom . . ." Bethie started to cry. "I'm such a dummy," she said, and buried her face in her hands.

Jo spoke carefully. "I assume you've considered your options?"

Bethie gave a mirthless snort. "You mean, did I think about trying to get the guy to marry me? Sure. Except the problem is, there's more than one candidate."

"Oh," said Jo, who sounded as if she didn't know what she was supposed to say to that. Bethie was sure that her sister was dying to ask what had happened, and how

Bethie could have been so careless, and exactly how many possibilities there were, but her voice was calm, even mild, as she asked, "Want to tell me what happened?"

Bethie wiped her eyes. Jo looked like she'd gotten taller on her trip, and her hair was longer than normal, pulled back in a twist that showed off the graceful length of her neck. Without raising her gaze from the bedspread—the same pink gingham check Sarah had bought when she was five—Bethie said, "I went to Newport. I took acid, and I had a bad trip, and there were these guys in a tree."

"Wait. What? Guys in a tree?"

"They'd climbed up there to see the stage," Bethie said. "One of them had a guitar, and one of them had some hash. They took me back to their tent. They had blankets and sleeping bags spread out on the ground, and I thought . . . I thought they were nice guys, you know?" Her voice cracked. "I thought that they wanted to help me."

Jo pulled Bethie close, until her sister was leaning against her, and put her arm around Bethie's shoulders. "Do you know someone?" Bethie asked. "Or do you think Shelley does?"

Bethie felt her sister's back stiffen. "Shelley and I had a bit of a falling-out," Jo said.

"Oh," said Bethie, feeling sorry for her sister and sorrier for herself.

"But I know other people," Jo said. "Let me make some calls." She got to her feet, with her familiar, athletic grace, and for the first time since she'd come back from Rhode Island, Bethie began to feel like maybe things would be all right.

•   •   •

Three days later, she and her sister were waiting in the lobby of the Atheneum Hotel in the Greektown neighborhood in Detroit. They sat on a love seat upholstered in some shiny, slippery fabric, red with gold stripes. Jo wore cuffed jeans and sneakers and a U of M T-shirt. Bethie had showered and pulled her hair into a ponytail. She wore espadrilles, a madras skirt that felt snug at the waist, and a light-blue blouse. She sat with her feet crossed at the ankles and her hands folded in her lap, looking prim and virginal. *As if it makes any difference*, she thought. *As if it matters now.*

The lobby was long and dimly lit, with a bar at one end, doors to a ballroom at the other, and the check-in desk in between. It smelled like smoke and the previous night's drinks. In the open area between the front doors and the reception desk were groupings of furniture, chairs and couches and low-set tables. Bethie imagined that, later in the day, the bar would be bustling. Waitresses would move through the room, offering cocktails; businessmen would sit at the tables and the couches, eating salted peanuts with their martinis, and the rumble of their voices would fill the cavernous room, but for now, the place felt abandoned, like a stage felt after a show. A single bored-looking clerk in a white shirt and a green vest stood behind the desk. A bellman, similarly uniformed, leaned against the wall just inside the revolving door. A man in a hat and a trench coat, with a suitcase in his hand, got off the elevator and walked through the lobby, his footfalls echoing. He tipped his hat to Bethie and Jo, returned the bellman's "Good morning," and pushed through the door.

Bethie sat, hands plucking at her skirt. The elevator doors slid open again. Heels clicked across the marble as a middle-aged woman approached. Her white hair was teased high around her head, and so thin that the weak light of the lobby shone right through it, and her pinkish-white skin was pleated with wrinkles around her eyes. She wore a brown skirt and a yellow sweater, and her stubborn, bulldog-like face and cat-eye glasses reminded Bethie of the vice principal back at Bellwood High. She looked the sisters over. "Which one?" she asked.

Bethie got to her feet. Jo also rose. "Can I come?"

The woman shook her head. "Wait here. I'll bring her down in an hour."

"Why don't you go for a walk," Bethie suggested, hoping that she didn't look as frightened as she felt. "I'm sure . . ." Her throat worked as she swallowed. "I'm sure I'll be fine."

"I'll be right here," said Jo.

The woman stood, waiting wordlessly until Jo realized what she wanted. Jo reached into her purse and handed her an envelope full of cash. It was, Bethie knew, the money Jo had planned on spending on her trip, visiting Goa and Udipalya, Jaipur and Dharamsala, Pushkar and Nepal. Jo had told her the names of the places, pronouncing each one with reverence and care. *I can't wait*, Jo had told her. *I can't wait to get out of here.* The woman opened the envelope and peeked at the money. Bethie couldn't look. She imagined that each bill in the fat stack represented a different city, a day or two that Jo could have been somewhere else. She imagined stretching out her hand, grabbing the money, driving Jo to the airport and telling her, *Go.* But then what? She couldn't imagine past that point. Where would she go? What would she do? How would she manage, alone with a baby?

The woman tucked the envelope into her purse. "Good luck," Jo whispered, and squeezed Bethie's hand.

Bethie tried to smile before following the woman to the far end of the lobby, where the elevator swallowed them up.

The woman didn't speak on their ride to the eleventh floor. In silence, she led Bethie to a room in the middle of the hall. There was a bed with a sheet spread out on top of the dull gold comforter, and two chairs set up at its base, with towels draped over their tops. The wallpaper was light-brown, with a repeating pattern of a bundle of stalks and fringes that Bethie thought was meant to be a sheaf of wheat. "Take off your skirt and your underpants, and lie back on the bed," said a man. He wore a blue jacket and a beige-and-red tie, and a white shirt, old but neatly pressed. His hands were bare. Bethie wondered if he'd washed them, and if he really was a doctor, like Jo's friend Shelley had said. "Legs up here," he said, indicating the chairs. He picked up a metal instrument, long and thin, and Bethie closed her eyes and wished she'd dropped acid, or smoked pot, or even had a gulp of vodka, anything to take herself out of her body, away from this moment.

"Hold still," said the man. "You'll feel a sting and a pinch." That, Bethie hoped, was the anesthesia. *She says it's a real doctor*, Jo had told Bethie, after Shelley had finally given her a name. *He'll take good care of you.* She felt the promised sting, felt the pinch, felt a faraway cramping sensation, like someone rummaging deep inside of her. "Please stop crying," she heard the man say. His voice was angry, but the woman just sounded bored when she told Bethie, "He needs you to hold still, hon."

An eternity crawled by. Bethie closed her eyes and tried not to hear or to feel. Finally, when it was over, the woman gave her a thick sanitary napkin and a bottle of pills, with the instruction to take one in the morning, one at night. If she developed a fever, she was to go to the hospital, and to tell them that she'd just started bleeding, that nothing had been done to her. "You were never here," the man said as the woman helped her to her feet. He looked her up and down, and Bethie called on her theater training. *Act like you're brave*, she told herself. She stood up straight and made herself meet his gaze, taking in his greasy hair and his small, squinting eyes. "Thank you," she said.

The man's face was expressionless. "Next time, try keeping your legs together," he said. Bethie gasped, but he'd already turned away to grab the edge of the blood-stippled sheet and pull it off the bed. The woman took Bethie by the elbow and led her back down the hall, back into the elevator, back to the lobby, where her sister was sitting on the love seat, holding Saul Bellow's *Herzog*, with her thumb marking her place. Jo got to her feet as soon as she saw Bethie, and hurried to take her sister's arm.

"Are you okay?" she asked, and Bethie nodded, leaning against her.

"I'm fine."

"I've got aspirin." She settled Bethie on the couch, got her a glass of water and a glass of Coke from an unfriendly bartender, and gave her sister aspirin to swallow. Bethie said that she was fine to walk, but Jo made her wait inside while she pulled the car right up to the door.

The whole way home, Bethie was quiet. She pressed her purse against her stomach and leaned her head against the window. The radio played, the Beatles singing "Ticket to Ride" and the Beach Boys singing "Help Me Rhonda" and Bob Dylan singing "Mr. Tambourine Man." As soon as Bethie heard his voice she reached down and clicked the radio off.

"Bethie?"

"I'm fine." Bethie's voice sounded like it was coming from a radio station whose signal they were losing. She felt that way, like she was fading in and out.

"Did you pick a major yet?" Jo's voice was cheerful. "Last time we talked, you were leaning toward English."

"I think I'm going to take some time off. At least a semester." Bethie didn't tell Jo that she wasn't going back to the U of M, not after this semester, not ever. She couldn't imagine walking the same paths she'd walked, strolling through the Diag, having a burger at the Union, sitting in the same classrooms in the Fishbowl where she'd sat as Devon Brady's girlfriend, a girl who was pretty and admired, a girl who hadn't been spoiled, raped, ruined.

"You're dropping out?"

In Bethie's head, the voice of the doctor—if that's what he had been—was loud as a shout. *Next time, try keeping your legs together.* She knew she'd be hearing that voice, those words, on an endless loop in her brain, maybe for the rest of her life.

"I can take some business classes at Wayne State. There's always a job for a girl who can type," she said, repeating the mantra of Mrs. Sloan, who'd taught Business Typing at Bellwood High. "You should go back on your trip," Bethie said.

Jo didn't answer.

"I'll pay you back," said Bethie. Just like that, a plan was forming. "I'll work at Hudson's this semester. Mom can get me a job. I'll earn enough money to give you back whatever it cost. You can go on your trip. You should go on your trip." The image of Jo's money in that awful woman's hands, the idea of Jo missing out on her chance to escape, the chance she'd wanted so much and had worked so hard for, tore at Bethie's heart. She could feel all her shame and sorrow gathering into a heavy knot at her center, an iron weight where her heart had once been.

"Don't worry about it," her sister said. "It turned out Shelley couldn't come after all. So, you know, it wasn't going to be what I'd thought." She was staring at the road, not meeting Bethie's eyes.

Bethie adjusted her grip on her purse, closing her eyes as her insides cramped. "Thank you," she said when Jo had pulled into the driveway. "Thank you for everything." She got out of the car, moving slowly, hunched over like Bubbe. It was the end of August, the air thick and humid and buzzing with the noises of lawn mowers and sprinklers and cicadas, those good, familiar summer sounds, beneath the wide, innocent Midwestern sky. Soon, school would begin. Kids would laugh and call in the early-morning light, mothers would pop their curlered heads out of front doors and yell at stragglers to hurry, or call kids back for homework and permission slips. Halloween would come, and costumed kids would knock on their door for candy. Then Thanksgiving, Chanukah, and Christmas. Snow would fall, snow would melt, grass would grow, be mowed, grow again. Mrs. Johnson across the street would bring over her squash and peppers and pumpkins, and Sarah would offer her roses and snapdragons and hydrangeas in return, and Bethie would always feel the way she was feeling, dirty and ashamed and unclean.

She went into the bedroom, pulled the shades to blot out the daylight, crawled into bed, and pulled her pillow over her head. She slept for an interval that could have been an hour, or eight hours, or a day. She woke, shuffled to the table, ate food she didn't taste, slept again. One morning, Sarah appeared in the doorway. "Bethie, you have to get up. You've got an interview in Housewares at eleven."

Bethie pulled herself out of bed, into the shower, and into the only dress she had that still fit, an old one of Jo's, green polyester with long sleeves. She couldn't fix her pasty complexion or the circles under her eyes, but she washed and set her hair, and put on lipstick and blush, and rode downtown with her mother, and promised the manager, one Mr. Breedlove, that she would work hard, and that she'd be grateful for the opportunity. When Mr. Breedlove smiled at her with yellowed teeth and said, "Happy to have you on the team," she felt a great weariness. *Time for another ride on the carousel*, she thought. Round and round again.

At lunch, Bethie ate cheeseburgers or fried chicken or the meatloaf special, while Terri and Marcy and Liz, the other girls on the floor, had salads or cottage cheese with pineapple. What was the point of watching her weight now? Once, she'd thought beauty was power, but now she could see that it was just trouble. A pretty face, a cute figure, a smile, all of those were weak spots. They were ways in, and Bethie wanted to be armored, defended, unbreakable. At home, she would poke and pick at her dinner, and when her mother and Jo were asleep, she'd pull ice cream out of the freezer, or a box of Bisquick from the pantry, add eggs and milk, and make pancakes, which she'd smear with margarine and douse with syrup and eat in big gobbling bites. The ice cream left her with headaches that made her feel like someone was driving an ice pick into her forehead, and the pancakes burned her tongue, and she knew that none of it was good for her, but she couldn't stop. Food filled her and soothed her, and even feeling stuffed to the point of sickness, even getting sick, was better than feeling the shame, remembering the abortionist's sneer as he told her to keep her legs together next time.

Another four bottles of Metrecal appeared in the pantry. Sarah began serving chef's salads for dinner and Jo, who'd gotten a job teaching history at a middle school in Detroit, would try to get Bethie to go on walks with her, or on bike rides, or to hit tennis balls at the park. One morning at Hudson's, Bethie's old high school friend Laura Ochs walked right past her, on her way to the semi-annual White Sale, and didn't even recognize her, and Bethie, her face burning with shame, locked herself in the break room for the twenty minutes she figured it would take Laura to buy discounted sheets or towels. She studied herself in the mirror. Her face was round and pale as the moon; her hair hung in lank strands against her cheeks. There were circles under her eyes, and her expression was exhausted, the look of a girl who knew that things were bad and that they would never get better.

My fault, she thought. *My fault for dropping acid, my fault for being stoned. My fault for being with Dev in the first place, and believing that he wanted to be with me.* That night, she joined Liz and Marcy for drinks at Tangier, a bar down the street from Hudson's, where the floors were sticky and the barstools' vinyl seats were torn, and the only nod to anything foreign or exotic was a single faded paper lantern that hung above the far corner of the bar. Bethie ordered a gin and tonic that came in a squat, smeared glass, and drank it as she listened to Liz chatter about her upcoming wedding, and Marcy complain about her husband.

"Uh-oh," Liz said, her voice low. "Gals, we've got

company." Bethie looked up to see Mr. Breedlove, the long strands of his sparse black hair combed across the brown-spotted dome of his skull.

"May I join you ladies?" he asked, squeezing his bulk into their booth. "Bartender, another round!" Another gin and tonic with an anemic wedge of lime arrived. Bethie sipped, breathing through her mouth to avoid Mr. Breedlove's stale coffee breath. He was telling them about his last trip to Miami, leaning so close that Bethie could see the blackheads that dotted his nose. "The gals there, whew, let me tell you," he said, and made a fanning gesture, to indicate their sexiness. "Talk about itsy-bitsy teeny-weeny bikinis!" Liz, who needed all the overtime he could pay her, giggled, and Marcy glanced at her watch, and Bethie excused herself to go to the ladies' room, where she spent another long spell studying her reflection. An idea was starting to come to her. Her face was still pale, but her eyes, instead of looking blank and exhausted, sparkled with mischief and bad intentions. She felt alive again, like a struck match fizzing into flame, the same way she'd felt slipping Uncle Mel's glass paperweight into her pocket, on the way out of his door. For the first time since she'd laid back on the hotel-room bed, Bethie could imagine possibilities. Doors were opening, and maybe she could walk through.

Mr. Breedlove was waiting for her, right by the telephone booth outside the restroom door. He crowded her into a corner, maneuvering his bulk to trap her against the wall, extending one arm and putting his hand by her head. "Want to grab a bite?" he was asking. Some part of Bethie's brain must have noticed one of his suit jacket pockets hanging lower than the other, and while her mouth was smiling and saying, "Of course, let me just freshen up," her hand was easing forward, dipping into his pocket, extracting the wallet and tucking it quickly into her purse.

Mr. Breedlove smiled at her, and gave her fanny a little pat as she disappeared back into the bathroom to powder her nose. Bethie locked herself into the stall and flipped open the worn black leather wallet, where she found sixty dollars and a Diners Club credit card, behind a plastic folder full of photographs of a woman who had to be Mrs. Breedlove, several small Breedloves, and a chocolate lab, by far the best-looking of the bunch.

She tucked forty dollars into her pocket, and put lipstick on her lips without meeting her own eyes in the mirror. On her way back to the table, she dropped the wallet on the floor and kicked it toward the bar, confident that one of the other patrons or Tangier's single weary waitress would discover it and give it back. "I'm so sorry," she said, picking up her jacket, which she'd draped over the back of her chair, "but I forgot I need to pick my mother up at the synagogue tonight. It's the anniversary of my father's death," she said, to sympathetic murmurs from Marcy and Liz, and a disappointed frown from Mr. Breedlove.

Outside, it was sleeting sideways, a wicked wind blowing off Lake St. Clair. Bethie shivered, pulling her coat closed, tugging her hat down over her ears. Forty dollars wasn't enough to pay Jo back, or even pay for a plane ticket back to London. But it would be enough for a one-way bus ticket to San Francisco. Dev had talked about California like the promised land, where it was always sunny, where it never snowed, where the Man wouldn't hassle you for burning a little rope. The next morning, she went to work as usual, but she left early, claiming debilitating cramps. She took the bus back home, and in the empty house, she found her sister's rucksack, gathering dust in the rear of their closet. Her blue-and-white dress still hung there, the pretty dress she'd brought on her visit to campus, the one she'd been wearing the night she'd met Dev. She left it hanging there, filling Jo's rucksack with the clothes that still fit her, underwear and bras and socks, a few books, a toothbrush and a comb, and walked out the door toward the bus station, and California, and whatever new life awaited her there.

Jo

"*L'chaim!*" roared three hundred wedding guests, as Denny Ziskin's heel came smashing down to shatter a napkin-wrapped glass.

Denny raised his arms in triumph, flushed with pleasure at the feat of breaking the glass, and of marrying Shelley Finkelbein. The crowd stomped and clapped and began to sing "Siman Tov U'Mazel Tov," and Denny grabbed Shelley's hand and danced her down the aisle, toward the reception hall doors, behind which, Jo knew, four thousand dollars' worth of delicacies awaited, including an ice sculpture of a Star of David, grapefruits topped with maraschino cherries to be served with a flaming brandy sauce, prime ribs of beef, twice-baked potatoes, a three-foot-long challah, and a reproduction of the Temple Mount constructed from chopped liver, olives, and carrot and celery sticks.

Jo was under the chuppah, wearing a bridesmaid's gown of apricot-colored satin with a white satin sash, white Mary Jane platform shoes, and a white headband in her curled and sprayed hair. She was holding Shelley's bouquet, in addition to her own. Shelley had given her a small, sad smile when she'd handed it over, before turning to the rabbi and taking Denny's hand. The bouquet was made of orchids and delphiniums and hydrangeas, all winter-white, and Jo had wanted to throw it, hard, preferably at Shelley's face, but she'd promised to behave herself. Her presence was the price that Shelley had exacted for giving Jo the name of a doctor who could help Bethie. "I'll tell you," Shelley had said when Jo had called, "but you have to be my bridesmaid."

Jo felt like she'd swallowed a stone. "No," she blurted. "Why?"

"Because I don't have any girl friends," Shelley had snapped, with a flash of her old spirit. "If you'll remember, I wasn't spending a lot of time senior year with my old sorority sisters."

Jo, who remembered exactly where Shelley had been spending her time, hadn't answered. "Denny was a Sammy. He's got eight fraternity brothers he wants to be his groomsmen. Plus his real brothers, plus his cousins," Shelley said. "I've got to come up with some more gals." Her voice had softened. "And I miss you."

I miss you, too, Jo wanted to say. *I miss you, I love you, I'll love you forever, I never stopped.* Instead, she swallowed and said in a stiff voice, "If that's what you want, I'll do it."

On the Thursday before the wedding, she'd left her house on Alhambra Street and driven to Shelley's house, where for three days straight she had been with Shelley, and if some evil demon had devised a perfect way to torture her, it could not have hurt worse. She'd accompanied Shelley to the beauty salon, where the girls in the wedding party had gotten manicures and had their hair styled. She'd sat next to Shelley at a bridal luncheon on Friday afternoon, and at Shabbat dinner with her family Friday night. They were always together, but never alone, and every minute, Shelley was right there, close enough to touch; lovely Shelley with her shining hair arranged in a graceful twist, amplified by lengths of fake hair the hairdresser had clipped in; Shelley with her pale skin and her sooty lashes, Shelley with her shining gray eyes and tobacco-scented breath, hugging Jo good night on Friday after dinner before dispatching her to the same blue guest room where Jo had slept during her visit the previous spring. That time, Shelley had snuck into Jo's bed at two in the morning. The night before the wedding, Jo lay awake, past midnight, past one o'clock, past two, waiting, hoping against hope that Shelley would come to her, that Shelley would say *I can't do this*, that Shelley would say *Let's run away together; let's just go.* Jo was ready. She'd filled her mother's car with gas before leaving home, she had her bag packed, the car keys on the bedside table. But Shelley never came.

On Friday afternoon, it had started to snow. Leo Finkelbein had stood by the living-room window, fretting about the guests who hadn't yet arrived and the foolishness of a January wedding in Michigan. By dinnertime, the snow turned into rain, which made Leo's mood darker. "Vurse," he had muttered. "It'll freeze!" The rain had frozen, but plows had cleared the roads and, on the morning of the wedding, the Finkelbein household arose to find the landscape transformed. Everything, from the ground to the trees to the rooftops, had been coated in a sparkling crust of ice. The whole world, especially the grounds of the West Bloomfield Hills Country Club, glittered as if sprinkled with diamond dust. The club sat on top of a hill above the golf course, with wide windows that offered a view of the sparkling slopes and the pine trees, with their boughs frosted with snow.

Jo told herself that she felt nothing as the happy couple came skipping down the aisle, Shelley, adorably gamine, and Dennis, gawky as a schoolboy in his heavy glasses and his white dinner jacket, with their guests clapping and stomping and singing, their hands clasped, arms raised triumphantly, as if they were boxers who'd just won a fight. She watched them and thought, *I want to die. I do not want to exist in a world where this has happened.*

"Jo? You okay?" That was Denny's sister Julie, pregnant beneath her apricot satin. Jo nodded, forced her lips into a smile, and followed Julie into the ballroom, where it looked like the inside of an ice castle. The tables were laid with pure white tablecloths, glittering crystal, and towering arrangements of white orchids and white ranunculus, creamy lily of the valley and white gardenias, peonies and hydrangeas, all mixed with gracefully curving branches that had been sprayed with white paint and glitter. Mr. Finkelbein, short and stout as a teapot in white tails, stood at the front of the room, in front of the nine-piece orchestra, patting his hands together, smiling in delight as Dennis and Shelley made their way onto the floor for their first dance to "Can't Help Falling in Love," which was followed by an exuberant hora. The guests formed circles, one inside of the other. Shelley and Denny were ushered to the center, seated on chairs, and hoisted to shoulder height by shouting, perspiring men, who hefted them up and down in time to the music. Dennis was beaming, and Shelley was smiling, clutching one end of a white handkerchief while Denny held the other end, looking as if this was all she'd ever wanted in her life.

Jo ignored the wedding guests who'd tried to grab her hand and draw her into the dance. She stood at the edge of the crowd, watching, her eyes on Shelley's face. When the hora was over, she went to the bar. She'd had two sloe gin fizzes, one more drink than she usually allowed herself, and was working her way through an unprecedented third, when a young man approached. He was tall and lanky, with thick, dark hair, a narrow, fox-like face, and an appealing smile. He pulled out the chair beside her, flipped it around so that he was straddling it, and took a seat, leaning forward, saying, "Hiya, babe."

"Babe?" Jo's voice was cool. The boy was undeterred as he nodded his head toward the dance floor, and a group of fellows in tuxedos who stood in a group by the stage.

"My buddies bet me that I couldn't make you smile."

Jo noticed his forearms: lean, sinewy, tanned golden-brown, so different from Shelley's pale skin. His dark hair was thick and shiny, and his eyebrows looked like emphatic dashes drawn above his eyes. She sighed and looked away, but the boy was undeterred. "So how about this?" he asked. He leaned close, lowering his voice to a conspiratorial whisper. "I'll tell you every joke I know, you'll laugh, my buddies will pay up, and we'll split the loot."

"You said smile."

"Beg pardon?"

Jo set her glass down on the white tablecloth. Speaking carefully, making sure not to slur, she said, "You told me your buddies bet that you couldn't make me smile. Not laugh. Smile."

"Well, look at that. You're smiling already."

"I am not." Jo waved her hand, like she was shooing a fly. "Go away."

"Before I've even introduced myself?" He shook his head in mock sorrow at his own bad manners and held out his hand. "David Braverman, at your service."

Jo's tongue was heavy. "I don't need any services."

"Then how about a dance?" He squeezed her hand, and Jo was so tired, tired of talking, tired of fighting, that she let Dave Braverman pull her to her feet. He was taller than she was, even in her heels, and it was not unpleasant to be held by someone taller, not unpleasant to feel small in his arms. Dave was an excellent dancer, guiding Jo through a smooth fox-trot as the band played "Runaround Sue."

She barely spoke, beyond telling him that she'd graduated in June, but Dave talked for both of them. Jo learned that Dave was a senior at the U of M, even though he was a year older than she was. He was the youngest of three, with an older brother and an older sister. His father owned an auto parts store; he had a semester left before he graduated, with an economics degree. She learned the name of Dave's fraternity, and that his dog was named Bingo, and that he drove a Mustang convertible. Had Jo heard the new Rolling Stones album yet? Jo shook her head. Had she seen *Dr. Zhivago*, which had premiered that Friday night? She shook her head again.

If Dave noticed her silences, or how she failed to do the girl's work of keeping the conversational ball aloft, he covered for her, maintaining an easy patter, answering the questions Jo would have asked him if Jo had been a normal girl, and not heartbroken and halfway to drunk.

"You okay?" Dave asked, as they danced close to the happy couple. Jo must have been staring. She hoped that, if Dave had noticed, he'd decide that she was pining for the groom and not the bride. She didn't say anything.

Dave danced her away, toward the other side of the ballroom, and his hands were gentle, his voice solicitous, almost as if they'd struck a bargain and he had agreed to take care of her, to see her safely through the wedding without leaving her side.

"My dad wants me to come work with him," he said, steering her gracefully past two elderly Finkelbein relatives, a man and a woman each the size of a small bear, clutching each other and shuffling in time to the music. "But it isn't what I want," he said, as Leo Finkelbein, pink-faced and light on his feet, cha-cha'd by, and stopped to greet her. "My Jo!" he said, holding her face in both of his hands and giving her smacking kisses on each cheek. "The beeyoudiful bridesmaid! Next time, your turn!"

"Hello, Mr. Finkelbein." He'd been busy for the past few days, a general preparing for a battle, taking telephone calls, dispatching Davis, his driver, to the airport to pick up visiting guests, reminding the caterer to make sure the champagne was chilled, sending his sons out to get their hair cut.

"Leo, Leo. To you, I'm Leo!" He looked at Jo, his expression turning serious. "I'm sorry you and my Shelley missed your trip."

"Oh," said Jo, feeling her cheeks heat up. "Well. Things happen." She waved her hand at the ballroom's glitter and grandeur. "Shelley had to get ready for all of this!"

Leo shook his head, his expression chagrined. "My Shelley. She could have anything. I wanted to give her the world."

Jo was aware that Dave was standing by her side, watching and hearing everything. "I guess this is what she wanted."

"Denny's a good boy," said Leo, brightening. He patted his small, plump hands together. "So a honeymoon, for now! And later, maybe, before the grandkids come . . ." He pronounced the word *grendkits*. "Your adventure. You and my Shelley, off to see the pyramids, and the whatdo-youcallems, the ashvams . . ."

"Ashrams." Jo's throat felt chokey.

Leo stood on his tiptoes, in his shiny formal shoes, kissed Jo's cheek again and danced off in search of his wife. Dave collected Jo's hands.

"Adventure, huh?"

"That's right," said Jo.

Dave spun her away from him and reeled her back, easing her into a showy dip before pulling her up-right. The band began to play "I'll Be There," and Dave snapped in time to the music. His hair had been tamed with some kind of pomade that smelled faintly sweet when Jo let her head rest on his shoulder. "So tell me the truth. Are you a magician?" he asked. One hand was on the small of her back. His touch felt calming, almost as if she were a baby he was trying to soothe to sleep.

"No. Why?"

"Because every time I look at you, everyone else dis-appears."

Jo rolled her eyes. "That's awful."

He shrugged, smiled, and said, "If I could rearrange the alphabet, I'd put U and I together."

"That's worse."

Dave made his face go comically sad before rubbing the lapel of his tuxedo between two fingers. "Know what this is?" Jo shook her head.

"Boyfriend material."

"Oh, God," Jo groaned, as she felt her lips quirk up-ward. Dave raised his hands in triumph.

"You smiled!"

Jo nodded wearily, as she remembered Denny and Shelley's triumphant arm-lift, how happy they'd looked as they'd come down the aisle, and the truth of the day came crashing back down on her. Shelley was gone forever; and Jo was alone, broke, and back in Detroit, in her mother's house, in her old bedroom. "Go on," she said, stepping away from him, intending to return to the table, and her drink. "Go collect your winnings."

"Oh, but this song's my favorite!" The band was playing "The Twist." Dave put his hands on his hips and began a sinuous wiggle, one that would have been sexy if his expression hadn't been so comical. "C'mon let's twist again, like we did last summer," the singer crooned from the bandstand, as the three colored girls in pastel dresses behind him ooh'ed and aah'ed the harmonies. Jo looked at Dave, who was graceful and handsome and light on his feet, and wondered, briefly, if he was like her; if he was no more interested in girls than she was in boys. There were, she had read, arrangements like that, marriages where a man and woman would keep up appearances, leading an outwardly normal life, even having children, while pursuing other interests on the side. Was Dave that way?

Jo decided that he wasn't. When he took her by the waist his hands were possessive, and when he looked at her, his gaze was frank and appreciative. It felt good. So did Shelley's shocked, frozen expression when Shelley noticed Jo dancing with Dave, and it gave Jo a mean little thrill. *Your fault*, Jo thought, settling her arm a little more securely around Dave's waist. *You could have chosen me.*

"Hey, you're good," Dave said, releasing his hold on her, dancing a few steps away, coming in close to twist, round and round and up and down. "We're good together. We should go out. Want to give me your number? We'll go into Detroit. We'll hit a jazz club, get a steak dinner."

"Maybe," Jo said. She let him lead her back to the table, let him hold out her chair, let him get her a drink from the bar: club soda, instead of the sloe gin fizz she'd been planning on. She listened as he dissected the band's song choices, remarking that they didn't seem to have learned anything after 1963, wondering if the Finkelbeins had expressly asked them to skip any kind of protest music. "Then again, I've got nothing against Phil Ochs, but it's not like you can really dance to his stuff." Dave had gossip about Shelley's sorority sisters, and Denny's fraternity brothers, and amusing observations about the wedding guests. "Look," he said, pointing at a little boy in short pants who was going from table to table, gulping down the dregs of abandoned cocktails, "it's me fifteen years ago!" He winked. "Or, you know, five weeks ago." He kept her glass full, and told her which of Shelley's aunts had caught her husband sleeping with the cleaning lady and which of Leo Finkelbein's associates were allegedly members of the Mafia. It turned out that Dave had grown up in Southfield with Shelley—"we're not quite as loaded as the Finkelbeins, but my dad's done okay."

"So why hasn't some lucky lady snatched you up?" Jo asked as the flambéed grapefruits were served. It could have been flirting, except her tone was conversational. She was not giving Dave shy glances from underneath her lashes, not dropping any coy reference to her own lonely nights.

"Haven't met Mrs. Right yet," Dave said easily, as he removed a segment of grapefruit and popped it into his mouth. "It so happens that I am in the market for a partner in crime." The band began to play again, "My Girl" by the Temptations, and Dave helped Jo to her feet. "I've got sunshine on a cloudy day," he sang, in a pleasant tenor. He moved in a circle around Jo as they danced, always keeping the beat, before spinning around and doing the steps backward, waggling his tuxedo-clad behind at her. "So what do you think?" he asked over his shoulder. "See anything you like?"

Jo found that she was smiling. "You're terrible," she said. But she couldn't deny that they fit well together. People were noticing them on the dance floor, two tall, graceful, dark-haired people, a male and female of a matched set. *It would be so easy*, Jo thought, as Dave pulled her against him and sang in her ear, as he walked her back to the table for the salad and the chopped liver and the prime ribs of beef, for the Viennese sweet table and the wedding cake. To not be the one making plans, to not be the one attempting to propel an unwilling partner forward, to not have to push through a hostile world. If she married a man, she could let him plan, let him push, let him maneuver; and the world they inhabited would welcome them. They would always have a place. It would be easy, and Jo was so tired. She closed her eyes, leaning into Dave, letting him take her weight. She felt half-drunk and weary, her heart aching and her limbs heavy with grief.

"You ready?" Dave asked her.

"Ready for what?"

Instead of answering, Dave put his hands on her shoulders and walked her toward the bandstand, into the crowd of girls that had gathered in front of Shelley. At the orchestra's flourish, Shelley raised her arms, and the girls around her squealed and she heard Dave cheer as Shelley Finkelbein Ziskin's bouquet arced through the air, over the heads of the eager bridesmaids, bounced off Jo's chest and fell into her reflexively outstretched hands.

Six weeks later, on Valentine's Day, Jo surrendered her virginity—such as it was—in a motel room in Detroit. Dave had taken her dancing at the Teutonia Club in Windsor, and he'd bought her the steak dinner that he'd promised at the London Chop House, a clubby, underground restaurant, all dark wood and leather booths with a telephone booth in the corner, caricatures of famous businessmen and politicians on the walls, and a pianist playing softly as they ate. By the time her spoon cracked the crust of the crème brulée he'd ordered for dessert, Jo's head felt like it was full of bubbles, and she was laughing at the story Dave was telling her, about a camping trip he'd taken with his fraternity brothers.

"So first, Roger says, 'There's no plumbing,' which I figure, okay, we'll use an outhouse. Then it turns out there's absolutely no plumbing, as in, no running water. And no electricity, and no insulation. But a beautiful view of the lake, Roger keeps saying. By the time we get there, it's pitch-black—so much for the view—and we've got one flashlight, and we're stumbling through the dark, when we hear gunshots. Turns out, it's bear season, which Roger also neglected to mention. So we start running . . ."

Jo smiled, half listening, enjoying the feeling of Dave holding her hand. All night, whenever they were walking, Dave had kept his hand on the small of her back, not pushing her, exactly, but supporting her, steering her, from her house to his car, from his car to the restaurant, where he tossed the keys to the valet, from the restaurant back into the car and from there to the lobby of a motel on Woodward Avenue, where they registered as Mr. and Mrs. Smith, and a humorless clerk slid a key with a heavy plastic tag across the counter. The room smelled of air freshener and, faintly, of mold. There was a dresser, a coin-operated black-and-white television set. The bedspread on the queen-sized bed had a synthetic sheen that reminded Jo of the love seat in the hotel lobby where she'd sat, waiting for Bethie. Jo wondered how many naked bodies had lain on that bed, how many heads had rested on the pillows. She felt Dave's lips on her throat and his hands on her zipper, her bra hooks, and, finally, her breasts, and she told herself to stop thinking. She pretended they were dancing, and she let Dave take the lead, undressing her, easing her down onto the bed, spreading her legs and working himself inside of her. It hurt, but not terribly. Jo stroked the smooth skin of Dave's back, his broad, muscled shoulders, the unfamiliar hair on his chest, and shut her eyes, trying to think of nothing or, at the very least, trying not to think of Shelley, until it was over and Dave lay beside her, propped up on one elbow, looking pleased with himself.

My first penis, Jo thought, considering the organ in question as it lay, limp and slick and sated, plastered to Dave's left thigh. There'd been a poem she'd read in college that began *My last duchess hangs upon the wall. My first penis sticks against Dave's thigh*, she thought, and she'd had to bite her lip to keep from laughing. Erect, it had been more impressive, a novel juxtaposition of hard and soft, with its glove of silky skin that slid against the stiff, veined flesh underneath. Dave had groaned when she'd touched it, had settled his hand over hers and showed her how to grip firmly at the base, how to tug the skin up toward the tip. He'd put on a condom, and she'd lost sight of her new friend for a while. When he'd withdrawn it was already beginning to wilt within its rubber sheath. Now it lay before her, dormant, soft, curved in the shape of a C.

"You were a virgin," Dave said, and Jo rolled over quickly, afraid that she'd been caught staring, and of what her expression might be telling him. He popped two cigarettes into his mouth, lit them both, and handed her one.

"Are you surprised?"

"A little, I guess. All the demonstrating you did, all those marches, I wouldn't have taken you for old-fashioned."

"Exactly what do you think happens at a picket?" Jo asked. The physical exertion and the champagne they'd had with dinner left her feeling relaxed and expansive, the way she'd felt after a tennis match, or after her basketball coach had made them run laps for miles. She also felt hopeful. She was, she recognized, not passionately attached to Dave the way she'd been to Shelley. She hadn't given him her heart, but that didn't mean she didn't have feelings for him. She enjoyed his company, and his touch, even if she could admit that the sex was just okay. If being with Shelley had been like a front-row seat at the best concert in the world, sleeping with Dave was like hearing music played on a phonograph in another room, the notes muffled by the walls. The pleasure was still there, it was just distant, more faint. But it wasn't as if she found him repulsive, or his touch unendurable. She liked Dave. She liked his wit, his loose-limbed grace, his easy conversation, his beaky nose and emphatic eyebrows, his thick, dark hair and his honey-colored skin. Most of all, she liked his confidence, the way he'd assumed responsibility for both of them; the way she'd been able to just nod and smile and go along with his plans: for dinner. For dancing. For finally having sex with a man. Maybe, even, for the rest of her life.

Dave put his arm around her shoulders, pulling her close. "I bet you had a million fellas sniffing around in Ann Arbor."

"Not a million," Jo said. *Not fellas, either*, she thought.

"So just one? Someone special?"

Against her will, Jo thought of Shelley. She remembered Shelley in her arms in the swimming pool, Shelley's long, dark hair fanned out in the water, the curve of her dark lashes against her pale, freckled cheek. The saucy tilt of Shelley's breasts, the bossy jut of her chin. Shelley in her wedding dress, her eyes hot and her expression wounded as she watched Jo dancing with Dave.

"Not really," she said, and prayed that her voice sounded casual, even as she wondered what rumors Dave might have heard. He was, she had learned, a consummate gossip, a man who prided himself on knowing everything there was to know about everyone who mattered. She was thinking of one night in particular, a Halloween party at the Tri-Delt house. Shelley had dressed like a cat, with furry triangular ears glued to a headband and the tip of her nose blackened with eyeliner. In the darkness of the basement, with the music so loud it was almost a physical thing around them, Jo had come within inches of easing Shelley into a corner and kissing her, right out in the open; kissing her until she purred, arching her back and pressing her breasts into Jo's chest. She'd contented herself with smoothing Shelley's hair under the guise of straightening her cat ears. In bed with Dave, Jo said very softly, "Not boys." Her body went stiff, prickling with goose bumps as Dave didn't answer, and she realized what she'd admitted. Then she thought, *Maybe he knew already*, and *It's better if he knows. If we're going to be together, I don't want to start out with lies.*

Dave was still for a minute. Finally, he brushed her cheek with his thumb. Jo let herself exhale. "Listen, lambie," he said. "Whatever happened before, whoever you were with, that doesn't matter now. We're a team. Get it?" He shifted so that he could look into her eyes, and Jo nodded, feeling grateful for this possibility, for the ease with which this door had swung open, revealing another world.

Naked, Dave left the bed, crossed the room, and picked his clothes up off the floor. He had a black velvet box in his jacket pocket. He pulled on his pants first, got down on one knee, and when he asked, "Will you?" Josette Kaufman told him, "I will."

There were benefits to marriage that Jo hadn't even considered when she'd let Dave slip the ring on her finger: for the first time in her life, Jo had managed to make her mother happy. Not just happy: Sarah was overjoyed, flagrantly, embarrassingly, ridiculously pleased. She'd burst into tears when Jo told her the news, throwing her arms around Jo's shoulders and hugging her for the first time Jo could remember in years. It was probably relief, Jo thought. Jo had been such a disappointment, for so long, and after everything that had happened with Bethie, up to and including her sister's abrupt departure for California, Sarah was probably understandably desperate for something to go right.

"We just want a small wedding," Jo told Sarah. She could tell that her mother was working herself into a frenzy, probably preparing to buy an entire trousseau with her Hudson's discount, borrow money to throw a catered dinner for two hundred, and hire a private detective to find Bethie, who'd sent them a single postcard from Albuquerque, New Mexico, and hadn't called home in six weeks. "Just a ceremony in the rabbi's study," Jo told her mother. A small, quick wedding would make her sister's absence less noticeable. They would spend a night in a hotel, load up Dave's car, and be on their way. Dave had a friend who'd moved out to the East Coast to work in a real-estate office in Boston, and had offered Dave an entry-level job.

"Boston?" Sarah asked. "But that's so far!"

Jo didn't answer, but she thought that, as far as she was concerned, the moon wouldn't have been far enough. She was ready to go, ready to leave her job teaching fractious seventh-graders, in a middle school where the hormones formed a palpable fog, ready to leave the little house, where the couch was still covered in plastic, where the bare patch in the kitchen-floor linoleum got wider and the lines in her mother's face got deeper every year, where every breath of air felt like it had already been in and out of her lungs a thousand times. Dave had spun her a story of life in New England as vivid as any of the fairy tales she'd told her sister: a cottage on top of a dune at the edge of an ocean, trips to New York City to see the shows, or to go dancing at the nightclubs. He knew how to sail—he'd picked it up one summer working as a waiter in Charlevoix, a resort town in Northern Michigan—and he ice-skated, and told Jo he'd teach her how to ski. "We're going to have adventures," he said, with his glinting smile, and Jo found herself unable to resist smiling back.

Jo submitted her teaching application to a dozen school districts within an hour's drive of Boston, and scheduled interviews at three of them. She packed up her bedroom, as well as the boxes from Ann Arbor that she'd never emptied, and loaded them into the back of Dave's Mustang. They made arrangements with the rabbi at Adath Israel for a Sunday-morning ceremony in his office, a luncheon for both families at the Caucus Club downtown, a night in the brand-new Pontchartrain Hotel.

The Saturday night before the wedding, Jo told Dave that she wanted to be alone.

"Old-fashioned," he said, and lifted her hand to his mouth for a kiss. "All right. Whatever my lambie wants." He'd moved out of the apartment in Ann Arbor that he'd shared with three other fellows and was "camping out," as he put it, with his older brother Danny.

Jo spent a long time in the bathroom that night, curling her hair, applying her eyeliner, flicking the pencil up at the corner, into a little wing, like Shelley had taught her; putting on lipstick, rubbing it off, and putting it on again. Her best outfit was the kilt and forest-green sweater she'd worn to Passover at Shelley's. She got dressed, left her bedroom without looking at her wedding dress, which hung on a hook on the back of the door, called "goodnight" to her mother, and stepped out into the first warm night of spring.

She couldn't remember where she'd heard the name of the bar. Gigi's, it was called, and it was just off Congress Street in downtown Detroit. Jo drove as if she were in a dream. She parked the car on the street, made sure it was locked, and walked down three steps, through an unmarked door, and into the bar, where the lights were dim and the air was a fog of cigarette smoke, hairspray, and perfume. A dozen stools were lined up around the bar, six wooden booths stood along the wall, and it smelled like every other bar that Jo had ever been in, a mixture of tobacco and the sour tang of beer. Peggy Lee was on the jukebox, singing "Fever," and a man behind the bar was drying glasses with a white towel. The man's hair was cut so short that it stood up in bristles, and the sleeves of his shirt rolled up to reveal an anchor tattoo. At the end of the bar, two women were talking, their heads so close together that their temples almost touched. Four women sat together at a table toward the back. Behind them, in the small cleared space, two other women slow-danced.

"What can I get you?" Jo blinked, and saw that the man behind the bar was actually a woman. At least, she sounded female, and what Jo had translated as stockiness was probably breasts, bound tight. The bartender looked at Jo, took in her startled expression, and smiled kindly. "First time?"

Jo nodded and asked for a Grasshopper.

"Are you meeting someone?" the bartender asked as she poured and shook and stirred. Jo sipped her sweet, frothy drink and shook her head. *This was a mistake*, she thought. What if she saw someone she knew? What if one of the girlfriends she said she'd been out with called the house and her mother, or Dave, learned that she'd been lying? What if she crashed the car on her way home, and . . .

Someone tapped her shoulder. Jo turned and saw a woman with bobbed dark-blond hair, a man's buttondown shirt, and a vest on top. Her body was shapely and solid, and her eyes were bright and interested.

"Do I know you?" Jo asked.

"Would you like to?" the woman replied. Jo could see the strong line of her jaw, but her voice was feminine, light and teasing.

"Yes," Jo said. It felt like she was watching someone in a movie, a college girl who'd left her parents' house the night before her wedding and had driven into the city, to a bar where women came to meet women, to dance with them, to kiss them in dark corners and maybe, later, to do more. "Yes, I think I would."

The woman put her hand on Jo's waist. She led Jo toward the back of the room and wrapped her arms around Jo's waist. They swayed together to Etta James. Jo could feel the other woman's breasts against her own, could feel the other woman's inhalations, and the warm puffs of her breath on her cheek, and it felt good, and right, not something she'd have to convince herself that she wanted, not something that could be, at best, dimly pleasant, but something as naturally and sweetly delightful as taking the first deep breath once your bra and girdle came off, or jumping into a cool lake on a hot day.

"Kiss me, honey," the woman said, as the jukebox played "How Long Has This Been Going On." The woman stood on her tiptoes, and Jo bent her head, and they were kissing, lips pressed together, tongues brushing lightly. Jo settled her hand against the back of the woman's neck, trying not to think of Shelley, and how Shelley had touched her in the same spot. The woman slid her hand around to cup Jo's cheek and pull her close and whisper that she had a place, a room, not far.

"Yes," Jo said. She sounded like she was gasping, like she was a drowning woman who'd managed to pull just enough air into her lungs to call for help, one last time. "Yes, please."

The woman pulled back, laughing a little. "Aren't we the eager beaver."

"That's an awful joke," Jo said sternly.

"I didn't mean it," the woman said. "I'm a terrible tease." She took Jo's arm and guided her up the stairs, out of the bar, down the street, through the doorway of a narrow redbrick row house. Her door on the third floor opened into a small, neat living room and a galley kitchen. Hanging over the stove's handle was a red-and-white dish towel, a twin of the one Sarah used in their kitchen at home.

"I'm Cal," said the woman, pouring Scotch into a glass. She took a sip and kissed Jo, letting Jo taste the burn of the liquor on her tongue. Cal had a narrow, foxy face, thin lips, and deep-set brown eyes.

I'm lonely, Jo thought. *I'm so lonely.*

Cal was looking at her closely, her head tilted to the side. "You okay?"

"I'm getting married," Jo blurted.

Cal's eyebrows lifted. "Oh?"

"Tomorrow," Jo confessed. She felt a great weight pressing down on her chest, and she struggled to breathe. "There was this girl . . . my girlfriend." *My Shelley.* "We were going to go away together, to travel, but she changed her mind." Jo couldn't bring herself to say the rest of it: how she'd spent a chunk of her money on her last-minute ticket home and the rest on Bethie's abortion, how she couldn't afford to go to New York like she'd planned, how she'd met her husband-to-be at her girlfriend's wedding, how she'd given up on her dreams. How she'd given up on herself.

Cal was looking down at her glass, turning it around in her hands. When she looked up, Jo could see faint lines around her eyes, twin grooves between her eyebrows. In the bar, she'd thought that they were around the same age, but now she could see that the other woman was at least in her thirties, maybe older than that. "This life,"

Cal said. "You have to give up a lot. I have family who won't see me. It's hard. It's not for everyone."

Tears were streaming down Jo's face, and her throat was too tight for her to say the words, *I thought I was one of the brave ones. I thought that this could be for me.*

"Come here, honey," Cal said. She took Jo's hands and led her to a neatly made bed covered in a stiff wool blanket. She unfastened Jo's shoes, unbuttoned her sweater, lay Jo on the bed, and curled around her, and held her as she cried, sobbing like her heart was breaking and thinking, *I can't marry Dave, not when there is this in the world; I can't settle for just that.*

She did. Of course she did. The next morning, feeling hollow and hot-eyed, her temples and the center of her forehead throbbing with a headache, she put on a Playtex girdle and her mother's wedding gifts: a newly purchased suit made of golden-tan tweed wool and a pair of brown leather pumps that pinched her toes. At ten o'clock in the morning she stood in front of the rabbi's desk in his office at Adath Israel with her mother beside her and her sister God only knew where and Dave's parents and brother and sister standing with him, and promised to love David Braverman in sickness and in health for as long as they both shall live. Neither of them had invited any friends. Even if Jo had wanted Shelley there, Shelley Finkelbein Ziskin was still on her honeymoon, taking a three-month tour of Europe with her husband. "I do," she said. "I will." Dave slipped a gold band on her finger, and Jo tried to feel the appropriate emotions—love, excitement, anticipation of the years to come. Instead, all she felt was a grayish exhaustion, and a thin relief. *That's over*, she thought. *And now I'll be safe.*

three

1974

Bethie

As her flight from Madrid touched down in Detroit, Bethie bet herself that it would take her mother less than five minutes to start yelling at her, and less than ten to start crying. She followed the shuffling crowd down the airplane's narrow aisle and through the Jetway. When she stepped out into the airport, with Jo's backpack on her back and her embroidered duffel bag slung over her shoulder, there was Sarah. She was dressed in a turquoise chenille suit and black pumps, with clip-on pearl earrings and a necklace that matched. Her hair looked freshly set and sprayed, and her face was as immobile as if someone had sprayed that, too. Bethie tucked her hair behind her ears. She hadn't cut it since she'd left Detroit, and it hung down to the small of her back in shiny waves; her best feature, by far. She wore a loose-fitting peasant-style blouse with embroidery at the yoke; bell-bottom jeans; her old red cowboy boots, the pair that Jo had given her, now scuffed and creased and run down at the heels; and a battered brown felt hat that she'd picked up . . . in San Francisco? Barcelona? She couldn't remember. It had belonged to some boy, some boy she'd met in some bar. She'd sat down beside him, plucked the hat off his head, put it on her own, and worn it all night. When she'd woken up in the morning, the boy was gone, and the hat was crushed under her pillow. She'd pulled it out, shaken it into shape, and worn it ever since.

Sarah pressed her lips together as she eyed Bethie. "Do you have any luggage?"

"Just this." Bethie tugged the embroidered bag more securely over her shoulder. The bag had come from a street vendor in Cherripond, and it currently contained the sum of her possessions: a few pairs of jeans, a few shirts, underwear, and a bra. Her wallet, a comb and a toothbrush, the Swiss army knife that she always kept close, and, most important, two ounces of extremely good hash that she planned on selling to her former Detroit acquaintances.

Sarah scrutinized the bag. Bethie could follow the path of her thoughts, so she wasn't surprised when her mother asked, "What are you wearing to the wedding?"

"I thought I'd pick something up at Hudson's."

Her mother gave a single nod. Her lips were so tightly pursed that they'd disappeared, leaving only a slit in their place. She walked stiffly along the fluorescent-lit corridor, with Bethie a few paces behind her. Bethie wondered if people who saw them even thought they were together, and if Sarah would want them to know. Probably not, she thought, as they pushed through the glass doors and out into the Michigan night.

Bethie breathed deeply, smelling dirt and grass and growing things, the essence of Midwestern spring. The essence of home. Barbara Simoneaux had always wanted to be a June bride, and she'd gotten her wish—her preferred month for the wedding, her chosen man for the groom, and Bethie, her best friend since forever, to stand with her under the chuppah.

Bethie followed her mother to the parking garage and got into the passenger's side of a car she didn't recognize, a Buick sedan in an ugly shade of beige. "New car?"

"New used car." Sarah's voice was neutral, but Bethie could remember when their father would come home, every few years, with the new model Chevrolet. They'd pile into the car for a slow ride around the neighborhood, breathing the new-car smell, listening to their father talk about the car's construction, what made the New Car better and safer than the Old Car. Sarah put her key into the ignition, gripped the wheel tightly in both hands, backed out of the parking space, and said, "You look like that Mama Cass." Her jaw trembled and her nostrils flared, as if she were preparing to say more, or cry. Bethie checked the dashboard clock and saw that she'd won her bet with two minutes to spare.

"Mama Cass is rich and famous," she said, trying to keep calm. She did her best to avoid mirrors, and her own reflection, but she knew how she looked, how far she'd come from the pretty, peppy, trim teenager with shiny hair and a big, bright smile. She tried not to let it bother her. A body was just a body, just a vessel for her soul, and she was under no obligation to keep her body looking any certain way, no more than she was obliged to do anything just because it was customary, or traditional, or expected of women in America. She didn't have to get married, she didn't have to have kids, and she didn't have to be thin.

"If you were rich and famous maybe you could get

away with it." Sarah's voice was waspish. "But you're not. Unless I'm missing something. Do you have a hit record in Nepal?"

"I haven't been in Nepal for a year and a half, Mom."

"You look like a slob."

"It's nice to see you, too." Bethie was determined not to let her mother draw her into a fight, and she'd taken a quaalude an hour before, just to make sure things stayed mellow.

"How long since you've been to a dentist?" Sarah asked.

Bethie shrugged.

"I made you an appointment with Dr. Levin for to-morrow morning at ten. And at Mister Jeffrey's at two o'clock."

"I don't want my hair cut."

"Just a trim, I told him."

"Mom, it's my hair. I can do what I want with it."

"What is Barbara going to think when she sees you looking like this?" Bethie didn't answer. She'd tried not to think about it. "It's disrespectful," Sarah continued. "It's the biggest day of her life, and you're going to show up looking like the Wreck of the Hesperus."

Bethie smiled. She'd heard her mother use that phrase a hundred times, but only about Jo.

"Did you even comb your hair?"

"Leave it alone, Mom."

Sarah made a huffing sound and gripped the wheel even more tightly. Bethie rolled down her window, feeling the softness of the misty air on her face. *The new world*, the settlers and the Pilgrims had called America when they'd first arrived, and Bethie felt, or imagined she could feel, how it was different from Europe, how there was a fresh, unspoiled quality to the air. Or maybe it was just a lack of history. In Italy and Spain, she'd walked on cobbled streets that had been there for centuries, slept in buildings that had stood when Columbus set sail for the Indies. In Michigan, things were considered old if they'd been around in 1924.

The house on Alhambra Street was unchanged. There was the beige carpet and the boxy television set in the living room, where the couch lived its life beneath a shroud of plastic; there was the worn linoleum and the red-and-yellow tablecloth in the kitchen, and the faded yellow curtains at the window above the sink; there were the twin beds, now covered in white chenille bedspreads, in the room she'd once shared with her sister, although the closet was now filled with Sarah's clothes.

"Are you hungry?"

Bethie shrugged. It was eleven o'clock at night in Detroit, which meant it was approaching breakfast time in Madrid. If she'd stayed, there would have been strong coffee and crusty rolls with butter and jam, wedges of hard cheese, and ribbony pink-and-white slices of *jamón*. Bethie hadn't wanted to eat the ham at first— the only pork she'd ever had back home had been at the Chinese restaurant, and the bacon that Barbara's mother made when they had sleepovers. Eventually, she'd gotten used to it.

In the kitchen, Sarah pulled two plates out of the cupboard. With short, angry jerks, she opened a can of tuna fish, dumped it into a bowl, and cut a lemon into wedges. Bethie sat at the table, watching, as her mother tore half a head of iceberg lettuce into chunks and spooned tuna on top.

"Delicious," Bethie said mildly. "Is there any bread?"

Sarah started to cry.

"What?" asked Bethie, even though she knew. Sarah

just shook her head, pulled a tissue out of the box near the sink, and wiped her eyes. Bethie ate her lemon-juice-doused tuna and every bit of lettuce on her plate. When she pulled a package of Gitanes out of her leather pocketbook, Sarah set out an ashtray, and when Bethie went to the bedroom, she could tell that her sheets had been freshly washed and ironed. *So there's that*, she thought, rolling onto her side as the mattress creaked a protest. She'd get tears, and criticism, and probably nothing more than dry tuna and lettuce to eat. Sarah would never say *I love you*. She would let Bethie know what a disappointment she'd become in a hundred different ways . . . but there would be fresh sheets and pillowcases on her bed. A dentist appointment, a hairdresser appointment, and a new dress, in a size larger than Sarah would ever wear, hanging in her closet in time for Barbara's wedding on Saturday morning.

It had been a long road back home. After she'd stolen her boss's money, she'd bought a bus ticket to San Francisco, but she'd ended up in New Mexico. There'd been a guy on the bus who'd gotten aboard in Chicago and had taken the seat next to Bethie. For the first hundred miles she'd ignored him, shaking her head in refusal when he offered his flask, pretending to sleep while he read a Raymond Chandler paperback. At some point she'd dozed off, and when she'd woken up, she'd been humming "Blowin' in the Wind." "Hey, you're good," the guy had said.

"I was at the Newport Folk Festival, where Dylan sang it live." The dream was returning to Bethie in snatches, the way she'd seen slivers of the glittering ocean when they'd driven into Rhode Island. "In Newport. With Joan Baez."

"Well, aren't you a lucky duck." The guy had introduced himself as Drew van Leer, and said he was meeting some friends in New Mexico, and that they were going to put together a band and that, as it happened, they were looking for a singer. He spent five hundred miles convincing her, and, finally, she got off the bus with him in Albuquerque, which was flat and beige, arid and empty. Bethie felt like she'd landed on the moon.

Drew lived in Santa Fe, and while they waited for the rest of the band, Bethie got a job cleaning up in a fancy Japanese-style bathhouse, and she slept in Drew's parents' guest room. Two weeks later, when the drummer still hadn't turned up, two of the other cleaning ladies proposed a camping trip in the high desert of Taos, Bethie packed Jo's backpack and tagged along . . . and instead of going back for her scheduled shift on Wednesday, she stayed in Taos, sharing a rented room with a girl she'd met on the camping trip, washing dishes and waiting tables in a diner that sold pupusas and chiles rellenos. Three weeks later when a group of college students came through en route to Vegas, Bethie joined them and moved along.

In Las Vegas Bethie sang sometimes, in bars, with bands, or in parks, with a hat out for money, and when she decided she'd had enough of the heat, she followed a guy to Portland, Oregon. She sang, and he played the violin, and they put together a set of Pete Seeger songs that they performed in Pioneer Courthouse Square. She cleaned houses and hotel rooms. She waited tables. She did the low-pay, low-status jobs that a young woman with no college degree and no fixed address could do. She did acid and mushrooms, smoked pot and hash, but only when she felt safe, usually when she was alone, and never so much that she'd have to worry about losing control. She earned money and sometimes, when she was feeling especially low or especially angry, she stole it.

There were always men around, some of them mean and some of them gullible, men who'd fall asleep after the fucking was done, with their wallets on the nightstand, or in the pocket of their pants, discarded on the floor.

After Portland was Seattle. After Seattle were Barcelona and Paris. Sometimes, in spite of her best efforts, Bethie would catch sight of her reflection, in a bus window or a bathroom, and see how big she'd gotten. Once, years ago, she'd overheard her mother discussing some cousin. *It's a* shande, *the way she's let herself go.* Bethie puzzled over that phrase, wondering how you could let your own body get away from you, like it was a car speeding away out of control. Now she understood. You stopped weighing yourself, stopped restricting yourself to small meals and salads, stopped picking French fries off your friend's plate and started ordering your own. *It doesn't matter*, she'd tell herself, but she never really felt free of the shadow of her larger body, the irrefutable evidence of her appetites and her weakness, unless she was high, or singing. With her eyes shut and the music all around her, she could give voice to her pain and her sorrow, and imagine herself as pure emotion, not a body at all.

From Paris she flew back to Los Angeles, and from there she finally made it to San Francisco, joining the throngs of hippies drawn there by the Mamas & the Papas song, finding that, instead of a sun-dipped, golden-hued paradise, the skies were gray, the streets choked with trash and glittering with abandoned needles. There were kids everywhere, panhandling, shooting up, nodding out, lining up at Glide Memorial Church on Ellis Street for free dinner at five o'clock every night. Eventually, Bethie saved enough money to fly to London, and from there she'd gone on to Amsterdam and points east. With Jo's rucksack on her back she traveled the route that Jo had meant to take, making her way through Tehran to Kandahar to Kabul to Peshawar and Lahore. It was easy for Bethie to attach herself to a group of college-age kids, to travel with them for a few days or even a week and then break off from the group, sometimes with some of their money or belongings in her pocket. Every once in a while, she would see a man, and the shade of his skin or the set of his shoulders would remind her of Harold Jefferson, and her heart would lift, but none of the men were ever Harold. Bethie would tell herself that it was better that way. If Harold could see her now, he'd be disgusted.

She trekked through Nepal with a bunch of kids from Sweden, and slept outdoors, in Chitwan Park, in a hammock, while monkeys swung and chattered overhead. She spent six months at a mandir in Puttaparthi, where Sai Baba himself had paused on his walk through a crowd of a thousand white-clad penitents to place his hand, in benediction, on her head. In Milan, she'd met a guy who'd said he was in the import-export business and hired Bethie to bring leather goods to New York City. Bethie loaded up her suitcase with wallets and handbags, wrote "gifts and clothing" on her declaration form, breezed through Customs, and followed the guy's instructions. She went to the shop whose address he'd given her and turned the handbags and wallets and belts over to the man behind the fingerprint-smeared glass counter, who gave her a hundred bucks in limp twenties that reminded her of the bills Uncle Mel had paid with. "Your cut," he said. Bethie flew back to Italy, where the guy was delighted to see her. "I figured you'd rip me off," he said. "Who, me?" Bethie said. For almost a year, she made the circuit every six weeks, bringing over larger and larger quantities of goods. When the guy trusted her completely and sent her with her largest shipment yet, instead of taking the wallets and purses and bags to the little shop, she'd brought them to a different place, where the sign said FINE LEATHER GOODS and the owner didn't ask questions.

When her mind was clear, which was not very often—pot and hash were cheap and plentiful in the circles in which she traveled, and did wonders when she couldn't turn off her brain, when she couldn't stop thinking about that night in Newport—she could understand herself. Every man she stole from or ripped off was standing in for Uncle Mel, for Devon Brady, and for the guys who'd raped her. *Make them pay*, she'd think, and pull her top down a little lower, and smile a sweet, tremulous smile at some man she met in a tea shop or at a bar or in a park or on a bus, and the man would smile back, happy and oblivious. Even if she was fat, there were men who wanted to fuck her; men she could rob. It was like a game, and Bethie almost always won.

Barbara Simoneaux had dated a fellow named Larry Krantz from the start of junior year through high school, and had followed him to Michigan State. Larry was a nice guy who'd grown up with three older sisters and, thanks to them, had a talent for styling girls' hair. At the end of their dates, Bethie remembered, he would roll Barbara's hair up in empty orange-juice containers after he'd kissed her good night. Everyone thought that they'd be together forever, but Barbara had met someone she liked better. Ronald Pearlman had been her brother Andy's freshman-year roommate at the U of M. Barbara had dumped Larry, who, she said, had taken the news with his usual Larry-like equanimity. She and Ronald had gotten engaged the previous June.

"Remember when Andy used to want us to play Mister Potato Head with him?" Bethie asked as Barbara fussed with her dark-brown bouffant in the mirror.

Barbara nodded. "And then he got older and he'd hide under my bed when you came over and try to look up your skirt."

"Really?" Bethie asked, and Barbara laughed.

"Don't be flattered. He did it to everyone." Barbara turned, peering at her teeth in the mirror, making sure she hadn't gotten any lipstick on her incisors. They were in the bride's room of Adath Israel, the synagogue on Rochester Avenue where Jo had gotten married and where, once upon a time, Bethie had wowed the crowd with her improvisational performance as Queen Esther. "So, what's it like to be back home?"

"Strange. Everything looks too big." It was true. The cars looked enormous, the yards looked as big as some of London's parks, and the roads were as wide as football fields.

"How's it going with your mother?" Barbara's voice was sympathetic. Of all of Bethie's friends, Barbara was the one who knew the most of the story. She knew how Bethie had gotten pregnant, and how she'd ended the pregnancy; she knew how Bethie had run, how she'd missed her sister's wedding, and how Sarah had let it be known, after Bethie's departure, that Bethie had broken her heart.

"Oh, just great. She's happy that I'm back." Bethie braced for questions. Barbara had to know that, even if Sarah was delighted to have her younger daughter home, she was surely less than delighted with Bethie's appearance, and her lack of a college degree, or a husband, or a job.

Instead of asking, Barbara turned back to the mirror, twisting left, then right.

"Am I a beautiful bride?"

"You are." Barbara had chosen a simple sheath-style wedding gown that fell just past her knees, with no train, a fingertip veil, and white pumps that she was planning on dyeing some other, more practical color after the wedding. Bethie was wearing the less awful of the two choices her mother had brought home from Hudson's, a shapeless dark-blue polyester tent that fell almost to her ankles, with a high neck, long, full sleeves, and a large paisley print that made it look like a slipcover. Mister Jeffrey had clucked at her hair, had trimmed off an inch—"just the dead ends, hon"—and had styled it to what were undoubtedly Sarah's specifications, so that it obscured as much of Bethie's round face as possible. Her jaw ached from having to remain open for so long, as her dentist tut-tutted over the state of her teeth. Her feet hurt because they were crammed into a pair of beige patent-leather shoes with a kitten heel. Bethie hadn't worn any kind of heels since she'd ditched Michigan, and when she walked she felt like a lurching freight train, graceless and huge.

Barbara's mother, in her pale-pink mother-of-the-bride dress, stuck her head inside the door. "You gals ready?" Bethie saw the way Mrs. Simoneaux's eyes shone when she looked at her daughter, and how her expression became sympathetic when she turned to look at Bethie. Anger surged inside her, and Bethie tried to push it aside. *I could have this, if I wanted it,* she told herself. She could starve herself thin again, cut her hair, find a guy, buy a little house in a neighborhood full of identical little houses. She could have everything Barbara had, everything her sister had, only she didn't want it, not any of it.

"All set." Barbara rolled on more lipstick, smacked her lips together, and smoothed her dress over her hips. Bethie stood up. She fluffed her friend's veil, picked up her bouquet, and followed Barbara out into the sanctuary.

After the wedding, there was a luncheon at the synagogue. After the luncheon, the guests saw Barbara and Ronald off in a shower of rice, and some of the younger ones went to Suzy Q's on Woodward Avenue for burgers. After the burgers, they adjourned to a bar, and by eleven o'clock the crowd had thinned to Bethie, Barbara's brother Andy, Andy's friend Art Lipkin, Art's girlfriend Suzanne Loeb, and Leonard Weiss, Jo's old high school boyfriend.

"She's married?" Len asked. Bethie had spent the last hour or so telling stories of her travels—the ashram in India, the beaches in Goa, the forests in Nepal, where you'd fall asleep to the sound of monkeys swinging overhead in the trees.

"Married," Bethie confirmed. She could still barely believe it herself. She'd met Dave Braverman once, in New York City. She had found her sister's husband handsome and charming. Maybe a little too handsome and a little too charming. She'd felt his eyes on her chest and her backside when Jo introduced her, when she took off her coat and sat down at their table. She'd been thinner then.

Leonard lowered his voice and brought his head close to Bethie's. "Hey, so, uh . . . you got any weed?"

Finally, Bethie thought. "Yes. From Amsterdam." "Amsterdam" was the magic word. Everyone assumed that, because pot was legal there, it was better than anything they could buy at home. "I've got Thai sticks and sinsemilla." Bethie kept her voice businesslike, remembering how Dev used to speak to his clients. "I can sell the pot by the lid, or it's a hundred dollars for an ounce."

"A hundred dollars?" Leonard's voice was incredulous.

"Worth it," Bethie said, and smiled into his eyes. "I promise."

She reached into her handbag. Leonard bounced from foot to foot.

"Tell you what," he said. "I've got some friends who want to buy. They can meet us out back. Can I call them?"

Bethie nodded. Leonard went outside to find a phone booth. Ten minutes later, he checked his watch and nodded at her. They went outside to where a beat-up Mustang was sitting with its engine on. There were two guys up front, another two in the back seat. Leonard opened the door, and Bethie was just getting ready to climb inside when a cop car pulled into the parking lot with its lights flashing and its sirens blaring.

"Shit!" Leonard yelped.

"Step out of the car," came a voice from the bullhorn on top of the police car. For a minute, Bethie thought about running . . . but where would she go?

She stepped out of the car, trying to remember what Dev had told her. *Don't raise your voice. Don't tell them anything except* I want a lawyer. *It's just another adventure*, she told herself as one of the officers escorted her away from Leonard's friend's car and into the back of his own.

•   •   •

Sarah didn't say a word as she led Bethie out of the police station on Livernois Avenue and into the car. Not a word as she steered onto Twelve Mile Road, not a word as she merged clumsily onto the freeway, slowing down, then speeding up abruptly, as cars honked and flashed their lights behind her. Bethie waited for tears, or shouting, but Sarah was silent.

"I'm sorry," Bethie ventured when they were on Rochester.

Her mother didn't answer.

"I'll pay you back for everything," Bethie said. She would need a lawyer, she thought. Maybe Dev would know one. If she could find him, and if he'd even take her call.

Sarah pulled into the driveway and turned off the car. Instead of getting out, she sat behind the wheel as the engine ticked. Bethie sat beside her, head bent, waiting.

"I thought you were the good one," Sarah finally said. "My good girl." Sarah shook her head. Her curls were still sprayed stiff from the wedding, but she had chewed off all her lipstick, except for a single splotch on the right side of her lower lip. "And now look at you. Jo's married, married to a good man, with a beautiful little girl and another one on the way. Jo has a home, Jo has a family, Jo's happy. And you!"

"I'm happy," Bethie said.

"You're selling drugs." Sarah's voice was a moan. "You came back here to sell drugs."

"I didn't come back here to sell drugs, I came for Barbara's wedding." The drugs had been a last-minute decision, after Bethie realized that she wouldn't be able to purchase a ticket to her next destination unless she scrambled up some cash, but she didn't want to tell her mother that.

"You're not too far away from turning thirty! And this is your life?"

"Maybe it so happens that I like my life this way."

Sarah groaned. She shoved her hands into her hair and started tugging, a gesture Bethie recognized from the night her father had died. "I wanted everything for you," she said through her tears. "Everything." She looked up, eyes streaming, mascara running in muddy tracks down her cheeks. "What did I do? Where did I go wrong?"

Bethie bit her lip.

"Your father died. That was hard, I know. It was hard for all of us. But I got through it, and Jo got through it, and you . . ." Sarah shook her head, as if her despair had reached a level beyond words.

Bethie kept her eyes straight ahead, looking at the front door. Sarah would stop talking eventually. Bethie would go inside. She'd take a long, hot shower. She'd sleep. Things would look better in the morning.

"And that boy, in college, and the rock show, and . . ." Sarah waved her hand in a shooing gesture that Bethie supposed was meant to represent her abortion. "I told myself, *She's been hurt. Give her time.* But it's been years." Sarah's voice cracked. "Is this what you want? Is this all you'll ever be?"

"I don't know, Ma." Bethie hadn't meant to say anything, but it felt as if some invisible force was wrenching the words out of her. Her throat was tight, and her eyes were full of tears, and all she wanted to do was to go backward, to unspool time, to erase her abortion, her rape, Uncle Mel's hands, her father's death. She wanted to go back to Adath Israel and be that pretty, smiling little girl onstage. She wanted to stand with her sister and her mother beside her, to feel her father's hands, warm and steady on her shoulders; to hear his voice saying, *My little girl was fantastic.* "I really don't know."

Sarah left her at the bus station. Instead of kissing her, she'd simply nodded when Bethie said "Goodbye." The *I-love-you* was the three folded twenty-dollar bills she'd pressed into Bethie's hand before Bethie climbed out of the car.

Bethie bought a ticket to New York City. When she got to Port Authority thirty-six hours later, she made her way out of the bus station and began walking downtown. An hour later, she'd found a club she'd remembered, a place where she'd once heard Phil Ochs. That night, a band called Television was making something that did not even sound like music. Bethie withstood an angry blast of cacophonous guitar as the lead singer—if you could even call him that—shrieked into the microphone. How had things changed so much? she wondered. How had so much time gone by, without her even noticing? How had she gotten so old? In the grotty ladies' room, she'd watched a woman with a mop of bleached-blond hair and tattered fishnet stockings loop a length of rubber tubing around her bicep while she held a loaded syringe clamped between her teeth, the way a pirate might have held a dagger. Pirates made her think of Dev, and thinking of Dev made her angry, and suddenly the woman was glaring at her.

"What the fuck are you staring at?" the woman had snarled, and Bethie had turned away, catching sight of her own face in the mirror. Her skin was pale, her lips were chapped, and her eyes looked haunted. She had forty-eight dollars in her pocket, and no idea where to go next.

She'd walked out of the club, ears ringing from the noise, and found a spot on a bench in Washington Square Park. There she'd sat, holding Jo's backpack against her chest, trying to decide what to do next, when she heard a woman's voice, almost in her ear.

"Hey, little sister."

Bethie's heart jumped. She remembered the twin bed in the house on Alhambra Street, with Jo in it beside her. *Princess Bethie was locked in the tippy-top of the tall stone tower, with thorns all the way down, and nothing but a stale loaf of bread and one tin cup of water.* She remembered the way she had leaned toward her sister, fingers hooked into the side of her mattress, her heart beating fast in the darkness, saying *Tell me how it ends.*

She turned. A woman was perched on the bench, her feet where Bethie was sitting and her bottom on top of the rail. She was tall, flat-chested, and slender, with wide-set eyes and dark-brown hair. Her long legs were encased in velvet jeans, and she wore a floppy, wide-brimmed black velvet hat.

"I'm Ronnie," said the woman, and pulled a joint out of her pocket. "Do you mind?"

Bethie shook her head.

"Were you here for the show?" Ronnie asked. She passed Bethie the joint. Bethie took a hit. Good stuff. Not as good as Dev's had been, but not bad.

"I heard Phil Ochs down here. A long, long time ago," Bethie said.

Ronnie was looking at Bethie, her eyes intent. Bethie turned away. When she turned back, Ronnie was still looking.

"Didn't anyone tell you that it's rude to stare?" Bethie snapped.

"Sorry," said Ronnie, sounding unapologetic. "I'm a healer. An intuitive." Bethie kept her face blank, but inside, she was rolling her eyes. She'd run the same game on unsuspecting guys all over the world. *Give me your hand*, she'd tell them, in the dim corner of some club or bar. *I can read palms.* She'd trace the lines on their palm with one fingertip, murmuring nonsense about their love or their health or their heart line while gazing deep into their eyes, sometimes while delicately removing their wallets from their pockets.

Ronnie must have missed Bethie's scorn, because she was still talking. "Sometimes I get senses about the people I meet. And I'm getting a very strong feeling that you're in a lot of pain. Psychic pain," she clarified, touching her spread palm to her heart.

Part of Bethie wanted to tell the woman to fuck off and go find another bench. Part of her wanted to ask for more details about this particular scam, because it had to be a scam, and figure out if she could use it herself. And part of her, a not-insignificant part, wanted to say, *Yes, I'm in pain. Can you make it stop hurting?*

"I feel like there's another presence around you. It's female," Ronnie continued. "Someone you've hurt."

Bethie rolled her eyes—for real this time. *Now she'll say it's my unborn baby, because she probably guessed I had an abortion. These days, who hasn't?*

"Not a baby," Ronnie said, surprising Bethie. She adjusted the brim of her hat, the better to consider Bethie with her wide eyes. "Someone young. Our age. A friend? Maybe a sister? There are regrets around the relationship. Things unsaid."

Bethie was so startled that she couldn't speak. *Jo*, she thought. *Except I tried to tell her . . .*

"Things unheard, maybe," Ronnie continued. Bethie felt her mouth start to fall open. She closed it fast. "Tell you what," said Ronnie. "Do you live around here?"

"I'm traveling," Bethie said, and left it at that.

"I live in Atlanta," Ronnie said. "Me and a bunch of other women. We're kind of a collective. A family of intention." She looked at Bethie expectantly, probably waiting for Bethie to ask what that meant, but Bethie just nodded. "We've got a great big garden." Ronnie extended the joint, its lit end glowing. "Grow a little bit of this, too." Bethie remembered the farm she'd visited back in college, somewhere near Pittsburgh. There'd been a little boy named Sky. He'd peed on Marjorie Bronfman's foot. The memory made Bethie smile, and Ronnie smiled with her and got to her feet. "I'm a trained hypnotist," she said. "We do this thing . . . well. I'll tell you about it on the way down. Sometimes it helps people get to the root of their pain and get better. You interested?" Bethie was all set to tell her no, that she was fine right here in New York City, but there was something about her, about the way she'd looked, or what she'd said about pain, or maybe just how she'd mentioned a garden, that made Bethie change her mind.

"Sure," she said, standing up and sliding her backpack's worn straps over her shoulders. "Why not."

Six nights later, Bethie found herself naked, curled on her side in the fetal position, tucked in a nest of pillows and blankets on the living-room floor of a farmhouse outside of Atlanta, in front of a tunnel of pink pillows arranged to represent a vaginal canal, preparing to reenact her own birth. Of all the ridiculous things she'd done in her life—and God knows, there had been plenty—this so-called rebirthing surely was the dumbest, she thought, as Ronnie began rubbing her shoulder and speaking in a low, soothing voice. There were women all around her with their hands on her arm, her hip, her leg, even her foot. Ronnie had begun by counting backward from ten, urging Bethie to take deep breaths, in and out, more and more slowly each time. She had taken Bethie through some of the childhood memories Bethie had described over the past few days: her first day of school, the day she'd learned to ride a bike and had steered straight into the Steins' mailbox because she'd been concentrating so hard on keeping her balance. She'd told Ronnie about her triumph as Queen Esther, the time she'd fallen while roller-skating and chipped her tooth, and the stories Jo used to tell her at night. She hadn't told Ronnie how she'd been molested by her uncle, or raped by a pack of strangers. She didn't mention her pregnancy, or her abortion, or how sometimes she felt as if she'd stolen her sister's life.

"You're in a crib, lying on your back," Ronnie intoned. "You can see the bars of the crib to the side, and a face. Someone's smiling at you! Can you tell us who it is?"

"My mom." Bethie took care to keep her own voice slow and dreamy. "She's got red lipstick."

"What's she saying?"

"For me to stop crying." Not that Bethie could actually remember what her mother might have said to her when she was a baby, but that sounded right. It was important that the women believe that she was buying this crap. Bethie's plan was to use the farm as kind of a way station, a place to rest, gather her strength, figure out her next move. The women of the community, Wren and Danielle and Kari, Jodi and Jill and a woman who called herself Rose of Sharon, welcomed Bethie when she tumbled out of Ronnie's car. That first night, they'd let her take a long soak in the farmhouse's single bathtub. "We make our own bath salts and soaps," Ronnie said, offering her a sampling, so Bethie had bathed like a queen, with orange-blossom-scented bath oil in the water, a lemon-and-sugar scrub for her heels and elbows, and a loofah to slough the travel dirt off her legs and her feet. They gave her a sleeping bag and a place on the braided rag rug on the living-room floor, and three vegetarian meals a day, and Ronnie told Bethie the story of how a nice Jewish girl from Massachusetts ended up in Atlanta. Ronnie had been in college, and she'd gotten a chance to be an exchange student at Spelman College, a historically black women's college. "My parents told me to concentrate on my studies, and not get in trouble. Which is why it took me a month, instead of ten minutes, to work up my nerve to go to the SNCC office." Bethie smiled politely, while inwardly she was thinking, *Ugh.* Another crusading do-gooder, like her sister. "They asked if I could type. That was how it started. I typed. I documented. I wrote down the stories of the voters getting registered, and I wrote press releases to get the word out when activists got arrested, and I wrote for the SNCC newspaper." Ronnie had gotten arrested herself. Laughing, she told Bethie the story of teaching her fellow SNCC members the hora while they were in jail. "Wow," Bethie managed. For years, Ronnie had been involved with the Movement. "Civil rights. Women's rights. Protesting the war in Vietnam." In between all of that, she'd gathered her "family of choice" around her, the women she called her sisters, fellow activists who stayed at this farmhouse, just outside the Atlanta city limits.

"You're welcome to stay. All we ask," said Ronnie, with

a twinkling smile, "is that you help out with the harvest." Bethie got the impression that donors sent money to support Ronnie and the others in their work. In addition, the women of Blue Hill Farm ran a pick-your-own business. Families would drive off the highway and pay for the privilege of gathering their own strawberries, raspberries, blackberries, blueberries, and even green beans and pole beans. They put their money in a coffee can (Bethie carefully noted where those cans were stored), and the women would direct them to the correct rows, to give them the cardboard containers, and to mind the supplies of the jams and jellies, soaps and scrubs and lotions that were also for sale.

At night, they'd cook vegetarian dinners (lots of salads, with fresh-picked or pickled vegetables; lots of tofu curries and black beans and lentils). They kept chickens in a coop out back, so there were always eggs, the yolks a yellow so deep they were almost orange. Bethie wasn't crazy about the fields—too hot, too buggy. But, after so long on the road, eating at restaurants, or fast food, or meals assembled from vending machines, she liked being back in a kitchen. She mastered the temperamental oven and made desserts, whipping egg whites into stiff peaks, creaming butter and sugar, sliding greased tins into the oven. She made pound cake, angel-food cake, marigold cake, and banana bread studded with walnuts, and the women praised her, saying that her treats were the most delicious things they'd ever tasted. "Like my mother's," said shy Danielle, who could barely look anyone in the eye. "Better than my mother's," said Jodi.

When dinner was over and the dessert plates had been cleared, the women would head outside. They would spread blankets on the grass and light joints and talk. *Consciousness-raising*, Ronnie called it, but to Bethie it was just a grown-up version of the once-upon-a-time stories Jo had told her when they were little girls. They would always start off with a question: *When was the first time you remember being treated differently because you were a girl? What would your mother's life have been like if she'd had the opportunities that we do? If you could tell men one thing about what it's like to be a woman, what would you say?* They'd go around in a circle, telling stories, and Bethie heard revelations that were as bad as, or worse than, anything she had to share. Danielle's father had beaten her bloody after he'd caught her in bed with a female high school classmate. Jodi's stepbrother had raped her from the time she was eight until the time she was fourteen and he left for college. Talia's mom had caught Talia rubbing herself on her stuffed bear's nose when she was four and had taken the toy away, doused it in the lighter fluid they kept by the barbecue, and burned it in front of the weeping, terrified little girl.

Bethie listened, volunteering nothing. She did not talk about her rape, although she was not the only woman in the house who'd been raped. She did not tell the story of her abortion, even though at least four other women had had abortions of their own, in settings that ranged from a pristine clinic in Puerto Rico to a blood-stained kitchen table in the Bronx. She listened and tried not to be moved by what she heard, or identify with the women she'd vowed to treat as targets. It wasn't easy. Not with Ronnie squeezing her hand and calling her Little Sister, or shy Danielle leaving a beribboned sachet of dried lavender on her sleeping bag, or when Jill said her butterscotch cake tasted like heaven.

Just get through this, Bethie told herself as she lay on her side on the living-room rug. They'd lit a fire in the fireplace to bring the room to body temperature, and the air was stifling. Talia had wanted to smear the pillow-fort vagina with Vaseline, so that it would really be authentic. Luckily, Danielle, who did most of the collective's laundry, had talked her out of it. Bethie could taste sweat on her lips and feel it trickling down her back, between her breasts.

"You're drifting further and further back in time now, back to a time before time even began for you," Ronnie said. "You are an embryonic life-form, growing and developing, but not yet aware of yourself as a person. Still, you exist. You exist here, in this warm, fluid, safe environment, completely aware of the sounds around you."

Someone pressed Play on the cassette player. The booming sound of a heartbeat filled the room. Bethie tried not to giggle.

"You are completely fulfilled, completely at ease. You have no wants, no hunger, no thirst, no desires. All of your needs are met. You are supported, safe, protected," Ronnie said.

Unexpectedly, Bethie felt tears spring to her eyes. *Supported, safe, protected.* When was the last time she'd felt that way?

"Nothing can hurt you. Nothing can harm you. But you feel constrained in this safe environment. You instinctively know that it is time to move on. I invite you to come forward in time," Ronnie said. "Come forward to the moment of your birth. Feel the beginning of this ending as you move toward the light, ready to be born."

Bethie found that she was shaking her head. She didn't want to move, she didn't want to leave. She didn't want to leave her safe haven and enter the bright, cold world.

"What do you feel?" Ronnie asked.

"Abandoned," Bethie whispered. The word was out of her mouth before she knew she was going to say it, and she was back in Uncle Mel's Cadillac, cruising past the house on Alhambra Street, where there was no car in her driveway. She was back in Newport, with a strange boy's hand on her wrist, and the boy was saying *Lie down, lie down, stop crying, shut up, you know you want it.*

"Breathe," said Ronnie. Bethie was trembling. She could feel hands on her shoulders, her hip, her thigh. The sound of her heart beating thundered through the room. Her hair was damp with sweat and her face was wet with tears. They were driving past the house, and the windows were dark, dark, dark. No one was home. No one was coming to save her.

"Bethie." Ronnie's voice was kind but stern. "It's time." Strong hands pulled her toward the pink pillow tunnel. Bethie struggled, shaking her head, squeezing her eyes shut. "Bethie," said Ronnie. "Be here with us, now. Whatever it is that's holding you back, that's keeping you stuck, it's in the past. It has no power to hurt you. Come be with your sisters. Come be free."

Bethie opened her mouth, intending to say *This is hot buttered bullshit.* Part of her could hear how ridiculous this all sounded; could see, clearly, the silliness of a naked adult woman preparing to wriggle through a pillow fort. But instead of a sarcastic denunciation, what came out of her mouth was a sob, and when she tried to speak she found that all she could do was cry harder. Snot ran out of her nose, and tears streamed down her face and rolled off her chin onto the rug. She wept, crying harder and harder, making horrible, guttural noises, as the women touched her bare arms and shoulders and stroked her hair and Danielle leaned down to hug her, whispering, "Shh, shh." Bethie was crying for everything that had been done to her, and everything she'd done; for every hurt she'd suffered and every hurt she'd inflicted. For her mother, who'd spent her life wrapped in a shrunken, tight-fitting shroud of unhappiness, her life limited by a handful of options and her lack of a man by her side. For her sister, whose wings she had clipped. For herself, for the bright-eyed, pretty thirteen-year-old she'd been, the girl who had dreamed of the spotlight, the girl who'd found the courage to say *Uncle Mel's hugging me too long*, a girl whose mother hadn't wanted, or been able, to hear what she meant and whose big sister hadn't been there to save her. The young woman who'd been raped, knocked up, and made to feel like nothing. Bethie wrapped her arms around her knees, rocking and crying, her damp hair sticking to her wet cheeks, and when Ronnie said, "It's time," she pushed herself forward, wriggling along the floor through the tight press of the pillows, before she came sprawling out onto the floor, into the light, laughing and crying as the women patted her and clapped their approval, telling her how well she'd done, how proud they were. *Maybe I'll stay*, Bethie decided. *Maybe I'll get stronger here. Maybe I'll figure out how to stop hurting. Maybe I can figure out how to fix what can be fixed.*

Jo

Jo patted her hair, freshly cut into a new, short feathered style, and checked her makeup, her single swipe of lipstick now augmented by mascara and foundation and rouge that she applied every morning. She could see the beginning of wrinkles, the way the skin of her eyelids seemed to have thinned and loosened. More than that, sometimes she'd catch a glimpse of her reflection and think she was seeing her mother. *Getting old*, she thought, without much regret, as her sister came loping out of the station, shading her eyes as she looked first left, then right. Bethie was resplendent in a pale-brown suede jacket with fringe that hung to her knees, a coat that would be completely useless in the New England blizzard that was on its way. She had no scarf or mittens, at least none that Jo could see. She wore tight-fitting jeans that flared out at her ankles, a fuchsia-colored sweater with a capaciously cowled neckline, dangly earrings, twists of wire strung with beads and bits of feather, and a pair of brown leather platform pumps with wooden heels. Her hair, parted in the center, hung in waves to the center of her back, and her weight seemed to have settled somewhere between the extremes of the lemon-water and Metrecal diets of her teenage years and the year or two after the abortion, where Jo was convinced that Bethie was piling on pounds deliberately, as a way of keeping men away. Her sister looked strong, at ease, comfortable in her own skin, even though their mother, Jo knew, was still riding her to lose twenty pounds. Jo blipped the station wagon's horn twice. Bethie waved exuberantly and trotted toward the car, tossing her luggage, a tote bag made of brightly colored squares of exotic-looking cloth, into the back seat and hopping into the front.

"The family sedan!" she said, mock-admiring the station wagon. "Jo, I guess you're in it for the long haul."

Jo felt her chest get tight and her cheeks get hot and reminded herself not to take Bethie's bait. "Of course I'm in it for the long haul. I have two kids."

"A woman at Blue Hill Farm has two kids," Bethie said. "Her husband was a total MCP. Male chauvinist pig," Bethie said, before Jo could ask what an MCP was. "The kind of guy who comes home from the office and expects to be waited on hand and foot, as if she hadn't been working all day long. She left him and took the kids with her, and she says she's happier than she's ever been in her life."

"Lucky for me I'm not married to an MCP," said Jo, mentally praying that Dave would not come home that night and immediately ask her for a beer, as was his habit. "Oh, here it comes," said Jo, turning on the windshield wipers as the first flakes of snow hit the glass, grateful to change the subject. She tuned the radio to WTIC, which gave the weather every ten minutes. "I hope you packed enough to stay a while. They're saying it's going to be the biggest blizzard of the decade."

"I love winter," Bethie said in the dreamy, blissed-out voice that figured in Dave's most savage imitations of Jo's sister. The name of the commune where Bethie lived was Blue Hill Farm. Dave called it Space Mountain, and referred to Bethie's fellow residents as the Space Cadets. At a red light, Jo looked at her sister, who was staring out the window, examining the pedestrians as if she were observing life on Mars. Maybe that was how it felt, Jo told herself. The Connecticut suburbs were probably as strange to her as Jo might have found outer space.

When they were growing up, if you'd asked Jo what her sister would do with her life, Jo would have replied, without hesitation, that Bethie, sweet, pretty Bethie, apple of her mother's eye, would get married and have children. But Bethie had gone her own way. In 1969, while Jo and Dave were sitting, rapt, in front of their television set, watching Buzz Aldrin and Neil Armstrong take those first buoyant, bouncing steps on the moon, Bethie had been in San Francisco, shacked up with some guy named Francis. *Nisht'unzer*, Sarah had sniffed, which meant *not one of us*.

When Jo found out that she was pregnant, Bethie was on Max Yasgur's farm in the Catskills, wearing a string of beads, a handful of mud, and nothing else. In 1972, when Jo and Dave were debating walnut versus cherrywood dinette sets and just beginning to hear about the Watergate break-in, Bethie was in Italy, and when Missy arrived, Bethie was in Atlanta, on the commune. She'd shown up for Missy's third birthday party with a crown of dried flowers in her hair and matching crowns for the birthday girl and her big sister, wearing a floor-length white dress of sheer, dotted Swiss cotton that turned out to be completely see-through in the sunshine. "I see London, I see France, I see your sister doesn't wear underpants," Dave had murmured, and Jo had pinched his elbow as her mother, tight-lipped, had escorted Bethie back inside.

"What do you hear from Mom?" Bethie asked Jo, with her face still turned toward the window.

"Same as usual. Work is hard, her feet hurt, and the car is still making that funny noise. She thinks the mechanics are ripping her off because she's a woman."

"She's probably right," Bethie said. Jo stifled a sigh. She was not unaware of the injustices in the world in general, or the unfairness of how women were treated specifically, but her sister saw sexism, discrimination, and chauvinism everywhere, and was not shy about pointing it out. *My eyes have been opened*, she liked to say. At the synagogue Jo and Dave had joined, or back home at Adath Israel in Detroit, whenever the rabbi would refer, in the responsive readings, to God as "he," Bethie would say "she," loudly enough for people in nearby rows to hear it. The last time they'd visited Blue Hill Farm, Jo made Kim leave her beloved Barbie at home, knowing that bringing it would mean a lecture on the unattainable physical ideal the doll promoted, not to mention the dangers of the phthalates emitted by plastic toys. Whenever Sarah referred to her granddaughters' beauty, Bethie would immediately chime in with praise of their intelligence or their humor . . . and the first time Bethie had visited in Avondale, she'd kept quiet the whole way to Jo's house before asking, "Are there any African American people here? Anywhere? Anyone who isn't white?" Dave had made some joke about how they were all on the other side of the tracks, and Bethie had smirked, and Jo hadn't known what to say, because the truth was,

Avondale, where she and Dave had decided to put down roots, was probably the least integrated place she'd ever lived. It was embarrassing. As a teenager, she'd wanted to change the world. She'd picketed and marched and sent what money she could to the voter-registration drives down South. Now, she lived on a street where not only was everyone white, no one else was Jewish, and the only African American and Hispanic kids her daughters went to school with were the ones bussed in from Hartford, as part of a program called ABC, for A Better Chance.

Jo tried to enjoy her time with her sister, to tell herself that she was glad that Bethie's dangerous, wandering years were over, and that at least one of them had grown up to do the essential work of changing the world. She made an effort not to roll her eyes at the tofu casseroles and the gender-neutral wooden toys and the unceasing earnestness of the women who lived on the Farm. Most of all, she tried to forgive Bethie for her role in Jo's own choices, for getting high and getting pregnant, for needing Jo's help and her money, for being, however inadvertently, a part of the reason Jo was currently the married mother of two. She tried not to think about the way Bethie hadn't shown up for her wedding, and had hounded her after she'd finally met Dave, insisting that he wasn't what Jo wanted, that Jo was not being true to herself. *Like I had that luxury*, Jo would think bitterly. *As if any woman like me does.*

Jo knew that it wasn't Bethie's fault. Her sister hadn't ruined Jo's trip, or her life, on purpose. Jo knew that. But what she knew and how she felt were different. Jo had never gotten to see the world, and maybe if attending Shelley's wedding hadn't broken her heart she would have found the strength to resist Dave's charms and move to New York City and try to make it as a writer, like she'd planned, instead of opting for the easy way out. It wasn't Bethie's fault, the way things had worked out, but Bethie was not entirely without blame, either, and it was hard to watch her sister flit around in love beads, with long hair, while Jo wore a girdle and a wedding ring; hard to watch Bethie move through the world exactly how she wanted, with no obligations or responsibilities, while Jo was stuck warming bottles and rinsing dirty diapers, emptying the refrigerator and filling it again.

There was also the way Bethie behaved around her, the sly questions, the way she would show up, smelling of sandalwood, dripping with sincerity, giving Jo a look that said *I know who you really are, and I know this isn't what you really want.* Jo loved her daughters: solemn, smart Kim, who'd been named for Jo's father, and graceful, fearless Missy. She loved the piping sound of their voices; she loved the feel of their plump thighs and arms and the sweet, musty way they smelled, like graham crackers and sun-warmed laundry. When the girls were toddlers she'd put a child's seat over the rear fender of her three-speed Schwinn, and she'd ridden them all around town. She'd taken them sledding on the golf course near their house, and had taught them how to ski and skate, and had coached their soccer teams when they were six and seven and eight, and gone to their classrooms every December to tell the kids about Chanukah (almost all of them were Christian and unaware that there were winter holidays other than Christmas or, in some cases, that there were religions other than their own). She couldn't imagine not being a mother. She was happy and fulfilled. Or, at least, she was happy enough, fulfilled enough. And yet, every time she tried to explain herself to Bethie, her sister just looked at her with a smug twist of her lips, a sarcastic tilt of her eyebrows, an expression that said, *You might say you're happy, but I know better.*

Jo kept her sister at arm's length. She saw her at Thanksgiving and Passover, when Sarah summoned them back to Michigan, and invited Bethie to Connecticut for the holidays Sarah ceded to her. She went to Atlanta for a week once every summer, and turned down any of Bethie's additional requests for visits as often as she could without being obviously unfriendly or rude. She'd given in this time because her daughters had begged to see their aunt Bethie, and because the neighborhood ladies had formed a consciousness-raising group, of which Jo was a member. They talked about feminism, and marriage, and men; they read (or at least skimmed) books by Betty Friedan and Kate Millett. Jo had mentioned the group to Bethie, and for years, Bethie had been offering to come and lead it, to tell Jo's friends about some of the issues the women on her commune discussed. "And you and I need to talk some things through," she'd said, words that made Jo feel deeply uneasy, and had kept her making excuses. What if Bethie decided, in the name of feminism or authenticity or just making trouble, that she needed to let Dave know about Shelley? *Dave already knows,* she wanted to tell her sister. *Dave knows I was with women, so you wouldn't be spilling the beans.* It was true, but still, a whispered confession after she and Dave had first made love was different from a blaring announcement, more than a decade into a marriage in which Dave's big dreams had, so far, been thwarted, in which they'd become increasingly distant, and where the frequency of their sexual activities had gone from every few days to every few weeks, with dry spells that had stretched for months after each girl's birth.

In the car, her good suburban station wagon, Jo turned

up the volume as the radio announcer began reading the list of school districts that had sent the kids home early. "I can't wait to see the girls!" Bethie said.

"They can't wait to see you," Jo said. Kim and Missy, ages eight and six, adored their glamorous aunt Bethie, who wore stacks of beaded bracelets on her wrists, delicate, dangling earrings, and ropes of jade and amber around her neck, and who smelled like the essential oils that she dabbed under her ears. *My aunt Bethie lives on the moon*, Kim had written in a first-grade essay on My Favorite Person. Jo had sent it to Bethie, the text accompanied by a drawing where Bethie looked like a black crayoned crane, with swirls of brown hair and enormous red lips. Jo had explained to Kim, who seemed to have been born without a discernible sense of humor, that her aunt lived on a commune, not the moon. "What is a commune?" Kim had asked, and Jo explained, "It's where lots of different people live together, like a family."

Kim's nose had crinkled in consideration before she'd nodded and gone back to the dining room to work on a book report that wouldn't be due for three weeks.

"So how are you?" Bethie asked. The fringed purse that sat in her lap was the same suede as her jacket, and her sweater must have been made of angora, fluffs of which were already drifting through the station wagon's interior and sticking to the fabric ceiling.

Here we go, thought Jo. "I'm fine," she said. She, too, wore jeans, their bottoms flared far less extravagantly than Bethie's, and a cotton turtleneck, green with thin blue stripes. She'd always kept her hair short, but after the babies were born she'd had her hairdresser chop it all off and style it into kind of an Audrey Hepburn–Mia Farrow crop. She had modest gold studs in her ears— with babies, you couldn't risk the kind of grabbable earrings her sister preferred, and Jo had never liked ostentatious jewelry, but next to Bethie she felt as drab as a pigeon, a housewife with a capital *H*.

"Fine?" asked Bethie. "That's it?"

"Fine is fine," Jo said, forcing her lips into a smile. "Fine's okay. I'm jogging." For her birthday, Dave had gotten her Jim Fixx's *The Complete Book of Running* and a pair of Nike shoes that she suspected he'd plucked off the shelf of one of the RePlay Sports stores. She'd laced up the shoes and barely made it to the end of the driveway before she realized how completely out of shape she'd become. She'd only gotten halfway around the block before doubling over with cramps, but she'd persisted, remembering how good it felt when her heart was pumping and her legs were burning and she was pushing herself farther than she thought she could go. She'd always played tennis whenever she could; she and Dave had skied and ice-skated, but she'd missed sports, and competition, and the way regular exercise made her feel. Now that the girls were in school, Jo ran five miles at a time, five days a week, racing in the Monday-night fun runs that the town held all through the summer and winning her age division more often than not. She played tennis on the town courts, and swam at the JCC in the wintertime, sharing lanes with her fellow housewives who were trying to shed the baby weight or keep the scale from creeping up as they left their twenties and thirties behind.

"Are you working?" Bethie asked.

"Just getting my toes wet." Just as she had in every town they'd lived in for longer than a few months, Jo had put her name down on the substitute teacher list in Avondale and three neighboring towns. Most weeks she only worked a day or two, and some weeks, not at all. But it was something. She also wrote the occasional piece for the local weekly paper, the *Avondale Almanac*, which she knew most people read only for the classified ads. So far, she'd interviewed a ten-year-old who'd been cast as one of the orphans in the Broadway production of *Annie*, a married couple who bred prizewinning Cavalier King Charles Spaniels, and the town's oldest resident, a surprisingly sharp 102-year-old who'd been eager for an audience to hear his thoughts on Jimmy Carter, whom he called "the peanut farmer."

"And what do you do all day?" her sister asked.

Jo made herself smile. "I cook. I clean. I read. I write."

"So you're basically Betty Crocker," Bethie said.

"Betty Crocker with a library card." Jo kept her voice mild. It was the reading—that, and the exercise—that let her believe that her life was different from her own mother's, and she needed to believe that there were differences. Sometimes, she would look up and see days that were essentially the same as her mother's days had been, endless rounds of cooking and cleaning and laundry, of checking homework and combing hair and ferrying her daughters to soccer practice and Hebrew school. The only difference was that her mother lived in an integrated neighborhood, with African American neighbors and colleagues, if not friends, and Sarah was minutes away from a big city, with its museums and orchestras, even if she chose not to go.

So Jo read. The Bravermans subscribed to the *Hartford Courant* and the *New York Times*, which came in the morning, and the *Farmington Valley Times*, which arrived in the afternoon, along with *Time* and *Life* and *Newsweek*, the *New Yorker* and the *Atlantic* and *National Geographic* and *Bon Appétit*, from which Jo attempted the occasional ambitious recipe (usually that would result in the girls turning up their noses, Dave cheerfully urging them to try some of whatever Mommy had worked so hard to prepare, and the three of them sneaking off to McDonald's while Jo scraped the leftovers into the sink). She kept up with current events, national and international, and most weeks she finished at least one book, sometimes two. Biographies, mostly, books about wars and dead presidents; everything but novels. She'd lost her taste for fiction. Sometimes she thought it was because spending even a few hours in an imaginary world would make it too tempting for her to consider other versions of her own story, other ways it could have unfolded. A different ending, a true happily-ever-after.

"Look at that snow," said Bethie, sounding as satisfied as if the weather had been arranged just for her. Jo drove them down the mountain, over a bridge that crossed the Farmington River, and along the two blocks that made up Avondale's downtown. There was a Catholic church, a glowering heap of brownstone, and down the street, a white clapboard Episcopalian church, with a cross thrust up into the wintry sky. The town's library, housed in a two-story Georgian mansion with the children's section in the basement, where Jo sometimes felt like she'd spent half of her life, listening to story hour and picking out books. Down the street there was a small supermarket, a liquor store, a five-and-dime called Fielder's, and the elementary school. Jo turned again, into a neighborhood of residential neat ranch-style houses and small Colonials with perfectly square lawns and even a picket fence or two. Jo saw Bethie taking it in and waited for some crack about "Little Boxes," or suburban conformity, but instead her sister kept quiet, her eyes on the sky and the snow.

"Dave's at work, in Hartford. I hope he makes it home." The truth was, Jo was hoping Dave wouldn't make it home. She liked the idea of hunkering down with her daughters and her sister, the four of them weathering the storm together. Already, she'd stacked three days' worth of logs by the fireplace and had a week's worth of old newspapers ready for the girls to roll and fold into knots. There were flashlights with fresh batteries and candles in every room, and she'd braved a trip to the supermarket that morning, where her fellow housewives were acting practically feral, grabbing for the last loaf of bread or gallon of milk or four-pack of toilet paper, as if everyone's snow-day plans included French toast and diarrhea.

"Wait until you see the girls," Jo said. "Kim writes poetry and short stories, with illustrations and everything. She's in a combined second- and third-grade class, but she's already done all the third-grade work, so they're talking about skipping her right to fourth grade. And Missy . . ."

Before she could continue listing Kim's academic achievements or describing Missy's prowess as a striker on the six-and-under Wildcats soccer team, Bethie interrupted. "And Dave? How's he doing? How are things?" There was the tiniest pause before Bethie spoke the word "things," and Jo heard what her sister was really asking. *How's heterosexuality treating you? Still living a lie?* Speaking rapidly, Jo said, "Dave's terrific. I mean, it took him a while to figure out what he was going to do. To figure out what would work. As you know. But I think this is it." Jo was sure that Bethie must have noticed by now her husband's inability to stay in one place, at one job, for very long. It hadn't taken Jo long to realize that her husband was all about the fast buck, the quick, easy score. *Behind every great fortune, there is a crime,* Dave liked to say. So far, Dave hadn't committed any crimes—at least, not that Jo knew about. But she worried, and she was careful not to ask too many questions when her husband pulled the suitcases from wherever Jo had stashed them and announced yet another new venture in another new town.

"He's selling used sports equipment?" Bethie's voice wasn't quite mocking, but it was definitely skeptical. Again, Jo told herself not to take the bait.

"I know. When he told me, I was thinking, 'How's that going to support us?' But people in New England are sports-crazy. Soccer, hockey, lacrosse, tennis. Everyone ice-skates, everyone skis. And everyone's kids outgrow their cleats and their boots and their poles and their bindings." Dave had started with one RePlay Sports store, which he'd opened with two of the fellows who'd gone in on his sports bar in Hartford and the guy who'd invested in the apple orchard in Vermont. She had to give Dave credit, Jo thought. He never held a job for long, but he never made long-lasting enemies, either, or left his former partners feeling so burned that they wouldn't give him seed money for his next project. The bar had only lasted for nine months and had left Dave with a permanent aversion to the food-service industry and, she suspected, some significant debt. But the sporting-goods store had been a success, and now there were three RePlays in Connecticut. After years of what Dave, in his arch and mocking manner, called "a certain degree of financial uncertainty," and one desperate six-month period that had culminated with the two of them piling their belongings into the trunk of Dave's car and leaving their apartment in Baltimore in the middle of the night, probably two steps ahead of the landlord, they had enough money to swing the mortgage on the three-bedroom ranch house on Apple Blossom Court. Already, Dave was eyeing the houses in the new developments on the west side of town, the center-hall Colonials where every house had four bedrooms, central air-conditioning, and an in-ground pool in the back.

"Dave's terrific," Jo said. "And I'm great."

Bethie sat for a long, terrifying beat of silence. "I saw you once," she finally said. "On campus. You and Shelley Finkelbein." Jo felt like she could barely breathe. Thinking about Shelley always made her feel like she was choking. "You were walking near the Union, and you were holding hands . . ."

"We were not," Jo blurted. She hadn't meant to say anything at all, but she had to correct Bethie's misperception. She and Shelley had been careful. They would have never held hands in public.

"You were," Bethie said. "Just for a minute, and you did it like a joke. You'd grabbed each other's hands, and you were swinging your arms, and I saw the way you looked at her, and the way she looked at you."

Jo winced. She couldn't remember the precise moment Bethie was describing, but she remembered very well the way she'd looked at Shelley, way back when. Quietly, Jo said, "It was a long time ago."

"How is Shelley?" Bethie asked, as if Jo hadn't spoken.

Without answering, Jo clicked on her turn signal and was careful not to stomp on the gas. Bethie waited until Jo was forced to answer.

"Shelley's divorced," she said.

"Oh?" Bethie's eyebrows rose toward her forehead. Even when her face looked surprised, her tone was still tranquil. "What happened?"

Jo shrugged. "You know what Mom always says. 'You never know what's going on in someone else's marriage.' I just hope she's keeping her married name. Ziskin was a definite upgrade."

Bethie smiled. Jo felt the bands around her chest unclench. Then they were on Apple Blossom Court, just behind the school bus, which opened its doors and disgorged Kim and Missy. The girls came sprinting down the street, lunchboxes banging against their legs, running through the snow and calling their aunt's name.

Bethie gave the girls their presents—candy necklaces, a pair of fancy barrettes, homemade fizzing balls, which would scent the bathwater with lavender, and got herself settled in Missy's bedroom. By then, the snow was falling so thickly that looking out the window was like peering into a cloud. Jo lit a fire and instructed the girls to fill the bathtub with water and make sure the flashlights were loaded with the fresh batteries and the candles were at hand. "We're like pioneers!" Bethie said. "Let's pretend we're in a covered wagon!" The girls had happily joined in the game, and Jo had gotten dinner started, seasoning the chicken and trimming the green beans.

Just before five, Dave called. "I think I'm going to be here for the night," he said. "They've closed Route 44, so even if I trusted the car to make it over the mountain, I'd be stuck."

"Just be safe," said Jo.

"Don't worry about me, lambie. I'm going to test out a few of the new sleeping bags we got in. I'll bunk down in the office. I've got a generator and a space heater and one of those propane cookstoves."

Jo suspected that Dave wouldn't be in his office for long. If she knew her husband, he would gather as many of his fellow stranded businessmen as he could and make an expedition to whatever bar was open before bunk-

ing down, or at least he'd find some whiskey to amplify
the space heater's warmth. Dave was a sociable man. He
loved a party, especially an impromptu, accidental one.
The best nights they'd had were in the summer, where
neighbors would all drift toward the night's designated
backyard. The kids would splash in the plastic wading
pool or run through the sprinklers, or use garbage bags
to construct a water slide. The wives would drink Tab
or white wine spritzers; the husbands would drink beer
and talk sports. Eventually, a few of the men would be
dispatched to raid refrigerators for hamburgers and hot
dogs and buns for the kids, and someone would go to
Fitzgerald's Market to buy steaks for the grown-ups.
Dave would preside over the grill; the wives, half-drunk
on wine and sunshine, would find paper plates and plastic cups and light citronella candles to keep the bugs
away. The kids would gorge themselves and watch *Three's
Company* or *The Jeffersons*, eventually falling asleep on
the family-room floor, and the grown-ups would sit out
in lawn chairs in the humid darkness, drinking, laughing, telling jokes. Dave always had a few new ones, and
he'd trot them out while he stood behind the grill in his
KISS THE COOK apron, with his tongs in his hand, holding
court. "So the son's standing at his father's sickbed, saying, 'Dad, squeeze my finger if you can hear me.' With
his last bit of strength, the dying father squeezes, and
then the son says, 'Dad, that wasn't my finger.'"

Sometimes, when dinner was over, Jo would put
on a cassette—Stevie Wonder or Linda Ronstadt or
Fleetwood Mac—and turn up the volume on the por-
table player. Dave would dance with the women: tense,
tightly wound Judy Pressman, with her hair in a neat,
low ponytail, or Stephanie Zelcheck, the youngest of
the wives, who'd just had a baby and was barely twenty-

five. Sometimes Jo would dance, but mostly she'd watch, sitting off to the side with one of her daughters or someone else's baby on her lap.

"Are you and my ladies all right?" Dave asked on the phone.

"We're good." Dave was still a handsome man, but he'd put on about ten pounds, and his hair was thinning. Jo noticed the way he would run his fingers through it when they passed reflective surfaces in bright sunlight, or in the morning, in the bathroom, after he'd gotten out of the shower. Dave was vain, a little lazy, perhaps not entirely honest, and money passed through his hands like water, gone almost as soon as he'd gotten it. But he loved their daughters, and he could still make her laugh or amuse her with a cutting observation. And, every once in a while, Dave made her remember her own father, with a sweet, piercing kind of pain. After their second baby had been a girl, Jo had braced herself for Dave's disappointment, but he'd been delighted instead. *Girls are less trouble*, he'd said, lifting the baby from Jo's arms and kissing her cheeks. *And I can already tell that this one's going to be a beauty, like her mom.*

"How about you?" her husband asked. "What's the plan? Did your sister make it in?"

"She's right here." Bethie was sitting on the couch, Kim and Missy on either side, an afghan pulled up over her legs, a small, inscrutable smile on her face. *She's like a tourist*, Jo thought. *A visitor in the Land of Suburbia.* "And we've got a fire going, and plenty of sandwich stuff if the power goes out. Don't worry about us. We'll be fine."

A few minutes later, the lights flickered, then went out. The girls clapped and cheered, while Jo put another log on the fire and tried to think of what she had in her freezer that might go bad. She was weighing the

risks of letting the girls roast hot dogs in the fireplace
when someone knocked at the door. She opened it to
find Nonie Scotto, her two-doors-down neighbor. In
her bulky winter coat, with her frosted blond hair tucked
under her hood, Nonie looked like a plump bear cub.
Snowflakes were melting on her eyelashes, and her face
was flushed pink from the cold. She had baby Amy
against her chest, tucked in a kind of zippered, fur-lined
sack, and she was pulling Drew, dressed in boots and a
snowsuit, on a wooden sled behind her.

"Whew!" she said, stomping her snowy feet on the
welcome mat. "It is really comin' down!" Nonie had
grown up in a small town in Alabama—"I'm a southern
belle," she'd say—and she had the honeyed accent and
disdain for winter to prove it. "Is your power out, too?"

Jo looked down the street, trying to see if anyone
had their lights on. "I think the whole neighborhood
lost power."

"We're having a snow day dinner party," Nonie said.
"At Judy's house. Come on, get your coat."

"A dinner party?"

"All the men are stuck over the mountain. We've got
to fend for ourselves. Just bring the kids and whatever
you've got to eat. You know, Judy's got that big fireplace,
so at least we'll all be warm."

"My sister's visiting. Okay if she comes?"

"No," said Nonie. "Leave her here all by herself in the
dark. Of course she can come! You should all pack your
jammies. It might turn into a slumber party. The radio
said it's not supposed to stop until tomorrow night, and
Lord knows when they'll get the power back on."

Jo told her daughters to find pajamas and tooth-
brushes, and to gather the flashlights, the candles, and
the extra batteries, and to pile some firewood on their

own sled. She took a flashlight into the dim kitchen and loaded a brown paper shopping bag with sandwich fixings, plus a jar of olives, a tub of sour cream and a packet of onion-soup mix, a box of Triscuits, a bag of pretzels, a kosher salami, and two bottles of white wine. "Excellent!" Nonie said, nodding her approval as Jo got Kim into her boots and coat and helped Missy zip up her snowsuit, and plopped both delighted girls onto the sled behind Drew. "Hold on tight!" she called. Together, the ladies ferried the kids and the food and the firewood across the street, bending their heads as thick, wet flakes tumbled down from the sky. In the Pressman house, a roaring fire was burning in the fieldstone-lined fireplace that opened onto the kitchen from one side and the family room from the other. Candles had been lit and set on every available surface, filling the house with a chancy, flickering light. Jo got her girls out of their snowsuits, while Bethie perched on the bricked ledge of the fieldstone fireplace and sat watching the women with a Cheshire-cat smile.

"Go on, just put the food on the dining-room table and lay your wet stuff in front of the fire." Judy had met them at the door, dressed in tweed slacks, a black wool sweater, and a pair of wool socks, her hair pulled back in a ponytail, her expression animated as she called out instructions. There were at least twenty people in the house, four or five women with their children, and there were dozens of pairs of boots drying by the fire. Big kids raced through the living room, playing hide-and-seek; little kids toddled after them or clung to their mothers' legs or hid under Judy's new coffee table, pearlescent Lucite in the shape of a shallow upside-down *U*. Faces glowed in the firelight, and the house was deliciously warm, smelling of woodsmoke and garlic and ginger, anise and cinnamon and cloves. Even without the power to force warm air up from the furnace through the house, it felt warm.

"Hot mulled wine," Judy said, zipping past with two mugs in each hand. "That's what you're smelling. It's in the kitchen, next to the stove. Help yourself."

"Don't have to ask me twice!" Nonie said, her voice merry. Jo stripped off her winter coat, unlaced her boots, and sent the girls on their way. "Judy, Steph, this is my sister, Bethie," Jo said, and Judy Pressman and Stephanie Zelcheck both said how pleased they were to meet her, and how much they were looking forward to their group.

Bethie had helped Jo carry her shopping bag into the dining room, where a feast had been laid out: wedges of cheese and bowls of crackers and nuts and olives, salami and pepperoni, cut-up cucumbers and peppers and carrots, bowls of chips and dips, and a steaming pot of some kind of chicken stew, bubbling over tins of Sterno. Beside the chicken was another pot of rice and a dish of mango chutney, and farther down the table, Jo saw cookies and brownies and a raspberry pie.

"Everyone just brought whatever they had," Nonie said, handing Jo and Bethie mugs of mulled wine. "I was making chicken in my slow cooker when the power died, but I'm pretty sure it's cooked through." She smiled at Jo. "Almost positive."

"It smells delicious."

Nonie waved her hand. "Easiest thing in the world."

"Well, it's certainly better than what we had planned." Jo found a bowl and a spoon in the kitchen, dumped her soup mix into the sour cream, stirred, and set the finished product next to an open bag of potato chips.

"Oh my goodness, is that onion dip? My downfall," said Arlene Dubin. Arlene, or Poor Arlene, as the other ladies called her, had two sets of Irish twins, a boy and a girl who were five and six, then two boys, three and four, and a husband who worked as an airline pilot and was almost never home. Arlene swiped a chip through the dip, popping it into her mouth and sighing with pleasure. Nonie finished her mulled wine and reached for the bottle of Chardonnay that stood open on the sideboard. "Here's to snow days," she said, filling her cup just as Judy came hurrying over.

"Everyone okay?"

"Perfect," said Jo.

"How'd you have all of this stuff lying around?" Nonie asked, nodding at the plastic glasses, the paper plates, the Sterno underneath the chafing dishes.

"Residents," said Judy. "Every year we host a bash for all the new surgical residents, and the caterers leave extras." She reached over to straighten a stack of crackers and readjust a cucumber circle that had dared to get out of line. Jo sipped her wine, which was rich and warm and tasted of cinnamon and cloves, and prayed her sister wouldn't give one of her soliloquies about non-recyclable plastic. "Drink up," said Judy. "We've got hot buttered rum for dessert."

Jo was careful to sip her wine slowly. She rarely allowed herself more than a single drink at parties. Alcohol made her joints feel loose and her body warm and elastic. It also lowered her inhibitions, and the last thing she wanted was to do anything that would arouse the suspicions of the ladies of Apple Blossom Court.

She was always so careful. Careful not to evince any special interest when the Stonewall riots were in the news. Careful not to pay too much attention to news reports about the Gay Pride marches and parades that were popping up in New York and Philadelphia. Careful not to look too long at any of the neighborhood ladies, even though those ladies were permitted to cheerfully leer at their friends' husbands, as well as Mark Shanley, the muscular teenager with long, frosted-blond hair who mowed all of their lawns, shirtless, in a pair of cut-off jean shorts. She was careful not to ever be the first to volunteer to rub sunscreen on someone's back in case anyone should notice and think that her eyes, or even worse, her hands, were lingering longer than normal. She did not let herself daydream about a night like this one, with snow falling outside and a fire burning inside and Nonie Scotto a little tipsy and no husbands in sight.

The kids were fed. The babies were diapered and put to bed in Judy's playpen. The dirty plates were cleared away. More bottles of wine were opened. At nine o'clock, when Kim started to rub her eyes, Jo led her up to Jenny Pressman's bedroom and made her a nest of pillows and blankets on the floor. Missy had insisted that she wasn't tired, but twenty minutes after her sister went up, she fell and banged her head on the arm of the couch and came running to Jo in tears. Bethie pulled her into her arms to kiss it better. "See, isn't the fire pretty?" she asked. Missy nodded, with her head resting against Bethie's shoulder. Jo reached out her arms. Bethie handed Missy over, and Jo stroked her daughter's wavy hair, feeling the exact moment when Missy's body went boneless with sleep. She gave her daughter a kiss on her temple, feeling emotion sweeping through her, almost bringing tears to her eyes. Had she ever loved anyone as much as she loved her girls? "What's that big brain thinking about?" she would ask Kim at breakfast, or at night, tucking her in, and Kim would say, "the person who figured out that horses could pull things," or "why do we cook food?" or "do you think dolphins can talk to each other?" And

Missy was so fearless, flinging herself at the soccer ball or the hockey puck, barreling toward the goal, with her legs and arms permanently scraped and bruised. Jo felt so connected to them. When they cried, she cried; when Missy scored the winning goal or Kim won first prize in her age group in the statewide science fair, she was as proud as she'd ever been of any of her own accomplishments. She loved them. More than that, she admired them. They would be better than she was: stronger and smarter, more capable and less afraid, and if the world displeased them, they would change it, cracking it open, reshaping it, instead of bending themselves to its demands.

Jo got Missy upstairs and settled next to her sister. Judy had a battery-powered radio in the kitchen, and every half-hour she'd turn it on to hear the latest news, then come out and stand in front of the fireplace to make reports. The governor had declared a state of emergency and ordered nonessential personnel to stay off the roads. The snow was still falling fast, with forecasters predicting that the region might get up to thirty-six inches. "I think we're all in for the night," Judy said.

When the last of the children had fallen asleep, the women arranged blankets and pillows for themselves on the floor. They spoke ruefully about the diets they were breaking as they nibbled brownies and drank Judy's hot buttered rum. Every once in a while one of them would say something about checking on her house. "I should at least get the walkway shoveled," Stephanie said. "What if Mike comes back?"

"He c'n shovel it himself, can't he?" Nonie asked. Her accent had become more pronounced with each glass of wine she'd enjoyed. She lay on her side on the carpet, basking like a cat in the fire's warmth.

"I guess," Stephanie said. Lucas, her baby, was asleep in her arms, scooched up with his head in the crook of her shoulder and his bottom sticking out. He gave a little whistle each time he exhaled, and Stephanie jiggled him up and down in a movement that Jo remembered becoming as natural as breathing when her own girls were small.

"Everything was delicious," said Jo, when Judy finally sat down. "Delicious," Bethie agreed, in her breathy murmur, as she drifted in from the kitchen. Her sister never walked anywhere these days, Jo thought. Bethie drifted, like she was a puff of milkweed, blown this way and that by the wind.

"Good food, plenty of drinks, the kids are all sleeping, and no 'Honey, can you grab me a beer?'" Judy said.

"Amen, sister," Nonie drawled.

"Think of it," Judy said, stifling a hiccup against the back of her hand. "All those men out there, realizing, on the same night, for the first time in their adult lives, that they can survive without someone fetching their beer and asking how their days went."

Jo turned her face away. For the early years of their marriage, she had asked Dave about his day, and she'd genuinely cared about his answers. In those early years, she and Dave got along; they enjoyed each other's company, and the sex, while not fantastic, was at least okay. After he'd decreed that they were financially secure enough to start trying for babies (the babies that he had assumed, without asking, that Jo wanted), she'd thrown away her diaphragm. She'd worried that she would hate being pregnant, that she would despise such a physical, visible confirmation of heterosexuality, and the way that her body would literally become a vessel, in service to the baby she was growing. To her surprise, she'd loved it. She'd barely had a moment's sickness, and had woken up every day feeling well rested, with her heart pumping strongly, ready to bound out of bed and accomplish everything on her list. Her hair grew thick and glossy, the whites of her eyes were so white that they shone, her skin glowed, just like the books said it would, and she never experienced swollen feet or heartburn or any of the common aches and pains she'd heard other pregnant women complain about. During her first pregnancy, with Kim, at some point every day she'd find a few minutes to lie in bed, one hand on her belly, feeling the skin thinning and stretching drum-tight, noticing her breasts getting bigger and the dark line of pigmentation stretching from her belly button to her pubic bone. She felt like a piece of fruit, something exotic and delicious, ripening in the sun, and she'd been certain, both times, that the baby would be a girl.

All through her pregnancies, Dave had been loving, thoughtful, and solicitous. At night, Jo would lie on the couch, legs stretched out in her husband's lap, and Dave would rub her feet with castor oil—something Bethie had recommended, after some homeopathic healer she'd met had told her about it—and he'd tell her about his day, doing his expert imitations of his manager at the bar where he was working, a fat, wheezing, balding man named George Toddhunter, or the bartender, Gus, a preening college boy with feathered hair and John Lennon glasses who'd published a pair of book reviews in the local newspaper and fancied himself a novelist. They'd watch the news, sitting close on the plaid couch that they'd bought secondhand, and eventually, Jo would heave herself erect—"I am heaving myself erect," she'd announce—and fix dinner, which would typically be one of her mother's recipes, or some one-pot or one-pan dish from a recipe she'd found in one of the women's magazines to which she now unironically subscribed. Dave would set the table, Jo would clear it, he would wash the dishes and she'd dry, and she'd usually be snoozing on the couch before prime time, waking up only long enough to brush her teeth, splash water on her face, and get herself to bed. She'd sleep for long, luscious, uninterrupted hours, and wake up in the morning, stretching her arms over her head, feeling gravid, and heavy, and perfectly content.

Both of her deliveries had been easy—a few hours of discomfort, an hour of hard contractions. When they'd sharpened into actual pain, the doctors had given her a whiff of gas, and she'd woken up with a baby in her arms. Kim was born in 1970, a quiet, watchful, owlish little girl who hardly ever cried. Thus encouraged, Jo had gotten pregnant again when Kim was just over a year old. Their prize had been Missy, who never wanted to be in her crib or her playpen and would cry lustily when deposited in either one. Missy was creeping at four months, crawling at five, and taking her first tottering steps when she was nine months old. She started walking, Jo would say, and never stopped.

Her Avondale friends had no reason to suspect that Jo wasn't the same as they were: a wife and a mother, no different, or less content, than anyone else on the block. They didn't know about Shelley or Lynnette. When Dave wanted to sleep with her she'd let him. She even enjoyed it, at least some of the time, but the truth was, her girls, with their creamy skin, their milky breath, their plump limbs and gummy smiles, satisfied any need for physical intimacy that she had. For years, she hadn't wanted sex at all, from women or men, except in a dim, distant way that seemed to have more to do with memory than desire . . . which, as far as she could tell, was about the same as her neighbors felt.

Years had passed. The girls had weaned and toilet-trained, they'd started nursery school, then kindergarten, and began to wriggle away from Jo's embraces, or announce, *I can do it myself!* Now that Jo was finally coming out of the fog of new motherhood, she was seeing Dave differently, and finding that she had very little to say to him, and less interest in what he might want to say to her. "How was your day, dear?" she'd ask, out of habit, and he'd accuse her of being sarcastic, of not caring, of not really listening when he talked.

"Tell you what," Bethie said, unfolding herself from her cross-legged seat at Judy's fireplace. To Jo's eyes, her sister's long hair looked messy and uncared-for, and the slippers she'd brought with her to Judy's house, purple velvet with gold embroidery, looked ridiculous, so impractical that any grown-up would know better than to buy them and would certainly not wear them in a snowstorm. "I know we'd scheduled something for later in the week, but since we're all here, who wants to do a little consciousness-raising right now?"

Oh, God, Jo thought, cringing. *Oh, no.* Bethie in a contained setting, at an event with an official start and an end time, was one thing, but Bethie on a night like this, Bethie unbound, was quite another. Across the room, Jo saw, or thought she saw, Arlene and Judy exchange a smirk.

"We're drunk!" called Stephanie from her spot on the sectional.

"That might help," Bethie replied. "In vino veritas, right?" Jo felt her heart contract as the other women laughed, or murmured their assent. *They're being polite*, she thought, and mentally begged her sister to sit down.

Instead, Bethie stepped to the front of the room and stood on the fireplace's ledge. Her bracelets rattled as she straightened the hem of her sweater.

"So," Bethie said. "Who can remember the first time you realized that you were a girl?"

Silence filled the room as the women thought it over.

"I remembered the first time I saw my little brother in the bathtub," Nonie finally said. "I ran to my mama, screaming, 'There's something wrong with him!' I thought he was deformed. Like his insides were on the outside."

Everyone laughed. Jo forced herself to breathe. Stephanie said, "When I was six, we went to my mother's sister's wedding, and I had this beautiful dress. All crinolines and puffy sleeves. My brothers just had short pants. They looked like babies. And I thought I looked so grown-up." There were nods and sighs of remembrance. "Then we got to the party, and my brothers were racing all over the place, and I tried to go play with them, and my mom grabbed me. She said I had to be careful. I had to be a little lady."

"Ah," was all Bethie said. Jo, meanwhile, was remembering fights with Sarah, arguments about her clothes, her hair, the way she sat and how she sounded. *Why can't you act like a lady?*

"So who thinks things have changed?" asked Bethie.

There was another pause. "I got my kids *Free to Be . . . You and Me*," Judy said. Jo nodded. She'd gotten her girls the same book. The record, too. "And it says that girls can be anything. Be a doctor, be a lawyer, be an astronaut. Then Jenny asked me, if she grows up to be an astronaut, who's going to take care of her babies? What am I supposed to say to that?"

The women's voices rose, overlapping and passionate. "The nanny!" Valerie called, and Steph said, "Men and women should both be raising the children," while Nonie, who seemed a glass or two past tipsy, said, "Far as I'm concerned, men oughtta be kept as far away from kids as possible. The one time Dan tried to change a diaper, Andy rolled himself right off the changing table and got kaka all over his carpet."

Bethie sat with her back to the fire and her knees drawn up to her chest. Jo looked at her, wondering what her sister was thinking. That she'd dodged a bullet because she'd never been married? That she was better off than all the women in the room? Was it true?

"Jo?"

Jo blinked. "What say you?" asked her sister. "Do you think men should help raise babies, or do we have to find some other way?"

Careful, Jo told herself. She could see Nonie watching her and could feel her sister's gaze, too. "I love being a wife and mother. But I think that ideally women should have the same options men have."

"That's right!" said Stephanie, just as Nonie said, "It won't work," and Bethie asked, "What do you mean?"

Jo smoothed her already-smooth hair. "Well, I think some women are happy staying home with kids. Or they are when their kids are little. But some women don't want that. They'd rather work."

"You don't think that raising children and running a house is working?" Bethie asked, eyebrows lifted.

"Of course it is," Jo said, feeling her cheeks flush, angry at her sister for drawing her into a trap. "You know what I mean. Work outside of the home."

"Do any of us know anyone—any woman our age— who isn't married and a mom?" Stephanie asked. Jo thought of all the girls she'd known in high school, all the smart young women she'd met in college, the girl who'd edited the *Michigan Daily*'s opinion section, the girl who'd won the university's top academic prize. The newspaper editor had gone to law school, then gotten married, and the last Jo knew, she was working part-time. The prizewinner had gotten married and had children, right after college. Just like Jo. Just like Lynnette, and Nonie, and almost every woman Jo knew.

"I'm not married or a mom," Bethie said.

"What's it like?" Stephanie asked, her voice full of almost childlike curiosity. "Do you feel like you're missing out? Are you happy?"

"I am happy," said Bethie, with her beatific smile. "But, remember, I wasn't married first, like some of the women I live with, so it wasn't as if I can speak about what that life was like, or if I like what I have any better. I just did what felt right for me," she said.

Bullshit, thought Jo, feeling childish and resentful, and convinced that Bethie was lying. *You got pregnant, you had an abortion, you spent ten years drifting around, going to rock shows and smoking dope before you landed in your commune. You fell into your life, the same way I fell into mine.*

"Here's another question," said Bethie. "Are marriage and motherhood what you expected?"

For a moment, there was no sound but the hissing and snapping of the logs in the fire. "It's boring sometimes," Valerie Cohen finally said.

"'S boring all the time," Nonie said, and hiccupped.

"We can't say we weren't warned," said Arlene. Her voice was bleak. "Betty Friedan told us. She said it was going to be boring."

"She did," Judy said. "But did we have other choices? Real ones?"

Jo had considered that question a lot, when she was

busy doing something particularly rote and unpleasant: weeding the garden, loading or unloading the dishwasher, or trying, and failing, to fold fitted sheets. She would fold, or pull, or wash, and consider how, no matter how much the bra-tossers and the National Organization for Women and the Society for Cutting Up Men had done to point out the tedium of marriage and motherhood, they hadn't done much about offering other possibilities or smoothing other paths. The only option she could see was paying some other woman—most likely an African American or Hispanic one—to do it for her, the way her mother had, and that did not feel like progress at all.

"I feel so guilty." Valerie's voice was quiet. "My parents were immigrants. They came here from China with nothing. They have a dry-cleaning shop in Boston and they both worked fourteen hours a day, seven days a week, so that my brother and I could go to college." Valerie reached across Nonie, fingers groping for the wineglass she'd placed on the ledge in front of the fireplace. "My parents could never even have imagined a life like the one I have. All of the luxury, all of the ease. I mean, my mother never even had a dishwasher." Valerie paused.

"And yet," Bethie prompted.

"And yet," Valerie repeated, looking down into her wine, with her black hair falling in wings across her face. "I know it's not as hard, or as boring, as dry-cleaning clothes was. But some days, I just feel so . . ." She shook her head. "Depleted. Like Arnold and the kids just take and take and take and there's nothing left where I used to be." She fisted her right hand and rested it against her heart.

"That's it," said Nonie, sitting up straight, so fast that her wine sloshed in her lap. "That's it exactly."

"Do you think the guys feel this way?" Judy still spoke like a New Yorker, all flattened vowels and rat-a-tat-tat delivery. "Does everyone feel bored or empty?"

Jo tried to adjust her position so that she could see her sister. Her bones had that delicious liquid sensation that came with a few drinks, and the living-room floor did not feel entirely solid beneath her. Outside, the snow was still falling, piling up in drifts against the darkened windowpanes, which rattled as the wind gusted, but the room was almost too warm, the air rich with the smells of spices and wine, perfume and shampoo. She could feel her thoughts coming together, ideas she'd had, then shoved away; opinions she never let herself dwell on, crystallizing and solidifying, helped along by the storm, and the closeness, and the company, and the alcohol. "I think that men go out in the world and get filled up. They get praised for their work."

"They get paid for their work," added Nonie.

"They get to fly," said Arlene, perhaps thinking of her pilot husband, who'd leave his family on the ground ten days out of every fourteen.

"And they wear clothes nobody's thrown up on, and they get to eat with both of their hands," Arlene said. She shook her head. "Can you imagine? A whole meal where you don't have to cut up anyone else's chicken, or tell them to use their napkins or eat their vegetables."

"And that's just the husbands," Nonie said.

"And they come home," Jo continued. "And there's dinner on the table. And the carpet's vacuumed, and the bed's made, and the blue suit that they asked you to pick up is hanging in the closet. And they say thank you, and maybe they even act like what we're doing matters. But I'm not sure they believe it." Jo pressed her knuckles to her lips. Judy and Valerie and Bethie were all watching her, and she bet that Nonie, with her eyes shut, was listening, too. "I think that they believe that it's their due. That they're people, and we're not quite people. Like, we're maybe two-thirds of a person."

"Fuck 'em!" Nonie called from the floor, and lifted one fist in the air, as Arlene stirred, reflexively covering her son's ears with her hands, the way they'd all learned to do when Nonie had more than three glasses of white wine. "We should go on strike."

"I'll organize," Bethie offered. Judy suggested that they have snow day dinners once a week, where everyone brought their kids to one house to feed them, and Arlene asked if they had to bring the kids, if they couldn't just leave the children at home and show up to enjoy themselves.

"No kids works for me," said Nonie. "It'll be good for Dan to be in charge. Let him see how bad I've got it."

"I love my kids," said Valerie. "Only sometimes, I wish . . ."

"I wish," Stephanie repeated.

"I wish," said Jo, and Arlene and Judy joined in. The fire crackled, and the wind howled. The snow fell down, and the candles flickered, then guttered out, extinguishing themselves in puddles of wax.

By midnight, almost everyone was asleep. Jo lay on the floor, between Bethie and Nonie, as the logs burned down to embers. At one point, a baby's cries woke her, and she heard icy hailstones rattling off the windows, and Stephanie singing, "Hush little baby, don't say a word, Mama's gonna buy you a mockingbird," as she nursed her son in the rocking chair. Jo felt deeply content, so relaxed she felt like she could sink right into the floor. *Or maybe I'm just drunk.* She was drifting off again when she heard the rustle of blankets and smelled lavender and sandalwood—*essence of hippie*, she thought. She turned on her side, and there was Bethie, lying right next to her, whispering, "Tell me what happened with Shelley Finkelbein."

Jo closed her eyes. In 1976, she and Dave had been in Michigan for Thanksgiving. The United States was celebrating its Bicentennial, the news was full of footage of the Tall Ships sailing into New York City's harbor, and in what felt like the truest sign of a new era, Jo and Bethie convinced Sarah to buy a new slipcover-less couch. On Thanksgiving morning, Dave was off somewhere, meeting up with a few of what seemed to Jo to be an endless supply of fraternity brothers (and having a hair of the dog, Jo suspected). Bethie was meditating in the bedroom, sitting cross-legged on the floor, staring into a candle's flame. Sarah was stuffing the turkey and the girls were playing hide-and-seek in the backyard when there was a knock on the door. "Jo, can you get that?" Sarah called. Jo had opened the door, and there was Shelley. Her long, dark hair had been cut to shoulder length, and she'd lost weight that she hadn't had to spare. Her pink-and-white checked shirt's wide collar bagged open, exposing the sharp rise of her collarbones, and her white slacks billowed around her legs. She wore a short fur coat, glossy and cocoa-brown, and there was an expensive-looking purse slung over her shoulder. She held an Olivetti typewriter in its hard-sided carrying case. Her fingernails were short, unpolished, a few of them ragged at the top, like they'd been bitten, and she'd chewed off all the pink lipstick from her lower lip.

Shelley's eyes met hers. Jo felt her heart stutter to a stop. *She looks just the same*, she thought.

"Hi," Jo breathed. Shelley gave her a tremulous smile, lifting one hand from the box to give Jo a small, ironic wave, and Jo saw that her initial thought wasn't true. Shelley was still a beauty, she would still turn heads on the street, but she'd lost something, a bit of her confidence, an essential degree or two of her rich-girl swagger. "Can I come in?" she asked.

Numbly, Jo led Shelley to the living room. Shelley put the box down on Sarah's coffee table, took a seat on the new couch, and crossed her legs. "Okay if I smoke?"

"I wish you wouldn't." Jo nodded toward the backyard. "My girls are here." Over the years, Jo had thought about this moment, playing out dozens of scenarios, a hundred times apiece. She'd pictured herself gliding past Shelley in the supermarket, even though Shelley probably didn't do her own marketing, bumping into her on the tennis courts, even though Shelley didn't play. She'd imagined and reimagined the conversation, sampling versions where she was cutting and cold, versions where she was indifferent, versions where she greeted Shelley with a bland, generic friendliness that she thought would be worse than either coldness or indifference. But she had never pictured Shelley showing up looking like this, frail and sad and wounded.

"What's going on?" Jo asked.

"I left my husband," Shelley said without preamble. The fingers of her right hand went to the fourth finger of her left hand, massaging the space where her rings must have been. Jo saw hollows under her cheekbones, new circles under her eyes.

Jo tried to keep her face expressionless. "Oh?"

Shelley shook her head. "I thought that I could make it work. Be the wife he wanted." She looked down at her lap, then up, straight into Jo's eyes. "I couldn't, though. I couldn't stop thinking about . . ."

Jo pushed herself upright, standing so fast she felt

dizzy. She couldn't hear it; couldn't stand it if the next word out of her beloved Shelley's mouth was *you*. She wasn't sure where Sarah had gone, but she suspected her mother was somewhere nearby, lurking and listening. And what if Shelley said she still loved her? Would Jo throw herself into her arms? Would she gather Shelley close to her heart, would she say, *Take me now?* Of course not. It was ridiculous to even think it. She was a mother.

"I'm sorry to hear that," she said. "Would you like some coffee?"

There was a pause. "Coffee," Shelley finally said. "Sure." Jo went to the kitchen, where Sarah raised her eyebrows. Jo mumbled that Shelley had come to visit, feeling like an awkward teenager again as she poured water into the coffee machine, spooned grinds into a filter, collected two mugs, napkins, milk from the refrigerator, the sugar bowl from its spot on the counter, next to the stove. She'd braided Missy's hair that morning, and the musty-sweet smell of her younger daughter's skin was still in her nose, and she could picture solemn, brown-eyed Kim, who liked to climb into bed with Jo first thing in the morning to tell her mother about her dreams. "Light and sweet?" she called. Once, that had been a joke between them. Jo was dark and strong; Shelley was light and sweet.

"Just black is fine." Shelley's voice was toneless. By the time Jo carried the mugs back to the living room, the tentative, hopeful expression Shelley had worn when she'd come to the door was gone, replaced with a look of resignation.

"I made a mistake," Shelley said.

Jo sipped her coffee and said nothing, wondering if Shelley meant that she'd made a mistake marrying

Denny or if her mistake had been coming to Jo's house. Shelley gave her a thin twitch of a smile.

"I told you I wasn't brave. Remember?" She started rubbing her bare ring finger again. "And I'm not. It took every bit of courage I could scrape together to come here. I had to see you. I had to at least try." Her voice was ragged as she raised her face again and looked at Jo. "But I'm too late, aren't I?"

Jo was glad that her own voice was steady. "I'm married now, Shelley. I have two little girls. I have a life. I'm happy." A splinter of ice had lodged itself inside of her heart. Part of her wanted to be cruel, to parade her satisfaction, her happy, normal life, in front of the woman who'd broken her heart so completely that for months it had hurt to even breathe. "Maybe I should be grateful to you. If you hadn't gotten married, I never would have met Dave."

"You're lucky, then." Shelley gave that thin, trembling smile, so unlike the go-to-hell grin that Jo remembered, and raised her mug in a toast. "Lucky you."

"I hope you figure it out," Jo said, trying to sound kind, knowing that she just sounded condescending. "I hope you find the right . . ." The right man? The right woman? ". . . answers," she finally said.

"Yeah." Shelley looked down at the typewriter. "I want you to have this." She gave Jo a crooked smile. "I'm going to be moving, and I'm trying to travel light. Are you still writing?"

"Not so much these days." Jo thought that she understood the gesture. Shelley had taken away Jo's dreams of love. Surely this gift was meant to remind Jo of her other dream, to suggest that she could still be a writer, that at least a piece of the life she'd wanted was still possible. "The kids keep me pretty busy."

"Maybe someday, then," said Shelley. "You can keep it for someday." She sounded like she might have been crying. Jo made herself turn away, and when Shelley said, "I should go," instead of trying to comfort her, Jo said, "I'll get your coat."

"Hey," Shelley asked when she was at the door. When Shelley was wrapped in her fur again, Jo thought she could detect at least a little of her old love's familiar rich-girl insouciance. "Did you ever get to take that trip?"

Jo shook her head, pushing down the anger and resentment that the thought of her truncated travels always stirred up. "No. I spent a big chunk of my money on . . . you know, on that other thing." All this time, and she still couldn't say the word "abortion" out loud, even though abortion was legal and had been for almost four years. Nor had she ever told Shelley who the abortion had been for. That was Bethie's story, not hers. "And after that, it felt like I was ready to start the next part of my life, you know? Like it was time to move on. Time to grow up."

"Well." Shelley looked like she wanted to say more. Her mouth was trembling as she pulled her short fur coat closed. "Bad timing." She'd jammed her purse underneath her arm and pushed her hands in her pockets.

Jo shrugged. Part of her felt desperate relief that Shelley was going. With every second in Shelley's presence, looking into those luminous gray eyes, smelling the scent that was perfume and tobacco and Shelley herself, she felt the urge to just toss everything she had, everything she'd built with Dave, to leave her daughters in the backyard and her sister staring into a candle flame, her mother in the kitchen and her husband at some bar, to jump into Shelley's car and just go. But she couldn't go. She could never leave her girls. They were her loves now; they were her life. "Good luck. I hope you'll be happy," she said, and Shelley's voice was flat, her smile joyless as she said, "Yeah. You, too." Jo had closed the door gently behind her and stood, with her forehead resting against the wood, listening as Kim and Missy came in through the back door, needing to go to the bathroom, needing their snowsuits unzipped, their boots pulled off, their noses wiped, clamoring for hot chocolate, saying, *Hurry, Mama, hurry!*

"Jo?" On Judy Pressman's living-room floor, her sister nudged her. Jo could picture her sister's face, her eyes wide-open in the dark.

Jo didn't answer. Instead, she held still, making herself take long, slow breaths until, hopefully, she'd convinced Bethie that she'd fallen asleep. She couldn't risk talking about Shelley. Not to Bethie, not to anyone. She had her girls, she had her house, she had a husband, and work. A car to drive, food to eat, books to read, miles to run, people in her life who loved her. It was enough, Jo told herself. It had to be enough.

Bethie

Bethie Kaufman didn't know who her sister thought she was kidding, but Bethie was not fooled. All of Jo's talk about how happy she was, how she was fine, how everything was great, and she loved her life and loved her husband and, *oh, let's not talk about me, let's talk about the girls.* Or OPEC, or the weather, or disco music, or the democratic elections in Spain. As if Bethie couldn't see the way her sister's gaze followed Nonie Scotto whenever Nonie was around. As if Bethie hadn't noticed the small, subtle, possibly unconscious ways Jo found to put space between herself and her husband. If Dave was in the kitchen (rare, because he had a wife and two daughters, all well-versed in the art of beer- and snack-fetching), Jo was in the family room. If Dave was in the family room, sipping his fetched beer, munching on a plate of Wheat Thins and cheddar cheese that one of his women had prepared and watching *Wide World of Sports,* Jo was in the kitchen. If Dave was in the shower, singing Bee Gees songs loud enough for everyone in the house to hear, Jo was folding the laundry she'd washed or unloading the groceries she'd purchased or making dinner, or getting the kids' school lunches ready for the morning.

All the women in Avondale lived this way, as far as Bethie could tell. She'd opened Judy Pressman's pantry and seen canned goods lined up, as regimented as soldiers in an army, all the labels facing the same way, and she'd peeked into Arlene Dubin's purse and seen the bottle of Valium she'd expected to find, given the woman's blank face and exhausted eyes. In Bethie's opinion, Judy Pressman, with her intelligence and drive, should have been running an actual army, instead of just the PTA, and Poor Arlene should have told her husband to get himself snipped after their first two kids, and gone and gotten her tubes tied if he'd refused, if she could find a doctor who'd do it without her husband's permission. And her big sister shouldn't have been in the suburbs at all.

It made Bethie feel terrible. After all of her years of wandering and her symbolic rebirth, she had found her way to happiness, a life that left her fulfilled and connected—to the earth, to other women, to her country, to justice, to the world around her. Under Ronnie's tutelage, she'd found her place in the struggle, for civil rights and women's rights, for a world with no nukes and no wars, where every child was a wanted child and where abortion was legal and safe. Her life had meaning. She wrote pamphlets and ran off copies; she organized rallies and demonstrations and get-out-the-vote efforts, and cooked giant pots of *chana masala* and dal for the nights they had meetings or consciousness-raising groups at Blue Hill Farm. Even on the days where all she was doing was collecting cash for pints of raspberries or bushels of peaches, she knew that some of that money would go to help resettle Vietnamese orphans, or to help a scared, pregnant teenager who didn't want to have a baby and didn't have the money for even the bottom rung of Planned Parenthood's sliding scale.

Bethie knew that her life was unconventional—and if she hadn't known, she'd have her mother's monthly letters to remind her. *I'm glad you are Happy but I hope you will Settle Down and find a Good Man to take Care of you*, Sarah would write, using her own idiosyncratic capitalization and punctuation marks. Bethie knew that Sarah wanted her and Jo to both have what she'd enjoyed, however briefly—a man's patronage, his last name, his love and support, with all the benefits that conveyed. With a husband, Bethie would be able to own a house, take out car loans and credit cards, and avoid the dozens of pairs of politely raised eyebrows, the none-too-subtle glances at her bare ring finger that she encountered every day and week, the women whose expressions became sympathetic when they asked, *Oh? No husband? No kids?*

No husband, she would say, her own expression friendly, her voice firm. *No kids.* She had work, friends, a life with meaning, and, lately, a life with possibilities, if she could just convince the rest of the collective that the military-industrial war machine was not lubricated by the proceeds from selling peach jam. And what did Jo and her suburban sisters have? What did they do all day? Drive the carpool. Clip coupons. Buy groceries. Bleach the whites, iron the shirts, roll the socks into balls. Make the beds, make the meals, make their husbands happy. A few years back, Bethie had sent Jo a copy of Shere Hite's *Sexual Honesty: By Women for Women*, and a note saying *I bet this would make for an interesting book club discussion!* The book, with its thesis that normal women only achieved orgasm from clitoral stimulation, not intercourse, had prompted a lively discussion among the ladies of Blue Hill Farm. Bethie had even heard that there were workshops in New York City and its suburbs where the leaders would pass out hand mirrors and anatomy charts and show women who'd considered themselves frigid how it was done. Bethie assumed that Jo had to be sexually frustrated, and she worried, as soon as the book was in the mail, that her sister would simply attribute her lack of fulfillment to Dave's ineptitude, not her orientation, but if Jo ever read the book, she never said a word. A few months later, Bethie had sent *The Stepford Wives*, but again, if Jo had ever cracked the spine of the story of how a Connecticut engineer had turned the town's wives into docile, compliant robots, she never said so. Bethie was a liberated woman, and her sister was still in chains, and it was Jo whom Bethie thought of when she'd led a Passover Seder at Blue Hill Farm, using the Freedom Haggadah, the previous spring. *When one person is in bondage none of us are free.* Her job, as she saw it, was to break Jo's chains, to return Jo to the freedom that she'd lost, to let Jo have the kind of life she wanted, which, clearly, could not be the life that she currently had.

The morning after the blizzard, Bethie awoke to a world all in white. In Judy Pressman's harvest-gold kitchen, she made herself a cup of tea and watched out the window, sitting in the stillness, until the plows came to clear the roads and Dave made it back over the mountain, coming through the door like he was Alexander who'd made it across the Alps. Jo and Bethie and Dave and the girls spent the day shoveling out the driveway and digging a path from the driveway to the front door. Kim and Missy worked alongside their mother and father with kid-sized shovels, and Bethie enjoyed the cold, the wind's bite on her cheeks, the snowflakes sparkling in the sunshine. In the backyard, she and the girls built an igloo, tall enough for Kim to stand up in. Jo had helped for a while, before drifting back into the house to start dinner. The girls had set the table, Kim folding each napkin precisely, Missy flinging silverware in the general direction of the plates. Dave sat at the head of the table and made a production of tucking his napkin under his chin to protect his shirt. His nails were buffed, maybe even polished, Bethie saw, and his hair was suspiciously poufy, like he'd sprayed it with something before coming to the table.

"For what we are about to eat, may the Lord make us thankful," the girls warbled. When Bethie caught her sister's eye, Jo shrugged. "We do the blessings over the candles on Friday nights, and they're learning the prayer for after meals in Hebrew school, but they're not there yet."

"Godless heathens," Dave said, scooping a dollop of steaming noodles onto his plate, then serving the girls smaller portions before finally serving Jo. "I'm raising a pack of godless heathens."

"Daddy!" Kim giggled, as Melissa surreptitiously used her fingers to maneuver food onto her fork.

"What are we enjoying?" Bethie asked, helping herself.

"Turkey tetrazzini," Jo said.

"Ah. So Mom's noodle surprise is traveling under an alias."

"It isn't noodle surprise!" Jo said, affronted, as Kim giggled, and Missy asked, "What's an alias?"

"This has fresh basil."

"That's the green stuff," Missy muttered darkly. "It's yuck."

"Vegetables are good for you," said Kim, as she primly smoothed her own napkin on her lap. The dynamic between the sisters was the opposite of what it had been for her and Jo growing up. Kim was mature, a little mother, a perfectionist. Melissa was the troublemaker. Not that she went out of her way to cause trouble, she just went barreling through life, noisy and exuberant and full speed ahead. Just like her mother. Or, at least, just like her mother used to be.

Bethie watched as Melissa tweezed a bit of basil between her fingers and then, after making sure her parents weren't watching, rolled it into a ball and flicked it onto the floor. She saw the way the girls took their cues from Jo, the way Jo kept them quiet while Dave described his night in the back room of RePlay Sports and his perilous journey back home over Avon Mountain. She wondered if Jo had any idea about how much more relaxed, how much more herself she seemed when her husband wasn't around. Alone with her girls, Jo was cheerful and easygoing, always up for an adventure, whether that was a bike ride, or a picnic, or letting the girls sleep in the pillow fort they'd built. When Dave was home, Jo got quiet, and instead of asking the girls what they wanted, it was *Whatever Daddy says*. Bethie felt like the only time she really saw her sister, the Jo she'd grown up with, was when Jo and the girls visited her in Georgia in the summer. They'd pick raspberries and blueberries and help make jam in the steamy, sugary-smelling kitchen, and sit around the firepit out back at night, roasting hot dogs (or tofu pups, in the case of some of Bethie's compatriots) and making s'mores. At the end of every visit, they'd go tubing on the Chattahoochee. Jo would wear a faded black one-piece bathing suit that she'd had since college. She'd hold one daughter on her lap, and Bethie would take the other,

and they'd drift with the current, hands and feet and bottoms in the cool water, faces warmed by the sun.

Every time Bethie visited her sister, she would hope
that things had changed. She knew that Jo's unhappiness
was at least partially her fault, and she worried that, in
some mystical, scale-balancing way, Jo's misery was tied
to her own contentment. Maybe neither of them could
be happy at the same time; maybe one had to be down
for the other to be up . . . and, of course, Jo could never
be happy as long as she was married to Dave Braverman.

Bethie knew more than Jo thought she did. She'd
seen Jo with Shelley in Ann Arbor, and had not failed to
notice the way Jo had been when she'd come home from
Turkey. Even in the depths of her own terror and misery, Bethie had noticed how quiet Jo was, how she'd jerk
like she'd been electrocuted every time the phone rang,
how she'd look like she wanted to cry when the Ronettes
came on the radio. Jo told her that she and Shelley had
had a falling-out, but Bethie figured that Shelley must
have been the one who'd given Jo the name of the doctor,
and she suspected, even though Jo refused to confirm it,
that Jo's attendance at Shelley's wedding was the price
Jo's former best friend had exacted for that information.
Jo had met Dave at Shelley's wedding. And Dave was
not a good guy, like their father had been. Once you got
past his dark eyes and his glinting grin, once you'd heard
all his big talk about his businesses and his plans, you saw
that there was nothing there but hot air and hairspray.
Dave might have had some of their father's mannerisms,
and maybe even some of Ken Kaufman's kindness, but
Dave was mostly superficial glitter. Bethie had tried to
tell her sister these things, but Jo hadn't wanted to hear
them. *Leave me alone, Bethie. This is what I want.*

What happened to her sister? Jo had always been

the brave one, the strong one, the one who stood up to wrongdoers and jerks. Bethie might never know who, or what, had broken Jo's spirit, but she knew she would have to be strong for her sister. She'd have to do what it took to help Jo find that spark again.

The next morning, Dave went to work, and Jo and Bethie took the girls sledding. Together, they stood at the top of the hill on the town's golf course, watching Kim and Missy zip down on their strips of brightly colored plastic, shrieking with glee as they flew into the air after bouncing over the lip of a sand trap. "Sleds sure have changed," Bethie remarked. "Remember the one we had?"

Jo nodded. "Dave's got a four-man toboggan for sale at one of the stores," Jo said. "He keeps threatening to bring it home."

"The family that sleighs together stays together?" Bethie couldn't see much of her sister's face, between her knitted hat and her sunglasses, but she thought she detected a wince, and decided that this was the best opening she'd get. "Hey, so, listen. How would you feel about coming back to Blue Hill with me?"

"Back—when, now?" Jo asked. A crease appeared between her eyebrows as she frowned.

"No time like the present." Before her sister could give her excuses, Bethie said, "I could use your help. You know we've been talking about opening a shop, right?"

"I know, but . . ."

Bethie kept talking. "We found a place to rent on Peachtree Road. You can help us make labels for the jams and sachets and stuff. We've got the inventory, we just need a car big enough to move it all. And you've got a station wagon."

Jo frowned. "There's nobody in Atlanta with a station wagon?"

There was, of course, but Jo didn't need to know that. "I need your car, and I need your help. We've got to come up with a name, and figure out what the signs and the ads and the flyers should say. You're good at that stuff."

"What stuff?"

"Words," said Bethie. "Remember the stories you used to tell me?" A faint smile lifted the corners of Jo's lips. "And I get the feeling that you could use a break," Bethie continued.

The smile vanished. Jo pressed her lips together, then said, "Why would you think that?"

Because you find excuses to never be in the same room as your husband, Bethie thought. *Because you had to ask permission to take the car this morning and to change the channel on the TV last night. Because you're going to be thirty-six soon, and then forty, and your life is running out, and you've already missed so much.*

"Listening to your friends, it sounds like all of you guys could use a vacation." Bethie kept her tone light.

"I can't just leave." Jo was chewing on her thumbnail, the way she did when she was thinking. "The girls need me."

"Mommy, Mommy, watch us!" Kim called on cue, and Jo shouted back, "I'm watching!" Kim lay on her belly on her sled. She counted to three, and Missy flopped on top of her. Kim shoved off, pushing the toes of her boots against the snow, and the two of them went hurtling down the packed snow.

"What's so hard?" asked Bethie.

"Well, Kim's got school. And violin lessons."

"Can't Dave send her?"

"I'll miss book club . . ."

"What are you reading?"

"*The French Lieutenant's Woman*."

"I'll talk about any book you want with you," Bethie promised.

"And Missy's got tumbling class and indoor soccer. They're after school." Jo adjusted her hat. "But maybe I could ask Nonie to drive her."

"Or maybe she could skip. Just have her do some somersaults on the floor."

"Kids need routines." That, Bethie knew, had to be wisdom culled from one of Jo's parenting books. Her sister had a whole shelf full, Dr. Spock and Dr. Brazelton and even Dr. Dobson's *Dare to Discipline*. *She doesn't want to be Sarah,* Bethie would think, when she'd see her sister consult this book or that one, or when she'd overheard Jo ask *Why are you curious about that?* when Kim wanted to know if they were rich, instead of saying *It's none of your business,* the way their own mother surely would have. Jo's girls didn't get spanked or screamed at. They got time-outs, where they were sent to sit down and think about what they'd done. When Missy didn't want Jo combing her hair, Jo sat down and talked to her, explaining why she needed to look neat, promising to be as gentle as possible, offering to let Missy get a short haircut, if that's what she preferred. When Kim snuck a flashlight under her pillow, Jo gave Kim a speech on the importance of sleep for growing bodies. Jo told her girls that she loved them every night, at bedtime, and every morning, before they left the house for school. She was always touching them, stroking their hair, pulling them close for hugs and kisses. She loved them. But Bethie knew that Jo loved adventure, too. She had to regret having had so few of her own.

"You guys didn't go on vacation this year, did you?" Bethie already knew the answer, but she wanted Jo to hear herself saying it out loud.

"Nooo . . ." Jo admitted. "We were thinking about Disney World, but then, with the third store opening, it was just going to stretch us too thin."

Disney World, Bethie thought, and struggled not to roll her eyes. "So let's go now! You'll get a break! A little warm weather! It'll be an adventure!" Bethie braced herself for further arguments, but Jo surprised her.

"If it's okay with Dave." Shading her eyes with one gloved hand, she called, "Hey, Kim! Let me borrow your sled!" Kim handed it over and both girls watched, wide-eyed and impressed, as Jo lay flat on her belly and went zipping down the hill, faster than any of the kids.

Dave complained, but not as much as Bethie thought he would, which made her wonder if he had some chickie on the side, if the annoyance of having to care for the kids for a few nights was outweighed by the novelty of being able to bang his side piece on the marital bed. He actually helped them pack, and shooed Jo out the door. "Take good care of my lambie," he said, escorting the girls to the driveway so that they could wave goodbye. Bethie found herself almost liking him in that moment. Dave loved his daughters. It was possible, she acknowledged, that he loved her sister, too. Which was nice, but it didn't make him what Jo wanted. Maybe he'd never intended to become her sister's chains, but that didn't change the truth of what he was.

The road trip from Connecticut to Atlanta was as much fun as Bethie had had with her sister in years. Jo drove, and Bethie managed the snacks and the map, and took charge of what little navigation there was. They ate pretzels and drank Tab and sang along to James Taylor and the Eagles, and talked about people they'd known. One of the Stein boys was selling Toyotas, which made him the scourge of the old neighborhood, whose residents only drove American-made cars, and Barbara Simoneaux, Bethie's best friend, had become an EST instructor, which made both of them laugh.

The first night they stopped in Philadelphia, at a commune started by a former Blue Hill Farm member. Bethie directed Jo to Spruce Street, and she and her sister tromped along the snowy sidewalk and up three marble steps to the townhouse's door. The place had four stories and six fireplaces, and all of them were lit when they arrived. Bethie introduced Jo to Margot, her former Blue Hill Farm compatriot, who hugged Bethie warmly before taking Jo's hand in both of hers and intoning the word "Welcome" while looking deeply into Jo's eyes. They ate fresh-baked wheat bread and stuffed squash for dinner in a kitchen crowded with houseplants that grew in terra-cotta pots or dangled from macramé hangers. After dinner, Jo helped with the dishes, standing elbow to elbow with Margot, who was short and round and merry, and who looked a little bit like Lynnette Bobeck and a little like Nonie, Jo's Connecticut friend. When the cleaning-up was done, Bethie and Jo went to the living room and lay in front of the fire as a man named Derek sat on a goldenrod-velvet armchair, picking out "Smoke on the Water" on a guitar.

"What do you all do?" Jo asked. Margot was a teacher in an experimental free school and Robert was a public defender. Derek worked for an environmental group, Judy was in grad school at the University of Pennsylvania, and Sally stayed home with the four children who lived in the house. Bethie watched Jo's expression sharpen as she listened. She noticed the way Jo leaned forward when she asked questions, and wondered if she was imagining the way Jo's gaze followed the sway of Margot's hips as Margot moved through the leafy-green kitchen to get them all more tea.

They left early the next morning. By midnight, they were back at Blue Hill Farm. Jo and Bethie tiptoed into the house, where the porch light had been left on and the kitchen smelled of pumpkin bread and sourdough starter. In Bethie's bedroom on the second floor, they slept the way they had when they were girls, side by side in narrow twin beds, each one covered with a patchwork quilt that Rose of Sharon had sewn.

The next three days were busy. Jo worked with all the members of the collective: Ronnie and Rose of Sharon, Danielle and Wren and Talia and her husband, Philip, the commune's only man. Jo helped them write the copy for the newspaper ad for their new store, and affix labels to the Mason jars filled with Blue Hill Farm's peach preserves and blackberry jam and jalapeño jelly and honey; helped them load up the station wagon and drive the goods to the shop on Peachtree Street. At dinnertime, Jo and Bethie mashed peas and potatoes together to fill vegetarian samosas, and at night, when the community members gathered, to read or knit or crochet or fold laundry, Jo would read *Free to Be . . . You and Me* to Blue Hill Farm's three children, Indigo, Marigold, and Sasha. Her sister was especially fond of the story of Atalanta, the princess who was bright and clever and fast and strong, who outraced all of her suitors and, instead of marrying the young man who came closest to winning, parted from him after they'd agreed to be friends and went off to see the world. "Perhaps someday they'll be married, and perhaps they will not. In any case, it is certain they are both living happily ever after," Jo read, and the kids applauded together as Jo closed the book.

On Saturday night, Philip made his famous seitan and peanut–sauced rice noodles. Jo had seconds, and thirds, and then pushed back her chair and gave a contented sigh. "This has been wonderful," she said, and looked at Bethie. "Have you seen my purple scarf? I need to start packing."

"What's the rush?" Bethie kept her voice casual.

"My kids?" Jo said. "Kim and Missy? Remember them?"

"I bet they'd love it here." Bethie turned, indicatively, toward the fireplace, where Indigo and Marigold were working on a puzzle and Sasha was sprawled on her belly, reading a book. The room was warm with the glow of the fire and the lamps, and it smelled like sage and smoke and peaches.

"You know they love their visits." Jo stretched her arms over her head, yawning.

"You're always welcome," Bethie said. "Like, if you and the girls wanted to come for an extended stay. You'd be a great part of the community."

Jo gave her sister a look of fond exasperation. "Come on."

"You could do it," Bethie said. "You and the girls. For a week, or a month, or as long as you liked."

Jo's expression was changing from fondly exasperated to just exasperated. "Bethie," she said, "I have a life."

"But does it make you happy? Is it the life you want? Because I don't think . . ."

Bethie paused. Jo raised her eyebrows. "You don't think what?"

"I don't think that you're happy," Bethie said. She imagined a needle lancing a blister, a finger pressing down, expelling all the fluid. "I don't think you're happy being Suzy Homemaker in Connecticut with Dave Braverman."

"Well, thank you for your insight," said Jo, in a tone that didn't contain even a hint of actual gratitude. "But I'm fine."

"Jo." Bethie reached out to touch her sister's shoulder, but Jo stepped backward, putting herself out of reach. "I'm trying to help you here."

"I don't need any help."

"I think you do."

Jo turned toward Bethie, squaring her shoulders, planting her hands on her hips as Wren and Philip, who'd been finishing the cleanup, quietly edged out of the kitchen. Jo wore jeans, a striped turtleneck, boat shoes, the kind of loose-fitting, comfortable stuff that she liked best. Her hair was unsprayed, her face was scrubbed clean. Even in her anger, she looked relaxed, at ease in this place and in her skin, the way she never looked in Connecticut.

"So what's your rescue plan? You think I'm just going to move down here? Me and the girls? We'll just ditch Dave back in Connecticut and move in with you?"

Said out loud, in Jo's scornful, big-sister voice, it did sound kind of silly. Bethie lifted her chin and mentally spat on her fists, preparing for battle. "Whether you stay here or not, you should know that you have options."

Jo ran her hand through her hair. Her gold studs gleamed in her ears, and her wedding band shone on her finger. "I know I have options. I'm just not sure why you think I need them. Because I'm happy."

Oh, here we go, Bethie thought.

"I have two beautiful daughters, I have a husband who loves me, who's finally making enough money so that we can afford some nice things. I have friends . . . and classes . . . and a job. I have a life." Her voice rose on the last word, trembling with emotion. "I have a life," Jo repeated. "A life that I like very much. So, while I guess I'm grateful for your concern, it's completely misplaced. I'm fine."

"You're not," said Bethie.

"Why do you think you know me better than I know myself?" Jo asked.

"Because you're in denial! Or you're paralyzed! Or you can't be honest with yourself. You're sitting in Connecticut, making dinner, folding laundry, reading a zillion books and newspapers every day. You're not writing, and you always said you wanted to write. You're not really doing anything." *You're not being true to yourself*, Bethie thought, but she couldn't say that yet.

"Bethie." Jo's voice was low and calm and full of warning, but Bethie didn't stop; couldn't let herself stop. *I'll say it*, she thought to herself. I'll say it out loud, once and for all, and if she can't hear me, if she won't hear me, then at least I'll have tried.

"I know you loved Shelley. I know you loved Lynnette. I know you love your daughters." She pulled in a breath. "But I don't think you love Dave. And I feel responsible. I think I'm part of the reason you married him."

Jo's eyes were narrowed, her color high, and her voice was cool when she spoke. "I don't know what you're talking about."

"You came home from your trip because of me. If you hadn't come home, you wouldn't have met him."

"Then it would have been someone else," Jo said.

"Why?" Bethie demanded. Her voice had gotten loud. She wondered if her fellow Blue Hill Farmers were listening, if Ronnie or one of the other women might jump in and back her up. "Why did it have to be any guy? What happened to you? You used to be so brave."

Jo looked down at her hands, clasped at her waist. Her lips trembled, then firmed. "I got tired," she finally said. "I had to come home, to take care of you. Mom made that very clear, that it was my job, cleaning up your mess. And when that was over, I couldn't buy a ticket back. And I watched Shelley get married. And I just got tired of fighting all the time. I wanted things to be easier. I didn't want every single day of my life to be a struggle."

Bethie's mouth felt very dry. "I'm sorry," she whispered.

"It's not your fault." Jo shrugged, and tried to smile.

"I'm at least partly to blame that you came home." *And gave up.* "And I just want to own what I did. I hate carrying all this guilt around. I want to tell you I'm sorry that I hurt you, even if it wasn't on purpose." Bethie paused expectantly. Jo stared.

"Am I . . . supposed to be apologizing for something?" she finally asked. Her face was puzzled. Bethie felt her temper flare. "What did I do to you?"

"You really don't know?"

"I know I didn't get you pregnant," Jo said. "Or make you drop acid in a crowd of a few thousand strangers."

Bethie felt her face flush. Part of her must have known that Jo blamed her for getting pregnant, and for everything that had happened because of it, but hearing Jo say it felt like being smacked in the face. "You left me," she said. Her heart felt like it was swelling, hammering against her ribs. She hadn't planned on bringing this up, but now it felt like she couldn't have stopped talking, even if she'd wanted to. Her voice rose with every word. "You and Mom."

"What?" Jo had the nerve to look confused. "Left you where?"

"Left me alone," Bethie said. "With Uncle Mel. Remember? After Dad died? You were off at summer camp playing kissy-face with Lynnette Bobeck, and Mom was selling Better Dresses at Hudson's. I was all by myself."

"Okay, but as soon as you told me what was going on, we figured out what to do. Mel gave you that money, and we never saw him again after that."

"But you let it happen," Bethie said. "Both of you. All those weeks. Uncle Mel would drive me home, and the house would be empty, and he'd drive all the way to the end of the street and just sit there and paw at me. And if you'd been around, or Mom had been around, maybe it wouldn't have gone on that long."

"I was working!" Jo said. "Dad was dead, we were broke, and I was working! All summer long! How can you think that what happened to you was my fault?"

"You were with Lynnette all summer long." Bethie's heart was hammering, and her stomach was lurching, as if she was on a boat in the high seas. "And he was giving me ten dollars a week, and all Mom ever talked about was how much everything cost, how expensive everything was, and you weren't even there . . ." She stopped, trying to calm down and breathe. Talking about it brought it all back, the stink of Uncle Mel's breath, the feeling of his flabby, sweat-damp cheek pressed against her neck, his thick fingers on her skin. The sound of the vinyl car seat squeaking underneath his weight, the way the windows would fog up from his breath. The way the ten-dollar bills he'd press into her hand were always limp, greasy, warm from contact with his body. They always felt used and dirty, just like her.

"Bethie . . ." Jo reached out her hand, fingertips brushing her sister's shoulder. Bethie shook Jo's hand off, stepping quickly backward until the heavy wooden kitchen table stood between them.

"You think that I ruined your life? Well, I think you ruined mine." Bethie riffled through her purse until she found the station wagon's keys, and threw them down on the table. "Go home, Jo. Go home to your girls and your husband. Go be happy." Bethie watched as her sister looked at her, then shook her head, picked up the keys, and her pocketbook, and walked upstairs to collect her things. Bethie was sitting in the kitchen when Jo walked out the door, leaving without even saying goodbye. *And what did I expect?* Bethie asked herself as she heard the station wagon's engine start. When you give someone hard truths, you can't expect them to thank you.

She got to her feet, filled the pot, brewed herself a cup of chamomile tea. *Give her time*, she told herself. Maybe she'll come round right.

Jo

Dave was asleep in his La-Z-Boy when Jo unlocked the door at just after two o'clock in the afternoon. She'd left Atlanta right after the fight with Bethie, had driven until two in the morning, stayed at a Days Inn outside of Durham, North Carolina, and had gotten back on the road at five the next morning, hoping to make it back before her girls came home from school. In all of those hours, she'd been forced to admit the truth to herself, and she'd come up with a plan. She would tell Dave that she wanted a separation, that she needed some time by herself. *We've grown apart*, she would say. She would tell him that he deserved to be with a woman who loved him, who could give herself to him completely, the way Jo never had, and never could. She would say that they both deserved to be happy.

She'd expected the house to be empty, so that she'd have time to prepare herself. She hadn't thought that her husband would be home, or that Melissa would be sleeping in his arms. "Ear infection," Dave whispered, getting to his feet without waking her up. Jo could see Missy's flushed cheeks, the way her fine brown hair was plastered to her forehead. "Not to worry. We already started the amoxicillin. She'll be fine." Dave carried Missy through the kitchen, past the remains of Kim's homework, spread out on the table: a diorama of George Washington crossing the Delaware. Snips of construction paper and cardboard littered the floor; a bottle of Elmer's glue stood, uncapped, next to the shoebox. Kim had drawn a credible version of Washington, with his blue coat and curly white wig, and had propped the figure in the center of a construction-paper rowboat, with one of its arms extended, a finger pointing forward, toward the enemy lines.

Jo's heart twisted. She forced herself to lift her feet, to follow Dave down the hall and watch as he settled Missy into bed. Missy murmured something as he pulled up the covers and smacked her lips as he bent and planted a kiss on her cheek. *I can't*, she thought, and those two words formed a counterpoint to the booming refrain of *Tell him* that was thumping through her head. *Tell him. I can't. Tell him. I can't. I can't live like this*, Jo would think. *It's a lie, just like Bethie said.* That thought would be followed by another one, just as insistent. *I can't make my girls live without a father.*

Back in the kitchen, Dave uncapped a pair of beers and handed one to Jo. "Welcome home."

"Thank you." She sipped, feeling Dave's eyes on her.

"Good trip?"

"Interesting," Jo said. Her head and her heart were both pounding, the picture of Dave kissing Missy's fever-flushed cheek contrasting with an image of Margot at the kitchen sink in Philadelphia; the sound of her husband's voice mixing with the memory of Bethie's accusations. *I could be happy*, Jo thought, and then wondered, *But am I so unhappy now?* Was she unhappy enough to tear up everything they'd built; unhappy enough to take her girls away from their daddy?

Dave shuffled his feet. Jo looked and saw something in his expression, something furtive and shamed. "What's going on?" she asked.

Dave set his beer down on the butcher-block table. The overhead light shone through his thinning hair and gleamed off his scalp. "Well, as to that," he said. *Another woman*, Jo thought. It felt like a bolt of lightning striking her, illuminating her, not with pain but with a terrible kind of joy . . . because if Dave had cheated, if Dave was preparing to announce that he'd fallen for someone else, then Jo would be free. She wouldn't be the one to break up the family. Dave could carry that guilt, and she'd take her girls down to Philadelphia, to the big sunny house with its fireplaces and its kitchen full of plants and its shelves overflowing with books.

"Do you remember those papers I asked you to sign last fall?"

Jo had a vague recollection of Dave handing her some forms and asking for her signature. She'd scribbled her name on the line that said SPOUSE without even reading what she'd signed, feeling guilty that she didn't pay better attention to the family finances, hating how stereotypically female that was, knowing what Bethie would say about the way she'd just handed all of the money management over to her man. But Missy had been trying to find her shin guards for soccer, and Kim had announced that she was Snack Kid for her Brownie troop and would need brownies or muffins for twelve girls by that afternoon. Jo had signed her name and had gone on with her day.

"I think so. Why?"

"I took out a loan," Dave said. In her absence, he'd started growing a beard, bristling dark-brown hairs that provided patchy covering to his cheeks and chin. "And a second mortgage. I was trying to get the West Hartford store up and running. I figured I'd use the income from the first store to cover the interest."

Jo watched him. A heaviness was gathering in her chest, as if her body had started to absorb the bad news before Dave even finished saying it.

"It's going to be fine," Dave said, with an expression suggesting that he didn't quite believe it. "It's just that we're going to have to file for bankruptcy, to restructure the debt, and set up a schedule so we can—"

"Wait." Jo held up one hand like a traffic cop, hearing an echo of her mother in the sharpness of her voice. "Wait. Back up. Go back to the part about bankruptcy."

"It's just a word." *At least*, Jo thought, feeling dizzy and sick, *he had the good grace to look sheepish*. "I know it sounds scary, but really, it's just a way of putting all our debt in one bucket, and then setting up a schedule so we can pay it off."

"Our debt?" Jo asked.

"The debt from the businesses," said Dave.

"How is that our debt?" Jo asked. "How is that personal? I haven't taken out any loans." But even as she spoke, she was thinking about those papers, how one of them had gotten splashed with coffee on top. *Look in the hall closet*, she'd been saying to Missy, trying to remember where she'd seen the shin guards, and whether Kim would be embarrassed if her snack wasn't homemade.

"I should have explained it better. I should have told you what you were signing. And, really, I know it sounds like the end of the world, but it isn't." He kept talking, but Jo knew that she'd already gotten the salient piece of information. Dave had bankrupted them. Not only was there no money, but there probably wasn't even credit that Jo could use to start a new life.

"I'm going to take a shower," she said, interrupting Dave, who was saying something about nonexempt assets and five-year repayment plans. She walked past him, catching a whiff of beer and the concentrated essence of unbathed Dave. He reached for her hand.

"Jo." He grabbed her arm before she could pass. When he looked at her, she felt like he could see everything she'd thought about, everything she'd hoped for. "Hey. Are you . . . Did something . . ."

Happen, she thought, filling in the blank. He's going to ask if something happened when I was away, and I will have to decide if I should tell him.

But Dave didn't finish the question. He looked at her, and she looked back, feeling something inside of her crack open and spill, something dark as ink and toxic as venom. *Resignation*, Jo thought. That was what it was, the feeling of knowing that this was it for her—this house, this man, this life. There would be no escape, no second act. Just this. "We'll get through this," he said after a long moment. Jo knew that he meant more than their financial woes, more than this crisis. He knew that something had happened—not what, but something—and he wasn't going to ask. And, in return, she was going to stay. It was a push. Dave, who'd spent a lot of time in Canadian casinos during college, who'd run a poker game in summer camp and who'd managed to find a game in every town in which they'd ever lived, knew all about gambling, and he'd explained it to her once. A push was a tie between the bettor and the bookmaker, a game that concludes precisely on the point spread or in a draw. A game where nobody wins, but no one loses, either.

Push, Jo thought that night when they were in bed. Dave's whiskers scraped at the side of her face as he sent his palms gliding over her skin, skimming along her thighs, her hips, along the dip of her waist, then up and over her breasts. Over and over, slowly and deliberately, until she felt a heaviness gather between her legs and heard her breath come faster. When he touched her, she was wet, and when he entered her, she sighed, feeling pleasure, dim but palpable, and—she had to be honest—familiarity and comfort. When he buried his face between her neck and her left shoulder, she let the tears spill down her cheeks. Down the hall, she could hear Missy tossing in her fevered sleep. At the moment of his climax, Dave gasped out Jo's name. *You don't love him*, Jo heard her sister say . . . but she did. After a fashion. At least a little. Besides, she was old enough to know that love wasn't all that mattered. There were other things. Habit and routine. Comingled finances. Children. Letting someone else keep your secrets.

That was the night that their third daughter was conceived. Dave wanted to name her Dora, after Doris, his mother, but Jo insisted, telling him that there was a name she'd always loved, with maybe some small part of her realizing that a girl named Lila would end up with a nickname that sounded like *lie*.

Bethie

On a sunny June morning, Bethie put on a dress and one of the three pairs of pumps that the women of Blue Hill Farm traded back and forth, and arranged a pair of tortoiseshell combs in her hair. She'd taken the shoes and the combs with her when she'd left Blue Hill Farm and moved into her own place, the apartment above the shop on Peachtree Road. Rose of Sharon was supposed to meet with the bankers, but she'd gotten bronchitis, and so Bethie went to the ten o'clock appointment at the First Bank of the South all by herself, to see if the members of the Blue Hill Farm Collective could secure a line of credit, just in case the month ever came when they couldn't cover the rent or the payroll.

The fight that had brought her to this point had been terrible. "I refuse to be a cog in the capitalist war machine," Wren had said at the collective's monthly meeting. "Why are we even selling anything? Shouldn't we just barter?"

"Believe me, if I could trade jam for two-ply toilet paper, I'd do it," Bethie said.

"I don't see what the big deal is about toilet paper," said Phil, tugging at his beard, and Bethie said, "Of course you don't, you're not the one wiping with it."

"Hey! I wipe!" Phil said, and Bethie said, "Not like we do."

Wren stood up and said that she'd come to Blue Hill Farm to escape the hierarchies of capitalism, a world that arbitrarily assigned value to things and to people, and Bethie said, "So should we just give our jam away at the farmers' market?"

"Maybe," Wren said, her voice serene. Her straight brown hair fell down to her shoulders; her gauzy Indian-print skirt had bells sewn to its hem and jingled when she moved. "Why do we have to have more money? Don't we have everything we need right here?"

Bethie had to struggle not to shout. "Look," she said. "Every Sunday, we sell out at the farmers' market. Every week, we sell out at the shop. I've had three different restaurant owners ask if we can be their condiment supplier. There's a demand, but we don't have a supply. We need more people, and probably a commercial kitchen . . ."

Jodi's voice was low and clear. "This place is meant to be a refuge from that world, of commerce and value and buying and selling. And you want to drag us all right back into it." She put down the pile of angora yarn in her lap, stood, and pointed her finger at Bethie. "You're a sellout. A bougie sellout."

Bethie's face burned. "I am not a sellout! Look around you. This place is a mess! The wiring's old, and the bathroom's practically falling off the side of the house. The furnace needs to be replaced, and the kitchen sink leaks."

Bethie could have gone on, but Ronnie, her old friend, Ronnie who'd brought her to Blue Hill Farm, Ronnie who'd saved her, raised her hand. The room got quiet. Blue Hill Farm had no official leader, no hierarchies, but Ronnie was the one who'd found the farm and brought them all together. When she talked, the collective listened. Bethie held her breath, waiting for Ronnie to speak up and save her again. She watched as Ronnie, whose face was wrinkled and whose brown hair was mostly gray, got to her feet and said, "The only constant in the world is change." She put her hands on Bethie's shoulders. "Maybe Blue Hill Farm isn't your place anymore."

"What do you mean, this isn't my place?" But, even as she was asking, Bethie knew the answer. She could feel the truth, in Ronnie's hands, in Jodi's pointed finger, and in Philip's sullen stare. Maybe the status quo was okay for the rest of them, but she was tired of living in a house where the hot water ran out after the third person's shower; tired of the old-fashioned kitchen with its tilted floors and tiny sink and its temperamental oven. She was tired of every decision having to be made by consensus, tired of lentils, tired of tofu, and, yes, tired of wiping herself with cheap, scratchy toilet tissue. She'd been reborn here, she'd thrived here, she'd made peace with her own flaws and failings here; she'd found work, direction, meaning. Now, maybe Ronnie was right. She could hardly believe that she was even thinking it, but maybe it was time to go.

She'd left a week later, with permission to use the Blue Hill Farm name and recipes, and with Rose of Sharon, who'd decided that she'd also had enough. Rose of Sharon subletted a friend's apartment in Five Points, and Bethie moved into the rooms above the shop. In sixth months' time, they'd gotten more customers, hired two clerks, leased a larger kitchen. Now it was time for the next step, trying to secure a small-business loan. Phil had told Bethie he'd meet her there, but by ten-fifteen, Phil hadn't shown, and the secretary outside the bank's vice president's office was giving her the stink-eye, so Bethie rose to her feet.

"I'm ready, if Mr. Jefferson can see me now," she said. The woman outside of Mr. Jefferson's door looked at Bethie's dress and hair and pumps, gave a brief, displeased nod, and led Bethie into a plushly carpeted office, fitted with bookcases and an imposing desk. Behind the desk, in a suit and tie, with his close-cropped hair starting to gray at the temples but his uptilted eyes, and his smile just the same, sat not just any Mr. Jefferson, but Harold Jefferson, late of Ann Arbor and Detroit.

"Why, Harold!"

He smiled at Bethie, the grin that promised fun and trouble and put his white teeth on display. Bethie's heart leapt. "Well, well, well," said Harold. "I saw the name Elizabeth Kaufman on my schedule, but I wasn't sure it would be you."

"Where have you . . ." Bethie felt breathless, flushed and light-headed, like she'd been lifted by a hurricane, spun all around, and dropped into Oz. "You're a banker?"

"I am. Now. I was in the army after college."

"Oh." She hadn't known that Harold had been in the army. "I should have known that. I could have written."

"I wouldn't have said no to letters." Harold's smile faded, and Bethie bowed her head, feeling her eyes fill with tears. "Aw, c'mon, I'm not that bad, am I?"

Bethie gave a kind of gasping combined sob and giggle.

"No," she said, and shook her head. "You're not bad at all."

"So what can First Bank of the South do for you today?" Harold asked. Twenty minutes later, their line of credit secured and their business concluded, Harold offered her his arm and walked her to the bus stop and asked if he could see her Saturday night.

"So," Bethie began. "Tell me everything."

"Everything," Harold repeated, and gave her a wary smile. He'd arrived at her place in a blue-and-yellow plaid sports coat, a white shirt, a dark-blue tie, and polished loafers, carrying a bouquet of yellow roses, and Rose of Sharon, who'd come over to do Bethie's nails, had stared at him as if he'd just stepped off a spaceship. "This is Harold," she said. "We went to high school together. He's an old friend." Harold drove a Chevrolet, and he'd taken Bethie to an Italian restaurant called Nino's for dinner. Bethie had worn her best dress, light-blue silk with short sleeves and a long skirt, and a draped neckline that showed the very tops of her breasts. She felt, or imagined that she could feel, other diners looking at them as Harold held out her chair, before taking his own. Harold was still solidly built, wide shouldered and broad chested. His uptilted eyes still looked like he'd just finished laughing, his reddish-brown skin was still smooth—"Black don't crack," she remembered Harold saying—and he still had that familiar smell, of spice and soap. What she noticed most was how his posture had changed. He'd been graceful back in high school, with an athlete's command of his body, and even though he'd claimed to hate "prancing around in public," he'd been a good dancer. Now, he stood like she imagined a soldier would, his spine stiff, almost rigid, and he favored his right leg when he walked.

For dinner, they had split a chopped salad and garlic bread. Harold tried her ravioli, she sampled his shrimp, and they shared a bottle of Chianti. They talked about Atlanta, and how it was different from Detroit, and about Detroit's radical mayor, Coleman Young. Bethie filled Harold in on her sister, and Harold told her that he, too, had a sibling who'd gone East, that his oldest brother, James, had become a preacher and had gotten a pulpit at Mother Bethel A.M.E. in Philadelphia, the oldest African Methodist Episcopal church in America. Finally, with most of the pasta eaten, Bethie had asked what she'd really wanted to know—what had brought Harold to Atlanta and what he'd been doing since their last encounter.

"Well." His nostrils flared as he inhaled. "You know I was doing civil rights work, back in Ann Arbor. I helped organize the student strikes."

Bethie nodded, feeling ashamed that she didn't know more. She remembered her sister telling her that Harold had been in SDS; and she had vague memories of seeing him at campus protests, but during her time in Ann Arbor, the only things she'd cared about were her theater friends, Devon Brady, and LSD.

"After I graduated in 1965 I went back home to organize. I could see how the deck had been stacked against African Americans. All of the inequities that were built into the system. I wanted to change things."

Bethie nodded, remembering Jo's fights with her mother about the Civil Rights Act, about African American families moving into their neighborhood, and what it was doing to property values. *Do you think you can win a marathon if someone moves your starting line five miles back?* Jo would ask, and Sarah would stick out her chin and say, *Life isn't fair*.

"I painted houses for money, but my real work was in the community. Trying to educate people. Trying to show them a way out, to get them to vote, to come to city council meetings, advocate for themselves. My parents thought I was crazy." Harold made his voice low and gruff, adjusting his posture the way he had when he'd imitated his father, back at rehearsals in high school. "'Hard work, that's the only way up,' my pops used to tell me. 'Nobody handed me a damn thing. I worked for what I have. Any man can do the same.'" Harold shook his head, and Bethie thought about how much Harold's father sounded like her mother. "I'd ask him, 'How much more do you think you'd have if you'd been born with white skin?' Or 'How are folks supposed to pull themselves up by their bootstraps if they don't have any boots?'" Harold smiled a little at the memory. "Oh, we had some terrible fights. Then the riots happened." Harold's voice trailed off, and his gaze slid away from hers. Bethie nodded. She knew, of course, what had happened in Detroit in 1967, how the police had raided an after-hours bar, which had started a fight, and the city had burned for five days. Buildings, businesses, houses had all been destroyed. There'd been lootings, and beatings, more than forty arrests and over a thousand injuries. Eventually, the governor had called in the National Guard. *It is a Shame to see them burning their Own houses, destroying their Own businesses*, Sarah had written to Bethie. *I will never Understand.* But Bethie, who'd attended a few teach-ins by then, thought she could. *Imagine every single day you walk past a store full of things you can't have, can't buy*, Jodi had said. Jodi had been sitting at first, cross-legged by the fire, but as she'd spoken she'd gotten to her feet, a short, solidly built woman in bell-bottoms and a T-shirt with a Black Power logo.

The firelight had shone on the braids that fell around her face and had made her dark skin gleam. Imagine knowing that if you walk in that store, you're going to be followed and watched and treated like a thief. Imagine seeing your father and your brothers getting pulled over, getting arrested, getting locked up for nothing, trying to find jobs, trying to hold jobs, with everyone assuming they are criminals. Imagine every day you go to a school where the building's run-down and the textbooks are outdated and there's forty kids in every class, and you put your hand over your heart for the pledge—one nation, indivisible, with liberty and justice for all—but you know it's a lie, and there's no liberty for you, no justice for you. She'd widened her eyes, looking at the women and men who sat in a circle around her. Wouldn't you feel like burning something, too?

"I'd been arrested at demonstrations a few times by then, and it turns out the FBI had been watching me," Harold said. "They sent an agent to talk to me when I was locked up, and they gave me a deal. They wanted to plant me with the Black Panthers. Told me that for every person I helped them bring in, they'd pay me a few thousand dollars. I said no." He shook his head. "I hated the war."

Bethie shook her head, hoping her expression could adequately convey how much she, too, had despised the war.

"But I wouldn't inform, so they gave me a choice: the army or prison. I didn't want to fight, but I sure didn't want to get locked up, either. I knew I'd never be able to get a job once they let me out, and I figured, if I enlist, at least I'll get to be outside. Breathing fresh air, reading whatever books I wanted. You know? And my pops would be proud of me." He lifted his wineglass and took a long swallow. "I did my basic training in Fort Gordon, Georgia. First time I was ever on a plane. By January 1970, I was in Cam Ranh Bay, on the Cambodian border." He tapped his fingers on the tablecloth. His eyes were far away. "I don't know if you ever saw a picture, but it was all sand and palm trees. If you put up a resort there, you'd have rich people paying to stay." He reached across the table to top off Bethie's wineglass and to refill his own. "I started off as an armorer, in the Fourth Infantry Division. We repaired small arms, and we patrolled Highway 19 from Cambodia to Qui Nhon, trying to find caches of enemy food and weapons. They'd send us out. Clear this village, clear that one. When there was nothing else to do, we loaded sandbags."

"Were you . . ." Bethie licked her lips. Her mouth was dry, and her mind was churning. There were so many things she wanted to ask—what he'd done to get arrested prior to the riots, what had happened to him once they'd begun, and if he'd gotten hurt. How his parents and brothers and sisters had felt when he'd gone to Georgia, then to Vietnam. Was it as bad as she'd heard, was it as unfair, were the black soldiers given the worst assignments and put on the front lines, and if he'd had a girlfriend, or even a wife; a woman who'd loved him and who'd worried while he was gone. She wanted to tell him that she, too, saw the unfairness, that she was committed to trying to change things. She cleared her throat, sipped her wine, and finally managed, "What was it like, being a soldier over there?"

"You mean, did I kill anyone?" Harold's face was very still. "I never shot anyone face-to-face." He snorted. "You like that answer?" He lifted his glass, looked into it, and set it down without drinking. "I was afraid. That's what I remember most. Waking up scared, going to sleep scared, and being scared every minute in between." He pressed his palms against his face and moved them from his cheeks to his ears, back and forth, like he was washing his face. "My last month there, I was driving an amtrac— an amphibious tractor, like a tank. It wasn't technically my job, but they said they didn't have anyone else to do it. We hit a mine. Got blown straight up in the air. It was . . ." He paused, bringing his hands to his face again. "It was the loudest sound I'd ever heard in my life. The gunner and I got blown straight out of the trac, and when I came down, a piece of it—a piece of the metal—landed on my leg. And it was on fire." His voice was steady and matter-of-fact. "My fatigues . . . my leg . . . just burning."

"Oh, God." Her heart was pounding, and her face felt cold. She wanted to touch him, and wondered if she could, if he'd want that. She wondered if people would see, and if they'd stare, so instead of reaching for his hand, she said, "Harold, I'm so sorry."

He nodded without meeting her eyes.

"You don't have to tell me anymore," Bethie said. "I'm just so sorry. So sorry that it happened to you. It was a terrible, unjust war—"

"Yeah." He drew a long, slow breath as Bethie cringed at the inadequacy of her words, at how clichéd they sounded. "I was in a hospital in Japan for ten months. I don't remember a lot of it. I had surgeries and skin grafts. The doctors took off three of my toes, and for a while, they thought they were going to have to amputate my foot, but I got lucky. They said if I hadn't been young and strong going in . . ." Harold shook his head. "It could've been worse," he said. "It was for a lot of the men. Soldiers in the hospital with me, they lost their arms, their legs. One man, the whole side of his face was just gone. He'd been burned right to the bone."

"Oh, Harold. Oh, God." Bethie's stomach was clenched tight as a fist. She felt a great, impotent rage sweep through her, fury at the war, and the politicians who'd sent so many young men to be maimed or killed.

"When I was well enough to go, I came back here, to Georgia. To Fort Gordon."

"Not home?"

Harold shook his head. "My father said the army would make a man out of me. It took me a while to stop being angry about it. I needed some distance. My degree from Michigan was in economics. I got my discharge, and I took a job at the First Bank of the South." He looked up and gave Bethie a smile that she could tell took effort. "And I kept hearing about this girl who made the best peach preserves down at the farmers' market. This girl from Detroit. And when I heard that she needed a loan, I made sure I was the one to see her."

Bethie felt her cheeks turn pink. She wanted to touch him again, and contented herself with looking at him and, very quietly, saying his name.

Every Saturday night after that, Harold would come to her place, always in a pressed shirt, sometimes in a jacket and tie, and always with a little gift: flowers, or a box of chocolates, the new Aretha Franklin or Stevie Wonder album, and once, on her birthday, a set of combs inlaid with mother-of-pearl. He took her to the movies, always insisting on paying for her ticket, and to outdoor concerts in Chamblee. They ate pizza and drank beer and played Did You Know and Do You Remember, with Bethie realizing that there was very little overlap between the kids she'd known in high school and Harold's friends, or between the places she'd been to eat and dance and drive, and the places he'd gone. It was as if there was a city under the city, or two cities that existed side by side, both invisible to each other. Music was where they intersected. They both had grown up listening to Motown on the radio. Harold remembered every word to every song, and she'd try to get him to sing, when she could. They talked and laughed, but Harold never touched her. It left Bethie confused and unsettled, flushed and breathless, feeling constantly like she'd misplaced something important, her car keys or her wallet, and she was always having to turn her room or her purse upside down to find it. She liked Harold, more than she'd liked any man since Devon Brady, long ago. She liked his patience, his solidity, the way he smelled. She liked his smooth skin, his big hands, with their neatly clipped square-shaped nails; the way he'd harmonize, almost unconsciously, with every song on the radio when they were driving, while drumming a backbeat on the steering wheel. But did he care for her? Was a life with Harold possible? And if it was, would Harold even want it?

After months of Saturday night dates and phone calls more weeknights than not, Thanksgiving came. Instead of going home to Detroit, or waiting to see if Jo would invite her to Connecticut, Bethie asked Harold to join her at Blue Hill Farm. There would be friends, and friends of friends, relatives and children and always a few strays, people who had nowhere else to go. "Is there going to be turkey?" Harold asked. "Because turkey is nonnegotiable." Bethie promised him turkey, and Harold said he would bring macaroni and cheese, and he'd bake his mother's sweet potato pie.

On the appointed Thursday, he picked her up at her apartment, wearing blue jeans that looked brand-new and a dark blue sweater that lent a richness to his skin and made Bethie think about laying her head on the broad expanse of his chest. Ronnie and Jodi and Danielle had cleared the furniture out of the living room and set up rows of folding tables, covered in slightly mismatched white tablecloths. At four o'clock, twenty-seven people gathered around the table and held hands and thanked the Earth for Her bounty before tucking into the turkey, which Bethie made sure was near their end of the table, and baked stuffed squashes, mashed potatoes and sweet potatoes, corn bread and relish, biscuits and jam, and Harold's offerings.

When dinner was over, it was still warm enough to light a fire in the firepit out back. Blankets were spread, whiskey was sipped, a few joints were toked. Harold and Bethie sat side by side, and Harold caught her up on his siblings. "My sister Hattie's been married twice, to two different men named Bernard."

"Really?"

"Really. My parents call her new husband Bernard the Second."

"I bet Hattie loves that," Bethie murmured.

"She's just glad they're talking to her. They were not happy when she and the first Bernard broke up. 'Jeffersons don't get divorced!' my father kept saying." He sipped from the bottle of whiskey, passed it to Bethie, and said, "Last year my sister Ernestine brought a white boy home for Christmas."

Bethie felt her breath catch in her throat. She peeked at Harold's face, which was carefully expressionless. "I take it that was not what your parents were hoping to find under the tree?"

Harold gave a brief snort of laughter and shook his head. "So how'd it go?" she asked. The fire was blazing, and people were talking, and someone was playing a banjo, and someone else was blowing into a harmonica, but Bethie couldn't hear anything but her heart.

Harold said, "Um."

Bethie's heart sank.

"It didn't go well," Harold finally admitted. "I mean, my folks were polite while he was there. They let Ernie have it after he was gone."

"What'd they say?"

Harold was frowning. "Probably the same stuff your parents would've said to you."

Bethie winced, imagining that conversation and what her mother would say.

"They said that she was asking for trouble. That people would stare at them, or say things, or worse. That her life would be hard. That if they had kids, their lives would be impossible, because they'd never know who they were or where they belonged."

"Wow." Bethie's heart was beating hard. Was this Harold's way of letting her down easy, telling her that it could never be? "So what do you think?"

Harold turned to look at her, briefly, before returning his gaze to the fire. "I think you love who you love," he said. Before Bethie could let herself feel happy or hopeful, he added, "I think it's easier, for sure, if you love someone who's like you."

Bethie stared down at the grass, hearing her mother's voice. *Birds of a feather must flock together.* She knew, too, what Sarah had to say about Jews who married gentiles. Her mother had friends who'd refused to attend their own children's weddings in protest, friends who'd sat shiva when their children had married non-Jews, who'd had grandchildren they'd never even met. *Would you do that?* she'd asked her mother once, long ago. *Would you actually skip my wedding?* Sarah had given her a hard look. *Don't try me,* her mother had said.

"But for me . . ." Bethie saw Harold's shoulders hunch, heard him inhale. "Well. Maybe I'm putting the cart before the horse here, but I should tell you . . ."

"Tell me what?"

"That I can't have kids." His voice was quiet, and his body was very still. "In Vietnam, they used chemical defoliants. They found out later that the soldiers who were exposed to them would end up with cancer. Or they'd be sterile, or their wives would have miscarriages, or they'd have kids with birth defects. I knew I'd never . . ." He breathed again. "I knew I'd never want to try, knowing what could happen. I had a vasectomy a few years ago. Just to be sure."

Bethie felt sick, angry and sad, furious at what Harold had been cheated out of, at what that war had taken. "I'm sorry," she said, hearing her voice crack. "I'm sorry that happened to you."

He gave a slow nod. "I was angry about it for a long time. But now . . ." Another shrug. "I couldn't be as angry as I was forever."

"I had an abortion," she said into the silence. She felt like she needed to say it, to tell him what she'd never told another man, to let him see her clearly, all of her scars. To trust him with this truth as he'd trusted her with his. Sitting beside him, her eyes on her lap, she said, "I was raped the summer after my sophomore year. Dev took me to a concert, and I got high. And I got lost and ran right into a bunch of bad guys."

For a moment, Harold was silent. Bethie could feel tension, like the air was getting thick before a storm. Then—finally—she felt Harold reach for her hand. In a hoarse voice, he said, "I don't want anything bad to happen to you again."

Bethie shut her eyes. "Do you think . . ." Once again, Bethie's mind was whirling with questions. Do you think that this can work; do you think people will accept us; do you think we can find a place to be in the world? Where would they live, and what holidays would they celebrate, and would Harold want her to go to church with him, or convert? How would his parents feel about her? How would her mother feel about him? Would Sarah be glad that Bethie was with someone, even if that someone wasn't white and wasn't Jewish, or would she hiss *unnatural*, the way she had at Jo?

Part of her wanted not to think at all; to take him in her arms and into her bed, to hold him and let him hold her and tell herself that tomorrow was another day, and they'd figure it out as they went. Part of her— a larger, more sensible part—knew that Harold would never agree to that. Harold was careful, deliberate, and methodical. *Measure twice, cut once*, she'd heard him say. And he wasn't a risk-taker. He'd want to know exactly what he was getting into, exactly what he'd be gaining, and losing, by choosing her. Bethie closed her eyes, feeling sorry for herself, and feeling, too, a deep, aching sympathy for her sister, who must have asked herself all of the same questions when she'd been in love with Shelley. Where will we go, and how will we live, and is there any place on earth where we can be together?

"I want to be with you," she said, not caring that it was forward or unladylike. "I want us to be together."

For a long, awful moment, Harold didn't answer. In that time, Bethie imagined life without him. No more Saturday nights reminiscing about drag races on Woodward Avenue, or Coach Krantz, or the Thanksgiving Day parade. No more phone calls at nine o'clock just to see how she was doing; no more bouquets that she'd stick in empty Mason jars and smile every time she saw. No more daydreaming about how it would feel to have Harold naked against her; how it would feel to touch the glossy skin of his back and shoulders and the dense curls on his head, to see if he smelled just as spicy up close.

"It won't be easy," he said. She could feel his deep voice rumbling right through her.

"I know," she said.

"You don't," said Harold. He sounded glum, but he hadn't let go of her hand. "Maybe you think you know, but you don't. You can't." He looked around at the people sitting by the fire, some black, some white, and said, speaking slowly, "You think we come from the same place. We don't. My Detroit, my family, my history, it's all different." His chest rose and fell as he sighed. "Maybe it's okay here, for us to be together. But this isn't the world."

"I can be brave," she told him. When he didn't answer, she squeezed his hand and pulled him to his feet. "Want to see my old room?" she asked, remembering what he'd told her at that party long ago. *A closed mouth don't get fed.* Bethie led him into the house, up the stairs, and into the attic, where she'd stayed when she'd first washed up in Atlanta, broken and lost and hating herself.

Harold looked around. There were three single beds in iron frames, a blue-and-white rag rug on the floor and, on a table pushed underneath a window, a record player and a stack of albums. He knelt, flipped through them, pulled one out, and settled it onto the turntable. "Some enchanted evening," Bethie heard Frank Sinatra singing from *South Pacific*. "You may see a stranger, / You may see a stranger, across a crowded room." Tears stung her eyes. Harold turned to her, opening his arms, and Bethie stepped into his embrace, settling her cheek against his shoulder, which felt as solid as she'd hoped. She pulled him close, until he was leaning against her, letting him know, without words, that she could be strong, that she could support him, that she could be what he needed, just as he was what she needed.

Jo

Nana, Nana!" Lila shouted, racing out of the car and into Sarah's arms. Jo braced herself for scoldings, for her mother's pursed lips and pointed fingers, but as her teenagers emerged from the station wagon, stretching and yawning, she saw that Sarah was actually giving Lila a hug.

Kindred spirits, Jo thought, and immediately felt guilty for comparing her youngest daughter to her intolerant, censorious mother . . . but, if she was being honest, she had to admit that the two of them had a surprising affinity. *The Wicked Witch of the West has found her apprentice*, was how Dave put it, and Jo would flush with frustration, not knowing which one of them she was supposed to defend.

"I made rugelach," Sarah announced, leading Lila into the little brick house on Alhambra Street. In 1985, after twenty-five years at Hudson's, Sarah had taken a retirement package, but had refused to move, even though, by then, Bethie could have bought her a house in Bloomfield Hills if she'd wanted one. *Why should I move?* Sarah had asked. *Why do I need all those empty rooms to clean?* She gardened and played bridge and had a regular mahjongg game, and although she had no real friends, as far as Bethie could tell, she had a range of acquaintances. She'd joined the synagogue's Community of Care and delivered meals to new mothers twice a week. "I get to hold the babies. That's the best part," she'd say. For a while, she'd look meaningfully at Bethie's midriff when she talked about the babies. Bethie suspected that, at some point, Harold must have taken her aside and explained that no additional grandchildren would be forthcoming. Either that, or the passage of time had done the trick, because right around Bethie's fortieth birthday, the comments had stopped.

For this visit, to celebrate Sarah's seventieth birthday, the plan was for the girls to stay with Sarah, all three of them in the bedroom that had once belonged to Bethie and Jo, and Jo was already prepared for Missy and Kim to beg to be allowed to stay with the adults at the hotel instead. *It's so dark there*, Missy said. It was true that the maple tree had grown to a towering height, and that its leaves kept most of the house in the shade, but that wasn't what Missy meant. Over the years Jo and Bethie (mostly Bethie) had paid for improvements to the property—a new roof in '82, new carpeting the year after that, and all new kitchen appliances the year after that. The driveway had been repaved, the landscaping redone, but for all that, the house still felt unchanged. The new kitchen floor was tile, not linoleum, but somehow there was already a worn spot in front of the sink, and Jo suspected that her mother purchased the lowest-wattage light bulbs on the market to save money, which kept the place dim.

"Come on in, everyone," Sarah said as Bethie and Harold arrived. While Jo and Dave had made the trip from Connecticut by car, her sister and brother-in-law had flown from Atlanta and rented a four-door sedan at the airport. "There's tea and cookies."

"Who is she?" Bethie whispered to Jo. "And what has she done with our mother?"

Jo smiled back, but it was a brief smile. Things were still tense between her and her sister, and had been for years. The blowout at Blue Hill Farm had been part of it. The card Bethie had sent after Lila's birth, fulsomely congratulating Jo on her commitment to her family, had felt like another slap. In the years since her post-blizzard trip to Atlanta, she'd spent time with Bethie at Thanksgivings and Passover Seders, in Connecticut or in Michigan, or over the last few years, at the beautiful home that Bethie and Harold had purchased in a neighborhood called Buckhead, where, Jo suspected, there weren't many Jews, even fewer blacks, and maybe no interracial couples at all. The summer visits to Georgia continued, with the rafting trips and the campfires behind Blue Hill Farm, where Bethie would take them to pick raspberries and spend the day. Jo had overheard the two older girls reminiscing, telling Lila how it had been when Bethie had lived on the farm. "It was like a great big slumber party that never ended," Kim had said. "All the kids slept in the attic, and you could stay up and talk all night."

"But the hamburgers weren't real hamburgers," Missy had added with a frown. "They were made of black bean mush."

As soon as Lila began nursery school, Jo started dropping the girls off with Aunt Bethie. She'd kiss them goodbye, give Bethie a list of what foods Lila was currently eating (it was easier to list those than to list the foods Lila wouldn't eat), turn the car around, and drive back home. She would tell herself that a child-free house was as good as a vacation, but all it did was emphasize how little she and Dave had to say to each other. The girls were what bound them and what gave them fodder for conversation. Had they saved enough for Missy's braces? Did Kim really need to buy a new dress to attend the prom at a different school, or could she just wear the dress she'd worn to her own school dance? Was it worth making an appointment with a psychologist, or would Lila figure out how to control her temper on her own?

Jo would always plan on using the free time to write, to finally begin the novel she'd always imagined writing, or even just a short story, or a poem, but it seemed she had no stories left, other than the ones about local residents that she wrote for the *Avondale Almanac* (her most recent opus had featured an area man who'd amassed the largest collection of *He-Man* action figures in all of New England). She'd sit in front of the Olivetti that Shelley had given her all those years ago. *Once upon a time*, she would type . . . and then her fingers would stop, and she'd sit, staring at that line, unable to think of what came next. "Write the stories you told us when we were little," Kim would say. "Those were great!"

But Jo knew her stories weren't special, or what anyone wanted. Parents were the ones who bought children's books, and parents wanted sweet stories with beautiful princesses, brave princes, and happy endings, or trees that gave and gave until they were just stumps. They did not want stories like the ones Jo had told Kim and Missy, where the prince was a lazy bungler who kept falling off his horse, and the princess ended up saving both of them, then riding off into the sky for parts unknown with the dragon whose company she preferred to the prince's. And Lila had hated stories, and bedtime in general. She'd kick and scream at naptime and at night, wailing, "Not tired. NOT TIRED!" until she'd finally collapse, facedown in her crib, and when Jo had tried to pull Lila into her lap for a story during the daytime, Lila would indulge her mother for a page or two, then squirm away, looking for something to break. Jo was in her forties, officially middle-aged, and it was time to accept the truth. She was a reasonably good substitute teacher, and her stories for the *Almanac* were acceptable, but she would never be a writer. In fact, the only thing she felt like writing were the bits of doggerel that popped into her head and hung around like stubborn colds, when she was grading history tests or peeling more carrots that wouldn't get eaten. *A girl named Jo once had a life / But that's gone now; she's only wife.*

It might have been easier to endure if Bethie's success hadn't been so spectacular. In a few years' time, her sister had gone from making jam in the kitchen of Blue Hill Farm and selling it at farmers' markets to selling it at a little shop to supplying what seemed like half of the restaurants and hotels in the South. Jo wondered about the toll that might exact on her sister's marriage, but Harold seemed perfectly fine with things. It probably helped that he, too, had started his own business, a security consulting firm. At first, he ran it as a part-time venture, in addition to his work at the bank, but eventually he had more business than he could handle, and he left his job to run the firm, which now employed almost a hundred men and women, many of them veterans.

Bethie and Harold glowed, with success and contentedness, and with, Jo thought, a little meanly, the kind of well-rested good looks you could have only when you were childless. She'd asked her sister about it once, and Bethie had given a firm headshake, hinting that there was some kind of war-related health issue, some reason that they'd chosen not to have children. Jo hadn't pushed for details. Nor had she told Dave, who probably would have started making mean jokes about precisely what had been shot off Harold in the war. Dave himself had been a full-time student during the draft. Jo suspected that he'd taken a leisurely path to his bachelor's degree in order to stretch out his student deferment. He hadn't done anything close to illegal. Still, Jo was aware that this was one more arena in which her sister had bested her. Bethie's husband was not only successful, and a good provider, he had served his country, had been wounded in combat. As for her husband, he'd once been briefly hospitalized after breaking three bones in his foot when a ten-pound weight had fallen from a shelf.

Jo sighed. Her sister looked at her with a quizzical expression. Bethie had changed her hair again. The Glenn Close in *Fatal Attraction* perm was gone, replaced by a long, layered Diane Keaton in *Baby Boom* bob. Maybe they were just busy, Jo thought. She knew the story of Blue Hill Farm by heart, the myth that her sister had burnished in all of those newspaper profiles, how she and her partners had gone from making jam in small batches in the Blue Hill Farm kitchen to selling it at farmers' markets, and how one restaurant owner had asked them to make jam for his customers, then two restaurants, then three, then hotels. By 1981, Blue Hill Farm had a dozen wholesale customers, and they'd shifted their base of operations to a commercial kitchen in Loring Heights. The next year, they'd won an award for outstanding product line in the nation at the Specialty Food Show in New York City, and sent out their first catalog. Jo had paged through the glossy photographs and ecstatic descriptions and wondered if Bethie had missed her, and who she'd found to write about the various jams and dressings. The orders Bethie had written had surpassed every expectation, and two chain grocery stores had started to carry their wares. Bethie and her partners had hired a CFO, a bright young woman with a Wharton degree, and broken ground on construction of a building that would house a much bigger commercial kitchen, in addition to a shop, a restaurant, and a cooking school. On that afternoon, in 1987, Blue Hill Farm was producing around forty thousand jars of preserves daily, in addition to the new product lines rolled out twice a year. The farm itself no longer existed as a commune and had been completely remodeled, the peeling paint scraped off, the floorboards patched, the windows replaced, and a few new bathrooms added, along with modern plumbing. It was a shop/inn/tourist destination, and Bethie was the Blue Hill Farm co-CEO. She looked the part, too, with her hair cut and styled and highlighted, her peasant blouses and bell-bottoms swapped for shoulder pads and sharp Jil Sander suits. Jo knew that Bethie still fretted about her weight, with her anxiety usually cresting right around the times she knew she'd be seeing her mother, but Jo thought that Bethie still looked good, healthy.

These days, Bethie wore as much makeup as any of Jo's acquaintances, and she shaved and plucked all the places that Jo's friends shaved and plucked, and if she still thought bras and high-heeled shoes were tools of the patriarchy, she'd made peace with wearing them. "If you want to know the truth," Bethie had said when Jo had called to offer her congratulations on the *New York Times* piece, "I tell all the reporters that I paid attention to entrepreneurs, but the one I really learned from was Dev."

"Devon Brady?"

"He had a quality product. Distinctive packaging. He knew his customers. He couldn't advertise, but he certainly used word-of-mouth effectively."

"You should tell people," Jo said. "Who knows how many ambitious young drug dealers you could inspire?"

Bethie smiled. Jo smiled back. At the exact same instant, the sisters said, "Hey, do you remember—" They broke off, laughing, and Jo was about to say, *No, you go first,* when Sarah came through the front door. In the sunlight, Jo could see that Sarah's face was drawn, that her shoulders were hunched, and that, instead of keeping her usual brisk pace, she was walking slowly, like every step pained her. Worse, she hadn't put on a full face of makeup the way she did every morning, even if all she was doing was going to the stoop to retrieve the *Free Press*. Her cheeks were pale, her eyes sunken and glassy. Jo felt an icy finger draw a line up her spine. She looked at her sister and saw that Bethie was seeing what she was seeing.

"Girls," their mother began, "I have some news."

Bethie

Sarah had left them a letter, in the top drawer of her dresser, in a business-sized envelope, with both of their names on the front. After the funeral, Bethie and Jo were going through their mother's things. Jo was tackling the closet, and Bethie was in charge of the dresser, so she was the one who found it.

"Should we read it?" Bethie asked.

Jo bit her lip, thinking. "Tonight," she said. "When shiva's over."

That afternoon, the house filled up the way it had for the two days before, with Sarah's colleagues from Hudson's, her friends from shul, Mrs. Johnson from across the street. Dozens of women, all of them saying the same thing: *Your mother loved you girls so much.* Bethie and Jo would give each other the same quizzical look, as Marge from Better Dresses or Carol from the synagogue told one or both girls how Sarah had bragged about Bethie's business and Jo's children. *She loved you so much. She talked about you all the time. She was so proud.*

That night, after the rabbi led a minyan through the Kaddish prayer and the house finally emptied, Jo had found a bottle of schnapps, possibly one left over from their father's shiva. Dave and Harold took the girls back to the hotel for the night, and Jo and Bethie took the letter and the booze outside to the backyard, where Sarah had set up a wrought-iron table with four tiny, tippy chairs underneath the cherry tree. Jo and Bethie squeezed themselves into the chairs. Jo opened the letter, written in blue ink on lined notebook paper, in Sarah's firm, back-slanted handwriting, with her usual abbreviations, capitalizations, and other uses of punctuation. They read and learned that, just as there were things they had never gotten to say to their mother, there were things that Sarah Kaufman had chosen not to say to them.

Drs found Mass in my belly six months ago. That was how the letter began. No *Dear Josette and Elizabeth*, no *Jo and Bethie*, no *My darling daughters* or *These are my dying declarations*. "She sure knew how to get to the point," Jo said.

Did one round of chemotherapy and got sick as a dog.

"She went through chemo? And didn't tell us?" Bethie's eyes were stinging. Whatever she'd felt about her mother, whatever resentments she'd held on to, the thought of Sarah going through treatment alone made her want to cry.

"That was Mom." Jo's voice was bleak. "Even if we had found out, somehow, she wouldn't have wanted us there."

Bethie kept reading. *I know you'll be angry that I didn't tell you, but I am a private person and did not want to burden you with my troubles. Jo, you have your husband and your girls, and Bethie, you have your "big business" to run.*

Neither sister said anything about the way Sarah

hadn't mentioned Bethie's spouse, although Bethie was sure that Jo had noticed. Sarah had gotten very quiet after Bethie told her that she and Harold had gotten married in a small ceremony at City Hall in Atlanta. "I'm glad you've finally settled down," was all she'd said, but Bethie knew that having a daughter married to a non-Jew and black man had not been a part of Sarah's vision for her good girl. Still, she'd sent a wedding gift, a set of crystal wineglasses from Hudson's. She'd hosted Harold's family for holidays, and had visited them in Atlanta, and even if she'd never seemed entirely comfortable around Harold, Bethie recognized that her mother was trying.

I told my Drs. "no more." They gave me medicine for the pain. It didn't hurt much. I am sorry.

Here, there was a space, as if Sarah had paused to gather her thoughts, to figure out what it was that she was sorry for, and what else she needed to say.

. . . for any way I might have failed you. There is a Will in the safe-deposit box (key in drawer in bedside table). Freddie Barash is Lawyer. Left $ to Grandkids, Jewelry and Keepsakes to Bethie, except a few things marked for friends.

"Well," Jo murmured, "that's pretty cut-and-dried." She looked sideways at her sister.

Be good to each other was the last thing Sarah had written, before *Love, Mother.*

Jo folded up the pages and slipped them into the envelope. For a moment, neither of them spoke, and when they did, they both said "I'm sorry" at precisely the same instant. Bethie started laughing, then the laughter turned into a sob. She sniffled, wiping her eyes, and looked at her sister. "What are you sorry for?"

"For not being around when you needed me," Jo said. "For not being there when you were in trouble."

Bethie wiped dust off the bottle of schnapps, uncapped it, raised it to her lips, and took a swallow. Nine years ago, when they'd had their fight, she would have given anything for Jo to say those words, for Jo to take some responsibility for what had happened to Bethie. Now, between the therapy she'd gone through and Harold's perspective, she could see it differently. *You were kids,* Harold would tell her, in the deep, resonant voice that made even an observation that they were out of paper towels sound as portentous as a reading from the Bible. *Not even kids: teenagers. Of course Jo was all up in her own head. That's the nature of the beast. And your mom was probably just trying to keep the boat from sinking.* Bethie's therapist, whose name was Allison Shoemaker and whose voice was fluty and sweet, had urged her to consider the most benign interpretation. *Maybe she genuinely didn't notice,* Dr. Shoemaker had suggested. *When she found out, she behaved appropriately, right? She tried to protect you. She let you know that she cared.*

"It's fine," Bethie said. "You didn't do anything wrong."

"I could have done more."

"Maybe," Bethie allowed. "But, for that to happen, you would have needed to know what was going on. And you didn't."

"If I'd been around more, I would have noticed." Lynnette Bobeck, Jo's teenage distraction, had come to the shiva. She'd put on forty pounds since high school and dyed her hair an unbecomingly brassy shade of blond. Her oldest son was in college, a sophomore at the U of M, as hard as that was to believe. Bethie took another swallow of schnapps, wincing at the burn. "Ugh, what is this supposed to taste like? Mouthwash in hell?"

"Cinnamon." Jo extended her hand, wiggling her fingers, and Bethie passed her the bottle. Jo drank, winced, gasped, and said, "Ow."

"I know." Bethie looked out into the darkness, the velvety sky, the faint glow of the stars visible through the layer of pollution. "Do you think you'll miss Mom? She was so hard on you."

Jo drank again, coughed, passed Bethie the bottle, and said, "She was hard on both of us." Bethie nodded. Every December, she'd gotten a chance to see a different kind of mother/daughter relationship at Harold's house, just a mile to the south of Alhambra Street, a significantly bigger and more impressive house than the one she'd grown up in. She and Harold would visit every Christmas. The Jefferson house was always full of music, raised voices, the smell of something being braised or fried or simmered. Harold's mother, Irene, doted on her daughters and her grandchildren. She was liberal with her hugs and kisses, and happiest when she had her newest grandbaby in her arms. Every year, someone would be having some kind of crisis, either romantic or financial. Harold's mother would invite the suffering son or daughter up into her bedroom, where, Bethie knew, she'd dispense commands in the form of advice from her seat at her vanity. So far, Bethie hadn't set foot in the sanctum. Harold's mother was polite to Bethie, and she treated Harold like a conquering king whenever he came home. There'd be a party, and Luther Jefferson's famous barbecued brisket, cooked for twelve hours in a smoker out back, and games of dominoes and Spades, which Bethie had given up trying to learn. She always felt like an outsider there, no matter how polite Harold's mother was to her, so she ate her brisket, played with her nieces and nephews, helped with the dishes, and tried to stay out of the way.

"I wasn't the easiest kid." Jo had another sip. "Some days, with Lila, I know how Mom must have felt. It's like, I love her to death, but I also want to throw her out a window."

Bethie snorted.

"I feel like she's made it her life's mission to get under my skin. I bet Mom felt the same way about me."

"Still," said Bethie.

Jo raised her shoulders, shrugging.

"I'm sorry, too," said Bethie. "Your marriage was none of my business. I shouldn't have dragged you down to Atlanta and lectured you about how you weren't happy."

Bethie saw her sister's shoulders draw together, saw her pull her knees up to her chest and wrap her arms around them. After a moment, Jo said, "Marriage is hard."

"It is," Bethie agreed, even though her marriage, while of much shorter duration than her sister's, had been largely trouble-free. Harold was a good man, and she knew what he'd sacrificed to be with her. She knew it when his brothers went on trips to Vegas and didn't invite him; she knew it when, once, he'd called her from Mervyn's, where he'd taken Kim and Missy. His voice had been tight when he'd put Bethie on the phone with the security guard who hadn't believed that the girls were his nieces, and who'd needed a white woman's assurance that Harold hadn't kidnapped them. If he could endure that for her, if he could live with a wife who outearned him, if he could sit and applaud while she collected an award from the Chamber of Commerce, Bethie could deal with his snoring, or the way he'd leave the sports section unfolded on the kitchen table, or the card games that lasted until two in the morning and left the living room smelling like an ashtray. She held out her hand for the bottle and waited to hear if Jo had anything else to say. When Jo didn't speak, Bethie said, "I have an offer for you."

Jo looked at her. "Oh?"

"Your trip. The one you never got to take. Now that the business is doing well . . ."

Jo made a face. "Nice understatement."

"I want you to take a trip. Anywhere you want to go, for as long as you want to stay. You have to go by yourself, though. Or with a friend. No husband, no kids. That's my only condition."

For a long moment, Jo didn't say anything. When she finally spoke, Bethie wasn't surprised at her response. "I can't."

"Why not?"

"It's . . ." She turned her face away from Bethie. "It's not a good time right now."

"You don't have to leave right this minute. I'm just making the offer."

"It's not your job to take care of me." Jo's voice sounded waspish. Bethie wasn't surprised. With Dr. Shoemaker, and on her own, she'd spent a lot of time thinking about the ways that money can complicate relationships. *If you give someone a gift they can't hope to reciprocate, they can end up feeling resentful,* Dr. Shoemaker had said. *You have to give without expectation, without needing anything more than a thank-you.*

"It's not about taking care of you," Bethie said. "You missed your trip because of me. I owe you. All I want to do is give you what you should have had." When Jo didn't answer, Bethie said, "Actually, that's not the only thing I want. I want to be in your life, and I want you to be a part of mine." Her voice sounded rougher as she said, "I missed you, you know. Not that I don't enjoy spending time with my nieces . . ."

"They adore you," said Jo.

"And I love them. But you're my sister, and you're the only family I've got, and I miss you." She saw Jo's shoulders rising, heard her sister's inhalation, and Jo's voice, quiet but perfectly audible, when she said, "I missed you, too."

Jo

One afternoon in early March, Jo was running on the town's fitness trail when she heard someone call, "Hey, wait up!" She turned, and there was Nonie Scotto, in brand-new sneakers and a pink nylon track suit that whistled as Nonie approached.

"Fancy meeting you here," said Jo, jogging in place.

Nonie's face was pink and sweaty, and she looked miserable. "You have to help me," she said. "It's my twenty-fifth high school reunion coming up, and I can't go there like this." She made a stab at jogging in place, then gave up and stood still.

Jo studied her friend. It was true that Nonie had put on weight in the years that Jo had known her, years that Nonie had spent in a state that ranged from annoyance to anguished despair over what she never failed to refer to as her "figure." Every year, in January, and sometimes in May, right before swimsuit season, Nonie would sign up for Weight Watchers or TOPS or Overeaters Anonymous. She'd come back from the initial meeting with her purse full of literature and her eyes full of fire, convinced that the reason none of her previous attempts had resulted in permanent lifelong weight loss was because she'd failed the program, not because the diet she'd gone on was unsustainable. "This time, I'm going to see it through," she'd say, and she'd drop ten or fifteen pounds in the first three or four weeks. At that point, after squeezing into her size-ten designer jeans and collecting a round of compliments, she'd get bored, and hungry. A slice of pizza would turn into three slices, a cheat meal would turn into a cheat long weekend, and then Nonie would show up on a friend's doorstep, announcing, "I'm off the wagon. Want to get a banana split?"

"You know what my problem is?" she'd asked Jo once, after ending a three-month stint on Weight Watchers, through a mouthful of half-melted ice cream and hot fudge at the Farm Shoppe, Avondale's ice-cream parlor. "My problem is that a lot of things taste as good as thin feels."

Jo always tried to tell Nonie that she looked fine, that her curvy figure suited her. "Not every single person's meant to be thin," Jo said.

"Says the thin lady," Nonie retorted. On the fitness trail, a pair of joggers ran past them. Nonie put her hands on her hips, and squinted up at Jo. "C'mon. Tell me what to do. You teach PE, right?"

"I substitute-teach at the elementary school."

"Good enough. Let's go."

The town's fitness trail had just been completed the previous October. It was a two-mile dirt path that formed a loop around Avondale's recreation center and golf course. Every quarter-mile, there were stations with instructional signs, and bars for pull-ups, or logs under which you could tuck your feet for sit-ups. Jo normally just ran the loop, sometimes once, sometimes twice, but that afternoon she stopped at each of the stations, guiding Nonie through squats and lunges and jumping jacks. "Come with me," Nonie said when they were done, marching past the clubhouse and leading Jo to her car. Jo followed along, curious and amused and, of course, knowing that she'd follow Nonie anywhere.

"Look," Nonie said, arming sweat off her forehead, reaching into her purse, which she'd locked in the trunk, and removing a copy of what turned out to be her high school yearbook. "Wait 'til you see. I used to be beautiful."

"You're still beautiful," Jo said. Nonie gave a rude snort, opened the yearbook, and showed Jo a picture of herself, in a pleated cheerleader's skirt, performing a split in midair. Her slim legs were spread wide against the sky, and the guy who'd tossed her stood underneath her, arms cupped, head tilted upward, looking delighted at the prospect of her descent.

"You see?" Nonie asked.

Jo drummed her fingers against her thigh. She'd worn plain gray sweatpants and a navy-blue T-shirt, her usual workout gear. "I don't know much about diets . . ."

"Oh, that part's easy," Nonie said, waving her hand. "For breakfast, you have hot water with lemon juice and cayenne pepper and maple syrup. Then you have a hard-boiled egg and half a grapefruit for lunch, or a can of tuna with no mayo, and you eat what everyone else has for dinner, only you make yourself throw up, after."

Jo stared at her, horrified. Nonie stared right back.

"What? It's only for two weeks." She closed her yearbook, running her fingers over its hardbound cover, looking wistful. "Maybe three. And it works. My sorority sisters and I did it all the time."

Jo suspected that an eighteen-year-old girl would have an easier time shedding pounds than a woman in her forties, but she kept quiet. It was after four o'clock, almost four-thirty. She'd have to hurry if she wanted to get home before Lila. Her youngest daughter had a key, but she frequently lost it, and if Kim and Missy were still at school or at soccer practice, Jo would come home to find her forlorn ten-year-old sitting on the front step, scowling, as if Jo had been the one who'd screwed up.

"Anyhow," Nonie said. "You let me worry about the food. I just want you to give me some exercises. So I can tone up my problem areas." She patted her thighs, then frowned at the jiggle.

"You can't lose weight in just specific parts of your—"

"Oh, hush!" Nonie said, playfully putting her hand across Jo's mouth. "Let me cling to my dreams. Just tell me that you'll help me."

Jo considered. "I'll do it," she said. "But only if you promise you'll eat reasonably. No crash diets. No throwing up."

"Fine, fine," Nonie said, rolling her eyes.

"Okay," said Jo. "I'll work on a plan. Can you meet me here tomorrow at three-forty-five?"

"Same bat time, same bat station," Nonie said, smiling brightly, and Jo felt her heart lift and her cheeks get warm, and told herself that it didn't mean anything other than that she was excited to have a project and to help a friend.

That night, Jo asked Missy questions about warm-ups and cooldowns and strength-training routines that her soccer coach put the team through, and wrote out a simple routine. The next afternoon, she waited for Nonie in

the parking lot behind the golf clubhouse. Some of the
women on Apple Blossom Court had gone back to work
when their kids had started full days of school. Judy
Pressman was a reading specialist in the school district;
Valerie Cohen had become an interior decorator; and
Stephanie Zelcheck worked at the Cape Codder, a boutique in Avondale's two-block downtown that sold kilts
and Fair Isle sweaters, Izod shirts and turtlenecks im-
printed with tiny whales ("I'm mostly doing it for the
employee discount," Steph had confided, and Jo had felt
a sad pang, thinking of her mother and everything she'd
bought with her Hudson's discount). Nonie didn't work.
She was part of the book club, and she volunteered a few
mornings a week at the Congregationalist church that
she and Dan attended, helping watch the little kids at
Mother's Day Out, but other than that, her time was her
own. At 3:45, she pulled up beside Jo. That day's track
suit was black with bright-yellow trim. "I look like a
bumblebee," Nonie complained.

"You look fine," said Jo, handing over the workout.
Nonie tapped her tongue against the roof of her mouth,
studying the sheet.

"You'll do it with me?" Nonie asked. "You'll show
me how?"

"Absolutely," said Jo. They started off along the trail
at a brisk pace. A quarter mile in, Nonie was pink-faced,
huffing and puffing and using her terry cloth wristbands
to delicately dab sweat from her forehead. "C'mon!" Jo
cheered. "I'm dyin'," Nonie gasped, and clambered onto
the sit-up log. Jo counted. Nonie groaned. Jo tried to
get her friend to jog. Nonie complained. When Nonie
couldn't hang for even five seconds from the chin-up bar,
Jo wrapped her arms around Nonie's nylon-clad waist,
hoisted her up, and held her in place, trying not to pay at-

tention to the curve of Nonie's waist and hips, the warm
solidity of her flesh, or how she smelled faintly of Opium
perfume. "I hate you!" Nonie gasped as Jo urged her
across the finish line, increasing her own pace from a jog
to a run to a sprint. Nonie collapsed, bent over with her
hands on her knees, panting, before lifting her head and
saying, "We're going for ice cream. Do not tell me no."

For the next six weeks, three afternoons a week, Jo
and Nonie would meet at the fitness trail. They'd jog and
do rounds of push-ups and triceps dips, mountain climbers and jumping jacks. Every Friday, Jo would introduce
a new exercise—leg raises, jackknife sit-ups, single-leg
toe touches, burpees ("Oh, God," Nonie wailed after Jo
demonstrated the move, "you're trying to kill me, aren't
you?").

Jo was sure that Nonie would abandon the workouts
the same way she'd quit all of her diets, but Nonie stuck
with it. By the fourth week, a jogger they'd waved at a
few times caught up with them at the chin-up bar. "Is
this, like, an organized thing?" she asked. Jo told her it
wasn't, and Nonie said, "You're welcome to join us!" That
was how the fitness club began. By the end of July, on
most afternoons there were at least six women following
Jo along the trail, a funny, jostling, talkative bunch whose
ages ranged from early twenties to late sixties. Some of
the women wore the nylon track suits that Nonie favored,
accessorized with matching headbands and wristbands,
and seemed more intent on protecting the integrity of
their hairdos than they were on improving their fitness. Others came in sweatpants, or shorts and T-shirts,
with their hair tied back in ponytails, ready to work. Jo
charted their progress and celebrated their achievements:
the woman who hadn't been able to walk the two-mile
loop without stopping and who, six weeks later, could jog

the entire way around; the one who couldn't manage a single push-up at her first session and who could bang out a dozen by her eighth; the ones who told her that they could carry more groceries, or climb two flights of stairs without getting winded, or who just felt better in their own bodies. "Even if you don't lose a single inch, or a single pound, you've gotten stronger," Jo told Nonie, the morning that Nonie performed her first unassisted pull-up.

"Screw stronger," Nonie panted as she dropped to the ground. Dust puffed out around her running shoes, and the other women cheered. "The point of this endeavor is to dazzle my former classmates with my pulchritude, not beat 'em at arm wrestling." She paused, turning sideways, admiring her shadow. "But I am looking good." She gave a dimpled smile. "Dan approves." Jo nodded, not wanting to think about Dan enjoying her hard work.

On Friday after the workout, they were celebrating with their weekly ice-cream cone (child-sized, a single scoop on a sugar cone) at the Farm Shoppe. "You need to stop givin' this away," Nonie said. "All those ladies tagging along, you should make them pay you. Not me, of course," she added.

"Oh," said Jo. "I'm not a professional."

"You teach phys ed," Nonie said.

"I'm a sub. And I don't even teach gym that often. Besides, I think that if I was going to set this up as a business, I'd have to get some kind of certification from somewhere. I think." It was funny, but for all the years that Jo had watched Dave launch his various ventures and observed, from afar, her sister's ascent to the throne of Jam Queen of Atlanta, Jo had only a vague idea about what starting a business actually required.

Nonie nibbled the edge of her cone. "You know what I'd do is go to the rec department," she said. "That way, you can be on their insurance. They hire instructors all the time, right? The ladies can pay the rec department," Nonie said, licking strawberry ice cream off her fingers with her pointed pink tongue. "The rec department can pay you. That way it's not a problem if you're using their facilities and someone gets hurt, or twists her ankle and decides to sue." Jo, who'd never considered the possibility of injury, winced, and Nonie put a consoling hand on her forearm.

"Look, if you're doing it anyhow, you might as well get paid." Jo couldn't argue with that. Extra money would come in handy. After Dave had declared bankruptcy, Jo had insisted that Dave give up his dreams of business ownership and get a job with a salary and benefits. He'd grumbled, but he'd acquiesced. He called his line of work "pharmaceutical sales," but the truth was that he sold athlete's-foot creams and shoe inserts to drugstores across a four-hundred-mile territory. His job paid well enough, but Dave had expensive taste, in cars, in clothing, in restaurants and vacations, and it seemed like there was always some expense that they hadn't anticipated, whether it was the cost of soccer camp, or the Benetton sweater that Kim absolutely had to have, or the twenty thousand dollars they'd spent to get the roof replaced. Besides, it might be nice to have a little nest egg that was hers alone. The next Monday, Jo brought her résumé and the certificate she'd had to earn to teach elementary-school phys ed to the director of the recreation department, an avuncular, ruddy-faced fellow named Richie Barnes, who wore plaid shirts and suspenders clipped to his khakis and kept his work-booted feet propped on the green metal desk. "Sure, sure," he said, with barely a glance at her papers. "I've seen you out there in the afternoons. What are you thinking of charging?" he asked, his Boston accent broadening the word to *chaahging*. Eventually, they settled on Jo's rates: five dollars for a drop-in class, thirty dollars for a month's worth of unlimited classes, with one-third of the money going to the Avondale Recreation Department and the rest of it going to Jo. "You want my advice, make up some flyers and take 'em around to the gyms," said Barnes. "That new Nautilus place on Main Street, and the JCC in West Hartford." Puzzled, Jo said, "Aren't women at those gyms already paying to exercise?" "Yeah, but they're paying to exercise indoors. Have you ever been in one of those indoor gyms?" Richie made a face. "Fluorescent lights and bad ventilation, and pushy high school jocks and muscleheads strutting around like they own the place. Ogling the ladies." He pronounced it as *oogling*. "If I was a lady trying to get in a workout, and someone offered me a chance to breathe fresh air, with people I liked, I'd take it in a minute. But it's just a suggestion," Barnes said, swinging his feet onto the floor and offering Jo his hand. "Either way, I wish you the best of luck."

Jo drove home, barely hearing the Hall and Oates on the radio, running numbers in her head. Twenty dollars per woman per month. If she could get ten monthly members—and she was almost positive that she could—she would have two hundred dollars a month, all her own. It wasn't enough to live on, certainly not enough to leave on (not, of course, that she was planning on leaving), but it was something. A start.

Over the weekend, Kim helped Jo design the flyers, after Jo enticed her with the notion of putting "amateur graphic designer" on the résumé she'd send with her college applications. FITNESS CLASS NOW FORMING, they

read. JOIN INSTRUCTOR JO BRAVERMAN FOR AN INVIGORAT-
ING HOUR OF BRISK WALKING, JOGGING, AND STRENGTH
TRAINING ALONG THE AVONDALE FITNESS TRAIL. ALL AGES
AND FITNESS LEVELS WELCOME! GET LEAN! GET STRONG!
GET HAPPY! ("Lean" and "strong" were Kim's contribu-
tions; "happy" was Jo's.) Jo begged Nonie for permission
to use the yearbook shot of Nonie, from her cheerleading days, airborne and smiling, and Nonie agreed, after
making Jo swear on her mother's life that she wouldn't
tell anyone that Nonie was the woman in the picture.
"I'm still a before," she'd lamented, staring at herself in
the mirror, sucking in her cheeks and tilting her chin.
"No divulging my identity until I become an after."

On Monday morning, Jo went to Kinko's to run off
a hundred flyers on eye-catching hot-pink paper. Kim
and Missy helped their mother distribute them around
town, at the area gyms and the supermarkets, the library and the mall, while Lila sat in the car, complain-
ing and playing the handheld Simon game that Dave
had gotten her for her birthday. By August, when the
summer air was as thick as soup and many families
had taken off for beach vacations in Rhode Island or
on Cape Cod, Jo had almost forty students enrolled in
her classes, which she'd switched to the cooler morning
hours. At seven o'clock in the morning, the group would
gather in the parking lot near the golf shop and follow
Jo onto the fitness trail. Jo showed her older ladies, and
a pair of pregnant ones, how to modify the exercises,
demonstrating push-ups on her knees and low-impact
versions of jumping jacks and high-knee skips. She carried a first-aid kit in a backpack—she'd had a fanny
pack at first, but in an unprecedented show of unity, all
three of her daughters had told her "absolutely not"—
and she kept a close watch on her charges, praying that

no one would twist an ankle or break a bone, but so far, the worst things that had happened were Ruthann Bremmer getting stung by a yellow jacket and Connie McSorley, one of the pregnant ladies, ending up with poison ivy in a personal area after she'd had to duck into the woods to pee.

At the end of August, Nonie announced that she was going to visit her sister on Nantucket for two weeks. "I'm gonna fall off the wagon. Fried clams . . . lobster rolls . . . ice-cream cones . . . ugh, summer's just a disaster!" she lamented. Jo, who was familiar with her friend's taste for Halloween candy in the fall, Christmas cookies in the winter, and Cadbury Easter eggs when spring arrived, elected to keep her mouth shut. "Maybe you could type up the exercises for me. Oh, no, wait!" Nonie grabbed Jo's hands. "I know what! You can do a video!"

"What? No I can't. I don't have a camera."

"Doesn't the school have equipment?"

"I'll ask."

The next afternoon, Jo approached the tech teacher, whose name was Mr. Genova, to inquire about borrowing a camera. "No can do," he said, glaring at her as if she'd asked to borrow a hundred dollars from him personally. "Equipment doesn't leave school grounds."

"I could do the exercises in the gym," Jo said, and Mr. Genova showed her a sign-up sheet, and a waiting list, and a waiting list for the waiting list, and told her that he didn't think a substitute teacher should be allowed to jump the line. "He said 'substitute teacher' like it was 'child molester,'" Jo reported to Nonie, who tapped her tongue on the roof of her mouth, looking thoughtful. "Desperate times call for desperate measures," she finally said. "Is that room locked at night?"

Jo didn't know for sure, but she couldn't imagine that

the school would leave expensive equipment just lying around. "Do you have keys?"

Jo saw where this was going. "I do, but, Nonie . . ." Nonie held up her hand. "No 'buts.' No excuses. Isn't that what you say?"

"Yes, I tell you that when you're trying to cheat on your lunges, not when you're telling me to steal stuff."

"Not steal. Borrow. Big difference." She raised her voice. "Hey, Missy, want to help us pull off a heist?"

"Don't answer that," Jo shouted, just as her daughter called from the living room, "What are we heisting?"

"You see that? Your daughter can help you! I'll do your hair and makeup."

"Nonie, I know that you think this is a game, but I could lose my job."

"You won't need that job." Nonie's eyes sparkled wickedly, and her smile was as pleased as Jo had ever seen it. "We're going to make you . . ."—she spread her arms wide, like she was writing words on the sky—". . . a star!"

"I can't believe you talked me into this," Jo whispered the next morning. She and Nonie, dressed in black, were walking—creeping—toward the high school's entrance. It was five a.m. on Saturday. Their plan was to take the equipment, film the workout routine that morning ("Magic hour!" Nonie said brightly), and have everything back in place by eight a.m. Jo held her breath as she eased the key into the lock. The door swung open. Lights did not flash; sirens did not blare. She exhaled a little, turned, and beckoned for Nonie, who was waiting behind the wheel. Nonie put the car in Park and ran across the lot, breasts bouncing enticingly.

"I can't believe I'm doing this," Jo whispered as she

hurried to the second floor with Nonie at her heels. They both had flashlights. Nonie even had a black face mask, which her son Drew wore when he was skiing. "If anyone stops you, just say you left your purse in the classroom." That was Jo's plan, and it would work . . . unless, of course, anyone saw her leaving the technology center with what she assumed were thousands of dollars in equipment. She unlocked the tech center's door. The students' desks were empty. The teacher's desk was bare. "In here?" Nonie asked, waving her flashlight at a wall of locked cupboards. Nonie tugged one of the handles and made a face when the door was locked. She walked to the teacher's desk and pulled the top drawer open, and there, between a staple remover and a large pink eraser, was a small silver key on a tag labeled "equipment." "Here!" Jo shoved the key in the lock, opened the cabinet door, and hunted until she'd found the equipment Missy had told them to collect: a camera, a boom, a microphone, and a power pack. Jo handed the camera and the power pack to Nonie, tucked the long boom and the mic under her arm, locked the cupboard, replaced the key, and had just stepped into the hallway when she heard voices, and laughter, the sound of a crowd of people coming up the stairs.

"Oh, shit!" Nonie hissed. "The walkers!"

"What?"

"The old people!" Nonie spluttered. "The senior citizens. Shit, I read about this. They used to power-walk in the mall, but the mall kicked 'em out, so now they're here! C'mon, we have to hurry!" She grabbed Jo's hand as the first of a crowd of warm-up-suit-clad seniors crested the staircase and made their way down the hall. Jo and Nonie hurried away, but not before they were spotted by the woman at the head of the pack.

"Yoo-hoo? Who's up there?"

"Yoo-hoo?" Nonie muttered. "Seriously?" She started walking more quickly.

"I told you we should've just worn normal clothes!" Jo whispered. If she'd worn her teaching clothes, or even her own exercise gear, she could have turned, waved, given the seniors an explanation. But with the two of them in head-to-toe black, and Nonie in her ski mask, their arms full of electronics, they looked like what they were: thieves.

Turning, Jo caught a glimpse of white hair, turquoise-blue nylon, and a four-pronged cane with tennis balls at the base.

"What are you doing here?"

"Fuck!" Nonie stage-whispered. "Run!"

Jo raced down the hall after her friend. The yoo-hooing lady had been joined by a man who was yelling, "Stop, thief!" Jo and Nonie pushed through the doors and ran down the east staircase, with the race-walkers yelling at them to stop. "Come on," Nonie said, her voice urgent as she grabbed Jo's arm. They raced down the stairs, with Nonie whispering, "Come on, come on, I'm not getting arrested in the dumbest crime of the century."

"Stop . . . making . . . me . . . laugh," Jo wheezed as she ran. They made it through the cafeteria, Nonie carrying the equipment, until finally they were out the door, into the parking lot, and leaning against the cafeteria's Dumpsters, laughing until they couldn't breathe.

"We did it!" Nonie said, pressing her hand to her chest. "Shit, I think my heart stopped in there. Does fear burn calories?"

"Probably," Jo said.

"Excellent." Nonie unlocked her car. "And off we go!"

Because Jo didn't want to implicate her daughter in a crime, she'd asked Missy to meet them at the fitness trail. "That's what you're wearing?" Missy asked as Jo and Nonie climbed out of the car. Jo looked down at her black T-shirt and gray terry cloth shorts. "Why? What's wrong?"

"Nothing. It's just that the fitness ladies all wear, like, you know." Missy gestured toward Nonie. "Warm-up suits and leotards and stuff. Leg warmers. Stuff like that."

"I am not a fitness lady," Jo said, her voice emphatic. "And spandex doesn't have pockets. Where do you put your car keys?"

"Bra," Nonie said merrily. "God's pocket."

The three of them walked to the first station on the trail, which had a pull-up bar and a patch of soft, sloping grass for push-ups. "Okay. Stand there." Missy got Jo in position, peered through the camera, nodded, and said, "Three . . . two . . . one," and pointed at her mother. Jo looked at the camera. She felt oddly nervous, her mouth dry and chest fluttery, even though no one but Nonie would ever see the tape. She forced herself to smile. "Hi, Nonie. It's me, your old pal Jo, leaving you with no excuse to fall off the fitness wagon. Today, we're going to start with three sets of four different exercises, starting with your very favorite, walking lunges." By the third exercise, Jo had forgotten all about Missy. "Keep your shoulders over your wrists," she said as her daughter circled her with the camera during the planks. "Don't let your knees get past your toes," she counseled during the squats, and "Remember to keep your core tight" for the one-legged toe touches. "And that's it!" she said when she'd gone through a round of each exercise. "Do the entire circuit three times, and you're done. I'd like to thank my cameraperson, Melissa Braverman, who is also my producer and director. Nonie, I'll see you back on the fitness trail."

"And . . . cut! Hey, that was good," Melissa said with an enthusiasm she usually reserved for her soccer teammates.

"Really good," said Nonie. "You know what? You should sell tapes."

Jo was only half listening, already thinking about how she'd get the equipment back, and whether she'd taken out something to thaw for dinner.

"What?"

"You should sell these," Nonie repeated. "Your fitness tapes. Like Jane Fonda."

Jo shook her head. "I'm not Jane Fonda. Or Suzanne Somers. I don't even own a pair of leg warmers, remember?"

"There're famous people who make fitness tapes," Missy said. "But aren't there also regular people who got famous because they did fitness tapes? We can go to Blockbuster tonight and check out the competition."

"Do it," said Nonie, waving as she got into her car.

"Do you really think it could work?" Jo asked as she and her daughter got into their car.

Missy's dark-brown ponytail brushed her shoulder as she turned her head and slowly backed out of the parking space. "Dad's always saying, you just need one thing—a product, or a business, or a service, or a big idea—and you just keep looking until you find it. What if this is your one thing?" Jo's heart twisted as she listened to Missy parroting her father's advice, hearing the love and admiration in Missy's voice. She hoped the girls had absorbed Dave's ambition and not what she had come to see, over the years, as his allergy to hard work, his willingness to take shortcuts or tell lies in search of the big score.

"We can take a look," Jo said.

Melissa gave her a smile, a warmer, less toothy version of her father's glittering grin. "We'll get you some leg warmers, and you'll be all set." She pushed a button on the car's tape player, and the music of Duran Duran filled the car. "And a title. You need a good title." Jo had thought of that already. On Monday morning, she affixed a piece of masking tape to the videocassette's side and, using one of Lila's markers (left uncapped and discarded on the kitchen table), she wrote JUMPING FOR JO. "I like it," said Melissa. At Missy's insistence, Jo had watched Jane Fonda's *Lean Routine* and something called *Buns of Steel*. Alone in the family room, Jo had seen the shiny leggings and high-cut leotards, the headbands and the matching leg warmers, the heavy makeup and the sprayed and feathered hair. Everyone in the videos smiled, all the time, even in the midst of the most grueling series of glute bridges and walking lunges, and no one ever seemed to sweat. The videos were part workout instruction, part performance, and while Jo knew that she could handle the first part, the second part was beyond her.

But a part of her wanted to try. Maybe Bethie's success was a once-in-a-lifetime miracle, something that wouldn't happen again in the same decade, much less in the same family, but that didn't mean that there weren't a few crumbs left over for Jo.

Nonie came back from Nantucket in a brand-new track suit (lemon yellow and neon green), glowing and exultant. "I did that tape every morning, and guess what else? My sisters-in-law both want copies!" She paused. "Is it sisters-in-law or sister-in laws? I never know. Anyway, they love you." Nonie was beaming. "I think you should sell 'em."

"Told you," Missy called from the kitchen. Jo asked, "You really think that people would pay?"

"I know they would." Nonie adjusted her braided green-and-yellow headband. "You know what my sisters-in-law said? They liked that you were a real person. You weren't some fakey-fake actress with breast implants. You're just a regular gal."

Just a regular gal, Jo thought, and smiled, thinking, *If you only knew.* That night, Missy drove her to the Video Barn, where a sullen, pimply teenage boy ran off twenty copies for a dollar apiece. At the end of the Friday fitness trail class, Jo stood on top of one of the tree stumps they used for step-ups and hops and, with her cheeks burning, she announced that she had videos for sale, for five dollars apiece. "In case anyone's going on vacation, or just wants to be able to do the workout at home." She finished her pitch and braced herself for shuffling feet, averted eyes, and embarrassed silence. Ruthann Bremmer spoke up first. "Ooh, I want one." Connie McSorley, of poison-ivy fame, said, "Me, too," and Julie Carden bought one for herself and one for her sister in Massachusetts. In ten minutes' time, Jo had a hundred dollars in her pocket and no tapes left in the box.

"Go back to the Video Barn and have them run off a hundred copies," Nonie instructed. "And tell pizza-face you want a bulk discount this time."

"Oh, Nonie," said Jo.

"Do it." For all her Southern charm, Nonie could be ruthless when it suited her. "I'm going to send copies to my sisters-in-law, and you're going to sell at least another twenty at class. And there's the PTA sale in September." Jo tried to imagine selling tapes of herself to strangers. She'd barely been able to watch the tape, worried about how unfeminine, how mannish she'd looked, in shorts and a T-shirt, performing high-knee raises and jumping jacks. *Unnatural*, she heard her mother say, and she thought of all the jokes she'd ever heard about female gym teachers.

"I don't know."

Nonie was glaring at her, eyes narrowed. "I don't get it. What's the problem? Shoot, if I was as skinny as you, I'd have done that video naked!"

"You look great," Jo said. Nonie had gotten some sun on Nantucket. Her face and arms and chest, normally pale pink, had acquired a golden glow. She'd lost a little of her jiggle, but she was still deliciously plump, her thighs and upper arms rounded and firm and covered in the finest dusting of golden hair. *Juicy*, Jo sometimes thought. Like a ripe peach, where the juice would fill your mouth when you took a bite.

"Come on," Nonie said. "What have you got to lose?"

"My self-esteem? My dignity? However much I spend to get the tapes made?" Nonie was relentless. She drove Jo to the Video Barn, demanded to speak to the pimply teenager's manager, and negotiated the rate she wanted. She made Jo pose for pictures, doing the star jump over and over, propelling herself into the air with her arms and legs spread wide. "Smile!" Nonie called, until finally, Jo did, and when her friend showed her the shot, Jo had to admit that she looked okay. At least, not awful.

"Glamorous yet approachable," Nonie said.

Jo rolled her eyes. "If I end up with a hundred copies of Jumpin' with Jo sitting in my garage, I'm going to make you do burpees every day for a month."

"That's your prerogative," Nonie replied. "But you know what? I don't think that's going to happen."

· · ·

At the PTA sale, Jo set up her wares at a folding table in the high school cafeteria, underneath a poster that Kim had made, a blow-up of the video's cover featuring Jo's star jump. Beside her, Nonie was selling slices of pineapple upside-down cake. "It's my Meemaw's recipe," she'd tell customers, even though Jo knew that the recipe actually came from the back of the Dole can. When the shoppers came flooding into the gym, Jo readied herself for cold stares and hard questions; women asking about her qualifications, or what, exactly, made her think that she was selling anything worth buying. But the questions never came. Forty-five minutes later, Jo was sold out again. "See?" said Nonie, looking smug. "Told you so."

Over the weekend, Jo visited the library, learning everything she could about the billion-dollar fitness-video market, which, by all accounts, was large, lucrative, and still expanding—fueled by women her age, stay-at-home mothers looking to shape up. On Monday, she went down to the basement with a tape to show to her husband.

Years ago, Dave had turned their basement into a home office. Not, Jo suspected, because he had work to do at home, but because claiming a home office let him write off a portion of the mortgage and the utilities. That was Dave, Jo thought: if there was a way to save money, he'd find it. "What can I do for you, my dear?" he asked. Jo pulled up a chair.

"I have a business proposition," she began, and offered him a tape. Dave watched the tape the whole way through. He inspected the packaging. He listened to Jo patiently, at one point even grabbing a legal pad and taking notes as she walked him through the genesis of the workout routine, how she'd made that first tape (leaving out the part about boosting the equipment from the high school), and how Nonie's sisters-in-law had asked for copies. She talked about how she'd sold videos to the women who took her class, and more to strangers, at the PTA sale. "I know that you'd know more about this than I do, but I wonder if maybe this could be something," Jo said.

Dave set down his pen and notebook and leaned back in his chair, lacing his hands over the belly he'd developed in recent years as he contemplated the ceiling. Finally he shook his head. "Won't work."

Jo felt a rush of disappointment that was tinged with relief. She was sorry that she wouldn't make a fortune selling exercise tapes, but she was glad that she wouldn't be out there, exposed, embarrassing herself and her kids, the subject of a thousand dyke jokes that she might never hear but would be able to sense nonetheless.

Dave's voice was sympathetic. "The problem, as I see it, is that you're not an aspirational figure. Don't get me wrong," he said, raising his hands, as if Jo had tried to argue with him. "You look great. But great for a neighborhood lady. Great for the mom next door. But women don't buy these tapes because they want to look like the mom next door. They buy them because they want to look like Suzanne Somers."

"That's what I thought," Jo said. "Nonie just kept telling me . . ." Her voice trailed off.

Dave waved his hand negligently, a king granting a favor to a peasant. "Sell 'em at bake sales, or to the ladies who come to your classes. Make yourself some pin money." Jo nodded, and walked backward, out of his office and up the stairs, the way she remembered seeing her father walking in shul, after he'd been called to the bimah, returning to his seat backward so as not to turn his back, and his backside, on the word of God. *Pin money*, she thought, and smiled at her own folly, and started in on the dinner dishes.

The next morning, she told Nonie the news. Her friend was predictably furious. "Dave's full of it," she told Jo, urging her to ignore him, to think bigger. "Why not take out an ad in the *Hartford Courant*? Or call the local newspeople and ask them to let you do a segment on Sunday mornings?" she'd asked. Jo never did. She was content. She liked teaching her classes, being out on the fitness trail underneath the canopy of leaves, accompanied by the murmur of a foursome or the crack of a driver on a ball. Jo kept a box of tapes in her car. She sold them to her students and at the synagogue's fund-raiser. The money was useful, for Kim's college application fees, and when Lila, who somehow had both an over- and an underbite, required another year of orthodontia. *It's enough*, Jo told herself. It has to be enough. They had made their way out of bankruptcy, and they had enough to pay the bills. It was true that Jo had never gotten to live with the love of her life . . . but how many woman who loved women ever did? Maybe the ones with more courage could, the women who lived in big cities, or communes, but Jo no longer had that kind of nerve, or that kind of time. Her father had been dead before he'd turned forty-six; her mother had died at seventy-one. Soon she and Dave would be empty nesters, then retirees, and their girls would inherit the earth and have the kind of big life that Jo had once dreamed about. Maybe she'd never written a novel, maybe she and Dave would never move to one of the grand houses in Avondale Woods, or put in a pool, like the Pressmans, but at some point, Jo hoped, they'd at least have money to redo the kitchen. That would be enough.

That was what she was thinking about on a Friday

night when Dave summoned her down to his office, saying they needed to talk. Missy was out with her soccer teammates; Kim was out with Derek Rudolph, the boy she'd been dating since Homecoming. Lila, as ever, was glued to the TV, watching *Full House*. Jo descended the basement stairs, mentally making her case for replacing the kitchen appliances or, at the very least, the garish green-and-silver wallpaper, which screamed 1970s. Maybe they'd do it in stages, she thought, as she settled herself in a chair. Wallpaper first, and they could take out the wall that separated the TV room from the kitchen, and . . . "Jo." Dave was looking at her, leaning forward, still in the suit he'd worn home that afternoon. His expression was grave. *He's sick*, was her first thought and, to her great shame, she felt a surge of relief. She'd be rid of him; she'd be single. And maybe she wasn't a young woman, but she wasn't old, either. There was plenty of life ahead, years that she could make use of, and . . . "I'm so sorry," Dave was saying. His face was red, and he appeared to be crying. Jo realized that she'd missed something important. "Sorry for what?" she asked, and tried to look appropriately solemn. Dave was staring at his desk, as if he could barely look at her. Jo felt the atmosphere change, the way it did in advance of a storm. She'd clenched her fists, bracing for whatever was coming, when he looked up and said, "You know things haven't been good between us for a while."

Jo didn't answer. Her hands and face felt cold. *Things have been fine*, she thought. What did I miss? Dave's shoulders heaved, and he gave a single bark of a sob, then said, "Jo, I want a divorce."

Jo's lips were numb, her hands icy, head swirling with a tangled skein of emotions—shock and fear and anger and, yes, relief. Underneath it all, relief. Dave wouldn't be dead, but he would be gone. She would be free. For a few blissful seconds, Jo let herself enjoy that relief before she thought to ask the obvious question. "Is there someone else?" Dave gave a single, shamefaced nod.

"Who is she?" Jo made herself ask, and Dave had the grace to at least look ashamed when he said, "It's Nonie Scotto."

five

1993

Bethie

There she is," Bethie said, pointing as a tall, skinny girl with a mop of tangled black hair emerged from the Jetway. Her niece was in that awkward place that Bethie remembered from her own adolescence, where you were done being a girl but you weren't quite a teenager, and where it felt like half of your body parts had declared for Team Adolescence and the other half hadn't caught up. Lila's narrow shoulders were bowed beneath the straps of her backpack, and the duffel bag she had was so heavy that it made her lean to the left. Every few steps she'd have to correct her course, or risk banging into the wall.

Four years ago, Bethie had bitten her lip, hard, to keep from saying *I told you so*, when her sister had called to tell her that Dave was leaving, and she'd had to bite it again to keep from gasping when Jo told her who Dave was leaving with. "What can I do?" Bethie had asked. She'd offered to lend Jo money, to buy Dave out of the house so that Jo and the girls could stay there, but Jo was adamant about doing things on her own.

"Besides, I can't stay. Nonie lives down the street, and Dave's moving in with her."

"Oh, God."

Jo's voice wobbled as she said, "I just want a fresh start, somewhere else. In Avondale, though. I'll stay here, at least until Lila finishes school."

So Jo and her girls had moved into a condo. Kim, then Missy, had finished high school and started college. Every year, Bethie had invited her sister and her nieces to come for a week or a month or even the whole summer, and for three years running, Jo had turned her down until finally she'd agreed to send Lila.

"I should warn you, she's pretty miserable," Jo said.

"We'll be fine." Bethie asked when school ended, bought a ticket in Lila's name, and lined up a summer's worth of activities for her niece. "We'll take care of her," she'd told Jo. Jo had just sighed.

Bethie knew that Lila had always been a challenge. She figured that any unpleasant behavior on Lila's part was surely a result of her father's abandonment, of Dave Braverman ditching her mom for that evil minx of a Nonie Scotto. "I never trusted him," Bethie had railed to Harold the night she'd gotten the news. She'd been pacing through their living room, making a circuit from the gas fireplace at one end to the newly installed French doors at the other, with her manicured nails digging into the meat of her palms. "And you know what else? I sent that bitch a jam sampler for Christmas!" Harold, in his deep, sonorous voice, had told her, "Let it go, hon." He'd grabbed her, midpace, squeezing her shoulders until she could laugh at herself.

"I'm glad it's Lila," she'd told Harold as they'd waited at the gate. Of all her nieces, she felt the most connected to Jo's youngest, who seemed to be struggling more than her sisters. Kim and Missy had sailed through school, both of them distinguishing themselves in academics and extracurriculars, while Lila was floundering, and did not seem to have evinced any special skill or talent. Nor had Bethie failed to notice the timing of Lila's birth. Jo must have gotten pregnant right after their big fight. Which meant, Bethie supposed, that she was at least a little bit responsible for Lila's existence, the same way she was at least a little bit responsible for Jo's marriage and life in the suburbs.

There was also the way Bethie had found herself thinking about her own childlessness more frequently, as she had slipped from her thirties into her forties. Early on, she and Harold had talked about adoption, or about becoming foster parents, but between her business and his work, plus the charities to which they both gave not just money but time, they were busy and, it seemed, neither one of them wanted children enough to make an aggressive case for them. Bethie was also not certain how eager an adoption agency would be to place a child with a biracial couple. So she contented herself with her extended family. With six siblings, Harold had more than twenty nieces and nephews, ranging from toddlers to young adults, in addition to Kim and Missy and Lila. Bethie loved her work, she loved her husband, she loved her nieces when she got to spend time with them . . . and, she could admit, she also loved it when her guests went home, and it was just her and her husband again.

She wondered if that made her—to use her mother's old word—unnatural. Every time she talked to a reporter—and, lucky for her, Blue Hill Farm had done well enough that she'd been interviewed half a dozen times in the previous few years, four times for print outlets and twice on TV—the subject would come up. Do you and your husband have any children? The why not was never spoken, but it was absolutely implied. Bethie always gave the same answer, one that she'd arrived at over time and had fine-tuned with a media coach. My husband and I were friends in high school, but when we reconnected, my biological clock had just about wound down. I'm lucky to have three beautiful nieces who spend part of the summer with me, and I'm a mentor with Big Brothers/Big Sisters.

"I wonder what would happen if I said, 'I just never really wanted kids'?" she'd said during their first media-training session, and both Rose of Sharon, who, by the 1980s, had shortened her name to just Sharon, and the media coach, whose name was Beverly Husner, said, "Don't say that!"

"Why not?" Bethie and Sharon had rented a conference room in the Doubletree Hotel for the afternoon, in preparation for their interview on CNN, which was doing a piece on "The New Entrepreneurs." Beverly had brought her own camera, and her own lights, and had borrowed a television set from the hotel. For two hours, she'd played the reporter, peppering Bethie and Sharon with questions, recording their answers, then playing the tapes back to show them where they'd said *um* or *uh*, *I mean* or *you know* or *like*, or where they could have brought their answers back to Blue Hill Farm, which they'd been instructed to mention, by name, as often as they could. "I mean, seriously," Bethie continued. "Would it be the end of the world if I just said I never wanted kids?"

Beverly cleared her throat and fiddled with the VCR remote. Sharon said, "It makes you sound unfeminine."

"Unnatural," Bethie murmured, remembering her history with that word, the way her mother had flung it at Jo across the Thanksgiving table all those years ago. "Seriously? In this day and age?"

"Seriously. In this day and age," Beverly said. "The world still expects women to want babies. And if you're a successful businesswoman, they don't want to think that you sacrificed the pitter-patter of little feet for money."

"It's not fair," said Bethie, and Sharon said, "Hey, think about the dumb stuff I get asked." Sharon lowered her voice to a contralto and leaned toward Bethie with an expression of fake solicitous concern. "So how do you do it? How do you manage? How do you balance everything? What happens if you're out of town at a business conference or on a sales call and little Amanda gets a fever, or Ryan gets in trouble at school?" She snorted. "Name me one man who ever gets asked if he misses his kids while he's working. And I can't just tell them the truth, which is—duh—I've got a nanny. And a cleaning lady. And my mom comes most weekends. There's no way I'd be able to do this without them."

"It's ridiculous," Bethie said. "They don't expect men to do everything. They don't care if men have help, and they don't ask men if they have regrets."

"They surely do not," said Beverly, fitting her camera into its hard-sided plastic case. "And someday, the world might change. Someday, they might ask Bill Gates why he's not at his kid's spelling bee instead of inventing computers, and they might let a successful female CEO off the hook for not having babies, or maybe even for not getting married at all. But we're not there yet. Not even close."

Beverly clicked her case shut, and Bethie had gathered the printouts she'd been given, about not wearing patterned clothes or dangling earrings and hiring a professional to do your makeup, even if the station told you they had a makeup artist, because you never knew what kind of time they would have or what kind of job they would do.

"Lila!" Bethie called, waving. "Over here!" Lila's head lifted, and she gave a wan, limp wave and began plodding, head bent, toward her aunt and uncle. *Poor thing*, Bethie thought. Lila looked lost in her oversized black hooded sweatshirt. An angry crop of pimples studded her forehead. Her nose looked too big for her face, her feet looked too big for her body, and in spite of her braces, she still had an overbite. A bright yellow Walkman protruded from the pouch of her hoodie, and its earphones were slung around her neck. Bethie opened her arms, saying, "Hi, honey. We're so glad you're here!"

By Lila's third day in their house in Buckhead, Bethie decided that her niece was clinically depressed. After five days, Bethie was convinced that she, too, was going to end up needing professional help if she couldn't get Lila out of her funk. And after a week of Lila in residence, Bethie was starting to wonder if Lila had endured some trauma similar to what had happened to Bethie when Bethie had been her age, if some tragedy or violation, not just the divorce, was making the girl so sullen and sad.

Lila rarely smiled and never laughed. There was no light in her eyes, and nothing, no trip or treat, no music or movie, no restaurant or television program, seemed to bring her joy. No matter what Bethie and Harold proposed—a visit to the Coca-Cola museum, an afternoon at a Braves game, even shopping at the Lenox Square Mall for new clothes, which both Kim and Missy had loved at the same age—Lila would assent with the same sigh, the same resigned nod, and she'd go through the day with the same plodding, head-down shuffle. "They're okay, I guess," she said when Bethie brought Esprit shirts and Gunne Sax dresses to the changing room.

"So should we get them?" Bethie asked, her hands on the stack of clothing that Lila had tried.

Lila shrugged.

"Do you like them?"

Lila shrugged again.

"Is there anything else you want to try?"

That time, Lila had shrugged and sighed, and Bethie had sighed, too, gathering the clothes in her arms and handing the salesgirl her credit card. "C'mon, let's split a Cinnabon," she said. The smell of the pastries perfumed the entire lower half of the mall, and she could already taste the sugary icing. Lila followed along behind her, carrying the shopping bags like they were full of rocks and not pretty new sweaters and dresses. In the food court, she picked at her half of the bun and answered Bethie's questions about school and friends and her sisters with grunts, single-syllable responses, and another spate of sighs. NYU, where Missy was enrolled, was "fine, I guess." Philadelphia, where Kim was in school, was "okay." School was fine, her friends were okay, the new apartment was "okay, I guess."

"And how about Nonie?" Bethie still couldn't fathom the speed with which her brother-in-law had upended his family . . . or how Jo restrained herself from driving over to where Nonie and Dave lived together with a can of lighter fluid and a match. "Do you like her?"

Lila fetched a sigh from the depths of her scrawny frame and poked at the remnants of her cinnamon bun. "She's fine."

"And how about her kids?" Bethie asked. "She's got a boy and a girl, right?"

"They're okay, I guess," Lila said. "It's fine."

"Fine, fine, everything's fine," Bethie had murmured to Harold that night in bed. They'd assumed their usual position, with Harold on his back in the middle of the bed and Bethie on her side with her head on his chest. "Except it isn't. There's no way things are fine."

She'd been—she could admit it now—anxious about having a child in the house, even just for the summer, afraid that she wouldn't be up to the job of taking care of a girl on the cusp of being a teenager. She remembered how, when her nieces were little, minding them took every minute of every day. Bethie had watched her sister scuttling around in a permanent crouch, with a baby on her hip, ready to grab Kim or Missy before they fell into a swimming pool or ran into the street, and when they finally went down for a nap or went to sleep at night, Jo's second shift would begin, the cooking and the cleaning, the laundry and the shopping.

"What's the saying?" Harold asked, his deep voice rumbling in Bethie's ear. Over the years, he'd gotten good at channeling his father, from the puffed-out chest, to the preacherly cadences, to his endless supply of wise sayings. "Little kids, little problems; big kids, big problems?"

Bethie sighed, thinking she would have preferred a toddler trying to put everything in her mouth to Lila's wall of sullen silence. She and Harold would talk, and laugh, and play Motown music while they cooked or cleaned or puttered, but even with the music and the conversations Lila was sucking every particle of joy and light out of the house. She seemed to carry her own cloud of gloom around with her, and her sighs and muttered answers could stop a conversation cold.

Bethie wanted to ask Jo for advice, but Jo had enough

to handle without her sister calling to say, "I think your kid needs help." *I can do this*, Bethie told herself. If she'd figured a way to go from selling jams with hand-lettered labels at farmers' markets to supplying restaurants and hotels all over the South, she could surely pull one little girl out of a funk.

Except she couldn't. During the week, Lila attended High Meadows Day Camp, where Sharon sent her kids. "They've got everything," Sharon had said. "Swimming, archery, kickball, soccer, waterskiing, canoeing, gymnastics, arts and crafts . . . shoot, I want to go!" At eight in the morning, Lila got on a bus, which took the kids out to Roswell, where the camp was spread out over forty acres, with a creek, and hiking trails, and a farm with goats and pigs. She got a nice tan, but on the days when Bethie came home early to meet her, she'd climb off the bus looking as miserable as she'd been when she'd gotten on, with her hair in tangles and her mouth set in a frown. How was camp? *Fine*. What did you do? *Nothing*. Lila never brought home anything she'd made in the craft cabin, even though Sharon said that her own house was overrun with braided lanyard key chains, carved wooden plaques, and ceramic pinch pots. Lila never mentioned any friends, or asked to visit other kids on the weekends. When they went over to Sharon's house, Sharon's boys, Luke and Jonah, would cannonball into the water of the backyard pool, or race each other from end to end, and little Annie, who was six, would follow Lila everywhere, her eyes full of adoration, desperate for even a crumb of attention from the older girl. Lila ignored Annie, and ignored Lucas and Jonah, and even Sharon. She'd wear her black hooded sweatshirt or sometimes, as an exciting change of pace, her navy-blue hooded sweatshirt, and she'd sit in the shade, with her hood pulled up over her ears and her hem pulled down over her knees and her Walkman headphones plugged into her ears, scowling at the bright-blue water as if it offended her.

After two weeks, Bethie called the camp counselors, who said that Lila was quiet but seemed to be enjoying camp. "Enjoying camp?" Bethie repeated that night when she and Harold were in bed.

"It probably just means she's not making any trouble," her husband replied. He smelled like Crest, and he was wearing his soft plaid nightshirt, which came down past his knees. Bethie called it his nightie, and Harold would shrug and say, *I'm secure in my masculinity. Go ahead and laugh. This thing's comfortable.*

"What can we do?" Bethie asked, her voice fretful. Harold took her in his arms.

"Not much more than what we're doing right now," Harold said. He slipped his warm hands underneath her pajama top and rubbed her shoulders. Bethie gave a happy sigh and closed her eyes. "We let her know we're here for her. She knows that we'll listen if she wants to talk."

"Big 'if,'" grumbled Bethie.

"That's all we can do," Harold said. "She'll come to us when she's ready."

But after another week, Bethie decided that she couldn't wait. On Saturday night, she went to the guest room where Lila was staying and sat on the edge of the bed. In anticipation of Lila's arrival, she'd fixed up the room with a new pink-and-yellow bedspread and boxed sets of Trixie Belden and Sweet Valley High books, which, Sharon assured her, were all the rage for girls Lila's age.

"Lila," she began, "is everything okay?"

"Everything's fine," Lila muttered.

"And you're sure camp's all right? Because, if it's not, we could find you something else."

"I could just stay home," Lila volunteered. "I could help Sidney make dinner. I could help Isobel clean."

Bethie shook her head, frowning. "I don't want you working. I want you to enjoy yourself." Sidney was the young man who prepared dinner for them four nights a week, which was expensive but cheaper than eating out. Even though Bethie enjoyed cooking, she was rarely home early enough to get dinner on the table. As for cleaning, she'd been thrilled when she'd been able to afford a housekeeper. Isobel vacuumed, changed the bed linens, even did the laundry, and Bethie paid her handsomely, feeling relieved that those chores were no longer her responsibility.

"I don't want to interrogate you. I know there's a lot going on at home. But you don't seem happy," Bethie said.

Lila bit her lip and didn't answer.

"Is there anything you want to talk about?"

Lila shook her head.

"Anything I can do?" Another headshake. Bethie tried to breathe through her mounting frustration and said, "If you need anything, you know where I am. I love you, honey."

Lila didn't respond. Bethie waited until she was sure that she had nothing to say before slipping out of the girl's room, down the hall to Harold.

"How'd it go?" he asked.

"Everything's just fine," Bethie said, imitating Lila's hangdog droop, moving across the room in Lila's bent-shouldered shuffle, reciting Lila's Eeyore-like refrain. It reminded her painfully of her own wandering years, when she'd regarded everyone with suspicion and tried to hurt them before they could hurt her. She wanted to save Lila the way Jo had saved her from Uncle Mel, the way Ronnie had pulled her through the pillowed birth canal and into another life, but Lila wouldn't let her get close enough to try.

"Poor kid," Harold said quietly.

"Poor kid," Bethie replied, pulling on her robe. She took her time in the big bathroom, with its his-and-hers sinks, its spacious, glassed-in shower, its deep soaking tub and the separate commode, all of it done in creamy white marble, and the forest-green tiles, hand-painted in Mexico, that had taken six months to arrive. She'd told Harold how surprised she'd been when Jo had announced her third pregnancy, how she'd been convinced, after Jo's visit to Blue Hill Farm, that her sister was preparing to make a change in her life. When Jo had called three months later, her voice unusually shy, saying, "I have some news," Bethie would have bet a week of the jam shop's proceeds that Jo was calling to say that she was leaving her husband. Instead, she'd said, "Dave and I are having a baby." As if Dave would be right there in the hospital, giving birth.

And that birth had changed her sister. The next time Bethie had seen Jo, Jo had been lying in bed, in a bathrobe, the baby in her arms, looking different than Bethie remembered after the previous births—smaller, quieter, utterly exhausted. It had been a hard pregnancy, Bethie knew, followed by a difficult delivery that had ended in a C-section and kept Jo in the hospital for six days, but it wasn't just that. Bethie knew the truth. Jo hadn't wanted another baby. Her sister would never say so. She probably didn't even let herself think about it. But somehow, Lila must have picked up on her mother's discontent and felt unwanted. And unhappy. So unhappy. The only time, all summer long, that Bethie saw even a hint of excitement or joy was when the Salters down the street hired Lila to babysit. Lila had come home at eleven o'clock on Saturday night beaming, with twelve dollars in her pocket and plans to sit for Alex and Meghan the following Friday. "Are you sure?" Bethie asked. "We didn't invite you down here to put you to work."

"No, no," Lila said. "We had fun!" With more animation than she'd displayed since her arrival, Lila told them about how they'd had a board-game tournament, and how she'd made Mickey Mouse–shaped pancakes for dinner. A few mornings later, Eileen Salter had hailed Bethie as Bethie was retrieving the paper from the end of the driveway.

"Your niece is a miracle worker," Eileen said, bouncing up and down as she jogged in place in her bright-blue tank top and black Lycra biker shorts. Eileen said that Lila had managed to get her daughter to comb her hair and her son to sleep in his own bed. Bemused, Bethie said, "She seemed to enjoy it," and Eileen, who'd always been a little frosty toward Bethie (Bethie was never sure whether that had to do with her black husband or her lack of kids), said, "She's amazing. You're so lucky." Bethie had high hopes for a regular engagement, but at the end of July Eileen and Bill took the kids to visit her parents in Rehoboth, and that was the end of that.

The last two weeks of August felt like they took two months to pass. Bethie's shoulders would tense every time she heard Lila sigh; she'd have to fight the urge to shout *Just talk to us!* every night at the dinner table. *Talk to us!* she'd think. *Let us help!* But Lila never did.

The night before Lila's departure, Bethie made one last foray to her room. Lila was sitting on the bed, her back against the wall. Her hairbrush sat on top of her dresser, and her backpack slumped next to her bed. The Sweet Valley High and Trixie Belden books were still lined up on the shelf, untouched.

"I'll bet you're looking forward to going home," Bethie said, sitting on the edge of the bed, hoping she looked cheerful and that she didn't sound like she was happy that Lila was leaving. Lila turned to her and grabbed her hands, startling Bethie, who didn't think Lila had touched her, voluntarily, even once, all summer long.

"Can I stay here?" Lila asked. "With you and Uncle Harold?"

Bethie was so shocked that she almost couldn't think of what to say. "You want to stay here?" she asked.

"Please," said Lila. "Please, can I?" She leaned forward, her eyes shiny with tears. "I wouldn't have to go to private school. And you could fire Isobel and Sidney. I could do the cooking and cleaning, I could even buy groceries on the weekends—"

"Whoa, whoa!" Bethie was shocked by Lila's words, and by Lila's unrelenting grip on her hands. "What's wrong?" Bethie asked. "Why don't you want to go home?"

"Because my mom hates me," Lila said.

Bethie stared at her niece. "Oh, honey. Your mom doesn't hate you."

"She does." A tear spilled down Lila's cheek. "Why do you think she sent me here? She wanted to get rid of me."

"She doesn't want to get rid of you," said Bethie. "We asked if you could come! It's true that your mom's going through a hard time right now, and maybe she hasn't been herself. Maybe she hasn't made you feel like she loves you, but I know she does. And Harold and I love having you. Your mom was doing us a favor!"

Lila shook her head, once to the right, once to the left. Her voice trembled. "She likes Kim and Missy because they're smart and good at stuff. I'm not smart . . ."

"Oh, Lila. Of course you're smart."

"I'm not," Lila said, raising her voice. "I'm not in any of the accelerated classes, I got a Needs Improvement in math. I hate school, and I'm not good at anything else. Missy was good at sports and writing, and Kim was good at drama and debate, and both of them got good grades, and I'm just . . ." Lila raised her hands and let them fall, a dismayingly adult gesture of resignation. "I'm *ordinary*," she said.

"Lila." Bethie kept her voice low and calm. "You are not ordinary, you are wonderful. You're a very smart, very special girl."

"I'm not smart. Or special. I'm just regular, and that's not good enough for my mother. She's always talking about how Kim and Missy are going to have big lives, how they go to these great colleges, and they'll have big careers, and, and do things. And I won't. I can't."

"Lila, listen to me." Bethie looked into Lila's dark eyes. "No matter where you go to college or what kind of job you have, your mother will still love you. And so will I, and so will Harold, and so will your dad and your sisters."

Lila shook her head, her expression woeful. "You don't know. You're not there, so you don't hear her. She'll never be proud of me."

Bethie kicked off her shoes and stretched out on the bed, with her back against the padded headboard and her legs out in front of her. She put her arm around Lila's shoulders, feeling the girl tense, then lean into her. "When your mom and I were your age, there weren't a lot of options for girls. Like, you know how your mother's always telling you that you can be anything you want to be when you grow up? That wasn't what we heard. Men could be doctors or lawyers. We were just supposed to marry them."

Lila blinked. "My doctor's a lady," she said. "So is the principal of my school."

"Yes," said Bethie. "Some girls did grow up and became doctors and lawyers and school principals. And then, some of those lawyers couldn't get jobs once they'd gotten their law degrees. And if you ask your doctor the next time you see her, I'll bet a lot of times people thought she was a nurse. I bet people still think that your principal is a teacher. A few girls did grow up and do things, and got those jobs, but for the rest of us, we were told that the most important thing was to be married, and be a mother."

"So my mom didn't want to get married or be a mother?" asked Lila.

Careful, Bethie thought. "I think your mom loved your dad. I think he loved her. And I know your mother loved being a mom, more than anything. She loved being pregnant, she loved taking care of babies, she loves all three of you girls. If you want to be a wife and a mother, she'll be proud of you. She just doesn't want that to be the only choice you have."

Lila shook her head. Carefully, as if she was approaching a feral cat, Bethie reached out to stroke her hair. "Your mother loves you," she said. Lila turned her face to the wall and didn't respond. "I love you, too," said Bethie. She heard, or thought she heard, Lila saying something, but Lila didn't speak again, or look at her. After a while, Bethie gave Lila's shoulders a final squeeze, then got off the bed, padded across the floor, and turned off the lights. In her own bed, she whispered to Harold what had happened, and Harold told her that she'd said all the right things, that she'd done everything she could, that Lila would get through this and come out of it fine.

The next morning, Lila was gone.

"We have to find her," Bethie said, pacing the length of the kitchen with the cordless phone in her hand.

"We will. The police are coming," said Harold. "Can you find a picture? They'll want that."

Bethie half walked, half ran to her home office. In the top drawer of her desk were copies of the photos that she'd taken and sent to Jo every week, documenting Lila's adventures in Atlanta. *Our Lady of the Scowls*, she'd told Harold as they'd flipped through the images: Lila frowning at the zoo, Lila frowning in the pool, Lila squinting into the sunshine from underneath a Braves cap, Lila glowering at the camera from her black inner tube. Bethie's stomach lurched. "Where could she be?" She could imagine possibilities from the benign (Lila in the Conaway family's tree house at the end of the street) to the horrifying (Lila lured into some strange man's car). Lila had left her suitcase by the bedroom door, but she'd taken her backpack . . . and, Harold reported, a hundred dollars in cash from his wallet. Bethie's face burned as she remembered sliding her long-ago boss Mr. Breedlove's wallet out of his pocket, and all the men she'd stolen from, all those years ago. Were such things hereditary? Was that skill buried somewhere deep in Lila's genetic memory, along with resentfulness and mistrust?

"Should I call Jo?" she asked.

Harold considered. "How about we give ourselves 'til noon to find her. If we can't, then we'll let your sister know."

Bethie nodded, already dreading that conversation. *You lost her?* Jo would ask. *Bethie, how could you?* It would be another terrible addition to the long, long list of things that Bethie had ever done.

The two police officers, both men, arrived at a few minutes after eight o'clock. Bethie and Harold led them into the living room and answered questions as best they could. No, Lila hadn't made any friends that they knew of. No, she hadn't been talking to any boys or men. "She's a kid!" Bethie had said, and one of the policemen, an older, heavyset man who'd introduced himself as Officer Beasley, said, "Ma'am, you'd be surprised." No, they couldn't think of anywhere she could have gone, anyone who might have taken her in, or taken her away. No, she didn't do drugs. Yes, she had access to a bicycle, but the one she'd ridden that summer (glumly, the way she'd done everything else) was still in the garage. No, she couldn't drive.

The officers advised Bethie and Harold to look anyplace that might have meaning to Lila, anyplace they thought she might have gone. "Should we put up posters?" Bethie asked. "Do we offer a reward?"

"Give it a few hours," Officer Beasley said. "Most of them come home on their own." He told them that the police would check with the phone company to see if any calls had been made after Harold and Bethie had gone to bed, or before they'd gotten up. He urged them to check the mall and the video arcade. He wished them luck.

"I'll stay home in case she comes back," Harold said. "Unless you want to?"

"No," said Bethie. She'd gotten an idea after the officers had left, and after a quick turn around the neighborhood and a short, embarrassed conversation with Eileen

Salter, who was still in her bathrobe with her hair uncombed, and who confirmed that she hadn't seen Lila, she climbed into her car and sped off. Part of her thought that there was no way Lila could have gotten herself all the way out there. Part of her decided that there was nowhere else for Lila to go.

She found her niece on the porch out behind Blue Hill Farm, which had once been a commune and had then been their commercial kitchen and was now in the process of being turned into a restaurant and bed-and-breakfast, Sharon's pet project, a laboratory and showcase for their products. Lila sat on the steps, her knees pulled up to her chest, and appeared to be staring out at the fields, where they grew blueberries and raspberries and, still, a little marijuana. Bethie walked up behind her and touched her shoulder and said her name. Instead of answering, Lila just sighed.

"How'd you get here?"

"Bus." Lila's voice was flat. Bethie felt herself exhale, imagining she could feel her heartbeat slow.

She stepped inside to call Harold, who said he'd tell the police. In the refrigerator, she found a pitcher of iced tea and two glasses, which she filled with ice and a sprig of mint. She carried the glasses and the pitcher outside, set them on a small wooden table, and sat in one of the white wicker rocking chairs they'd put there, waiting until she was sure she had Lila's attention before she spoke.

"When I was a few years older than you, my uncle started touching me."

Lila turned around. Her mouth was hanging open, and her eyes were wide.

"Which uncle?"

"You never met him. He died before you were born. He started doing this to me after my father died, and when I told my mom, she didn't believe me. Do you know who got him to stop? Your mother."

Lila's eyes got even wider. To her, Bethie thought, this must have sounded like a movie, one of those lurid ones that sometimes showed up on TV.

"Your mother was working that summer."

"At Camp Tanuga," Lila said. She'd absorbed at least that much of the family's history, Bethie thought.

"That's right. When she came home, I told her what Uncle Mel was doing to me. Your mom was ready to kill him. We figured out a plan. Your mom drove me to his house and went in with me. I told him if he ever touched me or any other girl again, I'd report him to whatever board was in charge of eye doctors. That's what he was, an eye doctor. Your mother saved me." Bethie took a sip from her glass of tea, wondering if Lila was old enough to know the story of the other time that Jo had saved her. She decided that she was. "And later, when I was in college, I was raped."

"Oh my God." Lila's eyes were glassy, and her expression was stunned. Bethie tried to remember being thirteen, when there was no pain as big or as consequential as your own pain, when you were at the center of the world, and other people just orbited in the distant periphery.

"I was raped, and I got pregnant. Abortion wasn't legal then, but there were ways to get it done safely, if you could afford it. Your mom and her friend were going to travel all over the world, and instead, she came home, all the way from Turkey, and she used the money she'd saved to take care of me. That's the kind of person your mother is. If she loves you, she'll do anything to help you. Give up anything she has; make any sacrifice she can make." Bethie looked at Lila and tried to keep from crying. "Your mother missed out on so much because of me."

"Like what?" Lila's voice was suspicious, but at least it wasn't flat, or bored.

"Well, most of the 1960s, for starters," Bethie said. "While I was roaming around, protesting the war and dancing at Woodstock, she was married. When the world started to change—for everyone, but especially for women—she was already a mother. She missed everything."

"Misses everything," Lila said, and gave the faintest smile. "It's like a joke. Like, there should be a Mister Everything somewhere."

Bethie found herself wanting to grab Lila by her scrawny shoulders and shake her.

"It's funny, unless you're the one sitting on the sidelines, living your life for other people."

Startled, Lila said, "Is that what my mom did?"

"You tell me." Bethie's voice was sharper and louder than she'd let it get over all those long weeks of the summer. "Your mom wanted to be a writer. She wanted to see the world. She wanted . . ." She stopped herself, thinking that it was for Jo to tell Lila exactly what she'd missed, if Jo ever felt moved to do so, and made herself breathe. "All I'm saying is that your mother is going to love you no matter what you do, because you are hers."

Lila didn't look entirely convinced, but she also looked less suspicious than she had since the day she'd gotten off the plane. "But she didn't have to miss everything. She could've gone on that trip, when you were . . ." Lila paused. "Better."

Bethie shook her head. "She used her money to help me. That was part of it. And I think that after she came home, she lost something. Her momentum. Her courage." What fairy tale was it, Bethie wondered, where you could fly as long as you thought lovely thoughts, but as soon as you stopped you came crashing back to earth?

"Whatever you want to be, whoever you want to be, your mother is going to love you and support you. I've known your mother all my life. I know who she is. She loved me even though I spent ten years just . . ." Bethie raised her hands and shook her head, searching for the right words. "Just wandering around, singing on street corners, stealing from people. Hating myself. She doesn't care if you have a big life or a small one, Lila. She just wants you to be able to be whoever you want to be, and love whoever you want to love."

"That's not true," Lila said, but her voice was wavering, lacking the all-out conviction that Bethie had heard before.

"She loves you," Bethie said again, and stood, stretching out her hand, waiting until Lila took it, thinking that if they hurried they could tell Jo that her flight had been delayed and get her home by the end of the day, without her mother knowing that anything had gone wrong.

Jo

In the years after her divorce, Jo had a mantra that she'd repeat to herself every morning, every night, and every bad moment in between: *At least it can't get worse.*

She'd gotten both her daughters into college, cosigning their student loans after Dave said he couldn't. She and Lila lived in a two-bedroom condominium, in a complex full of divorced people, where the walls were as thin as cardboard and the carpet was a sad, flat, industrial gray. Jo had done what she could to make the place cheerful, hanging brightly colored posters on the off-white walls, covering the carpets in her own wool rugs. She took Lila to Girl Scouts, which Lila claimed to hate, to the dance lessons that Lila abandoned after three months, and the piano lessons she quit after just six weeks, ignoring Lila's scowls and dirty looks, her daughter's muttered assertions that Dad's place was nicer, that Dad was more fun, that Nonie was a better cook and Dave was a better parent than she was.

It can't get worse, she'd think, even though she was exhausted all the time, aching with longing for her former life with Dave, who'd been her husband, however imperfectly, and for Nonie, who Jo believed had been her friend. The world felt like a terrible place. Everything hurt. In the morning, she'd wake up with her body aching like she'd run three circuits around the fitness trail in her sleep. She tried not to think about the pain or the disappointment. Dwelling on the past was a luxury she couldn't afford, along with new shoes, or new tires for the station wagon, or a rug large enough to cover up all of the sad grayish stuff in the condo's living room. She plodded through her days, putting one foot in front of the other, then did it again and again and again, getting up every morning, fixing breakfast, packing lunch, going to work, coming home, cooking dinner, washing clothes and dishes, grading papers, going to sleep, then waking up and doing it some more. She wouldn't let herself think about Dave and Nonie, or about Margot in Philadelphia, with the strawberry-blond curls, or about Shelley, who'd come to find her all those years ago.

She continued teaching her classes on the fitness trail. She wanted to quit, because every step along the path, every sit-up and leg-lift, reminded her of Nonie and of Nonie's betrayal, but the truth was that she needed the money. So she went, sometimes dragging Lila along. At fourteen, Lila was small for her age, all knees and elbows and beaky nose, with the same dark eyes and emphatic eyebrows as her father. Her dark-brown hair was tangled, her expression was guarded and suspicious, and her mouth seemed to be stuck in a permanent scowl. Lila was angry at her mother. She was angry about having to leave Apple Blossom Court and her only good friend, Amy Seligson; angry about having to switch schools, angry that her sisters had gotten to live with their father for all of their lives while she only got to see him every other weekend. On the door of her bedroom in the condo was a hand-drawn sign that read GET OUT. The wall next to her bed was covered with pictures of their old house, their old street, and her old school, and all of her old class pictures.

Jo tried to help. She mustered energy she didn't have and went to talk to Lila's teachers, telling them about the divorce, and the move, and how Lila's father had moved on with Jo's former best friend. She found Lila a therapist, a bosomy woman named Ellen Leong, who had an office full of toys and who told her, "Lila is working through her feelings of abandonment and disappointment," and charged Jo eighty dollars a session, which insurance didn't cover and which Dave refused to pay. ("She's fine!" he said. "She's just being a kid!") She took Lila on trips to see Broadway shows in New York City, where Lila claimed to be bored, or hiking in the Berkshires, where Lila said that she was bored and bugbitten, and after saving her pennies, on a spring break mother-daughter jaunt to Florida, where Lila got so badly sunburned after a few hours on the beach that the bulk of their stay was spent in the hotel room, with Lila in a bathtub full of lukewarm water and baking soda, and they only got to spend a single afternoon at Disney World.

Finally, after months of dealing with Lila's sulks and silences, she'd heard Lila laughing at one of the ladies in her fitness class, and she'd snapped. "What is wrong with you?" Jo asked Lila as they drove home from the fitness trail. It was April, crisp and windy, as they drove past the road that would have led them to Apple Blossom Court, Lila turned, and stared, and heaved a noisy sigh.

"I hate getting up early," said Lila. "Why can't you just let me sleep?"

"I can't leave you home by yourself."

"So just leave me in the car."

"Not safe. And don't change the subject. You were mean. How do you think Mrs. Futterman feels when you laugh at her?"

Appealing to Lila's empathy did no good. Jo wasn't even sure the girl had any. "If she doesn't want people to laugh at her, why doesn't she lose some weight?" Lila asked. She stuck out her bottom lip and exhaled hard enough to lift her bangs briefly off her forehead.

"It isn't that easy," Jo said. Lila muttered that it didn't look like Mrs. Futterman was trying very hard, and Jo said, her voice sharp, "If you can't be kind, how about you just be quiet?" She hated the harshness of her own voice, hated the way she had somehow started not just to look but even to sound exactly like her own mother. Had she been that impatient with Kim or Melissa? Had she spoken to them that way?

"And if your bed isn't made, no TV tonight," she said as they pulled into the Briarcliff parking lot. TV was on the schedule every night. Lila said that cards and board games were boring. She claimed she hated to read. She would roll her eyes if Jo suggested anything else—doing a craft project, learning to knit, running errands or baking cookies together.

"Hey," said Lila, shading her eyes. "Who's that?"

Jo looked and saw Missy waiting at the front door, with her backpack by her feet. Her heart sped up. When she'd talked to Missy on Sunday night, she had been fine, and busy, full of talk about her classes, and a boy she'd met, and some drama between her roommates. Now here she was.

Jo hurried out of the car, leaving the door open and the keys in the ignition and Lila still unbuckling her seat belt. Missy offered a limp wave and attempted a smile. "Hey. Um. I need to tell you something."

She's pregnant, Jo thought as her mouth went dry. *She got fired. She's on drugs, and I'm going to have to pay for rehab.* "Um. So I went to the video store last night . . ." Jo saw Missy's throat move as she swallowed. "Maybe we should go to Blockbuster and I can show you."

The video was in the center of the "New Arrivals." The woman on the box had feathered blond hair and a brilliant, pearly grin, but among the lineup of fit, tanned, long-legged, hard-bodied instructors, she stood out, with her rounded thighs and hips and warm smile. Instead of the high-cut leotard and ubiquitous leg warmers, she wore a plain white T-shirt and a pair of blue leggings. *Get Fit with Nonie!* read the words written in gold above her head. Jo heard herself starting to laugh. She picked up the box, laughing louder and louder. *Can't get worse,* she thought. *Well, I guess it can.*

Missy said, "Mom?" and Jo just kept laughing, a shrill, witchy cackle, clutching her own shoulders, rocking on her heels with tears streaming down her cheeks until a clerk in a Blockbuster T-shirt came over and said, "Ma'am, are you all right?"

"I'm fine," Jo gasped, wiping her eyes. "I'm fine." She flipped the box over and saw Nonie, her old friend, smiling as she stood, not in a meticulously lit exercise studio, but in what looked like someone's living room. Behind her were six women of varying shapes and sizes, some in leotards, others in shorts and tank tops, one in sweatpants and a T-shirt. "Finally, a fitness video for the rest of us!" read the copy on the back of the box. "Follow along at your own pace as Nonie takes you through a series of simple moves that use your own body weight to build strength and aerobic fitness! Nonie's assistants will demonstrate modifications for all fitness levels so that any BODY can do this workout! It's EASY! It's FUN! It's FITNESS FOR EVERYONE!" Jo had to search, and squint, before she found her husband's fingerprints, but they were there, in the small print at the bottom of the box: *A Dave Braverman production.*

"Oh, Mom," said Missy, and put her arm around Jo's shoulders, and even Lila, instead of muttering something mean about how it was Jo's fault, gave her mom's arm a small pat. Jo couldn't stop laughing. She laughed and laughed until tears poured down her face, aware that people were staring, aware that she was making a scene. The clerk came back and said, "Ma'am, I'm going to have to ask you to leave," and Missy had said, "We're going, okay? We're going right now," and with her arm still wrapped around Jo's shoulders she steered her mother out into the parking lot.

"Wow. I'm really sorry," said Mary Ellen Weems, the lawyer who'd handled Jo's divorce. "But I'm not a copyright expert." Mary Ellen got Jo the name of a man in New York City. When Jo finally got him on the phone, the man had her explain the situation, slowly, then go back and explain it again. By her third time through the story, Jo was starting to suspect that the man charged by fifteen-minute increments, and that he was stretching out their conversation to hit the half-hour mark. Finally, he asked if she'd trademarked "Jumpin' with Jo." "The name? The concept? The jump that you do at the end? Any of the moves?"

"The moves are just basic things. Squats and jumping jacks. Anyone can do them. That's the point!"

"Which may be a problem," said the attorney. Jo tried to picture him, imagining a plump, middle-aged man in a three-piece suit, a man who'd never done a squat or a star jump in his life. "If your husband claims that these are exercises that any kid who's ever taken a gym class learned, you're going to have a problem proving that he stole proprietary material from you."

Jo closed her eyes. "Sir," she said. "I know you can't see it. But I made a tape called *Jumpin' with Jo* that starts off with me saying 'Anyone can do these moves' and ends with me doing a star jump and, in between, includes exactly the same routine that Nonie is doing. A routine that she learned by taking a class that I teach. With the same modifications for women who are older, or who have bad knees. It's my routine, sir." Tears had squeezed out of the corners of her eyes and were dripping down her cheeks. She didn't think she'd ever been so angry in her life, at least not since Bethie had told her that she'd been raped.

The man quoted Jo the price of his retainer. She stifled a gasp and said, "I'll get back to you," and hung up the phone and held it, breathing deeply, before squeezing her eyes shut and punching in the Atlanta area code. She hated asking her sister for help, but she had nowhere else to turn.

"Oh, God," Bethie said then, after Jo had gotten the whole story out. "That motherfucker. That bastard. Tell me what you need."

"I need a loan." The words felt like dead worms in Jo's mouth.

"I don't know why you didn't ask me to finance the business," Bethie said, and Jo murmured that yes, in retrospect, that would have been a very good idea indeed. She hadn't gone to Bethie because she hadn't wanted Bethie to confirm that it was a bad idea or, worse, to have her sister lie and say that it was a great idea, and invest, and lose her money, just to show that she believed in her sister, that she thought that Jo was as smart and as savvy as she herself was, when, clearly, Jo was not. Bethie was the winner, the family success story, the one who'd turned peaches and sugar and hand-labeled Mason jars into a fortune. Jo was the loser, the punch line, the one who'd had her one big idea stolen by her unfaithful ex-husband and her former best friend. *Can't get worse.* What a dummy.

"But never mind. Let's not look back. Do you like the lawyer you talked to?" Bethie asked.

Jo gripped the phone hard, wrapping the cord tightly around her index finger. "He was fine. Expensive, though."

"Let me help." Bethie's voice was firm, and kind, and full of a righteous rage that left Jo weak with gratitude.

"Okay," she whispered.

"I don't get it," Lila drawled from the couch, once Jo had hung up. Lila had taken advantage of her mother's inattention and helped herself to a pint of Ben & Jerry's. Her mouth was lined in chocolate-brown, and Jo saw a chocolate chunk melting on the couch's blue upholstery. She'd told Lila, over and over, to please not take food out of the kitchen, but Lila didn't listen. "If it was really your idea, why didn't you register it or something?"

"I never imagined that your father would try to steal it." Jo knew she wasn't supposed to bad-mouth Dave in front of the kids. That was Divorced Parenting 101. No matter what your ex did or how enraged it made you, you weren't allowed to complain about the man who was, after all, the father of your children. But Jo couldn't stop herself.

"Dad's smart," Lila said, shrugging. "If you were smart, you would have figured out how to turn it into something by yourself." She unfolded her skinny legs from the couch and sauntered into the kitchen, and it was all Jo could do not to yank the phone out of the wall and hurl it at her youngest daughter's head.

The New York City lawyer, whose name was Robert Rhodes, subpoenaed both Dave and Nonie. Rhodes got to depose Dave Braverman. When Dave had tried to argue that he and Jo had come up with the concept together, Rhodes delivered a blistering cross-examination. He'd asked Dave exactly which moves he'd thought of, how many times he'd taught or even attended one of Jo's classes, and if he knew how a burpee was performed, or how to modify the move for someone with bad knees, or where one parked to access the fitness trail where the class had originated. Dave had mumbled through his answers, seeming to flinch from the video camera. When his deposition ended, his lawyer had huddled with hers, and by the end of the day, Dave offered Jo a lump-sum settlement. Jo suspected that the money wasn't even close to how much he'd already earned from his first-ever successful entrepreneurial endeavor. But it would be enough. She'd be able to pay off the loans she'd taken out for Kim and Missy. She'd be able to move out of the sad, thin-walled condo and back into a real house, and put enough away so that Lila could attend whatever college would be lucky enough to get her.

When the check finally arrived, Jo bought a three-bedroom house, new construction, a ranch-style home set on a quarter-acre lot, with a screened-in back porch, a lush green lawn in front, and, out back, the swimming pool that she'd always wanted, complete with an in-ground hot tub.

"Take a trip," Bethie had told her when Jo called to say that they'd settled. Bethie had waved off all of Jo's attempts to pay back the money Bethie had lent her for the lawyer. "I owe you more than I could ever repay. Send Lila down here again. Just go see the world. You've waited long enough." Jo packed a bag and drove Lila to Atlanta. She spent the night at the house in Buckhead where Bethie and Harold lived, endured Lila's murderous glances across the breakfast table, and said, "See you in August!" As soon as Lila was out of sight, Jo exhaled, feeling a lightness in her chest, a sense of hope for the first time, her shoulders drop down from her ears, where they'd been permanently hunched.

In the driveway, she sat in the driver's seat, her hands resting on the old station wagon's steering wheel. Missy was in New York, where she would spend her summer interning at a literary magazine. Kim was in Philadelphia, finishing her second year of law school. Jo was forty-nine years old, a woman of a certain age, with money in the bank. She didn't have to rush home to try to scramble up some summer-school classes, or teach on the fitness trail. She could buy herself a ticket anywhere in the world. Or, she thought, as the first real smile she'd smiled in what felt like years moved across her face, she could buy two.

At a Sunoco station, she gassed up the car, and at the register, asked the clerk if they had a map of the United States. "You're in luck," said the guy behind the counter as he slid a folded map across the counter. "Just got the one left." Jo thanked him, paid, and climbed back behind the wheel. She cranked up the air-conditioning and turned up the radio and, as the opening chords of "Jump" by Van Halen thundered from the speakers, Jo Kaufman turned her car west. She couldn't remember where, or when, she'd found out that Shelley Finkelbein had moved to Colorado, but she knew that that was where her old flame was living.

Maybe she's with someone, Jo thought, as she made her way across the country. *Maybe she's gotten married again*. She imagined dozens of scenarios, each one more painful and humiliating than the last, but she kept going, driving to Colorado in all-day, seventy-mile-an-hour gulps, driving from dawn until midnight, collapsing into bed at roadside motels, telling herself, *All she can say is no.*

There were no Finkelbeins in the phone book, but there was an R. Ziskin in the Denver phone book, with an address on Willow Court. Jo drove down her street, parked the car, and walked up the driveway of a neat little bungalow with pots of bright-red geraniums by the door.

Jo knocked. The door swung open, and there was Shelley, as if she'd been standing there waiting for Jo's arrival. Her skin was still creamy, faintly freckled, although lined around the eyes and lips. Her hair was short, still dark and glossy, curling in wisps around her cheeks. She wore jeans, acid-washed and fashionably high-waisted, and a billowy bright-green button-down blouse tucked into them. A heavy silver and turquoise necklace hung around her slender neck. Her feet were bare, and her nails were painted red, and Jo saw a silver ring on one toe, but no rings on her fingers. Jo drank her in, her scent, the shape of her body. Shelley's small, capable hands, her luminous eyes, her quick, inquisitive glance and the tilt of her head.

"Shelley?" Jo cleared her throat. She'd barely spoken in the long three days of her drive. Her voice sounded rusty. She was aware of how she must look, rumpled and road-weary, her hair sticking up in spikes and her hands and face sticky with sweat and dust. A scrap of a poem moved through her head: *Come live with me and be my love.*

"Jo." Shelley's cheeks flushed, faintly, and she opened her arms. She still smelled like flowers and cigarettes, and she still felt just right in Jo's arms. "I never stopped hoping," she said.

2006

Jo

"Come on," Shelley called. "If we don't go now, we're going to hit traffic." Shelley was dressed for Thanksgiving dinner at Kim's house in black cotton leggings and a midnight-blue velvet tunic, with her short silvery hair brushed up into spikes. She wore black patent-leather clogs, "my dress-up clogs," as she called them, the ones Jo suspected had been chosen because they'd aggravate Kim's mother-in-law. Once, Shelley had owned a collection of high-heeled shoes that would have rivaled any boutique's. Now she had arthritis and flats.

Jo slipped silver teardrop earrings through the holes in her ears that had gotten longer as the years had passed, and gave herself a quick check in the mirror, making sure her gray wool pants weren't wrinkled and that her black cashmere wrap didn't have cat fur on its sleeves. As Shelley put her coat on, Jo pulled her contribution to the Thanksgiving meal out of the refrigerator and gave it a shake, watching with satisfaction as the shimmery surface of the cherry-flavored Jell-O gave an obliging wiggle.

"It's going to be okay," Shelley told her as they walked down the driveway. It sounded, Jo thought, as if Shelley was trying to convince herself as much as Jo, but she made herself nod and say, "I know everything's going to be fine."

And even if it wasn't, Jo thought, as she turned on the car and pulled onto the street, she'd had such happy years with Shelley. She thought, sometimes, that everything she'd experienced, the years in the suburbs, the bankruptcy and financial uncertainty, the collapse of her marriage, Dave and Nonie's betrayal, Lila's endless misery and scorn, that all of it had been the price she had paid for the life she had now. Thanks to the settlement, she had enough money to maintain the house in Avondale and live nicely. The plan was to move to New York City after they'd both retired, if they could find a way to do it affordably. For now, they could go to the city once every month for a day or two of theater and museums, although sometimes, at Shelley's insistence, they'd go to Foxwoods, the new Indian casino up by New London, where Shelley would play poker and Jo would wander the casino floor, sometimes playing nickel slots, sometimes people-watching, sometimes just sitting with a book. Every summer, they did a big trip. So far, she and Shelley had toured Venice and Copenhagen and Barcelona. They'd taken a cruise on a barge through Holland, when the tulips were in bloom, paddled kayaks beneath glaciers in Alaska, and ridden bicycles through the countryside in Provence. On their first day, after a hilly, fifteen-mile pedal through the rolling countryside, they'd stopped at a winery for lunch. Jo had limited herself to a few sips of white and a single swallow of red, admiring the cool, cave-like interior of the stone farmhouse where they were dining, and enjoying her Niçoise

salad and fresh baguette. Shelley, meanwhile, had insisted on tasting everything they poured, finishing her
glasses and Jo's, sampling whites, reds, rosés, sparkling
wines, even dessert wines. "I'm just having a little bit!"
she'd said, flushed and indignant, when Jo pointed out
that they'd have to get back on their bikes when the
meal was over. By the time they stepped back into the
afternoon sunshine, Shelley was past tipsy. She'd put
her helmet on backward, waved off Jo's help, climbed
on her bike, wobbled maybe ten yards down the
smooth dirt of the winery's driveway, and then rolled,
very slowly, into a shallow, grassy ditch. Jo ran after her
and found her lying on her back, helmet askew, laughing so hard she was crying.

"BUI!" she'd gasped. "Biking under the influence!" Jo
had laughed and held her, and they'd drowsed together,
under the lemony sun, and Jo had spent the rest of the
ride pedaling solo, with Shelley sobering up in the van.

Over the years, Jo had imagined a hundred different
lives for her lost love. She'd pictured Shelley in a jewelry studio, her small, fox-like face intent as she used a
blowtorch to twist metal into earrings and pendants, or
Shelley onstage, performing monologues, or Shelley as
a poet in loose-fitting black clothing, walking through a
forest bright with fall leaves. She'd been amused when,
with a combination of pride and chagrin, Shelley told
her that she'd become a speech therapist. "I had to do
something practical after the divorce," she explained on
their first night in Colorado. They'd been in bed, where
Jo had been delighted to find that Shelley smelled just
the way she remembered, that same intoxicating combination of flowery perfume and tobacco, even though
Shelley claimed to have stopped smoking in the 1970s.
She'd put on weight since the last time Jo had seen her,

and she'd been careful to keep a pillow or a length of sheet over her midsection, until Jo had pulled her hands away and kissed every silvery stretch mark, every inch of yielding skin.

"Speech therapy?"

Shelley lifted her chin. "I was broke." Her father had died by then, of colon cancer, the year after Shelley's wedding, and her mother wouldn't have been supportive, even if Shelley had asked.

"No alimony?"

Shelley bit her lip, a gesture Jo remembered well, and said, "Denny wasn't in the mood to be generous." More lip-nibbling ensued, before Shelley said, "He found me in bed. With someone else."

"The pizza delivery boy?" Jo teased.

"More like the pizza delivery girl," Shelley confessed, ducking her head, as Jo felt jealousy flare in her chest at the idea of some long-ago stranger. "Denny was furious. He felt like I'd pulled some kind of bait and switch on him. That I knew I was . . ." Jo saw her throat work as she swallowed, before saying, ". . . gay before I married him. That I never intended to have kids, or be a mother, and I lied to him."

Jo hadn't meant to ask, but the words were out before she could stop them. "Did he have any idea? Did you ever tell him about—"

"You?" Shelley gave a sad smile and shook her head. "Of course not. He thought you were my friend. That was all." She shook her head again. "You were the brave one, remember?"

"Not so brave that I didn't end up exactly where you were," Jo said.

Shelley sighed and reached for Jo's hand.

"I took what he gave me, and I didn't want to move

back home, so I took out loans and I went back to school, and I have spent the last fifteen years teaching children how to pronounce their diphthongs."

"Come here, you diphthong," said Jo, opening her arms. Later, she'd whispered, "Do you forgive me?"

"For not running away with me?" Shelley answered, plucking Jo's thoughts from her head with that old, familiar ease. "Please. You had two babies. I don't know what I was thinking. It was a fantasy."

Jo had rolled onto her side, pulling Shelley close. "I'm here now."

Shelley had put her condo on the market and took the first good offer that she got. In Connecticut, she'd rented her own apartment, telling Jo that they shouldn't rush into things, that maybe they'd changed and wouldn't get along as well as they once had, but she'd ended up spending almost every night with Jo in Avondale, and when her lease was up after the first year, she hadn't renewed it. She found a job as a speech therapist in a school district two towns over, and Jo continued as a permanent substitute teacher. They took their big trips in the summer and shorter ones throughout the year, skiing in Vermont or driving up to Northampton or down to New York City to see exhibits or concerts or shows. They hung the bright, abstract paintings Shelley had collected on the walls, and spread her Navajo-style rugs on the floors, and crammed her clothes—so many clothes—into Jo's bedroom closet, putting the overspill into the room where Missy and Kim slept when they were home. Shelley met Jo's friends—brisk, take-charge Judy Pressman; peppy, preppy Stephanie Zelcheck; Valerie Cohen, who was working on a PhD in romance languages at the University of Connecticut. The women welcomed Shelley into the book club, and marveled at her and Jo's story, and pointedly did not mention Nonie Scotto, who'd once read books and sipped wine and raised her babies alongside them. Years went by, and they were happy. Except for Lila.

Jo understood her youngest daughter's anger. She could see things from Lila's perspective, and could appreciate how she had been less than entirely attentive toward her maternal responsibilities in the months and years immediately after Shelley had come back into her life. She had been love-drunk, besotted, which meant that Lila's needs, her homework projects and her school lunches, had seemed, at the time, far less important than Jo's desire to be with Shelley and only Shelley, every minute of every day. Jo cringed, remembering how, in those first months and years, she would send Lila to her father's house or to spend a weekend with one of her sisters, or even down to Atlanta to stay with Bethie for the weekend, the better to have uninterrupted time with her beloved. It pained her to remember how she'd even left Lila home alone a few times when she and Shelley were traveling and Lila was just fifteen. She'd given Lila money and the telephone numbers for all of the neighbors, and Lila, of course, had been all for it, promising to take care of the house and Shelley's cats, swearing that she'd be fine. When Jo and Shelley came home, one of the cats had been missing and the house had smelled like beer. The vodka that Jo kept in the freezer had tasted like water; there was a cigarette burn on one of the paintings and a suspicious stain on one of Shelley's good rugs. "I had a few people over," Lila muttered, her voice sullen, her eyes downcast. "So what?" Jo knew she should have talked to her, sat with her until Lila opened up, maybe even forced Lila to go back into therapy, but she couldn't muster the energy or the interest. Kim was working as a lawyer by then, with a coveted job in the U.S. attorney's office in New York, and Missy was taking a summer publishing course at Radcliffe and interning for a literary agent in New York City. Jo told herself that her older two were fine and that Lila would be okay, too, that Lila was just enduring the typical bumps and bruises of adolescence, and that she would emerge, eventually, as happy and well-adjusted as her sisters. It hadn't helped that, at the time of Shelley's return, Lila was at her most unpleasant and her least attractive. Her nose was beaky, her acne was awful, her braces always seemed to have chunks of food caught in the brackets, and every word out of her mouth was unkind. By tenth grade, she'd stopped calling Jo "Mom" or even "Mother" and began using her first name, and Shelley became Rochelle, or Ro. *Jo and Ro.* If the two of them were standing together, side by side, Lila would eye them up and down and say, "You guys look like the number 10." Shelley, who was sensitive about her weight, would flush, and Jo would touch Shelley's arm, warning her to be quiet, but that only made things worse, because even the most neutral physical contact would make Lila grimace, or roll her eyes, or make retching noises. Jo told her that rude behavior would result in the confiscation of her Discman or the elimination of her phone privileges, or later, no car, so Lila quit fake-vomiting and began using a nature-show announcer voice to narrate their actions. When she'd see Shelley touching Jo's hair, or Jo rubbing Shelley's feet, she'd announce, "In the wild, the silverback gorillas groom one another as a social ritual." When Shelley would make enchiladas for dinner, Lila would poke at her plate and mutter, "That looks like a one-way ticket to Shitsville," just quietly enough to pretend that Jo misheard her when Jo asked, "What did you say?" When Shelley gave Lila gifts—handmade amber earrings for Chanukah, a glass jewelry box with pressed flowers in the lid for her birthday—Lila would mutter "thanks," and they'd find the present in the trash, still in its box and wrapping paper, with the card still attached.

The worst was when Jo and Shelley had taken a weeklong sailing trip in the Bahamas, with an all-female company called Womanship. "Womanship!" Lila had repeated, when Jo told her where they were going. "Oh my God. Are you kidding me? So is everyone on the boat gay?"

"I don't think so," Shelley said. She tried to be patient with Lila; she tried to be kind. Lila's mockery hurt her, but it hadn't stopped her from trying to build a connection, which made Jo love her. Unfortunately, Shelley's efforts only seemed to make Lila despise her even more. "I think maybe it's just women who want the experience of learning to sail without men around. Men tend to take over things sometimes."

"Oh, Ro, I know," Lila said, her tone thick with fake sincerity. "Aren't men just the worst?"

Shelley had looked at Jo. "Lila," Jo had said, and Lila had widened her eyes. There was a fresh pimple on Lila's forehead, red and protuberant. Jo tried to find some affection for her daughter, some sympathy, but all she felt was weary disappointment. Wordlessly, she held out her hand, and wordlessly, Lila handed over the car keys and stomped up to her bedroom.

"Yeah," Jo had heard Lila saying later that night, when she'd passed by Lila's bedroom door. "It's called the Womanship." She'd snickered her mean-girl laugh, then said, "Where do you think they go onshore? The Dyke Dock?"

Lila had graduated from high school in the bottom

quarter of her class. She'd enrolled at Emerson College in Boston, but had flunked out after a semester. Next, she'd done a semester at the University of Hartford, with similar results. By the early aughts she was enrolled at Tunxis Community College, still trying to earn a degree, still with no idea of what she wanted to do with her life. The braces had come off, the acne had cleared up, and for her eighteenth birthday, Lila had gotten a nose job, with Dave's money, and over Jo's strenuous objections. "Your nose gave you character!" Jo had lamented, wondering what her parents, with their ethnic features, and especially her dad, with his Yiddish accent, would have made of her youngest daughter, who looked, she'd overheard Kim saying to Missy, about as Jewish as a ham sandwich. "I didn't want character," Lila had said. Her eyes were still ringed with dark circles from the surgery; her face was still bandaged. "I wanted to be pretty."

By her twenties, Lila had gotten her wish. She was a striking young woman with a limber, coltish figure and a wide, mobile mouth. Her hair was a thick, shiny dark brown; her nose and cheekbones and chin all had an arrogant, upward tilt. She carried her face like a cameo, something with undeniable value. Boys and men buzzed around her, her phone was always ringing or vibrating with incoming calls and text messages. Lila was pretty and popular, but she still hadn't finished a degree or found anything resembling a career. She worked part-time jobs and depended on the kindness of her family and the kindness of strangers. Especially, Jo suspected, strangers of the male variety.

Jo sighed. The public radio station played quietly, filling the car with news about the housing bubble's recent burst and the waves of foreclosures. Shelley squeezed her hand. Three weeks ago, Jo had found the lump in the shower, and she hadn't wanted to worry Shelley, but Shelley could tell, just from the look on her face as she'd come out of the bathroom, that something was wrong.

"Does this feel weird?" Jo had asked, guiding Shelley's fingers to the lump. Shelley had pushed, prodding gently, and said, "See if Dr. Mellors can see you today." After that, there'd been a mammogram, a needle biopsy, a diagnosis, and a plan for surgery, radiation, and chemotherapy.

She'd told Bethie her news, and when Bethie had asked what she could do, Jo replied, "Can you come for Thanksgiving? I'm going to tell the girls then," and Bethie had promised that she and Harold would be there.

Jo merged onto the Merritt Parkway and let herself consider her successes, the daughters she hadn't screwed up. Kim had soared through law school and was doing well at the U.S. attorney's office. She'd gotten married when she was only twenty-five, which struck Jo (who'd married at twenty-two) as unreasonably young, but Kim said she was sure about Matt. Kim had met him at the University of Pennsylvania. He had boyish good looks and a close-knit family, which, Jo thought, her daughter found alluring, given what had happened to her own parents. She and Matt, who seemed to be making obscene sums of money on Wall Street, had left New York City and moved to a suburb in New Jersey. Three months previously, she'd had her second baby, a little girl named Leonie.

Melissa had gone from NYU to the Radcliffe publishing course to an internship with a literary agent, which turned into a paying job ("not a well-paying job, but at least she's supporting herself," Jo told her sister). Five years ago, she'd left the agency and gone to work for Lester Shaub, one of the most famous editors in America. Lester ran his own imprint at one of the big publishing houses, and every year at least one of his books won some major award. Two of the American authors most frequently mentioned as potential Nobel Prize winners had been Lester's discoveries, and he counted Booker Prize, National Book Award honorees, and the occasional bestseller among his authors. Lester was in his seventies, still healthy and spry, with a handsome mane of curly white hair and a brownstone on the Upper East Side, where he hosted a summer solstice party every year. The most famous authors, editors, and agents in America came to sip cocktails, nibble hors d'oeuvres, and gawk at Joan Didion or Salman Rushie or the other bold-faced names. As Lester's right-hand woman, Missy sat in on meetings with Lester's authors. She met with their agents, if they were alive and writing, or their literary executors if not. She took Lester's notes and typed up his memos and made sure advances and royalty payments were sent promptly. She read every manuscript that Lester edited, offering her own suggestions. Each year, she acquired and edited a few projects of her own—a poetry collection, a debut novel—but the understanding was that she would work with Lester for seven or eight years, then go on to become an editor in her own right.

Missy was still single. She dated a lot, but she'd never settled down, and Jo worried that Missy thought that all men were faithless, duplicitous sneaks, like her father. Better to be single than to settle, and try not to worry about whether that was what Kim had done.

Jo believed that the girls were happy. Kim said that she loved being a mother, and Jo would smile, remembering how besotted she'd been with her own babies. Melissa would tell her about whatever project she was working on, or whatever problematic author she was wrangling, and Jo would glow with pride, remembering her own happiness at being completely engrossed in a book or a lesson plan or a class, or even one of the feature stories she'd written for the *Avondale Almanac*. As for her third daughter, Jo told herself that Lila was still in her twenties. Maybe it wasn't so strange for the youngest sibling of two such accomplished older sisters to be a bit of a late bloomer, to have a hard time finding her way. *She'll get there*, Jo told herself, as Shelley plucked the MapQuest printout from her purse and peered at it, first lowering and then lifting her chin. Shelley had worn bifocals for the past few years, but she still hadn't gotten the hang of them. "Turn here," Shelley said, and Jo turned, cruising slowly down the street and parking the car at the curb.

Kim and Matt's new house was enormous. "Stupid big," had been Lila's assessment, the first time she'd seen the place, and Jo had never come up with a more fitting description. The house wasn't of any particular architectural style, unless "More" counted as a style. It looked like it might have started its life as a Colonial, only the architect had kept on going, adding a wing here, a portico there, a four-car garage on one side and a turret swelling on the other. There were rows of rectangular windows, dormer windows, bay windows, and a soaring entryway that led to the inevitable two-story great room, as big as a basketball court. Worse than the aesthetics was the way the house's size seemed designed to encourage every member of the family to operate independently. The children had their own wing, complete with nanny's quarters and a second kitchen, and Matt had turned the basement into an expansive man cave that included a home theater, a wet bar, and a gym. A dozen people could live in that house and go weeks without seeing one another. Jo wondered if that was the point.

She and Shelley entered through an echoing foyer that could have easily served a boutique hotel. A grand arrangement of fall-colored blooms, leaves, and branches stood on the polished wooden table in the center of its black-and-white marble floor. Other than that, the room was empty, save for a fleet of wheeled and push-able vehicles, scooters and strollers, a tricycle and even a skateboard, lined up along the wall. A toddler-sized pink helmet hung from the scooter's handlebars.

Past the foyer and down a hall was the kitchen, which stretched the length of the back of the house. A table for twelve stood beneath a slanted glass ceiling, the baby's high chair sat at the outermost curve of the marble is-land, and Kim, with the baby in her arms, was standing by the farmhouse-style sink, conferring with three uni-formed caterers. "Mom!" she said, shifting the baby to her hip. "Shelley!" Kim had Jo's dark hair and olive skin, Dave's emphatic brows and rounded chin, and a curvy build more like Bethie's than Jo's own rangy frame. Her hair had been blown out smooth, and she'd done her makeup and dressed up in brown tweed wool pants and a wine-colored sweater. Jo wrapped her arms around her daughter and the baby, holding them for as long as Kim would let her. "It's good to see you," Kim said, kissing Jo's cheek and disengaging from her embrace. She gave Shelley an air kiss and whirled away. "I'm just going to make sure the table's set!"

Of course the table is set, Jo thought. Kim had prob-ably done that over the weekend, in between making the carrot mousse, ironing the napkins, and shifting the organic heirloom turkey from the wet brine to the dry rub. Her oldest daughter had always been a perfectionist, she thought, as a tiny voice shouted, "Grandma!" and her elder granddaughter raced into the room and launched herself at Jo's midsection. Flora wore a blue velvet jumper, with a round-collared white shirt and white tights underneath, and patent-leather Mary Janes. The bulky appearance of Flora's backside would have let her know, even if Kim hadn't told her, that Flora had experienced a setback in her toilet training after the new baby's arrival.

"Hello, sweetheart." Jo scooped Flora into her arms. The little girl had big brown eyes and wavy brown hair and deliciously chubby pink cheeks.

"Granny!" Flora crowed. She let Jo kiss her, then held out her arms so that Shelley could take her. When Kim had announced her pregnancy, she'd asked Jo what she wanted her grandkids to call her, and Jo, who hadn't given a single second's worth of thought to the question, said, "Oh, I don't care. Whatever you want is fine with me."

Kim had rolled her eyes. "Matt's mom is going to be Mimi."

"Oh?" said Jo. She knew, from friends and from her own intuition, that bashing her son-in-law or his family was a sure route to trouble, so she kept quiet whenever the subject came up.

"When we told her we were having a baby, I told her she could be Bubbe," Kim said.

"How'd that go over?" Jo asked, and Kim had snorted and said, "About as well as you'd expect." Jo had wanted to ask Kim what, if anything, her children would call Nonie. It turned out that the answer was Nonie. So she was Grandma, Shelley was Granny, and Matt's mother, whose name was Sandra and who, Jo suspected, would sooner be shot with poison-tipped arrows than voluntarily assume any title that even whispered of old age, was Mimi.

"Incoming," Shelley murmured. Jo heard the front

door open and close, then Matt's booming bass voice, welcoming his mother.

"Incoming!" Flora repeated. "Incoming! What is incoming?"

"Oh, it's just a way of saying, Look who's here!" Jo gave Shelley a stern look, then smiled as Sandra swept into the room. Ropes of seed pearls wrapped around her neck, disguising any droop, and a massive diamond glittered on her left hand. Her slim-cut navy pantsuit was immaculate, and her high-heeled shoes clicked against the tiled floors as she approached her granddaughter, arms extended, smiling as widely as the injectable fillers allowed. She reminded Jo of Shelley's mother, who still looked forty from a distance and older the closer you got.

"Flora, kiss your Mimi," she ordered, bending down to greet the little girl. "No, not too hard, you don't want to smear Mimi's makeup. HelloJoShelleyhowareyou? Flora, do you want to see the present Mimi brought you?" Sandra extended her hand, Flora took it, and Jo and Shelley exchanged a look. Most of the people they knew were welcoming or, at least, tolerant of the two of them as a couple. Sandra Grissom was the exception. She acted as if Jo and Shelley disgusted her, and she made no attempt to disguise her disdain. Jo had learned, years after Matt and Kim's wedding, that Sandra told her son that if the plan was for Shelley to walk Kim down the aisle, or play any kind of role in the ceremony, she, Sandra, would consider it a travesty and would stay home. Jo had decided that Sandra was a monster, and Sandra had never given her a reason to change her mind.

Jo waited until the caterers were occupied before sliding her Jell-O mold into the refrigerator and washing her hands at the kitchen sink. "Kim, what can I do?"

"I think we're all set." Kim pulled a BlackBerry out

of her pocket and scrolled through what was undoubtedly one of her checklists. "The turkey's coming out of the oven in an hour, the wine's chilling, the side dishes are heating up."

"Can I bring anything to the table? Light the candles?" As soon as Jo had asked the questions, two caterers bustled by, one carrying a cut-glass bowl of cranberry relish, the other holding a long electric lighter.

"How about the baby?" Kim said. Smiling, Jo stretched out her arms and accepted the sleepy, warm weight of her granddaughter. *Leonie's such an easy baby*, Kim had told her, with her voice full of wonder. She actually nurses, Kim had said. No nipple shields! No bad latch! It's nothing like it was with Flora.

"Lucky you," Jo had said. When Flora had been born, Jo had offered to stay and help for as long as Kim needed her. As a substitute teacher, Jo had a flexible schedule, and she'd invested the money she'd won from Dave with care, waiting for the day that she became a grandmother. Her plan had always been to take a few months off and help when her daughters had babies. She'd nursed all three of them, even before nursing was fashionable, so she could have helped Kim figure out how to do it, even though Jo didn't remember breastfeeding as being especially tricky or difficult. *Girls today*, Judy Pressman had told her. *They act like they're the first ones to have done any of this. They've got to reinvent the wheel, and make everything ten times harder than it has to be.*

Kim and Matt had still been living in Manhattan when Flora was born, but their apartment had a guest room, with its own bathroom attached. Jo had offered to come and stay, or even rent her own place. *I can be there as much or as little as you need me*, she'd said. *I'll do whatever needs doing.* She'd made her offer in the hospital, the day Flora was born, and Kim, who'd had a C-section and still had an IV poked into the back of her hand, had eagerly agreed, until Matt had crossed the hospital room to stand behind his wife, giving her shoulders a squeeze.

"We've got that baby nurse, remember?" he said. "And the lactation consultant."

Lactation consultant? Jo thought, and made a mental note to ask Judy what on earth that was.

"Right," Kim had said, "but that's just for, what, a week or two?"

Jo had watched Matt's hands tighten on Kim's shoulders. "We can keep her as long as you need her," he'd said, before looking at Jo. "And my mom's right around the corner."

Jo had driven back to Connecticut and tried not to feel slighted. Kim had called her every day to describe Flora's struggles to nurse, Kim's worries about whether she was making enough milk, how Flora wasn't gaining weight or sleeping more than ninety minutes at a stretch, and how Sandra seemed to expect the baby nurse to wait on her. "She'll say, 'Oh, let me hold the baby,' but she'll be all dressed up in, like, a cashmere twinset, and even though she'll have a burp cloth on her shoulder, Flora always manages to puke on her somewhere."

Good for Flora, Jo thought.

"And Sandra asks Marisol to get her coffee, or a snack. She calls her 'the girl,'" Kim reported. She sniffled, and Jo wondered if Kim was crying. "Like, 'The girl can go pick up a few things at the drugstore.' Except she can't. It's part of her contract. No housekeeping, no errands, just baby stuff."

"Honey, if you need extra hands, I can be there in two hours," Jo said, and Kim paused, then sighed. "No. No, thanks. We'll figure it out."

The year of Flora's birth, Matt had gotten an annual bonus even more obscene than usual (Jo wondered if the mortgages his bank had given to people who couldn't make their payments was the reason). He'd put their apartment on the market, made a profit, and moved his wife and daughter from Manhattan to Fort Lee, where many of his fellow masters of the universe laid their heads. They'd hired a full-time nanny, and when Flora was three months old, Kim had gone back to work. "It's awful," she'd told Jo during her lunch break her first day back. "I don't miss her at all," Kim said, her voice cracking. "I was so relieved to hand her off to someone else. I'm so happy to be back." She paused, inhaling. "I'm a terrible mother."

"Oh, no, you are not. That's normal!" Without thinking, Jo had dropped her voice into its lowest, calmest register, the tone she took to let her students know that what she was discussing was important, that yes, it would be on the test. "Every new mom feels exactly the way you're feeling."

There was a pause. "Is that how you felt?" Kim asked.

"You were an easier baby than Flora," Jo said. "And there weren't as many options back then. None of us had jobs to go back to."

"I want to really be there for Flora. Really be present for her, you know?" Kim had said. Jo had murmured assent, wondering if there was a critique hidden in that assertion, if Kim thought that Jo hadn't been present for her. "But, my God, I was so bored!"

"It can be boring," Jo said. That part she remembered very clearly, the gray sameness all the days had, the endless, repetitive rounds of chores. Mashing bananas, mixing water into rice cereal, walking a screaming baby back and forth through the house, or scraping shit off cloth diapers into the toilet before tossing them into the diaper pail. Jo thought her daughter was lucky, to be able to enjoy Flora for part of the day, then pass her off to competent, capable help. She thought it was, as they said, the best of both worlds.

Jo settled Leonie against her and walked back through the house, looking for Flora. She was halfway down the hall when she heard the quick taps of Kim's heels.

"What?" asked Jo, when she saw the expression on Kim's face. "What is it?"

Kim pulled Jo into the dining room, where, of course, the table was perfect, draped in a pressed white cloth, with an arrangement of miniature pumpkins and branches of bittersweet in the center. The room, the paintings on the walls, the silver and crystal and Kim's wedding china, all glowed with a mellow patina that spoke of money, comfort, ease.

"It's Lila," Kim whispered.

"Ah," said Jo. It was always Lila.

"I don't want to worry you," Kim began.

"I'm a mother," Jo said. "Worrying is what I do."

Kim gave a brief smile. "Lila stayed over last Saturday night. I was in her room—I'd lent her some earrings, and I went to get them back, and I swear I wasn't snooping, but she left her laptop open, and she was on this website," she whispered.

"What?" Jo asked.

"It was a website for sugar daddies. You know. Rich guys who want to spoil young girls."

"By 'spoil,' do you mean . . ." Jo let her voice trail off, unwilling to complete the sentence, unwilling to say the words *pay them for sex.*

"I don't know," Kim said, shaking her head. "I don't know how it works. I don't even know if she's, you know, registered or whatever. And if she has, I don't know if she's met anyone, or what she's doing with him. All that stuff gets negotiated in private."

"How can that be legal?" Jo asked.

"Because it's technically offering companionship, not sex. But I think someone needs to talk to her."

Jo knew, of course, that she'd be that someone. She wondered what she'd say . . . and also exactly what else Lila was qualified to do that could earn money . . . which was probably the exact thought process that had led Lila to Sugardaddies.com, or whatever it was.

"I wish she hadn't left the way she did," Kim said, sounding wistful. "She was terrific with Flora." Lila had spent part of the previous summer taking care of Flora and helping with the new baby. Jo remembered that most of Lila's moments of competence and kindness had been reserved for the Maderer kids who lived down the street. She'd been their regular sitter, starting when she turned thirteen and continuing through high school. Even when most of her weekends were devoted to parties, she'd sometimes forfeit a Saturday night out to go stay with Taylor, Alexa, and Zach. At first, Jo had been anxious about the idea of Lila caring for anything more fragile than a goldfish, but Lila had surprised her. She was patient with baby Taylor, who was only six months old when she started, and inventive with Alexa, who was four. She'd make up elaborate games, pretending they were pioneers crossing the country in a covered wagon, or she'd turn the Maderer kitchen into a restaurant, and Zach, the oldest, would help her take the orders. She'd even, on her own, earned her Red Cross certification in first aid and infant CPR. Jo had told her more than once that if college wasn't for her, there was no shame in being a nanny or working at a nursery school or a day care. Lila had always answered by turning up her refurbished nose, shaking her gorgeous mane of hair, and asking, *You think that's all I'm capable of doing? Thanks a lot, Jo.*

Jo had hoped that when Kim had hired her to help with Flora, Lila would rediscover her love of little ones and maybe make that her career. At first, Lila had been just as great with Flora as she'd been with the little Maderers. But eventually, she started spending more time in Manhattan. After too many late nights, followed by too many mornings when she slept through the alarm clock and missed Flora's drop-off at preschool, Kim had told her that it wasn't going to work, and Lila had packed up her stuff and moved to New York, where Missy had gotten her a temp job with Lester Shaub.

"I'll talk to her," said Jo.

Kim went back to the kitchen, and Jo walked to the foyer, where she found Flora riding a scooter made of purple and pink plastic that picked up momentum as Flora wriggled and shifted her weight.

"What's that?" Jo asked.

"Plasma car!" Flora said. Her eyebrows were drawn, her little face was intent, and she looked just like her mother had when she'd been little, sawing away at her violin.

"And where are you going?" Jo asked.

Flora looked at her like she was crazy. "To over there," she said, and pointed.

"Oh," said Jo. "I thought, because it was a plasma car, you might be driving it to outer space." For years, Jo had offered to host Flora in Connecticut. *I'll come down and pick her up. You can put the car seat in my car. Shelley and I would love to spend some time with her.* Kim always had an excuse. Flora was sick, or was just getting over being sick, or she was starting some new playgroup or class that she couldn't miss. "It's not like they're grading her," Jo finally said, kidding but not-kidding, when Kim said that Flora couldn't skip Music Together. "Let me take her. You and Matt can have a break."

Kim's response had been cool. "I work so much. When I'm here, I really want to be here. I don't want a break. And I love being with her. Honestly, I do."

"I don't get it. Nobody loves being with a baby every minute of every day," Jo had told Shelley. Shelley had been in the dining room, working on one of her thousand-piece puzzles, and she'd answered without looking up.

"I bet they think we're recruiting."

At first, Jo hadn't known what Shelley meant, and when she figured it out, she'd said, "Oh, no." Shelley had given Jo a cynical smile, saying, "Maybe Kim doesn't think it, but I'll bet Matt and that mother of his do."

Jo didn't believe that Kim was keeping Flora home because she thought that Jo and Shelley would send her home in a onesie decorated with rainbow triangles, or with a special affinity for the girl babies in her Tumblin' Tots class. What she actually thought was worse: Kim was spending as much time as she could with her daughter because she was trying to make up for Jo's deficiencies. Kim was determined to give her daughter the focused, loving attention that she'd decided she'd never received . . . and the truth was, her daughter wasn't entirely wrong. Jo hadn't been entirely engaged in Kim's childhood. She'd been exhausted, she'd been bored, she'd been frantic for just thirty seconds by herself in the bathroom, without the knocks and cries of *Mommy, Mommy*, just so that she could change her tampon and wash her hands. Dave had been good with the girls, even if he'd called it *babysitting*, but Dave had been at work five days a week, and there were no extra hands for Kim and Missy, no one to say, *Oh, let me take them, you go take a shower, or a nap.* That house, that life, that husband, none of it had been what she'd really wanted, and Kim must have sensed that somehow.

Jo turned as she heard the door open. "Aunt Bethie!" Flora said, and began wiggling toward the door. Bethie's brown hair was styled in layers, with blond highlights around her face. She wore a plum-colored wrap dress, black suede boots, a single gold cuff on her right wrist, and her wedding and engagement rings. Harold stood behind her in a sport coat and sweater, flannel pants, and polished cordovan loafers. He'd gotten broader in the chest as the years had passed, and his hair had turned a distinguished silver, but his smile, warm and welcoming, was just the way Jo remembered it. She felt tears prickling her eyes as Harold hugged her.

"You look terrific," Jo told Bethie, thinking that Bethie could have passed for forty-five. She'd lost a little weight, too. The Zone diet, Jo thought. "I'm Zoning," Bethie had said the last time Jo had visited. She'd been eating the same grilled chicken and fish and salads that she'd eaten on every other diet. She didn't think there was a single eating plan or program that her sister had missed . . . and except for the diets that let you eat butter and heavy cream, they were all the same. Grilled fish, chicken and salad, no breads, no desserts, no fun.

"I stay out of the sun," Bethie said. Jo handed the baby to Shelley and took Bethie into the living room, where a gigantic sectional sofa and a glass coffee table the size of a small skating rink failed to fill the empty space, and where artwork that Jo guessed had been bought for its scale and not its beauty barely covered a quarter of the walls. Persian carpets lined the floor, including one in shades of cream and gold and gray that

Jo knew, because she'd seen the price tag, had cost more than Kim's first semester of college, and an enormous television set stood in an equally enormous cupboard against the wall.

"Did you tell them yet?" Bethie asked.

Jo shook her head. "After dinner, I think. I'll sit them all down together."

"Are you feeling okay?" Jo nodded. Bethie looked at her, hard, then said, "You know I'm here for you. Anything you need."

"I know. Thank you." Jo felt tears threatening. She heard the front door open again, and Flora yelled, "Aunt Missy!" A minute later, Melissa was hugging her aunt and her mother hello.

"Look at you!" Bethie said, her voice approving. Melissa had never cared much for clothes, unlike her sisters, who'd always wanted this brand of jeans or that kind of sweater. Like her mother, Missy had always been the most comfortable in her T-shirts and sweatpants, but she'd figured out a uniform that worked for her in New York and was dressed in a version of it that afternoon: a crisp white blouse, open at the throat, high-waisted black trousers, and lace-up black patent-leather oxfords. The shirt and the shoes were both styled like menswear, and Melissa wore a man's heavy watch on her wrist, but her tumble of shoulder-length curls and dangling, delicate gold earrings were feminine counterpoints to her masculine attire. She carried a leather messenger-style bag slung over one shoulder, bulging with manuscripts and advance reader's copies of books that she'd distribute to her mother and her sister.

Kim poked her head into the room.

"Does anyone know where Lila is? I told her dinner was at four, and she promised to be here."

Jo sighed, pulling her cell phone out of her purse and punching her daughter's number. Unsurprisingly, the call went to voice mail, with Lila's smart-aleck voice saying, "You know what to do," and then a beep. Jo had offered to give Lila a ride to New Jersey, but of course Lila had plans for Wednesday night. "Everyone from high school's going to be home, and a bunch of us are going out. I'll probably sleep in and take a train," she said.

"I guess we can wait . . ." Kim was wiping her hands on her apron when Matt came up behind her, in boat shoes and jeans and a dark-blue polo shirt. His round pink face had gotten rounder and pinker over the years, his fine blond hair had gotten thinner, and, as he put his hands on Kim's shoulders, his expression was almost smug. That, thought Jo, hadn't changed at all.

"Not too long," he said. "Don't want the turkey to dry out!" He shook Harold's hand and kissed Bethie's cheek, treating them both with the kind of respectful deference that, Jo supposed, their wealth afforded them.

Kim looked at her mother. "Mom, what do you think?"

Jo gripped her phone, considering her son-in-law's impatience and her own news. "Let's get started," she said. "Lila can eat when she gets here."

The dinner was delicious. Jo couldn't find fault with a single dish: not the creamy pumpkin soup or the sausage and pecan stuffing, not the velvety, lumpless gravy or the roast turkey, its skin lacquered a gorgeous dark brown, not the salad of arugula and baby spinach and fennel, with a tart, citrusy dressing, which cut the richness of the turkey and the honey-butter served with the biscuits and the corn bread. Jo didn't have much appetite. The announcement she'd soon be making sat like a lead ball in her belly. She kept one eye on the door, looking for Lila, thinking that, as tasty as the food was, none of it had history. Jo thought about the turkeys that her father used to baste with melted margarine and teriyaki sauce, and wondered what Kim would say if she'd offered her daughter that recipe, and whether the hydrogenated fats in the margarine or the corn syrup in the teriyaki sauce would strike her as more offensive. She remembered how, years ago, Bethie and Harold had hosted Thanksgiving, and Harold had deep-fried a turkey in the garage of their house in Buckhead. That bird had been succulent, the skin crisp, the meat meltingly tender, so good that she'd snuck out of bed for a midnight snack and found Harold, his father, and two of his brothers in the kitchen, all of them happily gorging on turkey sandwiches, biscuits and gravy, and sweet potato pie.

She looked down the table and was unsurprised to see that her Jell-O had gone untouched.

"Flora, want to try some Jell-O?" she asked. Flora frowned, asking, "What is Jell-O?" and Jo, hoping Kim wouldn't start grilling her about preservatives and Red Dye No. 3, scooped a bit onto Flora's dish.

"So, Kim," Jo asked. "How much longer does your maternity leave last?"

Kim, who'd been holding Leonie on her lap, exchanged a guilty look with her husband. "Actually," said Kim, "I'm going to stay home for a while."

"For how long?" Jo asked.

"I'm not sure," said Kim, who, Jo knew, was sure of everything, from precisely how many pounds the turkey had weighed to how much money, to the penny, she had in her checking account. "It's kind of open-ended."

"She quit," said Matt, popping a forkful of stuffing

into his mouth. "Decided to let me be the breadwinner for a while."

"You quit?" Jo repeated.

Kim glared at Matt, then turned to Jo. "I decided it was time to look for a job with more flexibility. I'll be home for a while, and then I'll find something else."

"But you loved your job!" Melissa said, which was exactly what Jo had been thinking.

"It was just a lot," Kim said. She was trying to smile, doing her best to sound happy. "If I went back I was going to be the lead attorney on a new case they were bringing to trial. It would've meant fourteen-hour days, plus commuting, and I just couldn't." She smoothed her free hand on her napkin, then patted her hair and repeated, "I just couldn't." She looked at her mother, and for the first time Jo could see the dark circles beneath Kim's concealer, the pallor beneath the blush. "And I want to be here for my daughters. I'll never get these years back if I miss them. I missed Flora's first step . . . her first word . . ." Kim's voice was cracking, and Jo, keeping her voice light, said, "You saw her second step. And you heard her say 'Mama' that night instead of that afternoon. Flora knows you're her mother. She knows you love her. And, honey, if you're not happy, she's going to know that, too."

"I'm going to be happy." Kim sounded like she was making a promise, although Jo wasn't sure if she was making it to her, or her daughters, or herself. "I'm going to be here for them, and I'm going to be happy."

Jo and Shelley looked at each other, and Shelley took Jo's hand. "You know I'm free if you ever need help," said Jo, and Sandra put down her wineglass and said, "And I'm just down the street!" *Which she was*, Jo thought, *Goddamnit*. She poured herself more wine, wondering if she had it in her to make her announcement here at the table. Maybe it would be better if she told everyone individually—Kim first, then Missy, and Lila, if Lila even showed up. She was thinking it through when the door slammed, heels clicked across the marble floor, and a voice called, "Let the games begin!"

And there was Jo's youngest, her baby, in a tiny, clinging Lycra miniskirt, black tights, black boots with stacked heels, and a black leather jacket over a crop top that revealed a sliver of smooth belly and the glint of a new piercing. Lila's hair was piled on top of her head in a messy bun, with tendrils escaping to brush her cheeks and the back of her neck. Her lips were painted a vivid red, and her eyes looked unfocused. Down at the opposite end of the table, Jo saw her son-in-law and his mother exchange a look as Lila sauntered toward the table.

"Auntie Lila, sit near me!" Flora crowed.

"Jo, Ro, and Flo!" said Lila. She pulled out the chair beside Flora. "What'd I miss?" she asked, helping herself to a biscuit.

"Well," Kim said, with a tight smile. "I just told everyone that I'm going to be extending my maternity leave and looking for a new job."

"Oh?" Lila's eyes glittered as she cocked her head, looking like a curious, malevolent bird. "The Stepford Wives of Fort Lee finally got to you?"

"I don't know what you're talking about," said Kim, smoothing her napkin.

"Bitch, please," Lila drawled.

"Language," Sandra murmured. Lila ignored her.

"You know exactly what I'm talking about. Every single woman on this street went to an Ivy League school, and most of them have advanced degrees, and all of them stay home full-time with their kiddos. They drive around in Range Rovers and take the kids to Tot Shabbat." Lila filled her glass with red wine, took a swallow, and reached for the turkey as Kim said, "It's true, some of the women have put their careers on hiatus . . ."

"Hiatus!" Lila hooted.

Kim's voice was high and indignant. "But they're going to go back to work. I am, too."

"So what's your plan?" Lila's voice was silky. "You're going to take five or six years off and then walk back in there and pick up exactly where you started?"

"Maybe not there," Kim said, "but I can find a job that's more flexible. I've got skills. I've got experience."

"Sure you do," said Lila. "And what's a little five-year vacation when you've got skills and experience?" She paused for a swallow of wine. "Personally, I think Melissa's the one who's got it figured out. No kids. No husband. Excuse me, no spouse," she said, giving Jo and Shelley a look of exaggerated apology. "Nothing on her plate but the great Lester Shaub. Right, Missy?"

Jo thought she saw Missy cringe. Lila's voice became dangerously soft.

"Whatever Lester wants, Lester gets."

"Lester is a legendary editor," Melissa said. "I'm lucky to work for him."

"Sure," Lila said, in that deceptively calm voice. "You're lucky. But he's lucky, too. He gets whatever he wants. Doesn't he?"

Matt's voice was bluff and hearty. "Sounds like you've got some good publishing gossip."

"Oh, I've got stories," Lila said. "Who here read *Stone Soup*?" *Stone Soup*, Jo knew, was Lester's latest big book, written by a twenty-six-year-old wunderkind named Isla Clare. The book had been written up everywhere, with the stories accompanied by a photograph of the young, dark-haired author in some sultry, sloe-eyed pose, with her hair tumbled around her shoulders and her tattoos on display.

"I bought it," Matt said.

Of course he did, thought Jo.

"Of course you did," said Lila.

"I read it," Shelley said quickly. "It was fantastic."

"Lester thought so, too," Lila said. "Of course, it needed some changes. He put the author up in the St. Regis, and he'd visit her every afternoon. To help her with the edits, he said."

"That's how it works," said Melissa. "Lots of editors don't even edit. They just acquire books, and they don't even try to make them better. Lester's different. He sees writing a novel as a partnership."

"A partnership," Lila repeated. "Except in a partnership, both people get something, right? Although maybe it was a partnership. Isla Clare got the best editor in America to make her book as good as it could be. And Lester got Isla."

"That's enough." Missy was half out of her seat, her face flushed.

"Lucky Lester," Lila said. "To have such a loyal second-in-command. Someone who defends him, no matter what he does. Or who he does it to."

"Shut up," Missy snapped. "And, just FYI, Lila, Lester told me that you were the one who came on to him."

Lila's cheeks and neck flushed an ugly shade of red. "Oh, as if. Like guys in their seventies with hairy ears who smell like Vicks VapoRub are really what I'm into."

"You're into anyone who can pay your bills," Missy said. "You're allergic to actually holding a job."

"No, I'm allergic to old perverts who think they've got a right to grab my boobs."

"Is that why you're on that website?" Missy asked sweetly. She turned to Kim. "What did you tell me it's called. Sugarbabies? Is that it?"

Lila lurched to her feet, glaring at Kim. "You fucking snoop."

"Oh, Lila," said Kim, as Lila stood up. In her heels, she had to be at least six feet tall.

"You're a narc," she said, pointing at Kim, then turning to Missy. "And you're a bitch."

"Girls," said Jo.

"Language," said Sandra.

"Get a job," Melissa spat at her little sister. "Stop being a freeloader. You're going to be thirty soon. It's getting embarrassing. Men aren't going to just pay your bills forever."

"Yeah, well at least I'm not pimping out my own sister to keep my boss happy."

Beside her, Jo heard Shelley suck in a shocked breath.

"I was trying to help you," said Missy. Her voice was quiet. "I thought maybe you'd like getting paid for honest work. For a change."

At the other end of the table, Kim's head was bent, and Matt was smirking.

"Could everyone just settle down?" Kim said. "Lila, let me fix you a plate."

"I wouldn't eat your fucking turkey if I was starving," Lila snarled. Jo saw Lila's gaze move over the table. She could practically hear the calculations. *Oh, no*, she thought, and stood up so fast that her chair fell over behind her. Just as Lila made her move, Jo grabbed for her Jell-O, but Lila was quicker and had gotten a better grip. She wrenched the platter out of her mother's hands, turned, and hurled the quivering mass at Missy's face. Only Missy still had her athletic reflexes and managed to simultaneously duck and turn sideways. The Jell-O flew over her head and hit the wall, and the abstract oil painting, behind her with a loud, liquid splat. Kim shrieked, handed Sandra the baby, and raced around the table, calling into the kitchen for rags and seltzer. Matt was red-faced, pointing at Lila, bellowing about insurance; Flora had started to cry, and Missy was glaring at her sister. "You bitch," she said as Sandra grabbed Flora's hand, trilling, once more, "Language!" as she hustled the little girl out of the room.

Lila straightened herself up, gave her hair a shake, turned, and strutted toward the door. "Wait," Jo called.

"Leave me alone," Lila called back, quickening her pace. Jo hurried after her.

"Lila."

"They don't want me here."

"Lila, wait," Jo said, and Lila's heel must have caught in the fringe of the antique Turkish rug in the hallway. One minute she was upright, the next she was airborne, and the minute after that, she was on the floor, clutching her ankle, yelling, "Shit, shit, shit!"

Bethie

Kim and Matt tried to sponge off the art—it turned out that it wasn't a painting but an encaustic collage, the work of some rising star on the New York art scene. It had cost six figures, or so Matt kept yelling. Missy sat at the table, white-faced. Bethie and Harold went to tend to Lila, who was writhing on the floor, with Jo on her knees beside her.

"Why don't Harold and I take you to the hospital?" Bethie said, thinking that the smartest thing to do might be to get Lila away from the drama. Jo nodded.

"Fine," Lila muttered. Bethie and Harold helped Lila up off the floor and supported her as she hopped down the walkway and into the back seat of their Audi sedan. Bethie loved her car, with its rich-smelling leather interior and its seat warmers for the handful of mornings in Atlanta cold enough to warrant their use, but she'd bought it with a twinge of shame, knowing what her father would have said about her buying an import, and a German one at that. Harold got in the driver's seat,

Bethie climbed in beside him, and Lila rolled onto her back, groaning.

"Well!" Bethie said. "That was memorable!" *Poor Lila*, she thought. Jo's youngest daughter reminded her of herself during her years on the road. Of course, Bethie still didn't know if Lila had a story beyond the divorce, and the teenage embarrassment that must have gone along with having your father ditch your mother for the lady who lived three doors down, then having your mom fall in love with a woman. Kim and Missy only had to put up with all of it for a year or two before they went off to college, where they could tell their new friends as much, or as little, of the story as they cared to share. They had the luxury of seeing their mother's new life unfold from a distance. Lila hadn't had that option. High school couldn't have been easy, Bethie thought, and Jo's youngest had never seemed especially mature for her age. *Lila's taking longer*, Jo would say. But there was taking your time, Bethie mused, and then there was this. Her niece was clearly drunk, or high, or both . . . and what, exactly, had she been yelling about?

"Do you want to tell me what you were talking about with Missy?" Bethie asked. Instead of an answer, she got Lila's familiar glowering silence. Bethie tried again. "I guess your internship with Lester didn't end well?"

Lila gave a scornful snort.

"What happened?" Bethie asked.

"It doesn't matter," said Lila. "It's over."

"It matters," Bethie said. "It matters to me."

Harold steered the car around a curve, humming a little under his breath, the way he did when he was nervous. The silence stretched, so long that Bethie didn't think her niece would answer. But, finally, Lila started to talk. Her tone was arch and cynical, but Bethie could hear the hurt underneath.

"Lester's imprint or whatever was moving offices. Two floors down. They needed people to help pack up the books, and people's desks, and whatever. It was a three-week temp job. Missy got them to hire me." Lila hissed in discomfort. Bethie heard the leather creak as her niece shifted in the back seat. "Lester figured out right away that I wasn't a book nerd. I can't even remember how. I probably pronounced some word wrong, or didn't know who Thomas Pynchon was, or I mixed up the Jonathans. But he figured it out. All the other editors and interns, he'd ask them what they read over the weekend. He'd ask me what I did. Where I went. He said he valued my connection to the real world." Lila's voice was becoming bleak. "Then he'd started inviting me into his office by myself, and asking me about my personal life. Who was I dating; were they treating me right. He'd ask about . . . you know, personal stuff. Was I happy. Was I satisfied."

"Oh, boy," Bethie said. She knew where this was going.

"We had a pantry in the office, with snacks and a fancy espresso machine. He'd come in to fix himself a coffee, and he'd always find a way to bump into me, or he'd give me a squeeze with his arm around my waist, only his hand would be up near my boob. Sorry, Uncle Harold."

Lila sighed. "Everyone in the office hated me, because Lester liked me so much. They were all jealous, except Missy. She was thrilled. I guess Lester would tell her how glad he was that I was there. How I was his conduit to millennial culture or whatever." Lila shifted, giving another pained hiss. "I didn't want to get Missy in trouble.

But I didn't want to have to, you know . . ." Her voice trailed off. Rain had started pattering against the sunroof and the windshield. Harold flicked the windshield wipers on. "Anyhow. The first Friday of every month, Lester would take everyone for drinks at the King Cole Bar in the St. Regis. The martinis cost, like, twenty dollars. Lester would run a tab. Sometimes, writers would come, or agents, or other editors, or book scouts. Important people. At least, Melissa said they were important. They all looked like schnooks to me. One Friday, I was coming out of the ladies' room and Lester was there waiting for me."

Bethie swallowed hard, remembering her uncle, his smelly breath, his scratchy face. She was old now, so old that sometimes her own face in the mirror startled her. She'd attended her thirtieth high school reunion; she'd celebrated her sixtieth birthday; she'd survived the deaths of both of her parents. In all those years, she'd forgotten all kinds of things, names and faces and tastes and sensations, but she knew that she would never forget how it felt to be in Uncle Mel's car, the stench of his breath, the foggy windows, that feeling of being trapped, of how nothing she could do would free her.

"So Lester kisses me. He jams his tongue down my throat, and I push him off me, and he laughs, like it's some game. He says he likes feisty women, and I tell him if he ever touches me again I'll go to HR." Lila was talking fast and breathing hard.

"Did you tell your sister?" Bethie asked.

"Not until tonight." Lila's voice was tiny. "Missy worships him. She would talk about how great he is all the time. How he was Philip Roth's first editor, how he and John Cheever were drinking buddies. How everyone who's worked for him goes on to have a great career because of his connections. Lester knows all the publishers, all the agents. I didn't want to get her in trouble or, you know, make her choose. So I just left." Lila sniffled. Bethie couldn't see her niece's face in the darkness of the back seat, but it sounded like she was crying. "He probably found someone else to move the rest of the books the very next day, someone from Smith, or Vassar, or one of those places. He's probably grabbing some Seven Sisters boobs in the pantry."

Bethie heard the echo of her mother's voice in her head. *But you can forget about those East Coast colleges, those Six Sisters. Seven Sisters,* Jo had said. *That's okay. The U of M is fine.*

"You remember something like that happened to me," Bethie said.

"I remember," Lila said. "You told me about it. The summer I came to Atlanta."

In the back seat, Bethie saw Lila push herself upright. "So, what?" she asked. "I'm supposed to tell Missy what happened? You think Missy's going to save me?"

"I think you should give her a chance to do the right thing."

Lila gave a sigh. "Yeah," she said as Harold pulled the car underneath the portico by the entrance for the emergency room. "Yeah, that'll happen. Because I matter just as much as her career."

"Of course you do!" said Bethie. Lila snorted again and didn't say another word until they helped her out of the car.

In the waiting room, Lila hobbled over to the receptionist, waving Bethie and Harold over to the seats along the wall. "Do you know if she has insurance?" Harold asked, his voice low.

"No idea," Bethie whispered back, so Harold went up to the counter, telling the woman behind the desk that they'd pay for whatever Lila needed. Bethie sighed, thinking about how much she loved Harold, and that he would take care of her, of Lila, of whatever he could. She'd gotten so lucky with him.

Lila filled out forms on a clipboard and sat with her uninjured leg pulled up against her chest. She leaned against the wall, underneath a poster about food-borne illnesses, and closed her eyes. Bethie called her sister to give her an update, and she and Harold sat with Lila as the television set played overhead and the room filled and emptied with a procession of the walking wounded: men who'd cut themselves carving the turkey or gotten their noses broken during family fights, a little boy who'd shoved a walnut up his nose. After an hour, Lila was finally loaded into a wheelchair and taken away. Bethie took out her phone, intending to call Kim's house again, when Jo, with Shelley behind her, came hurrying into the room.

"Everything okay?" Jo asked.

"They just took her back. How are things at Kim's house?"

"Everything's fine but that painting," Jo said. "Or the artwork, I guess you call it. It's not a painting. Matt was extremely clear on that point." From the capacious tote bag that she carried instead of a purse, she pulled a Tupperware container, paper plates, paper napkins, and a fistful of plastic forks. "You guys missed dessert, and, I have to say, all things considered, the bourbon pecan pie was amazing." Jo took the lid off the container. There was pecan pie, pumpkin pie, apple pie, fresh whipped cream, and even a few chocolate-chip cookies.

"Hey," said Bethie after Jo had distributed the plastic forks, and she'd savored a mouthful of pie. "Did Lila ever talk to you about what happened with Lester Shaub?"

Jo shook her head. "Not a word. But I think I can fill in the blanks. Missy's furious." Jo lowered her voice. "She said Lila came to work looking like she was dressed for the club, and that she flirted with everyone."

"So she's saying that it's Lila's fault?"

"Not exactly." Jo shook her head, looking miserable. "She said she isn't sure that anything even happened. She said that Lila exaggerates. Which, unfortunately, is true. Or at least it's been true in the past."

"Do you think that Lila's exaggerating?"

"I don't know." Jo shook her head and raised her hands to her temples. "She's my daughter, and I love her. But if I'm being honest, I can imagine her coming to work dressed inappropriately. I can imagine her flirting. But coming on to a seventy-two-year-old man? A guy who's her sister's boss, too?" Jo shook her head. "Lila's judgment isn't always great, but I have a hard time thinking she'd do that."

"So you think Lester tried something inappropriate."

Jo sighed, twisting her hands. "Maybe. Or maybe Lila misinterpreted. Or maybe she's exaggerating. Maybe he did make a pass at her, which would be gross, not to mention inappropriate, because he's her boss, only maybe—"

"How's the patient?" asked Harold, his voice loud and hearty. Bethie looked up and saw Lila coming toward them. She had crutches under her armpit, a boot on one foot, and a loopy grin on her face. "Guess who got Vicodin?" she singsonged, pulling a plastic bottle out of her pocket and rattling it happily. Beside her, Bethie heard her sister give a long, resigned sigh.

"Hey," Bethie said, remembering. "Don't you need to tell Lila something?"

"Oh," Jo said, looking stricken, shaking her head. "We can do that later."

But Shelley surprised her. "No," she said. She put her hand on Jo's shoulder, and Bethie saw Lila roll her eyes. "No, I think you need to tell her now."

"What's happening?" asked Lila. It came out like *Wuss happnin*. Bethie watched as Jo smoothed her short hair, quickly touching her fingertips to each earring and then her chest.

"Well," she said. "It turns out I've got a little touch of breast cancer."

Lila didn't say anything, but her eyes got big. Bethie took her sister's hand. Shelley started talking about upcoming appointments, chemotherapy and radiation and long-term survival rates. Harold said, "We're all here for you, Jo," and Bethie said, "Anything you need," and Lila, finally, in a small broken voice, said, "Oh, Mom." When Jo stretched her arms open, Lila closed her eyes and leaned against her, resting her head on her mother's shoulder.

seven

2016

Jo

The Avondale fitness trail had been demolished in 2012, the trees cut down and the path paved over to make way for a neighborhood of McMansions, each one bigger than the last, but in Jo's dream, she was running on it again, underneath the canopy of the oaks and elms and silver maples that flaunted their abundance of glowing-green leaves. She could smell the cedar chips under her sneakers, could feel her heart pounding, pushing oxygen-rich blood to her muscles, and she could hear her own breath, steady as she ran. Jogging around a corner, the trees gave way to a clearing, and Jo could hear a baby crying, even though she was alone on the path. The cries swelled, then receded, then grew again, but no matter which way she turned or how fast she went, Jo could never manage to find the baby, or give it comfort. *It means something*, she thought as she opened her eyes.

Shelley was sitting in the seat beside her, the in-flight magazine open in her lap. When Jo sat up, Shelley took her hand.

"Hi," Shelley whispered.

"These drugs are amazing," Jo whispered back.

"I'm glad you think so." She reached over and adjusted the silk scarf Jo wore over her head, tucking in the edges without meeting Jo's eyes. Shelley hadn't been happy about Jo's decision to stop treatment. They'd had what was, by far, the worst fight of their relationship about it. *There's an experimental protocol they're doing at the Menninger Clinic . . . or we could try Avastin again. No,* Jo had said. The first time she'd been diagnosed, after a mastectomy, the exhausting, nauseating rounds of radiation and chemotherapy had left her bald and eyelashless and so weak she could barely stand up long enough to fry an egg. She'd had ten years, ten good years, and she had no desire to go through that again, especially when the doctors told her that treatment might buy her maybe another year, but no more than that. She wanted to be comfortable; she wanted to say goodbye while she was clearheaded. She'd had wonderful years with Shelley, her partner, the love of her life; she'd done her best with her girls. It would have to be enough.

"Please fasten your seat belts as we begin our final descent into Atlanta," the pilot said. Jo closed her eyes. Around the time that the fitness trail had been demolished, Blue Hill Farm had been completely redone, converted into a five-star bed-and-breakfast, a place that had been booked solid as soon as it had opened, where you had to call six months in advance to get a room. Bethie had worked some magic so they could all stay there together. Jo didn't like to think about what it must have cost her sister to buy out the place, and get the customers who'd made their reservations to agree to leave. *Let me worry about it,* Bethie had said, and Jo had agreed to let her sister take care of everything, from coordinat-

ing with Jo's doctors and arranging nursing care to buying first-class tickets to Atlanta for Jo and Shelley and
the girls. She'd wanted to hire a private jet, but there Jo
had drawn the line. All she wanted was to see her girls,
all together, once more before she went—and Bethie
had promised that she'd try.

A plush limousine that seemed to glide over the highway took them forty-five miles from the airport to the
farm. Jo was directed to the living room, where, once
upon a time, Bethie had gone crawling, naked, through
a vaginal canal made of pillows. They'd transformed it
into a bedroom, complete with a hospital bed that could
be raised or lowered at the touch of a button and a side
table for Jo's medications, the bottles arrayed on an antique silver tray. A miniature refrigerator in the corner
held the emergency pack: a shot of morphine, for break-
through pain; a shot of Haldol, in case she began to hal-
lucinate. There were DNR posters taped to the door, to
the end of her bed, and to the wall above her. *Can't be too
careful*, the hospice nurse who'd met her there had said,
adding grimly that there were always paramedics who
wanted to rush in and be heroes.

Jo napped as soon as she was lying down and woke
in the late afternoon. With her back propped up by pillows, she could look through the windows, out at the
rolling fields, the grass a green so rich and deep it almost
glowed.

"We used to grow the best dope out there," Bethie
said. When Jo laughed, Bethie touched her hand. On
the television, Hillary Clinton, in a sapphire-blue pantsuit, was chatting with supporters before turning, giving
a practiced wave, and climbing the steps to her plane.

"Preparations are underway for the Democratic National Convention in Philadelphia, where Hillary Clinton will make history, becoming the first female presidential nominee from a major party," the news anchor said.

"Can you believe it?" Bethie asked. "Did you ever think we'd see the day?"

"Now she just has to win," said Shelley, knocking on wood, and Jo waved her hand, knowing that Hillary was practically a lock, feeling sad only that she wouldn't be alive to see it.

Bethie was holding a pot of lotion, Blue Hill Farm's latest product line, a rich cream scented with lavender grown a few hundred yards away. "How about a hand massage?" Gratefully, Jo let her sister put a dollop of lotion into the center of her palms and spread it up her wrists and over her fingers, rubbing gently. She let her eyes drift shut, thinking that during these last few weeks she had been more moisturized than she'd been in all her life. Someone was always offering to rub her hands, her calves, her feet. She could feel the pain, down deep, but it was muffled and distant, far away, for now.

"Mom."

Kim was first, of course. Kim was always early; Kim hated people who were late. *It's disrespectful*, she'd say. Jo opened her eyes and smiled.

"Hi, honey." She hoped that she didn't look awful. She'd lost weight, and her hair again, of course, but she was wearing a light-blue linen tunic and, under her blankets, a pair of loose pale-gray pants. She'd insisted on real clothes, not a hospital gown, and had even allowed Shelley to smooth foundation on her face and brush some color on her cheeks and lips, and she'd hoped she looked all right, but she could see the truth in Kim's startled expression, the way her eyes had briefly widened with shock. There was a couch on one side of the hospital bed, a daybed on the other. Jo had imagined the girls and Bethie sitting there, reading to Jo, sometimes talking or telling her stories, the way she'd told them stories when they were girls.

Kim came over and stood by the side of the bed. "How are you feeling?"

"Not bad, considering. How are you?" Jo looked at her daughter's face, searching for signs of tension or sadness, the way Kim would press her lips together tightly, like there were words she didn't want to let out. Kim's daughters were behind her, Flora, tall and lanky, with her spill of honey-blond hair and the lips that she kept closed over her braces, and solid, dark-eyed, curly-haired Leonie. Soon, Flora would have her bat mitzvah, and Jo wouldn't be there. Jo inhaled slowly, trying to think of all the time she'd had with her granddaughters, and not everything that she'd miss.

Kim and Matt had gotten divorced when the girls were six and three years old. "I can't be the kind of wife he wants," Kim had said when she'd showed up on Jo's doorstep with her suitcase and her girls. Jo got the story in pieces, learning that Kim had planned on going back to work full-time after Leonie started full-day nursery school. Matt had wanted her to stay home. "He wanted to take care of me. And I feel awful, because that was what I wanted when we got married. A man who'd take care of me. A man who'd never leave. And a life where I'd never have to worry about money." Jo had nodded, keeping quiet, thinking about how Kim must have chosen in reaction to her own parents' divorce. Matt, unlike Dave, would never leave her, and he certainly wouldn't leave her scrambling for money, living in a condo with flimsy walls and fraying carpet, paying for her kids' education with loans while he whooped it up with her neighbor. "But I don't want that anymore," Kim said. Kim had cried, and Jo had comforted her, had told her that she was a wonderful mother to her daughters, that people changed, and sometimes, marriages did not survive those changes, in spite of everyone's best intentions. "You're allowed to want to use your education," Jo said. "You're allowed to want to be more than a mother."

So Kim had gone back to work, first at the U.S. attorney's office and then as a public defender for young women, frequently young mothers, who'd gotten lengthy sentences selling or even just possessing quantities of pot that wouldn't have gotten a white kid anything more than a warning. Kim had needed Jo, and Jo was happy to be needed. For years, she would spend a few nights each week in New York City, where Kim had moved to be closer to work and to her sisters. Jo and Shelley helped with the cooking and cleaning and shopping. They'd become pros at riding the subway, escorting the girls to swim team and Hebrew school and cooking classes. Kim worked and struggled and stretched herself thin, the way all working mothers did. She felt guilty for enjoying her job, and she felt guilty when she missed some milestone, or when Jo and Shelley had to attend a choir concert or a parent-teacher conference or a doctor's visit in her stead. *You're doing the best you can*, Jo would tell her, over and over, and refrain from pointing out that Matt never seemed to torment himself when he was golfing the first time Flora rode her bike on her own, or reading the paper during Leonie's first successful dive into the deep end. Women had made progress—Jo only had to look as far as the television set to see it—but she wondered whether they would ever not try to have it all and do it all and do all of it flawlessly. Would the day ever come when simply doing your best would be enough? Her generation hadn't managed it, and neither had her daughters. Maybe Flora and Leonie and their classmates and cousins would be the lucky ones.

"We lost ourselves," she said. Her voice sounded sludgy and slow, and she must have fallen asleep, because the slant of light on her quilt had shifted. Flora and Leonie had disappeared, and Kim was the one at her bedside.

"What did you say, Mom?"

Jo's eyes prickled with tears, and her face flushed with the effort of remembering. Oh, there was so little time left, and so much more that she wanted to say! "We lose ourselves," she repeated, forming each word with care, "but we find our way back." Wasn't that the story of her life? Wasn't that the story of Bethie's? You make the wrong choices, you make mistakes, you disappear for a decade, you marry the wrong man. You get hurt. You lose sight of who you are, or of who you want to be, and then you remember, and if you're lucky you have sisters or friends who remind you when you forget your best intentions. You come back to yourself, again and again. You try, and fail, and try again, and fail again. She understood why Kim had married Matt, and why she'd left him. She understood how Melissa had failed Lila, and how Lila had hurt Missy. Try and fail and try again.

She held her daughter's hand and closed her eyes. When she opened them again, Bethie had taken Shelley's place in the chair next to her bed, a cup of tea that smelled of grass and lemon balm was steaming on the table, and Melissa was standing in the doorway.

"Hi," Jo said, pushing herself upright. Melissa looked awful, pale and drawn and tired. "What's wrong?"

Melissa looked weary, the way she had for years. Lester Shaub's fall had followed the pattern set by many of his fellow moguls, captains of industry, and CEOs. It had happened gradually, then all at once. A whisper here, a rumor there, and then one of the authors had filed a lawsuit, the HR director's records had been subpoenaed, and it turned out that, over the years, there'd been dozens of allegations, ranging from unwanted touches and kisses to rape. Lester, it emerged, also had instituted what the gossips delighted in calling a blow-jobs-for-blurbs policy, which explained why so many female authors' debut novels came ornamented with praise by one or another of Lester's stable of elderly literary giants, encomiums that turned out to have been written by Lester himself.

Through it all, Missy had stood by him, the staunch defender, the loyal soldier. "That isn't the Lester I know," she would say, telling reporters that Lester had never been inappropriate with her, pointing out the ranks of female authors he'd discovered and published and promoted. "Just because it wasn't happening to you doesn't mean it wasn't happening," one reporter had said, and Missy, shrugging, had said, "All I can tell you is what I know. Look, everyone's out there shouting, 'Believe women.' Well, I'm a woman, too." Jo had never mentioned Lila's story to Missy. The year of Lester's professional demise, she'd let others host the holidays, happy to have Kim at her in-laws' and Missy with friends and Lila wherever Lila went, while she and Shelley traveled to Vermont in the fall and Mexico in December. Better to eat apples and honey by themselves and tortillas instead of latkes than to have to listen to Lila say *I told you so* while Missy hung her head or shot back, "At least I have a job."

When Lester's misdeeds had finally been exposed beyond all reasonable doubt, he'd released a combative statement that proclaimed his innocence and announced his retirement. Missy, as promised, inherited the keys to Lester's kingdom, and all of his surviving authors, but it was as if she'd sat down at a banquet of rotten fruit and spoiled meat. She'd be forever tainted by her association and her loyalty. Last year, one of her authors had won the National Book Award. At the awards dinner, Missy, the author, and the author's husband had been seated all by themselves at a table for ten.

"Missy," Jo said. "How are you?"

"Okay. You know. Hanging in there." Missy sighed and shook her curls. A shaft of sunlight pierced the room, illuminating a wedge of Missy's cheek, a single eyebrow, one brown eye.

"Are you going to beat yourself up forever?" Jo asked. "Because I'm not going to be able to enjoy the afterlife if I know you're down here suffering."

Another sigh, another shrug. "How can I forgive myself?" Missy's voice was loud and anguished. "I knew. Or at least I suspected. And I looked the other way, because I liked my job, and I liked him. Do you know what I told myself?" Without waiting for her mother to answer, she said, "I'd say that all geniuses are flawed. Some of them drink, and some of them beat their wives, and if all Lester does is, you know, grab the occasional intern, on the grand scale of things, that isn't so bad." She rubbed her hands on the sides of her pants. "And when those women would go to hotels so Lester could edit them, I'd think they were dummies. I'd think, What do they expect to happen with a man in a hotel room?" She gave a short bark of laughter. "Some feminist you raised. The only woman I was looking out for was me."

"So you made a mistake." Jo wanted to tell Melissa more. She wished she'd spent more time teaching her girls that women should forgive themselves, showing them how to take care of themselves with kindness. The world was hard enough, would beat them up enough without them adding to the pain.

Missy was pacing now, her heels loud on the wooden floors. "You know that thing you used to tell us? That quote about how all it took for evil to flourish was for good men to stand by and do nothing?" Missy asked. Jo nodded. "That was me. A good person who stood by and did nothing." Missy's voice cracked. "A good person who stood by while her sister got hurt."

"So you'll do better."

Missy stopped, mid-pace, and hung her head.

"You can't fix anything that happened. You just have to try to do better from now on."

"I know." Missy smoothed her hair, untangled an earring from a curl. "I know."

Jo heard the door bang open and raised voices and footsteps approaching quickly. *Here we go*, she thought, gathering what strength she had. And finally, there was Lila, her baby, tanned and glamorous in peep-toe booties and bubblegum-pink lipstick. A short, sheer dress of pleated beige linen skimmed the tops of her knees, and aviator sunglasses hid her eyes. Jo felt herself exhale, felt the taut muscles of her back and shoulders unwinding. When she'd asked Bethie for this one last thing—the thing she wanted most, one last chance to talk to Lila— her sister had promised to try to track down Lila, but Jo hadn't been optimistic.

Lila was based in New York, at least nominally, but she'd spend months away, visiting points unknown, with traveling companions her family never met. For a while, Jo and Kim and Missy had been able to keep track of Lila by her social media accounts. Lila would post pictures of herself at a beach in Mexico, or she'd snap a shot of herself on a roof, and Kim or Missy would recognize one of the buildings in the background, or she'd show up in Atlanta, on Aunt Bethie's doorstep, and stay with Bethie and Harold for a week or two. Sometimes Lila took Jo's calls or returned her texts. More often, both were met with silence. Lila was angry. She was angry at Missy for not believing her about Lester Shaub; angry at Kim for kicking her out of her cushy au pair gig, for tattling to Jo about that sugardaddy website, and for taking Missy's side; angry at Jo for a list of sins too long for Jo to even remember most of the time. Leaving Dave, that was one, even though Dave had been the one who'd left her. Leaving their neighborhood—again, Dave's fault, but Lila couldn't see it. Finding Shelley and making a life with her. Jo would have to own that one. Not taking Lila's side against her sisters; not letting her live at home indefinitely, not giving her money, or the car keys when she asked, kicking her out when Shelley discovered that Lila had swiped the Percocet that Jo had been prescribed after her mastectomy. "Who does that?" Shelley had demanded, and Lila had pouted, standing hipshot at the front door, and said, "Someone who figured out she can sell them for twenty bucks apiece." Lila was angry, and if Lila did not want to be found, there'd be no finding her. Jo had prayed that her sister's money and connection to her youngest daughter could work some magic, and that she'd be able to say goodbye to Lila, to send her on her way with some advice, or at least the knowledge that her mother loved her and always had. She was leaving Lila her estate, such as it was, the money she'd saved and the money she'd invested over the years. Kim and Missy would administer the trust fund. Jo knew that Lila would be furious when she found that out. "I know how to handle money! I don't need a babysitter!" Jo could hear her shriek, but handing her youngest daughter a pile of cash, all at once, would surely end in disaster.

Lila swept across the floor, tall and glamorous, smelling like perfume and strong mouthwash, as if no more than a week had elapsed since they'd last seen each other, as if Lila had spent the last weeks and months taking Jo to her doctors' appointments and visiting her in the hospital, rubbing her back and moving the heating pads and offering her sips of water from the bendy straw, as devoted a daughter as Jo could wish.

"Hi, Mom," she said, bending down to kiss Jo's cheek, and, finally, Jo started to cry.

"So what do you think?" It was nine o'clock at night. Outside, the Atlanta sky was dark velvet. Jo could hear crickets chirping and cicadas humming, and the faint murmur of the air conditioner that kept the temperature bearable.

"About what?" Her voice was slow and slurred.

"Your youngest." Shelley had climbed into bed with Jo, had tucked her body around Jo's, and was holding Jo's hand. "You know there's something going on."

"I'm just glad she's here." Jo knew that Shelley was right. There was always some drama with Lila, and this would be no exception, but Jo had just taken one of her pills. Her body felt deliciously ethereal; the world and its troubles seemed very far away. "She'll tell us when she's ready."

"You mean when it'll make the most impact," Shelley said.

"Or then." Jo adjusted herself against the warmth of

Shelley's body. "I'll bet you're glad that you didn't have kids."

Shelley gave a dramatic shudder. "Yours have been plenty, thank you very much." Smiling, Jo squeezed her beloved's hands.

"Whatever it is, we'll manage it," Shelley said. "Me, and the girls, and your sister."

Jo nodded. She was tired, so tired, and soon she'd be beyond help and beyond care. All she could do now was hope. She hoped that Kim would stop hating herself for leaving her husband, for wanting to be free. She hoped that Matt would be a good father to his girls. She hoped that Melissa would forgive herself. She hoped that Lila would find her way, somehow. She hoped that things had changed, but she knew that they hadn't changed enough. All the demonstrations, all the consciousness-raising, all the protests, all the pickets, all the books she'd read, all the conversations she'd had, all the ballots she'd cast, all the *work* and here they were, still.

The door opened, admitting a spill of warm light onto the floor. Lila, barefoot, bare-legged, dressed in a T-shirt, with her face scrubbed clean and her hair pulled up in a messy topknot on her head, came traipsing into the room. Without a word, she padded across the carpet and perched on the edge of the bed, for once not acting disgusted that Jo and Shelley were in there together. Shelley got to her feet and looked at Lila with a narrow, suspicious expression. Jo didn't know what her own face looked like. She couldn't really feel it, or much of anything else.

"Mommy," said Lila, who'd quit calling Jo *Mommy* at some point around her third birthday. Her lower lip quivered as she stared at the floor.

"What, honey?"

"I need to tell you something."

Jo could picture Shelley rolling her eyes, thinking, *Here we go again.* "Okay."

"I'm pregnant." Even with her head sunk deep into down pillows, Jo could hear—or imagine—Shelley's snort. She could picture Shelley's disgusted expression, and knew that this was probably exactly what Shelley expected from Lila.

"Are you going to have the baby?" Her voice was a whisper.

"I think so," Lila whispered back. She shook her head, and said, "Honestly, after I found out, the first thing I thought was that it's not like I've got anything else to do."

"Is this what you want?" she asked.

Lila nodded immediately. "It is. Really. I think it's all I've ever wanted. I was a good babysitter, remember?"

Jo nodded. Questions were occurring: Where would Lila live? How would she support herself? Did Lila know the baby's father, and would he be part of things?

"I know I've messed up a lot, but this is what I want. I'm going to be a good mother." Jo heard Lila's voice catch. "I'm going to make you proud. And Aunt Bethie said I can stay here. Me and the baby. She said she'll find me a job at Blue Hill Farm, if I want one, when I'm ready. She said . . ."

". . . that I owe you one." Bethie stepped into the room and put her hands on Lila's shoulders, keeping her eyes on Jo's face. She'd changed her hair again, letting the gray grow in, and she wore it loose, down past her shoulders, the way it had been back in the 1960s.

We tried so hard, Jo thought. On the television screen, Hillary Clinton raised her face, smiling, as a thousand silver balloons came pouring from the ceiling. They'd tried so hard, and come so far, and still, there were miles and miles left to go, a whole journey that she'd miss.

"Take care." Jo hoped they all could hear what she meant. To Bethie: Take care of my girls. To Lila: Take care of yourself, and your baby. To Kim and Melissa: Take care of yourselves, take care of each other, be as good as I know you can be. To Shelley, I will always love you. I am sorry for all the years we missed, but glad for all the years we had. She could feel the darkness pulling at her, caramel-thick, candy-sweet, a cocooning, velvety silence . . . and faintly, from somewhere, the baby crying, and Lila's voice singing "Hush, little baby, don't say a word." *Oh*, Jo thought. *So that's who you are.*

She woke, and slept, and woke again, weeping, moaning in pain, saying, *Oh, Shelley, I'm sorry, make it stop, it hurts, it hurts so much. Shh, shh*, Shelley soothed her, and then there was a prick in the crook of her arm as someone gave her a shot. Time expanded and contracted, like a balloon being blown up, deflated, and blown up again. When she woke up in the morning, the tears had dried to a filigree of salt on her cheeks. On TV, Hillary Clinton, in a white pantsuit, was standing at the center of a stage, to the sound of cheers so loud that Jo imagined the building must have been shaking. The camera panned through the audience, picking out the faces of women her age. Some of them were crying. *Look*, Jo tried to say, but no one heard her. *Look what we did.*

"Mom."

Jo looked up at Lila. *It won't be long now*, she thought. *Hurry up please it's time.*

She closed her eyes . . . and then she was back in her bedroom, in the house on Alhambra Street. They'd just moved in, and her mom and dad were so excited! This was their step up in the world, the American Dream, and Sarah had let Jo wear her favorite pants and her most comfortable shirt instead of a dress, because pants were what Jo wanted. Jo's feet were bare, and she knew she could run around and shout as loud as she wanted. No one would get mad. Her mother would make Jo's favorite chicken for dinner, and Mae would come, to bake corn bread and sing along to the radio. Frieda would be there to play Cowboys and Indians with her, and at night her little sister would look at her, wide-eyed and excited and a little afraid in the new bedroom of the new house. Jo had promised to tell her a story. "But not too scary," Bethie had whispered, and Jo said, "No, not too scary, I promise." She loved her mom, she loved her dad, she loved her little sister. She wanted to make them happy and proud. She thought of dragons and princes and towers surrounded by thorns, of brave girls and happy endings. "Once upon a time," she began.

2022

Bethie

What's the name of this place?" Tim asked Bethie, taking his fingers out of his mouth long enough to ask the question, then popping them right back in. *Tiny Tim*, Lila called him, even though he wasn't tiny anymore and was getting too big to be carried, although he would still shout *God bless us every one* in his best cockney accent, if his mama asked him nicely.

"This is Michigan," said his big cousin Flora. Flora put her hands on his shoulders and turned him to face the redbrick house on Alhambra Street. "I go to college here."

"Right here?" Tim regarded the house dubiously.

"Not right here," said Flora. "Remember what I told you? I go to college in Ann Arbor, where my grandma went. This is Detroit, where Auntie Bethie and my grandma grew up."

Tim gave the house a moment of his consideration. Bethie wondered how it would look to him—just a house with a pointy triangle-shaped roof and a white aluminum awning. Down the street was a house he'd probably like better, yellow with green shutters, like the colors on the cover of *Frog and Toad Are Friends*. *Frog and Toad Are Friends* was his favorite book. They'd all read it to him a hundred times. *Not this again*, Lila would say, but she'd read it, patient as ever, as kind and doting a mother as Jo could ever have hoped.

"Did you live here?" Tim asked Lila.

Lila shook her head. Her long, dangling earrings chimed. The earrings used to belong to Bethie, but she'd given them all to Lila: bell-bottom jeans and soft velvet scarves, her traveling bag made of colorful squares of fabric that she'd bought in India.

"No," Lila said. "Aunt Bethie lived here. And my mom."

"Your mom was my grandmama," Tim said. "Only she died."

"She did," said Lila, as Kim sniffled and Missy looked away. "But she would have loved you very much."

Tim nodded. Of course he knew that Jo would have loved him, Bethie thought. Everyone loved Tim. Harold loved Tim, and Sharon and her kids and grandkids loved him. Everyone who worked at Blue Hill Farm treated him like a beloved mascot, making him nut butter and jam sandwiches, slipping him squares of chocolate, giving him piggyback rides.

"Do you miss her?" Tim asked.

In a choked-sounding voice, Lila said, "I wasn't always the best kid. I wish she'd known me now."

"Oh, honey," Bethie said. "You were fine."

Lila made a noise, somewhere between a laugh and a sob, and Kim patted her sister's back, and Missy took her hand.

"Are we going to get ice cream?" Tim asked.

"I can take him," Flora volunteered, "if you guys want to stay."

"No," said Bethie. She pulled her phone out of her bag, aimed it, and took a few pictures of the house that she and Jo had been so eager to escape, so certain that their lives would be bigger, and better. Tim was looking at her carefully.

"Are you crying, Aunt Bethie?"

Bethie shook her head. "Just remembering," she said. She watched as Lila lifted her son in her arms. Together, they walked back down the street to where the cars were waiting.

Acknowledgments

My thanks to Carolyn Reidy; Jon Karp; my agent, Joanna Pulcini; and Libby McGuire, my brilliant new publisher.

Thanks to the editors: Sarah Cantin, who was there at the beginning, and Emily Bestler, who was there at the end.

Kristin Fassler, Dana Trocker, and Ariele Fredman have been a pleasure to work with and have already worked wonders. Thank you for making this publication such a pleasure.

Thanks to everyone on the Atria/S&S team: Suzanne Donahue, Gary Urda, Lisa Keim, Chris Lynch, Paige Lytle, Katie Rizzo, Sarah Lieberman, and Elisa Shokoff; to Joanna's assistant, Jenna Walker, and to Emily's assistant, Lara Jones.

I'm grateful to James Iacobelli for giving this book such a gorgeous cover, and to Andrea Cipriani Mecchi for taking such a beautiful author photo.

Thanks to Dhonielle Clayton for her smart, perceptive read, and to Curtis Sittenfeld for her sharp suggestions, and for liking the sex scenes.

My assistant, the delightful Meghan Burnett, has always been invaluable, but never more so than for her work on this book.

Thanks to Moochie, furry muse, who curled up at my feet, slept while I wrote, and mostly kept the snores on the quieter side.

All of my love to my husband, Bill Syken, who makes me dinner, makes me laugh, and came up with the title, and to my delightful daughters, Lucy and Phoebe. You are my light at the end of the tunnel.

And thanks to Frances Frumin Weiner, mother, grandmother, inspiration, and all-time good sport, who was there. I love you, Mom. I hope I got it right.

Mrs. Everything

Jennifer Weiner

This reading group guide for Mrs. Everything *includes an introduction, discussion questions, and ideas for enhancing your book club. The suggested questions are intended to help your reading group find new and interesting angles and topics for your discussion. We hope that these ideas will enrich your conversation and increase your enjoyment of the book.*

Introduction

From Jennifer Weiner, the #1 *New York Times* bestselling author of *Who Do You Love* and *In Her Shoes* comes a smart, thoughtful, and timely exploration of two sisters' lives from the 1950s to the present as they struggle to find their places—and be true to themselves—in a rapidly evolving world. *Mrs. Everything* is an ambitious, richly textured journey through history—and herstory—as these two sisters navigate a changing America over the course of their lives.

Topics & Questions for Discussion

1. Jo and Bethie are very different people. But in what ways do you find them similar? Do their similarities outweigh their differences? How do their similarities cause problems in their relationship?

2. Forgiveness, of others and of the characters' own selves, is an important theme in the novel. Discuss how characters work through their conflicts and how they do or do not resolve the issues.

3. Compare and contrast how Jo and Bethie are influenced by their mother. Is there a defining element of their relationship with their mother? How does it weave its way into the sisters' lives?

4. *Mrs. Everything* spans half of the twentieth century and the early part of the twenty-first. What period details make you feel immersed in each decade? Were there any details that you remembered from your own past? Were there details about life

in earlier decades that surprised you? What effect did this have on your reading experience?

5. In *Mrs. Everything*, Jennifer Weiner has created many memorable secondary characters, from Mrs. Kaufman to Lila to Jo and Bethie's partners and beyond. Did you have a favorite? What qualities made them come alive for you?

6. Were you ever frustrated by the choices Jo and Bethie made? Did you empathize with their choices, despite feeling frustrated?

7. Literature is full of sisters with complex relationships. Do Jo and Bethie remind you of other favorite sister duos? What is it about the sister relationship that captivates us as readers?

8. What draws Jo and Shelley together? After they've reunited, what keeps them together?

9. What do Bethie and Harold learn from each other throughout their relationship?

10. Because *Mrs. Everything* takes place over several decades, it touches upon many political and social movements. Did you learn anything about American history while reading? Was there a cause or issue that particularly interested you?

11. When Lila visits Bethie for the summer, they have a heart-to-heart about the pressure Lila feels from her mother to be special and achieve great things. Bethie tells Lila that it comes from the lack of op-

tions the sisters had growing up in a different era: "Some girls did grow up and become doctors and lawyers and school principals. . . . A few girls did grow up and do things, and got those jobs, but for the rest of us, we were told that the most important thing was to be married, and be a mother. . . . She just doesn't want that to be the only choice you have" (p. 456). Though Lila does have more opportunities available to her than her mother and aunt did, she (and her generation) face new challenges. Did you relate to Lila's concerns?

12. How does faith—both religious and in a more general sense—inform Jo and Bethie? What does faith mean to the sisters?

Enhance Your Book Club

1. If your group hasn't already read Jennifer Weiner's novel *In Her Shoes*, consider reading it together and comparing its themes of sisterhood with those of *Mrs. Everything*. What similarities do you notice between the sisters in these two novels? What ideas and feelings does Jennifer Weiner explore in both?

2. Choose one of the eras from the novel and come to your book club dressed in clothes or donning fun accessories from the period. Pick a film set in that same decade and discuss how the director and Jennifer Weiner each evoke that moment in history.

3. Visit Jennifer Weiner's website at www.jennifer weiner.com to learn more about her and her books, and follow her on Twitter @jenniferweiner.

Turn the page for a look at
Jennifer Weiner's new novel

Big Summer

available from Atria Books.

ONE

2018

"OhmyGod, I am *so sorry*. Am I late?" Leela Thakoon hurried into the coffee shop with a cross-body bag hanging high on one hip, a zippered garment bag draped over her right arm, and an apologetic look on her face. With her silvery-lavender hair in a high ponytail, her round face and petite figure, and her emphatic red lipstick, she looked exactly the way she did on her Instagram, only a little bit older and a little bit more tired, which was true of every mortal, I supposed, who had to move through the world without the benefit of filters.

"You weren't late. I was early," I said, and shook her hand. For me, there was nothing worse than showing up for a meeting feeling flustered and hot and out of breath. In addition to the physical discomfort, there was the knowledge that I was confirming everyone's worst suspicions about fat ladies—*lazy, couch potatoes, can't climb a flight of stairs without getting winded.*

Today, I had wanted to look my best, so I'd worked out at six in the morning and cooled down for an hour, unhappy experience having taught me that, for every hour I exercised, I'd need thirty minutes to stop sweating. I'd arrived at the coffee shop Leela had chosen twenty minutes ahead of time, so that I could scope out the venue, choose an advantageous seat, and attempt to best project an aura of cool, collected competence. *#free lancehustle*, I thought. But if I landed this collaboration, it would mean that the money I earned as an influencer would be more than the money I made doing my regular twenty-hour-a-week babysitting gig, and possibly even more than my dog's account was bringing in. I wouldn't be supporting myself with my online work, but I'd be closer to that goal. In yoga that morning, when we'd set our intention, I'd thought, *Please*. Please let this happen. Please let this work out.

"Want something to drink?" I asked. I already had my preferred summer beverage, cold brew with a splash of cream and extra ice, sitting in front of me.

"No, I'm fine," said Leela, pulling the metal water thermos of the environmentally aware out of her bag, uncapping it, and taking a swig. *Oh, well*, I thought. At least my coffee had come in a glass and not plastic. "I'm *so glad* to meet you." Leela draped the garment bag over a chair, smoothed her already smooth hair, and took a seat, crossing her legs and smiling at me brightly. She was wearing a pair of loose-fitting khaki shorts, pulled up high and belted tight around her tiny waist, and a blousy white top with dolman sleeves that left her slender arms bare. Her golden skin, a deeper gold than I got even at my most tan, glowed from the sunshine she'd probably enjoyed on a getaway to Tahiti or Oahu. There was a jaunty red scarf around her neck, pinned with a large jeweled brooch. She looked like a tiny androgynous elf, or as if someone had waved a wand and said, *Boy Scout, but make it tiny and Southeast Asian and fashion*. I was sure that some piece of her outfit had been purchased at a thrift shop I'd never find, and that another had been sourced from a website I'd never discover, or made by some designer I'd never heard of, in sizes that would never fit me, and that it had cost more than one month of my rent. The entire rent, not just the half I paid.

Leela uncapped her bottle and looked me over, taking her time. I sipped my coffee and tried not to squirm, breathing through the insecurity I could feel whenever I was confronted by someone as stylish and cute as Leela Thakoon. I'd worn one of my favorite summer outfits, a hip-length pale yellow linen tunic over a plain white short-sleeved T-shirt, olive-green leggings with buttons at the cuffs, and tan wedge-style sandals, accessorized with a long plastic tortoiseshell necklace, big gold hoop earrings, and oversized sunglasses. My hair—regular brown—was piled on top of my head in a bun that I hoped looked effortless and had actually required twenty minutes and three different styling products to achieve. I'd kept my makeup simple, just tinted moisturizer to smooth out my olive complexion, mascara, and shimmery pink lipgloss, a look that said *I care, but not too much*. In my previous life, I'd dressed to hide, in a palette limited to black, with the occasional daring venture into navy blue. These days, I wore colors and clothes that weren't bulky or boxy, that showed off my shape and made me feel good. Every morning, I photographed and posted my outfit of the day (OOTD), tagging the designers or the places I'd shopped for my Instagram page and my blog, which I'd named *Big Time*. I kept my hair and makeup on point for the pictures, especially if I was wearing clothes I'd been gifted or, better yet, paid to wear. That had entailed a certain outlay of cash, on cuts and color and blowouts, in addition to a lot of trips to Sephora and many hours watching YouTube makeup tutorials before I'd found a routine that I could execute on my own. It had been an investment; one that I hoped would pay off.

So far, the signs were good. "Oh my God, *look* at you," Leela said, clapping her hands together in delight. Her nails were unpainted, clipped into short ovals. A few of them were ragged and looked bitten at the tips. "You're *adorbs*!"

I smiled back—it would have been impossible not to—and wondered if she meant it. In my experience, which was limited but growing, fashion people tended to be dramatic and effusive, full of oversized praise that was not always entirely sincere.

"So what can I tell you about the line?" she asked, removing a Moleskine notebook, a fountain pen, and a small glass bottle of ink from her bag and setting them down beside her water bottle. I tried not to stare. I did have questions about the clothes, and the collaboration, but what I really wanted to know was more about Leela. I knew she was about my age, and that she'd done a little modeling, a little acting, and that she'd made a few idle-rich-kid friends and started styling their looks. The friends had introduced her to celebrities, and Leela had started to style them. In a few years' time, she had amassed over a hundred thousand social-media friends and fans who followed her feed to see pictures of beautiful people wearing beautiful clothes in beautiful spots all over the world. By the time she'd announced her clothing line, Leela had a built-in audience of potential customers, people who'd seen her clients lounging on the prow of a yacht in the crocheted bikini Leela had bought from a beach vendor she'd discovered in Brazil, or walking the red carpet in a one-of-a-kind custom hand-beaded gown, or dressed down in breathable linen, handing out picture books to smiling children in poor villages all over the world.

When Leela had launched the brand she was calling Leef, she'd made a point of saying that her collection would be "size-inclusive." She didn't just want to sell clothes to straight-size women, then toss big girls a few bones in the form of a belated capsule collection or, worse, ignoring us completely. Even better, in the videos I'd watched and the press release I'd read on her website, Leela had sounded sincere when she'd said, "It's not fair for designers to relegate an entire group of women to shoes, hand bags, and scarves because the powers that be decided they were too big or too small to wear the clothes." *Amen, sister*, I'd thought. "My clothes are for every woman. For all of us." Which sounded good, but was also, I knew, a bit of a cliché. These days, designers who'd rather die than gain ten pounds, designers who'd rather make clothes for purse dogs than fat people, could mouth the right platitudes and make the right gestures. I would have to see for myself if Leela was sincere.

"Tell me what got you interested in fashion," I asked.

"Well, it took a minute," Leela said, smiling her charming smile. "I've always been drawn to . . . I guess you'd call it self-expression. If I were a better writer, I'd write. If I were a better artist, I'd paint or sculpt. And, of course, my parents are still devastated that I'm not in med school." I saw a fleeting expression of sorrow, or anger, or something besides arch amusement flit across her pretty features, but it was gone before I could name it; erased by another smile. "High school was kind of a shit show. You know, the mean girls. It took me a while to pull it together, but I made it out alive. And I figured out that I know how to put clothes together. I know how to take a ten-dollar T-shirt and wear it with a two-thousand-dollar skirt and have it look like an intentional whole." I nodded along, like I, too, had a closet full of two-thousand-dollar skirts and other components of intentional wholes. "So I found my way to working as a stylist. And what I found," she said, lifting her shoulders and straightening in her seat, "is that women still don't have the options that we should." She raised one finger, covered from knuckle to knuckle with gold rings that were as fine as pieces of thread. "If you're not in the straight-size range, there's nothing that fits." Additional fingers went up. "If you've got limited mobility, you can't always find clothes without hooks and buttons and zippers. If you're young, or on a budget, if you want clothes that are ethically produced, and are made by people who are paid a living wage. I don't want women to ever have to compromise," she said, eyes wide, her expression earnest. "You shouldn't have to decide between looking cute and buying your clothes from a sweatshop."

I found myself nodding along, feeling a pang of regret for every fast-fashion item I'd ever picked up at Old Navy or H&M.

"Once I started looking at what was available, it was obvious to me—I wanted to design my own clothes," Leela said. "I know how great it feels—and I'll bet you do, too—when you put a look together, and it just . . ." She paused, bringing her fingertips to her lips and kissing them, a clichéd gesture that she somehow made endearing. "It just works, you know?"

I nodded. I did know. Once I'd decided to work with what I had, not wait until God or the Universe or some magical diet granted me a different body, once I'd started searching out clothes that fit and looked good on the body I had instead of the one that I wanted, I had discovered exactly the feeling Leela Thakoon was talking about.

"I think everyone deserves to feel that way. Even if you don't fit the skinny, white, long-straight-blond-hair mold. Even if you've got freckles, or wrinkles, or wide feet, or you're one size on the bottom and a totally different size on top." She put her hand just above her breast, like she was pledging allegiance to inclusive fashion. "All of us deserve to feel beautiful." She looked at me, her eyes meeting mine, and I nodded and found myself unexpectedly blinking back tears. Normally, I would have had a hard time mustering much sympathy for women whose worst problem with clothes was that they were too big. You could always get your pants cuffed and your shirts and dresses taken in. You could even pick up things in the children's section, where everything was cheaper, but if you were plus-size, there wasn't much you could do if the size of a designer's offerings stopped before you started. Still, I respected Leela's attempt to offer kinship, to point out that even tiny, exquisitely pretty world travelers with famous friends didn't always fit into the box of "beautiful."

"So that's why!" She smiled at me brightly, asking, "What else can I tell you?"

I smiled back and asked the open-ended question I used at the end of all of these conversations. "Is there anything else you think I need to know?"

There was. "For starters, I don't work with sweatshops," Leela began. "Every single item I sell is made in the USA, by union workers who are paid a living wage."

"That's wonderful," I said.

"We use fabrics made from natural, sustainable materials—mostly cotton, cotton-linen blends, and bamboo—that's been engineered to wick sweat and moisture and withstand five hundred trips through the washing machine." She paused, waiting for my nod. "We recycle as much as we can. We'll have a trade-in program, where you can exchange a worn garment toward credit for something new. We've designed our manufacturing and our shipping with an eye toward keeping our carbon footprint as small as possible, and with annual goals for reducing it as well."

"Also great," I said, and found, again, that I was impressed in spite of myself.

"We are, of course, a woman-led company with a nonhierarchical management structure." She gave a small, pleased smile. "True, right now it's just me and my assistant, so it's pretty easy, but I'm going to keep it that way. We're small at the moment," she said with that beguiling smile, "but when we expand—not if, but when—we're going to be as inclusive as possible. That means race, gender, age, ethnicity, and size. I want to make clothes for everybody."

"That's terrific," I said, and meant it.

"Best of all," she said, reaching across the table and giving my forearm an uninvited squeeze, "the pieces are *luscious*." She popped to her feet and picked up the garment bag and held it in both hands, offering it to me. "Go on. Try them on."

"What, right now?"

"Please. It would be such an honor," she said, her smile widening.

Thankfully this coffee shop had a spacious bathroom that was covered in William Morris–style wallpaper, with fancy soap and hand lotion and a verbena-scented candle flickering on the reclaimed-wood table beside the sink. I hung the bag from a hook on the inside of the door. *Luscious*, I thought, bemused. It sounded like a brand-new code word for *fat*, like *Rubenesque*. But I'd take it. I'd always take a well-intentioned gesture toward kindness and inclusion over the rudeness that had underscored too many of my days.

I unzipped the bag. According to the promotional materials, each piece of the capsule collection had been named after a woman in Leela's life. They were all designed to work together, each could be dressed up or dressed down, and the collection could "keep a working woman covered, from office to evening, seven days a week." It was the impossible dream. In my limited experience, clothes didn't work this way. Yoga pants still looked like yoga pants, even if you wore them to the office with a blazer on top; a bridesmaid's dress was still a bridesmaid's dress, even if you hemmed it or dyed it or threw a cardigan over it and put it on for a trip to the grocery store.

I removed the first hanger from the bag and gave the dress a shake. It had an A-line silhouette, three-quarter-length sleeves, and a waistline that gathered under the bust. The fabric was a silky blend of cotton and something stretchy and synthetic, light and breathable, but with enough weight to drape well. Best of all, it was navy blue, with white polka dots. I adored polka dots.

I hooked the hanger over the stall door, shucked off my leggings and top, pulled the dress off, shut my eyes, and let the fabric fall over my head and shoulders, past my breasts and hips, unspooling with a beguiling, silky swish. I turned toward the mirror and held my breath.

For all women—or maybe just all plus-size women; or maybe just me—there's a moment right after you put on a new piece of clothing, when you've buttoned the buttons or zipped the zipper, but before you've seen how it looks—or, rather, how you look in it. A moment of just *sensation*, of feeling the fabric on your skin, knowing here the waistband pinches or if the cuffs are the right length, an instant of perfect faith, of pure, untarnished hope that *this* dress, *this* blouse, *this* skirt, will be the one that transforms you, that makes you look shapely and pretty, and worthy of love, or respect, or whatever you most desire. It's almost religious, that belief, that a piece of silk or denim or cotton jersey could disguise your flaws and amplify your assets and make you both invisible and seen, just another normal woman in the world; a worthy woman who deserves to get what she wants.

I opened my eyes, gave the skirt a shake, and looked at myself in the mirror.

I saw how my skin glowed, rosy, against the navy blue, and how the bustline draped gracefully and didn't tug. The V-neck exposed the tiniest hint of cleavage; the wide, sewn-in waistband gripped the narrowest part of my body; and the skirt, hemmed with a cute little flounce of a ruffle that I hadn't noticed at first, flared out and hit right beneath my knees. The sleeves were fitted, snug without being uncomfortable—I could lift and lower my arms and stretch them out for a hug, and the cuffs sat between my elbows and my wrists, another visual trick, one that made my arms look as long as the skirt made my legs appear.

I turned from side to side, taking in the dress, and me in the dress, from every angle the mirror would give me. I could already imagine it working with my big fake-pearl statement necklace, or with my dainty amethyst choker, with my hair in a bun, or blown out straight. I could wear this with flats, I thought. I could wear it with espadrilles or wedges or stilettos. I could wear it to work, with sneakers and a cardigan . . . or out on a date with heels and a necklace . . . or just to go to the park, sit on a bench, and drink my coffee. As Leela had promised, the fabric breathed. The dress moved with me, it didn't pinch or bind or squeeze. It flattered, which, in my mind, meant that it didn't make me look thin, or different, but instead like the best version of myself. It made me feel good, made me stand a little straighter. And . . . I slipped my hands down my sides. Pockets. It even had pockets. "A unicorn," I breathed.

"Knock knock!" called Leela, her voice merry. "Come out, come out wherever you are!"

I gave myself one last look and stepped out of the restroom. In the coffee shop's light, the dress looked even better, and I could notice little details, the subtle ruching on the sides of the bodice, the tiny bow at the base of the neckline, the embroidered rickrack along the cuffs.

"So what do you think?"

I thought about trying to be coy. I thought about trying to be as effusive as fashion folk typically were. In the end, I gave her honesty. "It's amazing. My new favorite dress."

She clapped, her pretty face delighted. "I'm so glad! The dress—we call her Jane—is the backbone of the collection. And there's pants . . . and a blouse . . ." She clasped her hands together and pressed them against her heart. "Will you try them on for me? Pretty please? I've only ever seen them on our fit model. This is my first chance to see them, you know, out in the real world."

I agreed. And, to my delight, every piece was just as comfortable, just as flattering, and just as thoughtfully made as the Jane. The high-waisted, wide-legged Pamela pants were chic, not frumpy, a world away from the palazzo pants that grandmothers wore on cruises; the white blouse, named Kesha, had princess seams and a clever hook-and-eye construction to guarantee that it wouldn't gape. I normally hated blazers, which always made me look boxy and approximately the size of a refrigerator, but the Nidia blazer was cut extra-long in the back and made of a stretchy brushed-cotton blend, with cute zipper detailing on the sleeves in a perfect shade of plum.

The last piece in the garment bag was a swimsuit called

the Darcy. I lifted the hanger, swallowing hard. Swimsuits would probably always be hard for me. Even after all this time, all the work I'd done to love my body—to at least accept the parts I couldn't love—I still cringed at the cellulite that riddled my thighs, the batwings of loose flesh under my upper arms, and the curve of my belly.

The swimsuit had a kind of vintage style. There was a skirt, but it wasn't the heavy, knee-length kind I'd remembered from my own mother's infrequently worn bathing suits, but a sweet flounce of ruffles that would brush the widest part of my thighs. *You can do this*, I coached myself, and pulled the suit on, over my underpants, and adjusted the straps.

Another deep breath, and I looked in the mirror. There were my thighs, so white they seemed to glare in the gloom. There were my stretch marks; there were the folds of fat on my back; there was the bulge of my stomach. I shut my eyes, shook my head, and told myself, *A body is a body*. Everyone has to move through the world in one, and mine was a body, like everyone else's, no better, no worse.

"Daphne?" Leela called. "Is everything okay?"

I didn't answer. *Deep breath*, I told myself. *Head up.* I slicked on red lipstick and slid my feet into my wedges. I made myself smile. Finally, I looked again, and this time, instead of seeing cellulite or rolls, or arms or thighs, I saw a woman with shiny hair and bright red lips; a woman who'd dive in the deep end and smile for the camera and live her life out in the open, as if she had just as much right to the world as anyone else.

Holding that thought in my head, I opened the door. Leela, who'd been bouncing on the tips of her toes for each previous reveal, went very still. Her hands, which she'd had clasped against her chest, fell to her sides.

"Oh," she said very softly. "Oh."

"It's perfect," I said, and sniffled.

"Perfect," she repeated, also sniffling, and I knew that not only had I found the swimsuit and the clothes of my dreams, but I'd landed a job, too.

Once I'd changed back into my own clothes, I returned to the table. Leela, beaming, extended her hand.

"I'd love to hire you as the exclusive face, and figure, of Leef Fashion." Her hand was warm, her grip firm, her gaze direct, her smile bright.

"And I'd love to accept. It's just . . ."

Leela looked at me, her face open and expectant.

"Why me?" I asked. "I mean, why not someone, you know, bigger?" *No pun intended*, I thought, and felt myself flush.

Leela tilted her head for a moment in silence, her silvery hair falling against her cheek. "I like to think that building a campaign is like putting together a great outfit," she finally said. "You pull a piece from here, a part from there. And everything has to fit. When I thought about who would fit my brand, I knew I wanted someone like you, who's just starting out. I want to make magic with someone I like; someone who is just at the beginning of her story. I want someone real," she concluded. "Well, as real as anyone ever is on social. And you're real, Daphne," Leela said. "That's what people love about you, that's why they follow you. From that very first video you posted to the review you did of that workout plan . . . BodyBest?"

"BestBody," I murmured. That had been a doozy. The company had sent me its workout plan, a sixty-dollar booklet full of exhortations about "Get your best beach body now," and "Be a hot ass," and "Nothing tastes as good as strong feels," and shots of slim, extraordinarily fit models with washboard abs and endless legs demonstrating the moves. I'd done the entire workout plan, all twelve weeks of it. I'd filmed myself doing jump squats and burpees, even though I'd been red-faced and sweaty, with parts of me flopping and wobbling when I did mountain climbers or star jumps (none of the models had enough excess flesh for anything to flop or wobble). My carefully worded review had alluded both to the challenging workouts and the punitive language, which I'd found distracting and knew to be ineffective. *Research shows that shaming fat folks into thinness doesn't work. And come on—if it did, most of the fat women in the world would have probably disappeared by now*, I'd written.

"You have an authenticity that people like. You're just . . ." She tilted her head again. "Unapologetically yourself. People feel like you're their friend," Leela said, looking straight into my eyes. "You're going places, Daphne, and I want to get in on the ground floor." She extended her cool hand. "So, what do you say?"

I made myself smile. I was delighted with her praise, with her confidence that I was going places. I was still thinking about the BestBody review and how the truth was that the workout had left me in tears, so disgusted with myself that I'd wanted to take a knife to my thighs and my belly. I hadn't written that, of course. No one wanted to see anything that raw. The trick of the Internet, I had learned, was not being unapologetically yourself or completely unfiltered; it was mastering the trick of appearing that way. It was spiking your posts with just the right amount of real . . . which meant, of course, that you were never being real at all. The more followers I got, the more I thought about that contradiction; the more my followers praised me for being fearless and authentic, the less fearless and authentic I believed myself to be in real life.

Leela was still looking at me, all silvery hair and expectant eyes, so I took her hand. "I'm in."

She smiled and bounced on the balls of her feet, a happy little elf who'd just gotten a raise from Santa. We shook and started talking terms—how much she'd pay for how many pictures and videos posted over what period of time and on what platforms. We discussed what time of day was best to post, which settings her viewers preferred. "Still shots are great. Colorful backdrops. Walls with texture, or murals. And fashion people love video," Leela said with the solemnity of a priest explaining the workings of a crucially important ritual. "They like to see the clothes move."

"Got it," I said, practically squirming with impatience. I couldn't wait to finish my day, get back to my apartment, and model the clothes for my roommate, to see how they worked with my shoes and my necklaces, to think about where I could wear them and how I could make them look their best.

"Oh, and outdoor is better than indoor, of course. Do you have any plans for the summer?" Leela asked. "Any travel?"

I breathed in deeply and tried to keep my face still. "I'm going to a wedding on the Cape. Do you know Drue Cavanaugh?"

Leela nibbled her lip with her perfect white teeth. "She's the daughter, right? Robert Cavanaugh's daughter. The one who's marrying the *Single Ladies* guy, right?"

"That's her. She and I went to high school together, and I'm going to be in her wedding."

Leela clapped her hands, beaming. "Perfect. That's absolutely perfect."